WALKIN

Anne Bennett v
in the Horefa
daughter of Ro ... immigrants,
she grew up in a tight-knit community where she was taught to be proud of her heritage. She considers herself to be an Irish Brummie and feels therefore that she has a foot in both cultures.

She has four children and four grandchildren. For many years she taught in schools to the north of Birmingham.

An accident put paid to her teaching career and after moving to North Wales, Anne turned to the other great love of her life and began to write seriously. *Walking Back to Happiness* is her fifth book.

By the same author

A LITTLE LEARNING
LOVE ME TENDER
A STRONG HAND TO HOLD
PACK UP YOUR TROUBLES

ANNE BENNETT

Walking Back to Happiness

HarperCollins*Publishers*

HarperCollins*Publishers*
77–85 Fulham Palace Road,
Hammersmith, London W6 8JB

www.fireandwater.co.uk

This paperback edition 2003

2

First published in Great Britain by
HarperCollins*Publishers* 2002

ISBN 978 0 00 787936 6

Set in Sabon

Printed and bound in Great Britain by
Clays Ltd, St Ives plc

This book is written for my mother
Eileen Josephine Flanagan
and is dedicated to her memory.

I have many people to thank for this book coming into being. First of all, there is my good friend Ruth Adshead, who helps me so much, and my husband and four children for their love, encouragement and support. Special thanks must go to Judith Evans at Waterstones in Birmingham city centre, both because of her enthusiasm for my books and introducing me to Peter Hawtin of HarperCollins in May 2001. Thank you, Peter, for being so positive about me. Many thanks too go to Susan Opie, my editor at HarperCollins, and Maxine Hitchcock, my assistant editor, both of whom helped me to take the book apart and put it together again, and my agent Judith Murdoch for believing in me and giving me positive feedback. I feel immense gratitude to you all.

Chapter One

Hannah Delaney looked down at her sister, Frances Mullen, and knew she'd never leave her bed again. She felt tears prickle the back of her eyes as she reached for Frances's yellow, emaciated hand, but she held them back. If Frances could be brave about her impending death, then so could she. 'You're a grand girl, Hannah,' Frances said in little more than a hoarse whisper. 'Thank you for coming.'

Hannah's face flushed at the implied reproach. 'You didn't bother when I sent for you when my husband, Paddy, was coughing his guts up in the County Hospital,' Frances might have said.

Hannah knew Frances must have been badly hurt but there had been a desperate reason why she'd not been able to come back when Paddy lay dying and one she could never share with Frances, nor with any of the family. Hannah had told Frances she had the 'flu and wasn't well enough to travel. She hadn't even come for the funeral and no one could guess how heartsore she was that she couldn't come and mourn the man who'd always been more of a father to her than her own and maybe be a measure of support to her sister.

The townsfolk couldn't understand it at all. 'People have the 'flu all the time and get over it,' they'd said to Frances. 'Why doesn't she come for a wee visit now to see how you all are?'

'Sure, isn't she rushed off her feet with the fine job she has?' Frances had answered the criticisms. But inside, she'd ached for the presence of her youngest sister. She'd reared her and had loved her like one of her own, but she seemed to have forgotten all that, for she'd not been near the place for three years.

But now she was here and suddenly to Frances it didn't matter any more. There was little time to waste on censure and argument and Hannah certainly had no wish to quarrel. She'd always loved Frances dearly and she was saddened that she had such little time left.

'Why wouldn't I come?' she said with a forced smile, giving her sister's hand a gentle squeeze. 'Aren't you the only mother I ever knew and don't I love you more than anyone in the whole world? If there's anything I can do for you, you only have to say.'

Frances gave a wry smile and a little sigh. So, she thought, God does answer prayers, some prayers. He couldn't spare her any longer and God knows at times she was tired enough not to care, but now Josie would be all right. She'd fretted about the child, worried to death that Hannah wouldn't come, that she wouldn't be able to ask her.

Frances studied her sister, while she framed the question she had to ask. She wasn't worried Hannah would refuse. How could she? She'd taken Hannah in when she was just a day old, when their mother had died of childbirth fever. Frances's third child, Martin, had been only a week old himself and she also had Miriam just fifteen months and Peter coming up to three yet she'd not hesitated to offer Hannah a home. And for that reason Hannah owed her a debt. 'It's Josie,' she said. 'Will you take Josie? Will you look after her when it's . . . when it's all over?'

'Josie?' That dark, secretive, plain child, the one Hannah hardly knew at all for she'd been born after she'd left the farm and always seemed to disappear whenever she'd come for her very occasional visits home.

She'd scarcely ever given the child a thought, for Frances had done what their own mother had done and had a large gap in the family and the nearest in age to Josie was Sam, who at twenty was eleven years her senior. Hannah knew from the letters her sister had written that Sam had been living in the mountains, working their grandparents' farm since he'd left school at fourteen. If Josie was to go there, she'd become a maid of all work, her childhood would be over and Hannah well knew that.

But for God's sake, there was a fine family of them. Surely to God one of them could look after their own sister?

But in her heart she knew she was the only one left. Peter had become a priest and was living away in the Scottish Highlands somewhere and poor Miriam was married to a man she had met on a brief visit to England. She returned with him to his home in Connemara where, according to Frances, they tried to scratch a living from the stones. At twenty-eight, she'd been married eight years and had eight children.

Miriam had not come home for her father's illness

or funeral either and gave the excuse she was almost on her time, but Frances had suspected she couldn't afford to come. Even if she'd have offered a home to Josie, Hannah knew Frances wouldn't have been happy sending her there.

But then what about Martin who was twenty-seven, the same age as herself, and Siobhan two years younger? Martin had coped with the farm single-handed since his father had died, but Hannah, who'd been brought up alongside him and understood him better than the others, knew he was no farmer. He'd always wanted to go to New York; he used to talk about it all the time. And now he and Siobhan had the chance. Their Aunt Norah had offered to send them the fare.

Martin had been unable to contain his excitement when he'd met Hannah off the train. 'It's like a dream,' he'd said, as he'd set the old pony pulling the cart to canter over the cobblestones. 'I thought I was stuck on the farm for years, you know, I mean with Da gone? I'd never have left Mammy and God knows I wished no harm to her but . . . well, the old place won't be the same without her.'

There was no place in bustling New York and their aunt's plush apartment for a child either. It hadn't been said openly, but it was understood.

That left Margaret and Ellen, only Margaret was now known as Sister Ambrose, one of the 'Sisters of the Poor'. If the war hadn't raged on for six horrifying years, she would already be in Africa teaching the heathens about the love of Jesus. Now that it was over, she was just awaiting a ship's return to civilian duties.

Ellen was twenty-one and getting married. But even

as Hannah thought of her, she immediately rejected the idea. She was marrying a farmer and would have to live with his parents and two sisters and a brother in a small farmhouse with only two bedrooms. A young sister in tow, too, would make the place even more cramped.

She wondered suddenly where she might have ended up if it hadn't been for Frances. She might have been pushed from pillar to post, one relative to another. Or left with her morose, sullen father who blamed her for her mother's death. There was the rub though. Frances had been there, solid, welcoming and loving, and now her dying wish was for Hannah to care for her youngest child.

The trouble was Hannah was marrying Mr Bradley in late summer and she didn't know how he'd take to her looking after Josie. They'd never talked about children, and she didn't know how he'd feel being landed with a nine-year-old girl.

Well, he'd have to put up with it, she decided suddenly, for she owed her sister and this was pay out time. 'Is it such a hard thing to ask?' Frances asked, and Hannah realised the silence had stretched out between them uncomfortably, while the thoughts had tumbled about her head. 'No,' she said untruthfully. 'No, not at all. I was just wondering how I'd manage being at work all day. And she doesn't know me at all. How does she feel about it?'

'She doesn't know. How could I tell her? I didn't know if you'd agree.'

'When does she think . . . I mean, does she know?'

'That I'm dying?' Frances said. 'Oh aye, she knows. At least I think she does. She's not a stupid girl. She's seen the doctor come and go and the priest and I haven't left my bed now for over a week. I haven't actually told her, but I think she knows.'

Frances was right, Josie did know her mother was dying. She'd listened at doors, a common practice when she wanted to know about anything she knew none of her family would tell her, and heard it said plainly. She wasn't totally surprised at the gravity of her mother's illness for she'd watched her become weaker and weaker and her skin and eyes take on a yellowish tinge, and she shed many tears that she'd kept hidden from her family.

But still she'd hoped and prayed. God, she'd spent so long on her knees and lit so many candles and said a special novena for the sick, she'd thought it just had to work. Father Mulligan said God answered prayers and if your faith was as small as a mustard seed you could move mountains. But Josie's mother got more and more frail with each passing day and Josie lost faith in the priest's words. She thought it a stupid thing to want to move mountains from place to place anyway, and surely to cure someone like her Mammy, who was so loved and needed, had to be easier than that.

But as her Mammy got worse instead of better, Josie had begun to feel lonely and afraid. She'd got used to her mother not being around by the time Hannah arrived, for she hadn't been well this long time and Siobhan and Ellen had seen to things. She knew it wouldn't last. Ellen was set to marry and Siobhan . . . she knew what was planned for her and Martin. Not a word had been said to her, it was amazing what people talked about when they didn't know you were there, and she shivered in fear, for she hadn't a clue who was going to look after her.

Josie found out who would the day after Hannah arrived, and then she stared at her mother in horror. She wanted to stamp her feet and shout and scream, but she couldn't do that in front of a woman as sick as her Mammy. But surely she could see Josie couldn't live with Hannah, someone she didn't know in a strange country? God, it was hard enough losing her mother, she'd barely come to terms with that, without leaving behind all that was familiar. 'Mammy,' she said in a voice thick with unshed tears. 'Mammy, I don't want to go to England and I don't want to live with Aunt Hannah – I don't know her.'

'You will, child. By the time it is all over, you'll know her.'

'Don't, Mammy.'

'Cutie dear,' Frances said gently, 'sit up here beside me,' and she patted the bed.

Josie sat, but gingerly, knowing how even a sudden movement could hurt her mother for she was so thin that the bones in her body were visible. And now one of those stick-thin arms trailed around Josie's neck as Frances held her daughter close. 'Oh, Mammy! Why have you to die?'

Frances was a little while answering. She battled with tears behind her own eyes at the unfairness of life. How she hated leaving this youngest child an orphan at such a young age. She'd have liked to have had a few more years till she was older, maybe married, certainly better able to cope. But it wasn't to be. She knew it, everyone knew it, and it would be no kindness to allow Josie to harbour any sort of false hope. 'I don't know why I have to die, Josie. Aren't we all in God's hands?'

'If you ask me, he's not doing a very good job of it,' Josie said fiercely and Frances didn't chide her for she'd had many of the same thoughts.

'If I have to go anyway, can't I go with our Ellen?'

'You know there will be no room for you there, child.'

'Granny's then?'

But even as Josie spoke, she gave a shudder of distaste. She hated her grandparents' farm high in the Wicklow hills. There was nothing cosy about the bleak, thatched cottage they lived in and no comfort to be had either in or out of it. She could never understand Sam liking the backbreaking work he had to do to scrape a living from the hills, or how he managed to live with his grandparents, their granda finding fault with everything and their granny not knowing what day of the week it was.

'There's no one to see to you there.'

'I can see to myself,' Josie retorted, bristling.

'Aye, and you'd have to see to everyone else in the place,' Frances said, adding bitterly, 'I had my share of it and I don't want it for you. Sam gets away with it for he's a boy. Believe me, Josie, your childhood would be over the minute you stepped over the doorstep and you'd skivvy every hour of the day.' She gave Josie a squeeze and pleaded, 'Come on, pet. Don't make this even harder for me.'

After that what could Josie do? She looked at her mother's saddened face and saw that her eyes were brimming with tears and knew that she couldn't add to her distress by arguing further.

Frances seemed to sink rapidly after her talk with Josie. Ellen and Siobhan took on most of the nursing of their mother, Margaret was released from the convent and Miriam was sent for. Josie, from the necessity of taking on many of the household jobs, often found herself working alongside Hannah. She wondered sometimes if Hannah had arranged this, but she didn't care if she had or not. All she knew was that her mother was losing her grip on life and there was damn all she could do about it.

Hannah tried to get her talking, asking questions about the farm and school and her friends and what she did with her free time, but Josie wouldn't play. She always answered her questions, she was too polite to ignore her altogether, but she did so tersely. She never introduced a subject herself and seemed not a bit interested in her aunt's life or the place where she lived.

The tense atmosphere between Hannah and Josie changed a few days later. Josie had crept in to her mother's bedroom, knowing for once she could see her alone. She intended to have one last try at convincing her Mammy that she couldn't live in a stuffy, alien city with an aunt she didn't know and didn't like much either and that surely there was a friend or relative she could stay with.

The Tilley lamp was turned low and the candle before the Sacred Heart of Jesus lent little from its flickering flame. The priest had been that day and the room smelt of the oils he'd used to anoint Frances. Awed and a little frightened, for Josie hadn't seen her mother since she'd told her she was to live with Hannah, she soundlessly crept nearer to the bed. 'Mammy!'

Josie watched her mother dragging her heavy lids open as if they weighed a ton and she stared at her daughter through pain-glazed eyes and without a spark of recognition. 'Mammy, it's me, Josie.'

Frances looked at her for a moment longer before letting her eyelids drop closed again and Josie stood in the room watching her, biting her thumb, while tears rained down her cheeks. It was if her mother was already dead. Josie fled from the room, hurtling down the stairs and out through the front door, avoiding everyone gathered in the kitchen.

It was teatime before she was missed. By then, Ellen knew she had been into their mother's room for she'd left the door wide open and none of the others would have done that. She said she'd have a few sharp words to say when Josie did come home.

Hannah put two and two together. She knew that Frances's drug dosage had been raised to try and give her ease from the intense pain, but Josie hadn't been told. Nor had she been told that Frances, drugged and pain-riddled, seldom knew any of them anymore. She thought for a moment and then without a word to the others, she slipped out into the yard.

She heard the muffled sobbing as soon as she opened the barn door and she followed it up the ladder leading to the upper floor, the very place she'd always made for whenever she was upset. Barely had her head pushed through the opening, than she saw Josie spread-eagled across the straw bales.

But despite the stealth that Hannah had used so as

not to startle the girl, Josie heard her. She raised her head, her face blotchy from crying, but her eyes flashed fire. 'What d'you want?' she spat out. 'Go away! Leave me alone!'

Hannah ignored the anger in Josie's voice, for behind it she heard the knot of raw pain. She eased herself through the hole and sat on a bale nearby, but not too near to Josie, who'd buried her head once more into the straw and refused to look at her aunt. 'I used to come here too,' Hannah said, conversationally. 'There's something comforting about the smell of straw.'

There was no movement from Josie, but Hannah knew she was listening intently. 'I'll miss Frances too,' she said. 'She was the only mother I ever knew. And I might as well have had no father either,' she added bitterly. 'Frances said he was so mad with grief, he hadn't even a name for me. The priest suggested Hannah. It was his mother's name.'

Josie knew the story. It had often been talked of in the family. 'Your daddy was like my daddy too,' Hannah went on. 'He used to talk to me if I got upset. I loved him dearly.'

Josie raised her head. 'Then why didn't you come to the funeral?' she asked, accusingly. 'Everyone was asking.'

'I was ill.'

'After, then. Mammy used to get upset and cry at night.'

There was a silence between them and then Hannah gave a sigh. 'There were reasons,' she said quietly. 'One day I may even tell you what they were, but what matters now is you and me.' And then, because she'd sensed the girl's antagonism towards her from the beginning, she asked, 'Will you hate living with me so much?'

Josie swung around and stared at Hannah and decided to be truthful. 'Yes, I will. I don't know you or anything about England and I don't want to know either. I don't want to leave here.'

Hannah thought that now was not the time to tell Josie she wasn't keen on looking after her either. 'We can't all have what we want, Josie,' she said. 'I've tried to get to know you the last few days, but you . . . Look, pet, we must make the best of it for your mother's sake. Give it a year? If after that you're still miserable, I promise we'll look at it again.'

And then what? Josie thought. Maybe she could induce Martin or Siobhan to send for her to go to America, but would she like that any better? 'At least when your Mammy died, you didn't have to leave the place altogether,' she cried.

'No, no I didn't, and like I said, I'll always be in your parents' debt because of what they did. After a while, people forgot I was really Hannah Delaney. I was known as one of the Mullens.'

'Did you care?'

'Not at first. I wanted to belong somewhere. My own sisters and brothers became like strangers till one by one they took the emigrant boats to the States till only my eldest brother, Eamonn, was left to farm the land with my father. He doesn't really know me though and I don't know him and for a time it was nice being thought of as one of you lot. It was as I got older that I resented Hannah Delaney being swamped altogether.'

'Is that why you left?'

'Partly,' Hannah admitted. 'I wanted to start afresh. Stand on my own two feet, just to see if I could. A good friend of mine, Molly McGuire, had left Ireland just the previous year and we promised to write to each other. She got a job easily in a hotel in Leeds. It was called The Hibernian, reputed to be the biggest, best and of course most expensive in the town. The wages weren't great, she told me, but the tips were legion. She said she could get me a job, straight off.'

Hannah stopped there, remembering her indecision. She didn't want to upset Frances, and she knew she would if she was to follow her friend. But she knew she'd regret it if she didn't go while she had the chance. As she dithered, Molly challenged her. Hadn't she always said she wanted to see something of other places? Hadn't she always said she didn't want to live the whole of her life in Ireland and wasn't there a big, wide world out there to explore?

And she was right. Hannah had said all those things and meant them, too, but the actual leaving was hard, especially when she loved Frances as dearly as she would any mother and Paddy and the others, too. She knew she would miss them all.

In the end, she poured her heart out to Paddy and he patted her hand and told her not to fret, that it was natural to want to spread your wings when you were young. 'But Frances . . .' she had wailed.

'Frances will come around, never fret, I'll talk to her,' Paddy had promised.

'Was Mammy upset when you left?' Josie asked, jolting Hannah back to the present.

'Very. I was sad too. God, it was a wrench to go.

People said I was ungrateful to leave when I could have been such a help to Frances at long last. Frances never said that and I doubt she ever thought of it, she wasn't like that. She said she'd miss me so much, but she wished me Godspeed. It broke me up and we cried together as we hugged, and for a while, my resolve weakened. It was your father who said to go and satisfy myself and to remember I had a home to come back to if it didn't work out.

'Not everyone saw it like that of course, but then all my life people have been telling me how grateful I should be to Frances and I *was* grateful to her. But that level of gratitude gets to be a heavy burden when you're reminded of it constantly. Not that your parents ever spoke about it, it was others, the relatives who hadn't wanted me themselves, or neighbours who felt justified to speak as they chose because they'd known me all my life.'

'And did you like it in this Leeds place?' Josie asked.

'I did not and that's the truth,' Hannah said, remembering her horror at the grim greyness of the place and how the opulence of the hotel unnerved her and the way she could barely understand the way the other girls spoke. She was achingly lonely and many, many times thought she'd made a mistake because she missed her family so very much. She missed the farm too and often longed for the sight of a green mossy hill, springy turf beneath her feet, and good clean air to fill her lungs with.

'I didn't mind the work,' she said. 'I was well used to work, but everything was so strange and when Molly got married and moved to London only months after

I arrived, it was worse. We wrote for a while, but in the end the letters petered out. A girl called Tilly Galston shared my room then.'

'Was she nice?'

Hannah smiled as she remembered the good friend she'd been and the way she pulled her out of the morose self-pitying attitude she'd been in danger of developing. 'I'd have gone home if it hadn't been for her,' Hannah said. 'She wouldn't let me.'

'How could she stop you?'

'Oh, she was very bossy,' Hannah said. 'But funny too, you know. She could always see the bright side of things and could always make me laugh. She bullied me into going out and about too and making an effort with the other girls. We were good friends.'

'Where is she now?'

Hannah shrugged. 'Still in Leeds, I suppose,' she said. 'At least she was there when I left and moved to Birmingham.'

'Don't you know?'

'Well, no I don't exactly.'

Josie made a face. She felt Hannah was a poor friend to not keep in touch with Tilly, but she wasn't about to argue the point. Tilly was in the past and it was the future she was worried about. She wondered if Hannah wanted to take her back to live with her. Maybe she was against the idea, too, and it had been forced upon her. Maybe it was gratitude rearing its ugly head again and suddenly she felt a bit sorry for her aunt. 'All right then,' she said in an effort towards compromise. 'Say I do come with you, where do you live in this Birmingham place?'

Hannah knew Josie was putting a brave face on it and replied, 'An area called Erdington to the north of the city. Many call it Erdington Village, which it was once, but now it's like a little town. It's not anything like here. You've never seen so many people and cars and buses, lorries and trams on the roads, especially in the city centre. But the guesthouse, where I work, is in Grange Road and that's not a bit like that. It's lovely. It's wide and tree-lined and the houses are set back behind privet hedges. There's even a small farm in Holly Lane, not that far away, and sometimes we can get hens' or ducks' eggs from the farmer, Mr Freer.'

She stole a glance at Josie and went on, 'I suppose living here you're thinking, "So what?" Believe me, if you'd been subjected to the rationing restrictions Britain has had to put up with, you'd know how wonderful getting the odd egg is. I've had a word with Mrs Emmerson and she doesn't mind in the least putting you up for a while. She's very kind and anyway, I'll be getting married in September.'

Married! That gave Josie a jolt. She thought Hannah would have given up all thoughts of marriage. She was old, almost as old as Miriam, and she'd been married for years and years and had a whole tribe of children now, though no one seemed pleased about that either. Still, that wasn't her problem. What was, though, was the man Hannah was to marry. 'Does Mammy know that?' she asked.

'Aye, she does,' Hannah said. 'We talked about it. He has a largish terraced house of his own. There'd be plenty of room for you in it.'

'And how does he feel about me?'

Hannah crushed down the worry she had about that and the less than welcoming letter she'd received just that day in answer to hers that she'd written, telling her fiancé what her sister had asked her to do. He'd written that he didn't want to take on the responsibility of a child and he'd been surprised at her making a decision without consulting him. It was, he'd said, no way to start married life.

Hannah would win him round, she had to, but now Josie needed reassurance. 'He'll be fine,' she said. 'Haven't I told you about the size of the house? Why would he mind you sharing a wee piece of it? He knows it's the right thing to do and Mr Bradley always does the right thing.'

Josie stared at Hannah. 'Mr Bradley!' she said incredulously. 'Hasn't he a first name? You don't call a man you're marrying "Mr".'

But it was how Hannah thought of him. Solid, rather dull Mr Bradley – Arthur Bradley – the one Gloria Emmerson told Hannah she must grab before someone else did. He was her stab, perhaps her only stab, towards respectability.

Not of course that Mr Bradley knew anything about Hannah's past. Oh dear me no, that would never have done. But Gloria knew and she liked Hannah and wanted the best for her.

That's why she found her a job in her thriving guesthouse and then latched on to Mr Bradley, a commercial traveller, who'd confided in her that he was sick of the road. 'To rise in the firm though,' he'd said dolefully, 'I need a wife. The boss thinks married men are more steady and reliable.'

If Gloria thought Arthur Bradley was just about the steadiest person she'd ever met, she gave no indication of it. 'But,' Arthur had gone on, 'I don't want to marry and anyway, I've nothing to offer a wife. The house went with my father's job, you see. After he died, Mother had the house during her lifetime, but when she died it went back to the firm. So I don't even have a permanent place to live.'

That had all changed a little later when out of the blue, Arthur inherited a large terraced house in Harrison Road, Erdington, after the demise of an elderly uncle. Gloria immediately began to think of him as a suitable catch for Hannah. First, though, she had to win Hannah round to her way of thinking, for she'd shown no interest in any men in the time she'd known her.

Hannah wasn't the least bit interested in Arthur Bradley either. She felt sorry for him at times but didn't really know why. He seemed a lonely sort of man, out of step with the rest of the world somehow. Gloria said it was because he'd lived all those years with his mother. 'How many years?' Hannah asked. 'He's not that old.'

'I'd have said he was going on for forty.'

Hannah was surprised. 'Do you think he's that old?' she asked. 'Was he in the war?'

'No,' Gloria said. 'He had flat feet or some such he told me. Anyway, it doesn't bother you him being so much older than you, does it? I mean, he doesn't look his age.'

He didn't, Hannah had to admit that. Despite Arthur Bradley's thinning brown hair and the wire-framed glasses perched on his long, narrow nose, he didn't look his age. She supposed that was because he was quite skinny, wiry almost, and he looked worse because he was so tall. His whole face was long, too, and had a mournful look about it, particularly his dull brown eyes, and Hannah realised while Mr Bradley didn't look his age, he certainly acted it.

'Don't you want to be a respectable married woman?' Gloria demanded.

'Of course,' Hannah said. 'If everything had gone to plan, I would be married now, but I don't want to marry just anyone.'

'Look,' Gloria said. 'I don't wish to be harsh, but your lad's body is lying buried in the sands of a Normandy beach. He isn't ever coming back and you have to accept that. Do you want a life of loneliness?'

'I don't love Mr Bradley.'

'Do you like him?'

'Aye, I suppose.'

'Then you'll rub along well enough, I'd say.'

'Gloria, there is more to marriage than that.'

'Yes, there is. One thing is, can he provide for you? Well, Arthur can. He has a good job and a fine house that you would be mistress of.'

'Those kind of things don't impress me.'

'Well, they should. Money is a hard thing to get along without.'

'How do you know, anyway, that Arthur will be for it?'

'I don't,' Gloria admitted. 'But the boss is on to him to get himself married and I know he's gone on you.'

'Don't be daft, I'm sure he's not,' Hannah snapped.

Gloria wondered why it was that Hannah didn't realise how truly lovely she was with that glossy mane of auburn hair, creamy-coloured skin and startling green eyes. And then Gloria had played her ace card. 'Don't you ever want a child, Hannah?'

Hannah wanted a child more than anything in the world, and Gloria knew that, but she'd accepted the fact that with Mike dead there would be no child. But now to have the chance to marry and to be able to have her own baby, a child, to hold in her arms, to love and to watch grow up . . . Well, it was more than she'd ever expected from life. Was it possible? Could she take Mr Bradley on for life, and it would be for life, in order to have that child?

Yes, yes she could, her whole being cried. She'd walk over red-hot coals if it would fill the empty void in her life and help heal the ache in her heart. 'All right,' she said at last. 'Sound Mr Bradley out if you must, but you may have a shock. He may not want to marry me at all. He doesn't strike me as the marrying kind.'

And that had been that. She had committed herself. But Josie was right, she must stop thinking of him as Mr Bradley. 'His name is Arthur,' she said, holding out her hand. 'Come on, dry your eyes and let's go in.'

'Will I get into trouble?' Josie asked tremulously. 'Will they all give out at me?'

'Maybe,' Hannah said. 'But I'll stick up for you, don't worry. It's you and me in this together from now on. You and me against the world.'

Josie liked the sound of that. She got to her feet, scrubbing at her eyes with the sleeve of her cardigan and dusting the pieces of straw from her clothes. 'I'm ready,' she said and she followed her aunt down the ladder.

Chapter Two

Frances's funeral was well attended and everyone spoke of the fine woman she'd been and what a great loss it was to the whole family. The eldest of the Mullens, Peter, officiated at the Requiem Mass. Hannah knew that would have pleased his mother and also too that Margaret had got dispensation from her convent to attend the service.

What would have upset her, though, would have been to see Miriam. Hannah had been so shocked at the young woman only a little older than she was herself who she hadn't seen for years. Miriam's face was gaunt, though ruddy in complexion, and deeply lined and her hair, which had once been burnished auburn like Hannah's own, had streaks of grey in it and hung in limp strands around her face. Her black clothes were respectable enough and Hannah guessed they were borrowed because her shoes were scuffed and down at heel. Beneath her coat was the swell of yet another pregnancy. Miriam resembled a woman nearly twice her age and Hannah felt sorry for the life she led.

But one of the worst aspects of that day for Hannah had been meeting her father. She'd made no move to visit him since she'd come over, knowing she wouldn't be welcome, and he greeted her with a curt nod as if she were a person he'd seen before, but never really knew. Her brother Eamonn took her in a hug that Hannah knew he'd done just because it was the thing everyone expected but in fact, she felt closer to Mary, his wife, who greeted her warmly and said she must come up to the house.

She knew she wouldn't go. Her father's continual rejection still hurt her, cutting deeply. Now, together with the pain of losing Frances, she felt misery almost engulf her.

She'd been in no mood for the riotous wake after the funeral and was glad that she and Josie were leaving soon. She told the others that work was pressing and that Gloria had written asking about her return and Hannah felt she shouldn't be away too long, especially as Gloria had been so good both about giving her so much time off and allowing her to bring Josie back with her.

Most of the family had been relieved that Hannah had agreed to take on the care of Josie as their mother had wanted, though little was said about it. Hannah thought it was probably embarrassment and guilt stopping their tongues. Only Peter and Margaret had said that Hannah's reward for her generosity would be in Heaven.

Hannah was tempted to say that was a long time to wait and ask Margaret what was so appealing about black heathens that she could turn her face towards them so stoutly and ignore the needs of her young orphaned sister.

But of course she said none of this. She just thanked them. Martin eventually spoke about it as he drove them to the station. 'It's really good of you to do this,' he said. 'Taking on Josie and such. I suppose you think me and Siobhan really selfish taking off for America, but it's what we've both wanted to do for years and it's been like a carrot dangled in front of me what with me being unable to take it, especially after Daddy died.

'If we don't go now,' he went on, 'we'll never go, neither of us. Siobhan is as anxious as me. She knows as well as I do that there's nothing here for me. She sees the life Miriam has and shudders, like I do myself. God! The man she married must be an inconsiderate brute.'

'There are inconsiderate brutes in America too,' Hannah reminded him. 'They are not the prerogative of the Irish, you know.'

'I know, I know,' Martin replied. 'But . . . anyway, we both think there's nothing to keep us here now and you agreeing to look after Josie has made it possible. You won't lose by it – financially, I mean. As soon as I'm settled I'll send you something for her.'

'Well, though I'm not saying the money won't be useful, the point is it's rationing that's the problem,' Hannah said. 'I'll have to see about getting Josie a ration book as quickly as possible.'

'There won't be rationing for ever,' Martin pointed out. 'And there might be a bit of money too once the farm is sold. The beasts are all but gone, your father's had some of them, and the farm goes up for sale tomorrow. 'Course it will have to be split between us all, but there'll still be a little.'

'However big or small, I'll put that away for Josie. She will want money in the future,' Hannah said.

'Aye. That's a good idea,' Martin said. 'Pity I'll not get to meet this man you're marrying. Fair sprung that fact on everyone. If you could put the wedding forward a month, it would be before we sail and me and Siobhan could come over.'

'It's all settled for mid-September,' Hannah said, and she was glad it was. She didn't want eagle-eyed and outspoken Martin over there increasing her apprehension about marriage, for she knew Martin would not find much to admire in Arthur Bradley.

But Martin did not know the whole story and never would. Martin could never know how Hannah longed not only for marriage, respectability and a baby, but also for a man of her own, who would love and cherish her above all others, like her father had never done. Mike had, and oh how she'd missed him and had shed bitter tears when she found out he was dead.

Josie, Hannah was to find out, was not a good sailor. Her face had taken on a greenish tinge even before the shores of Ireland had totally disappeared from view.

Josie had never felt so miserable in all of her life, nor had she ever felt so sick, had never been so sick either.

By the time she'd been half an hour on the boat, her whole stomach ached with vomiting. She leant against Hannah, who was sitting beside her on the bench on the open deck, braving the sharp winds that whipped the seas to rolling white-fringed breakers and carried the drizzling rain with it. Cold and damp though it was, it was better than inside which smelt of Guinness, cigarettes and vomit. Hannah felt a stab of sympathy for the child who must be feeling so lost and afraid and so sick, for her face was still wan and pale, her long brown hair straggly and glistening from the unrelenting mizzle which had thoroughly dampened both of them. But Josie took comfort in Hannah's arms around her, like she had when Hannah had held her head as she was sick over the side of the boat, pulling her hair back and wiping her face later with a damp cloth she had with her.

Ever since that day in the barn, Josie had felt differently about Hannah, but for all that, those last traumatic days of her mother's life were fraught ones and Josie was frightened of the future. But she now trusted Hannah and often sought her out. Hannah was frightened of the future, too, for Arthur's attitude to her bringing Josie home hadn't softened. He totally ignored all the reasons she'd listed for having to return with Josie in the second letter she'd written to him. Posthaste, his reply came back. Hannah was to leave the child in the care of the social services who would now be responsible for her welfare.

Hannah had been simultaneously horrified and angry and she'd hurled the offending letter into the fire, lest Josie catch sight of it. She thought the child had enough to put up with. She'd been wrenched from her home, with her parents dead and her sisters and brothers spread about the globe. She had only Hannah and she'd have to make Arthur see that. She wouldn't allow Josie to feel the rejection she'd always felt herself.

* * *

Josie would never forget her first view of Birmingham as they emerged from New Street Station. She'd recovered quickly once she'd left the rolling boat and had quite enjoyed the train, though she'd been very hungry and glad of the reviving tea and sandwiches Hannah had bought at the platform buffet at a place called Crewe, where they'd had to change trains.

She seen little of Dublin as they passed it on the way to the Port of Dún Laoghaire, but the noise and bustle seemed all around her as she surveyed Birmingham, her new home. Hannah had been right that day in the barn, Josie thought, for she *had* never seen so many lorries, or cars or people – hundreds of people thronging the shops, or alighting from large rumbling buses or swaying trams that rattled alarmingly along the rails set into the road.

Not that she had time to stand and stare, for she had trouble keeping up with Hannah's easy strides, especially hampered as she was by a case and a bundle. And all the time Hannah talked, pointing out this shop and that, and telling her she'd take her to something called the Bull Ring soon.

At last, they stood at the bus stop opposite the police station in a road aptly named 'Steelhouse Lane' outside a large building which Hannah told her was a general hospital. 'Used to be the workhouse, I'm told,' she said. 'Gloria Emmerson said the older people still don't like going in when they're sick or anything.'

Josie studied the grim building and honestly didn't blame them, but before she was able to reply, the bus screeched to a halt beside them. Josie was glad Hannah had chosen a bus. It was unnerving enough and nothing like the cosy single-deckers she was used to where you knew everyone on board, but the trams frightened her to death.

They sat upstairs, so that Josie could see more of the city she'd come to live in, while Hannah pointed out landmarks to her, like the large green clock at Aston Cross, and Salford Bridge that spanned the canal, unaware how horrified Josie was by everything.

She'd been as surprised and shocked by the back-to-back houses as Hannah had been when she'd first arrived and depressed by the grim greyness of the whole place. She looked with horror at the huge factory chimneys belching smoke into the spring air and became aware of the pungent stink that tickled her nose and lodged at the back of her throat. She thought the canal, that Hannah pointed out with such pride as she explained that Birmingham was ringed with such waterways, was horrible. She'd never seen such brown, oil-slicked, stagnant water and it made a sharp contrast to the rippling stream near her old home that had glinted in the sun as it babbled over its stony bed.

As the bus rumbled its way towards Erdington, Josie felt depression settle on top of her. She thought everywhere drab and without a blade of grass anywhere. Homesickness swept over her, so strong she felt tears prickling her eyes. She wondered how Hannah could stand living in such a place. She was frightened of arriving at her destination, frightened of Mrs Emmerson and her guesthouse where Hannah worked and wished with all her heart she was back in her home in Wicklow.

* * *

But Hannah had not exaggerated about Grange Road. It was lovely. The pavements were as wide as the road and had trees planted every few yards and that alone went some way to making Josie feel better.

Gloria Emmerson wasn't frightening either. She was plump and motherly. Even her face was round, but it was kindly-looking with a smallish mouth and a squashed-up nose and really bright sparkly eyes. Josie smiled at Gloria as she swept them into the house and through to her personal rooms at the back. She had a casserole cooking in the oven and the smell of it revived Josie's spirits somewhat as she realised that, despite the sandwiches and tea at Crewe, she was still very hungry.

Gloria watched them surreptitiously as they ate. Josie, she thought looked very pale, though she supposed that was from the upset of her mother dying and the tiring journey they'd had. She thought her a plain little thing with her large brown eyes standing out in her head and her brown, nondescript hair.

Not a patch on her aunt, she thought. Not that it had done her much good in the long run, she reminded herself with a sigh. She didn't know whether she was doing her a favour or not pushing her into marriage. But then, Arthur Bradley was nothing if not respectable and after all, it was the best she could expect in the circumstances.

Arthur was waiting for Hannah in the house he'd inherited in Harrison Road, just off Erdington High Street. It was a fine terraced house with three stone steps up to the front door, while an entry ran around to the back door and strip of garden.

Initially, it had given Hannah a thrill of pleasure to realise that, after her marriage, she would be mistress of such a house. The front door opened onto a marble-tiled hall with the door to the front room with a bay window to the right-hand side, which Hannah decided would be the parlour, and carpeted stairs to the left. Behind the front room was another slightly smaller room and at the end of the hall was the door to the breakfast room, leading through to the kitchen and scullery, while a large cellar ran from front to back beneath the whole ground floor.

It had originally had three large bedrooms upstairs, but at some time Arthur's relative had cut one of the double rooms in two to make a much smaller bedroom and an indoor bathroom and lavatory. It was an unheard of luxury, though Arthur said in the daytime, he would prefer the lavatory outside to be used so as not to spend time traipsing up and down the stairs and thereby wearing out the stair carpet.

Still, not to have to go out in the middle of the night was a bonus, and there was running water into the bath, provided you remembered to light the geyser. They had proper bathrooms at the hotel of course, one between four rooms, and Gloria had one in her living quarters which she allowed Hannah the use of once a week. Other times, Hannah had to make do with a bowl of water in her bedroom. What luxury to be able to have a bath when she liked.

In fact, the whole house would be a joy to care for. It was even adequately furnished. It wasn't her choice, but, in those austere post-war days with shortages and utility being the watchwords, she thought herself and

Arthur fortunate to have the problem of furnishing a house solved for them. 'In time, when things are easier, we might replace some of the furniture,' she told Arthur on her first visit.

'Hmph, yes, my dear,' Arthur had said. 'But you know money might not be so plentiful. I shouldn't want to go into debt for anything. This hire-purchase scheme is not one I should like to get involved in.'

Hannah, who'd never owed a penny in her life, agreed with Arthur's sentiments. Gloria, when she told her, said it just showed what a sensible man he was, and wasn't it just as well they hadn't to buy even the basics before they could start married life, though she advised Hannah to buy if not a new bed, then certainly a new mattress.

But that day, Hannah had more on her mind than a new mattress. She hoped Arthur would come to see that she had no alternative but to bring Josie home with her, without getting cross about it.

He wasn't the sort to rant and rave, but he could go very cold if he was displeased. And she knew this news would greatly displease him. He'd made his views adamantly clear in his last letter and would have presumed that Hannah would have carried them out.

That was why Hannah had asked him not to come to the guesthouse that evening after he finished work, but go to the house instead where she would meet him as soon as she could get away.

When she'd been a few minutes in the house, having told Arthur straight away about Josie, she knew she'd been right to come alone. He made no shout or cry of protest, but instead had gone very still, his mouth a tight line of disapproval, his nose pinched, his eyes coal black and sparking with anger, while a tic beat at the side of his temple.

Arthur Bradley had looked forward to seeing Hannah again after a few days away. He didn't love her – he'd never loved anyone but his mother, but he admired her.

Before he'd had the house, his mother having died some years before, he'd stayed often at Gloria Emmerson's guesthouse for he was more often in the Midlands area than anywhere else. For a start, the factory and head office he worked from was in Aston, just outside Birmingham. And then, Birmingham itself and the surrounding area being the home of light engineering, had many factories making the goods his firm needed to make the wireless sets they put together.

Arthur disliked the travelling and staying at indifferent guesthouses. He'd done it for years and he'd been complaining to Gloria about it yet again one day when she seized her chance. 'My boss, Mr Banks, is a family man himself, you see,' he'd told Gloria. 'He likes married men in the firm. Says you can rely on them. It's all the married men who work in the offices and seldom have to go on the road.'

'Maybe you should think about marriage yourself then?' Gloria had suggested.

'I never thought to marry,' Arthur had said. 'Anyway, I know no one suitable.'

'What about Hannah?'

'Hannah!' Arthur had noticed Hannah of course, he couldn't have failed to. Everyone who came to the place noticed Hannah.

'Well, if you've got to be married, you could look

further than Hannah and fare worse,' Gloria had said. 'She's a well set-up lass.'

'I know that all right,' Arthur had said. 'But I know my faults, none better. I'm a dull sort of chap for someone like Hannah.'

'She's not in the full flush of youth,' Gloria reminded him.

'I know that and I'm surprised. I thought someone would have snapped her up before now.'

'Aye, well there's been a war on, you know. The one who might have married Hannah never came back from it.' No harm, Gloria thought, in telling him that much. 'Ask her,' she urged.

She wasn't worried about Hannah's reaction. She'd already talked her round and she knew what her answer would be and hoped fervently that she'd done the right thing.

Arthur was overjoyed that Hannah had agreed to marry him. In the early weeks of their courtship, however, Hannah had often doubted her decision, even with the house that Gloria saw as such a prize, and it was always the thought of one day having her own baby that held her on course. Arthur Bradley wasn't a demonstrative man, nor one, as even Gloria was heard to say, to flash his money about overmuch.

He seldom took Hannah out and whenever he did, even when they were alone, he was so respectful, he appeared aloof and cold. There had been no snuggling for them in the back row of the cinema the odd times they'd gone together. There were no stolen kisses in the entries in the darkening winter nights, or cuddling on the sofa in Arthur's front room and taking comfort in one another. No further than that of course, but Hannah would have welcomed being held and caressed and kissed. That wasn't Mr Bradley's way, though, she told herself and anyway, she didn't need such things, after all she was no lovesick teenager.

A few weeks after their engagement, Arthur came to see Hannah in an ecstatic mood. He told her that they'd both been asked for dinner with his boss and his wife, Mr and Mrs Banks. Such a thing had never happened to him before.

The evening was a success. They all got on remarkably well, so well in fact that the Banks insisted Arthur and Hannah call them Reg and Elizabeth. Arthur could see how Hannah had charmed his boss and his wife. In fact, Hannah and Elizabeth had seemed like old friends together.

He knew some of his colleagues couldn't imagine what Hannah saw in him. He'd seen the looks of puzzled envy on their faces when he'd taken Hannah to the annual dinner-dance, just after she'd agreed to marry him. He'd thought himself a lucky man. If he had to have someone looking across the table from him every day, then Hannah he felt could do the job better than most. Added to her looks, she was compliant, eager to please and had never opposed him in anything.

And now . . . now she stood bold as brass and told him not only that she'd defied him and brought her sister's child home, but that she was to live with them and that she'd promised her sister on her deathbed that she'd look after her.

'You had no right to promise such a thing without consulting me.'

'Arthur, she was dying,' Hannah said, her voice rising in distress. 'Not long after that first day, she was having so much morphine she didn't know where she was and could recognise no one. Should I have asked her to wait while I wrote you a wee letter?'

'Don't shout, Hannah.'

'I feel like shouting,' Hannah snapped. 'Have you no feeling, even for the child? How do you imagine she feels, her parents both dead, her brothers and sisters scattered to the four corners of the world? She is alone, Arthur.'

'The authorities would . . .'

'I wasn't leaving her with any authorities,' Hannah said. 'How could you expect me to do that after promising my sister I'd see to her?'

'Well, I don't want her here and it's my house.'

'Then she won't come and neither will I,' Hannah said angrily, astounded at Arthur's uncompromising attitude.

'Do you know what you're saying?'

'Yes, I do. I won't bring her here under sufferance,' Hannah said. 'She's gone through enough. You were lucky to have your mother until you grew up. I never knew mine and without Frances and her abiding love for me, I would have been lost. I owed her so much and if you want to know I'm glad I have the opportunity to pay back some of it. If you can't see it that way, you're not the man I thought you were and maybe we'd better call the wedding off now before it goes any further.'

She removed her ring as she spoke and laid it on the sideboard. She'd not removed her coat and hat and without another word she turned and left, slamming the front door behind her.

On the way home, though, she wondered what she'd done. Gloria had agreed Josie could stay till the wedding, but she didn't know if she'd want her staying there for good. And if she didn't, Hannah would be out of a job and a place to live.

Back in the house, Arthur, too, was having second thoughts. What Hannah had said about his mother had hit home for he'd been devastated when she'd died. Then he thought of his work colleagues when he told them the marriage was off. He imagined the nudges and winks. 'Knew it wouldn't last. She was miles too good for him.'

And what of his boss? He'd think Arthur a failure for not hanging on to Hannah. And if they should ever find out the reason that Hannah had walked out on him, he had a horrible feeling that they'd see and understand her point of view, not his.

He was a devout man and eventually he walked along to the Abbey, his parish church, to ask the advice of one of the priests there. There were confessions every night till eight o'clock, so he knew there would be someone about.

Father Fitzgerald was pulling his coat about him as he stepped out of the church, for there was rain in the air, when he saw Arthur coming up the path. 'Can I walk with you, Father? It's advice I'm after.'

The priest's heart sank. He hoped Arthur Bradley wouldn't keep him long; the church had been chilly and he was also very hungry. But then, he told himself, Arthur wouldn't have known that. 'Talk away then, Arthur,' he said.

Arthur told the priest everything and though he told him of his own misgivings, he also told him the truth about Hannah's promise to her sister and the debt she felt she owed her and the priest listened without a word.

They'd reached the door before Arthur had finished and they stood with the wind gusting around them and yet the priest felt himself going hot with anger at Arthur's words and actions. He told him he'd been less than charitable and whatever his feelings, he should honour Hannah's promise.

'We have just fought a war of unparalleled magnitude,' he said. 'A time when there was much grief and loss of life, but also when there was more neighbourliness and helping one another. I'm ashamed that you even hesitated to take this poor orphan child in. You have a good job and a fine house, many have far, far less and yet would welcome that child. Your inability to share shows a serious flaw in your character and one that should be attended to.'

Arthur was shaken by the priest's condemnation of him, there was no doubt about it. But he was a man of honour and knew there was only one thing to be done. He went straight round to the guesthouse after leaving the priest. Gloria opened the door. 'Can I see Hannah?' he asked.

But Gloria had already heard an account of the quarrel from an indignant Hannah and she said sternly, 'I'm not having Hannah any further upset.'

'I'm not here to upset her.'

'Well that's as may be . . .'

'Please,' Arthur said earnestly. 'I'm here to apologise.'

Well, thought Gloria, that's more like it. She asked

him to step into the dining room, all the guests having now finished their evening meal, and that was where Hannah faced him a few moments later.

Arthur saw that two spots of colour stood out in Hannah's cheeks and her whole manner suggested that she would stand no nonsense. But Arthur wasn't there to spout nonsense. What the priest had said had wounded him deeply and had made him ashamed of his behaviour at the house. Though he made no mention of the priest, this shame is what he told Hannah as he asked for her forgiveness.

Hannah's eyes narrowed in suspicion. 'Why the sudden change of heart?'

Arthur still didn't mention the priest. He had the feeling it wouldn't help his case. 'I don't know,' he admitted. 'When you'd gone, I thought about what you said. I was wrong and I'm sorry, truly sorry, and sorry too if I upset you.'

In spite of herself, Hannah was impressed. It took courage for a person to admit they were wrong about something and ask for another's forgiveness.

'Please, take back the ring?' Arthur said, holding it out to Hannah.

But she had to be certain. 'And Josie?' she said. 'How do you feel about her now?'

Arthur was a truthful man. Eventually he replied, 'You must be patient with me. I know nothing about children, I've never had dealings with any.'

'I don't expect you to be a natural father,' Hannah said. 'I expect you to be welcoming, to be kind to her.'

'I'll do my best, I can't say fairer than that.'

'No,' said Hannah, slipping the engagement ring

back on her finger 'No, you can't.' But though she spoke the conciliatory words, Arthur's earlier attitude had shaken her. Despite her longing for a child, she knew if she hadn't got Josie's welfare to consider, she'd have probably called it a day with Arthur Bradley there and then and to hell with his fine house and steady job.

Chapter Three

Arthur and Hannah were married the second Saturday in September and everyone said it went off a treat. Gloria sat in the pew watching Hannah walk down the aisle on the arm of Tom Parry, the husband of her best friend and neighbour Amy, and thought it hard she had no one belonging to her but Josie at her wedding.

Why couldn't the two off to America have delayed their departure until after the wedding? Or the one she said was living with the grandparents, or the one that wasn't long married come over for a few days? Then she had to walk down the aisle on the arm of a comparative stranger when her own father was apparently alive and well. And it wasn't that he hadn't been asked. Hannah had written and asked him did he want to come and would he like to give her away, but his refusal had been brief to the point of rudeness.

It had been the same with her brothers and sisters. They were all in America except the one and he said it was a bad time to leave the farm, claimed he was up to his neck in the harvest and had a couple of cows ready to calve.

'It's a crying shame, that's what,' Gloria said angrily to Josie.

'Sure, she hardly knows them anyway,' Josie said. 'It's my family she grew up with.'

But deep down, she knew it had hurt Hannah. She'd heard her muffled crying in the attic room they shared when she thought Josie was asleep. She hadn't comforted her then, though she wanted to, because she had the feeling Hannah wouldn't want her to know. In the same way she wouldn't tell Mrs Emmerson she'd been upset, because she thought she'd be letting her down in some way.

In the time they'd been living together at the guest-house, Josie had drawn even closer to Hannah. She knew she'd taken her in because she'd been almost forced to, but she'd never shown her that. She'd always been kind and considerate. In those first early weeks, sometimes Josie had been so homesick, she could neither eat nor sleep. It had been Hannah then who wrapped her arms around her and promised things would get better, or sat by her bed, often for hours, stroking her forehead to relax her enough to drift into sleep.

Josie knew she'd never forget that. She wished, though, she wasn't marrying Arthur Bradley. Not that he bothered about her much, he mainly ignored her, and as the youngest in a large and busy family, she was used to being ignored, especially by men. Her father and her brothers were always either too busy to bother about her or off on business of their own and would hardly give her the time of day.

No, it wasn't the way Arthur was with her that

bothered Josie about the marriage, it was the man himself. Hannah was beautiful, truly beautiful, but much of her beauty came from the light that danced in her eyes that lit up her whole face. She'd seen heads turn when she'd gone into a room. Every guest who came in had been almost mesmerised by her and she'd even seen people turn to look at her at Mass.

And yet she'd bothered about none of them and certainly didn't encourage attention. In fact, there was a certain something Hannah had, a certain aloofness with men, that put them off slightly, though she was always polite. She'd wanted to ask her about it, but could never seem to find the right words, or the right time to say them. Still, Josie had the feeling that with the slightest encouragement, the men would be falling at her feet.

She knew all about the soldier Hannah had been engaged to who died on the beach in Normandy around D-Day. She'd heard it from Mrs Emmerson and it had been the first time she'd known it, for in the letters Hannah had written to her mother, she'd not mentioned a word of it. 'I think he took part of her heart with him and that's the truth,' Gloria said. 'That's why she wants no other.'

So why then did she pin the rest of it on Arthur Bradley? Josie thought. 'She doesn't love him,' she'd cried in protest to Gloria. 'She can't love him.'

'What's love, pet?' Gloria asked sadly. 'I didn't love my husband, but we got along all right. No children, and that was a blow to take, but it meant we were able to work hard. He had a shop then and it did all right. But when he dropped dead of a heart attack when we'd been married just ten years, I sold the shop, lock, stock and barrel and bought this place.

'I could have married a man I loved and one that loved me,' she went on. 'And there was one. But with him, I'd probably be living in some back-to-back slum with a squad of children and not a half-penny to bless myself with. I did what I had to do for me and Hannah's doing the same.'

'What happened to the other man – the one you loved?' Josie asked, intrigued by Gloria's revelations.

'He went to America,' Gloria said with a shrug, and a flush of shame coloured her face for a split second as she went on. 'Told me I'd broke his heart. Stuff and nonsense, of course. Don't you worry none about Hannah. She wants a home of her own and someone to care for her.'

But did he care for her? Privately, Josie doubted it. They didn't match somehow either. It was like a snail getting married to a butterfly.

Still, a wedding was a wedding. And something to write to Eileen Donnelly about. She'd been her friend at school in Wicklow. When she'd been so homesick, Hannah had advised her to write to someone and tell her how she felt. She said it might help.

And it did. Josie wrote reams and reams, covering page after page with how depressing the place was, the noise, the traffic, the squashed-up houses, the stinking factories that tipped their filth and waste into the sluggish brown canal. She told her of the greyness, the drabness, the absence of green meadows and mountains and streams, and she begged for news from home.

When Eileen's reply had arrived, Josie had been so

disappointed that she'd cried. Eileen said everything was just the same and her mother was having another baby.

There was so much Josie longed to know. So her next letter was full of questions which Eileen answered, but briefly and without elaboration in any shape or form.

By that time, Josie was well settled into the Abbey school. She'd thought her accent might have made her the butt of jokes, but she found many of the children were Irish, or from Irish families, and she was soon settled in. She got on well with the girls in her class and made a special friend of a girl called Mary Byrne who also lived nearby. She found the teachers very strict, not at all like the sleepy easy-going village school she'd gone to.

Her sisters always said she could count herself lucky, for there had been no village school for them and they were taught at the convent, almost three miles away, while the boys went to the Brothers' almost as far away.

But it wasn't the distance alone. They'd always told her that the nuns were the very devil and they'd beat the hands off you for the merest thing. The village school had come to Josie's rescue and although they might have been shouted at, Josie never saw anyone struck.

That wasn't the case at the Abbey school and she knew her sisters had been right about the devilish nuns that taught them being hot on punishment, for the headmistress at the Abbey was a nun from the nearby St Agnes Convent. She wielded a cane to help exert her authority and had no hesitation in using it. Sometimes, after playtime was over, there was a line of children, who'd been sent in by the dinner ladies, waiting outside the headmistress's room, to be 'dealt with'.

So far, Josie had never had the cane, but the prospect of it was held over their heads like the Sword of Damocles. But school didn't occupy her whole life and with the homesickness receding and with Mary at her side, she was finding out some of the advantages of city living and she wrote to Eileen and told her all about it.

Erdington village is no distance away. Soon, after Hannah's marriage, it'll be just at the end of the road. There are so many shops you wouldn't believe, and crowds of people, like the town on a fair day. But even better, they have a cinema. They do dances there as well, but that's for older people. They have special films for children on a Saturday morning and it costs sixpence, but most Saturdays Hannah lets me go.

If not, we can go swimming because they've got a proper baths and Hannah has bought me my first bathing costume. She says if you have no choice about a place then you must make the best of it and so I am. There's a library here too, a massive place with a proper children's part, and you can borrow two books and keep them for a fortnight.

She posted that letter with relish, hoping Eileen was consumed with envy on reading it for she was proving a great disappointment as a correspondent.

And now there was the wedding to brag about. She wished Hannah would be married in a white floor length dress made of silk and decorated with lace and little rosebuds so that she could describe her looking like a princess to Eileen. But she wasn't wearing white, nor a dress either. 'It wouldn't be seemly with everything in such short supply and a wicked waste of clothing coupons,' Gloria told Josie. 'That navy costume trimmed with cream is much more practical and it can be worn again. It will look nice enough, especially now Amy's decorated her hat to match the cream shoes and handbag Hannah has.'

Hannah looked more than just nice, she looked lovely, but then she always looked lovely. She didn't look like a bride, that was all. Josie supposed it was more practical, but did you want to be practical on that one day of your life? She did take on board the bit about clothing coupons, though. She knew they were a headache and one of the first things Hannah had to see to after her arrival was to fit her out with a ration book and a set of clothing coupons.

Josie, coming from the land of plenty in comparison, had imagined that now the war was over, everything would be back to normal, but it was far from that.

And yet Hannah had used some of those precious clothing coupons to get material for a dress for her that had been made up by Amy. It was pale blue and in shimmering satin that fell from her waist in soft folds. It was the nicest and prettiest dress that Josie had ever owned and she had an Alice band covered in rosebuds holding back her hair and pure white socks and black patent leather shoes.

That was another thing, her hair. Gloria had given her a hairbrush and said she must brush her hair one hundred times every night to make it shine and after a month or two, when it had got long enough, she rolled rags around it after her bath on Saturday, so that it would be wavy for Mass on Sunday.

Josie never skimped on the hundred brushes after she'd overheard Amy telling Gloria that Josie's hair was shining like burnished copper. Burnished copper! Josie said the words to herself, liking the sound of them.

Amy went on to say that her hair was her best feature, for she was a plain little thing, not a patch on her aunt, but if she made the most of herself as she grew up she'd make a quite presentable turn-out in the end. Josie hadn't been a bit offended by Amy's remarks for she knew she only spoke the truth.

She had no illusions about her looks and if she'd ever had, they'd have been dispelled the day her mother took her as a small child to visit her great-granny, who lived in the hills, and was ill in bed. She'd been taken by the hand into the bedroom where an old toothless lady with a bonnet covering her head had peered at her with small gimlet eyes in a face screwed up in a scowl. 'Is this the one?' she said. 'The afterthought?'

Then she'd turned her gaze from Josie and looked Frances full in the face and said, 'Well girl, I don't know what you've done with this one, but she's as plain as a pike staff.' And so, at the age of three or four, Josie had learned what she looked like. She knew her eyes were too big for her face, although they were deep brown and could have been attractive in anyone else, her mouth was too big as well, and her skin had a sallow look to it.

But then she'd learned that her hair, which no one had ever bothered much with before, was her best feature and that she might make a good turn-out after all, and for someone who'd thought she was plain as plain could be, that prediction was a soothing one.

So she'd walked behind Hannah down the aisle of the long church, filled with pride as she noted the numbers of people crowding the pews on either side. There was not a relative amongst them, but many of the neighbours and the friends Hannah had made in the area and in the church were there for her special day and Gloria had invited friends of her own to make the day more of an occasion.

Arthur seemed to have few friends and no relatives either. But he'd invited some work colleagues and his boss, Reg Banks, and his lovely wife Elizabeth, and with them all the church was almost full.

At the altar, Josie had taken the bouquet of roses and carnations from Hannah and slipped into the pew beside Gloria, who'd squeezed her arm in support, even while she dabbed at her eyes with a screwed-up lace hanky she held in her hand.

Hannah knelt at the altar beside Arthur, letting the Latin words of the Mass wash over her, soothing her, telling her she was doing the right thing. She didn't love Arthur, but she'd not deceived him. She'd never said she loved him, nor had he said those words to her. She'd known his reason for marrying her, he'd done it primarily to please his boss.

The boss's wife, Elizabeth, who Hannah had taken to straightaway, had confided in Hannah as they'd washed up in the kitchen the first time they'd been asked to dinner. 'Reg thought Arthur a bit of a cold fish. The sort of man married to his mother, you know the type?'

Hannah had nodded. 'He was very fond of her,' she said. 'It upset him greatly when she died. He told me all about it.'

'Oh, I know it did,' Elizabeth said, handing Hannah a plate. 'I'm not meaning to make light of it, but somehow while she was alive, he didn't seem able to let go and get on with his own life. You do understand me?'

Oh yes, Hannah fully understood.

'Of course, my dear, you've known him some time.'

'I wouldn't say I knew him well exactly,' Hannah said. 'After his mother died he'd come and stay at Mrs Emmerson's guesthouse when he had business in the Midlands, often for weeks at a time, but I'd never spoken to him more than mere pleasantries. Then, not long after he'd inherited the house in Erdington, he asked me to marry him. I had no idea he was interested in me in that way.'

'My dear, any man in the land would be interested in you,' Elizabeth said with a laugh. 'My own husband is quite besotted. Oh, don't you blush, my dear,' she chided, seeing the crimson flushing on Hannah's face. 'You must know how attractive you are. Tell me,' she went on, turning to Hannah in a confidential manner. 'Was Arthur your first love?'

Hannah swallowed deeply. She'd told no one about Mike, no one but Gloria, but she'd never been asked so directly before. 'Don't be upset or embarrassed, my dear,' Elizabeth said. 'It would never go any further than here.'

'There was someone,' Hannah admitted. 'I . . . I was engaged to him. We . . . We were going to get married by special licence, just in a registry office, you know. He had leave coming up, but we knew it was likely to be just forty-eight hours. We were due to tell his parents then, but we didn't foresee any problems. We'd met many times and they liked me well enough.'

Hannah had stopped even attempting to dry anything and stood with a plate in one hand, the tea towel held to her chest with the other, distress showing in every inch of her body. Her eyes were shining with tears and the sense of loss struck her suddenly and with such force, it almost took her breath away.

Elizabeth knew that Hannah was back there with her soldier and she made no movement, nor any attempt to speak. The room was very still and Hannah, her voice made husky with the tears that had squeezed out of her eyes and dribbled down her cheeks, went on. 'It was all arranged when suddenly all leave was cancelled and he was transferred south.

'Everyone was talking about the "Big Push", but although I wanted the war to be over, I also worried for Mike. He'd been injured before, but I had a funny feeling about this. I suppose I sort of knew when the letters stopped, but I hoped. You see, I had received no official news. That went to his parents.

'I didn't know that at first. When I'd had no letters for almost three weeks, I called to see them, frantically worried. They lived in Dewsbury in Huddersfield, quite a distance from the hotel where I worked then. I found their house in darkness. Boarded up! Empty!

'It was about another couple of months before I heard any more,' Hannah said, 'and that was from his friend, Luke,' remembering the letter Tilly brought to her just before she fled from the home. 'He told me Mike had been killed minutes after landing on the beach. He'd been caught in the blast himself and ended up in hospital on the south coast. He'd been out of it for a few months and not in any state to write to anyone.

'It was his mother visiting him that had given him the news that Mike's family had just disappeared. He'd not taken it in at first. He was very ill and still getting to grips with Mike being dead. They'd been special friends for years.

'It was afterwards he realised I would probably know nothing. He still couldn't write because he'd broken nearly every bone in his body in the blast and was in plaster up to the eyeballs. He dictated a letter to the nurse telling me everything he knew, which was precious little. I . . . I remember I went a little wild at the time.'

She looked at Elizabeth suddenly, her face contorted in grief, her eyes ravaged. 'I was beside myself,' she said. 'Half the time, I didn't know what I was doing. I knew I had to get away, everything in Leeds reminded me of Mike, places we'd been to together, people we knew. I couldn't stay.' She stopped and her voice dropped to a mere whisper. 'If I'd had Mike's parents' support, things might have been so different. As it was . . .'

'Is that why you came to Birmingham to Mrs Emmerson's?' Elizabeth asked gently.

Hannah barely heard the question. She remembered how fearful she'd been then, beaten down with shame, panic-ridden. Nowhere she could turn to. The plate she hadn't been aware she'd still been holding slipped through her fingers and shattered to pieces on the tiled floor.

Stupefied, Hannah stared at it for a couple of seconds before dropping to her knees and beginning to gather up the pieces into the towel while she gabbled, 'Oh, I'm so sorry, Mrs Banks, truly sorry. I really don't know what came over me. I just . . . I don't know how it happened. What must you think of me?'

'My dear! My dear!' Elizabeth said soothingly, lifting Hannah to her feet as Reg's voice called from the other room, 'You two women having a smashing time out there?'

Hannah looked towards the kitchen door, terrified Reg would appear there any second and order her and Arthur from the house. Elizabeth caught the look and made a dismissive flap of her hand towards the door. 'Don't mind him, that's his attempt at a joke. As for the plate, don't worry about it. It's just an old thing.'

It was no such thing, it was one of a Wedgwood set that Elizabeth was very fond of, but she felt Hannah had been so terribly upset by the revelations and remembrances that she'd urged her to tell, that she didn't have the heart to tell her. Elizabeth had felt the raw emotion running through Hannah, making her whole body quiver, as she'd helped her up and now she eased the young woman into a kitchen chair. 'Now you stay there,' she admonished. 'I'll make us a cup of tea and that broken pottery will be cleared up in no time.'

Hannah had been glad to sit, for her legs had shook so much and a roaring had begun in her ears and filled her head and she'd been afraid she was going to faint. But to her great relief, she didn't and eventually the pounding of her heart eased and her breathing returned to normal.

That incident between Elizabeth and Hannah was never referred to again, but it had forged a friendship between them. This had been noticed by both Arthur and Reg and while Reg had been pleased, Arthur had been delighted. He'd told Hannah over and over what an asset she was to him already.

So, kneeling beside her at the altar, Hannah knew Arthur thought he'd made a good bargain in the marriage. What of her? What had she latched on to Arthur for? She knew well why she'd married the man; because she wanted a home of her own and to be a respectable wife and most importantly, the desperate longing in her for a child.

She was glad Josie had come into her life when she did, although initially she hadn't wanted to look after her. Her coming had eased the ache Hannah carried inside her. This had especially been the case when homesickness had made her vulnerable and upset and Hannah could soothe her.

Eventually, she would have a child of her own, not that she imagined Arthur would make excessive demands on her, and although Arthur was a man who'd never touch her heart, she would be a good, dutiful wife. And then hopefully before too long, a devoted mother. Her life would then be complete and she'd be content.

Gloria watched the couple kneeling at the altar and wished Hannah and Arthur could have had a week at Blackpool, rather than just a mere three days. Josie had been keen to help, before and after school. The child had learned a lot since she'd come from Ireland and now she was a dab hand at many things in the kitchens and grand at serving the meals. She seemed to like doing it too, or at any rate she was always willing enough, so Hannah didn't have to worry about her.

But, somehow, she didn't think it had been Hannah's decision to have such a short honeymoon, but Arthur's. Hannah claimed he couldn't afford it, but Gloria was sure he could. One thing that did worry her about Arthur was his streak of meanness and she hoped Hannah could get him over it.

Gloria had told Hannah before the wedding that she should put her foot down. 'Start as you mean to go on, my girl,' she advised.

'He's saving for the wedding and honeymoon and all,' Hannah said. But Gloria was sure he'd have a bit put by, for hadn't he been working for years with only himself to see to and she could bet his mother left him something. And then his boss, so Hannah said, had promised him a rise on his marriage, when he would have a wife to keep.

Hannah, too, was afraid that Arthur was mean. She'd never told Gloria because she would go on and on about it. But the few times they'd been to the pictures, he'd never bought Hannah anything either going in, or in the interval. The first time, as the lights went up in the interval and the girls had gone down the aisles with the ice creams and such, Arthur had remarked. 'Never buy anything here. Places like these rip you off, don't they?'

They probably did, but there was something just so right about sitting in the cinema, eating sweets or licking an ice cream. That was what she'd enjoyed with Mike on his short leaves home, when she'd beg, cajole and bribe fellow workers at the hotel to change shifts to be with him as often as possible.

And after the ice creams, they'd take advantage of the darkness to snuggle together. Not that Arthur did that either. He sat stiff and erect in the seat beside her and never ever held her hand which she would have welcomed. It would have been comforting and Hannah, above all things in the world, needed comfort, comfort and tenderness.

But what odds now? Hannah thought, as she got to her feet as the organ began to play. The die was cast and it was too late for any regrets. Hannah was now Mrs Arthur Bradley and would stay that way for life.

Chapter Four

Hannah had been terribly excited to be going to Blackpool for her honeymoon and it was a shame that it turned out to be such a letdown for her. Her pleasure had been sustained in the train journey, especially when Arthur sat and held her hand, and had only begun to slip when she stepped out of the taxi outside the small and rather dingy hotel where they were to stay.

The crabbed woman who described herself as owner showed them to their room and issued them with a list of hotel rules and regulations and did so without even a show of welcome from her sullen mouth and hard, cold eyes.

Hannah circled the depressing room. The paintwork was a drab brown, the faded wallpaper was peeling in places and the bed, she tested by plumping herself down on it, was lumpy. She glanced up at Arthur and said, 'Not very nice is it?'

She was immediately sorry when she saw Arthur's face colour. 'It wasn't easy finding anywhere,' he said.

'I know. I'm sorry. That sounded very ungrateful,' Hannah said, contrite.

'And at least we have the meal to look forward to,'

Arthur said. 'They usually serve dinner at one o'clock, but I persuaded them to cook us a full meal when we arrived as a special favour. I knew we'd probably be hungry.'

Maybe a meal would put a new complexion on the matter entirely, Hannah thought. Maybe food would also still the panicky doubts that she'd done the wrong thing in marrying Arthur that were making her feel a bit sick. She pushed the doubts away, stood up and forced a smile on her face. 'You're right, Arthur. It's hunger making me so miserable. Shall we go down?'

Just a little later, Hannah was to sit in the dark, unwelcoming dining room and think that while the hotel staff might have agreed to serve them a full dinner, they were doing so begrudgingly. Arthur and Hannah were the only ones in the room, for high tea – the usual meal at that time of the evening – was well over and the guests had dispersed either to their rooms, the residents' lounge or the small bar their landlady had pointed out on their arrival. Hannah couldn't blame them, glancing around the room as she waited for the food to arrive. She knew it wasn't a place she'd have chosen to linger in.

And then the insipid, unappetising meal came and Hannah felt her spirits plummet. It was served by a girl with a sulky face and lank, greasy hair who laid the plates before them in a 'like it, or lump it' style.

And Hannah did not like it. The grey meat was tough and stringy, the vegetables over-cooked, the mashed potatoes lumpy and the whole lot of it covered with glutinous gravy that was barely warm. However, she refused to get totally depressed by it, even when the apple pie she'd ordered had more pie than apple. The custard she'd declined, remembering her experience with the gravy. Never mind, she told herself, we shan't spend much time in the hotel. Except, a little voice inside her said, for the bedroom.

She glanced across at Arthur and her stomach contracted as she thought of what lay ahead. Arthur caught her look and smiled. 'Do you fancy a walk, my dear?'

Hannah was glad that Arthur seemed to want to postpone the moment when they'd have to retire to that uninviting and chilly bedroom as much as she did and she agreed eagerly.

Once outside though, she wondered at the wisdom of such action, for the wind was fierce and snatched away all attempts of conversation. But as they neared the promenade clutched tightly together from necessity rather than desire, she heard the tantalising music of the fair.

Anyone who'd ever been to Blackpool told her about that fair, the Golden Mile they called it, and she'd caught a glimpse of it as they'd passed it in a taxi earlier that evening. But it was one thing to pass it quickly in the dusky half-light, quite another to come upon it in its full glory, ablaze with flashing lights of all colours, now that night had fallen over the town. Music from various rides was thumping all around them, mixed with screams and laughter.

Hannah had never seen anything like it and her eyes were everywhere and wide with astonishment. Beautiful carousel horses pranced round and round with laughing people astride them and just feet away, there were other carriages attached somehow to a huge big wheel spinning wildly, those inside them screaming like mad. And no wonder, Hannah thought. 'Oh, Arthur,' she said, breathless with the excitement of it all. 'I'd be frightened to death on that.'

Arthur laughed and squeezed her hand. Hannah passed many rides that night that alarmed her. One had little cars running around a track, which dropped so suddenly that Hannah gave a little cry of terror, sure a car would be thrown from the tracks, spilling out its unfortunate occupants. Arthur hugged her tighter, touched by her fear brought about by her inexperience of such things.

She stood mesmerised by a small area where cars darted about and seemed intent on bashing into other cars. They were attached to wires or something in the roof, she noticed, which sparked in a frightening way. 'What are they?' she asked Arthur. 'And what are they doing?'

'They're bumper cars.'

'Don't people get hurt?'

'Not often,' Arthur said. 'Look at the thick rubber around them. That's the whole point of it.'

Other booths advertised the 'Ghost Train', or 'House of Horrors', or 'Hall of Mirrors' and Arthur and Hannah were encouraged to sample the delights inside. 'Come on, sir,' said the woman outside the Ghost Train. 'Dark as pitch inside and filled with goolies. Gives you a chance to hold your young lady tight.'

Smiling, Arthur shook his head and turned away and then Hannah saw her first pink candyfloss. 'Oh, what's that?'

'Candyfloss.'

'It looks like cotton wool.'

'It tastes nothing like it. It's spun sugar,' Arthur told her. 'There are toffee apples too.'

But he didn't offer to buy Hannah either and she was too shy of him to ask, but she felt disappointed and told herself not to be silly, she couldn't sample all the delights of the place on her first evening. Arthur didn't offer to take her on any ride either and in fact, told her firmly that they were a waste of money.

Hannah supposed they were, but they appeared such fun. 'People seem to enjoy them though, Arthur,' she ventured.

'Hmph. A fool and his money are soon parted,' Arthur said pompously.

'But we could spend a little, couldn't we?' Hannah said. 'To sort of get value out of the place.'

'"Value out of the place!"' Arthur repeated. 'My dear, we've just had a wedding which was not cheap, despite the help Mrs Emmerson gave us and there was the train journey here, and the lodging house we're staying in. Believe me, there is little over for indulging in a fair. Never mind,' he went on consolingly, as he patted her arm. 'Women are not supposed to understand such matters.'

Hannah opened her mouth to argue, but shut it again. She'd paid for Josie's outfit and her own, but the small reception in the room behind the Lyndhurst pub afterwards had been paid for by Gloria on her insistence. The honeymoon was Arthur's contribution, and maybe it had cost a lot and there was little over, but surely just one or two rides wouldn't break the bank?

'Tomorrow,' Arthur said, 'we'll take a walk along the front. That at least won't cost us a penny. And now, I think we should make for home. I'm ready for bed myself.'

Hannah felt her face flame. The pleasures she'd lovingly shared with Mike Murphy she could now share legally and properly with her husband. She hoped he'd never need know that she wasn't a virgin, for she knew a man like him would expect her to be.

But Hannah needn't have worried. They returned to the hotel frozen, their red cheeks and dishevelled clothes showing the power of the wind. Arthur smiled at her as she took off her coat and tried to flatten her hair. 'Leave it,' he said. 'You look lovely. Would you like a nightcap?'

Hannah had never cared overmuch for any alcohol she'd ever tasted, so she said, 'Not for me, Arthur. I'm chilled through and I'd really like a cup of tea.'

Arthur laughed. 'Really, my dear. You can't have a cup of tea. If you want warming up, I'll buy you a brandy. That should do the trick, but don't get too much of a taste for it. It's very expensive stuff.'

Hannah, from the first sip, knew she'd never develop a taste for brandy. She thought it was like the worst medicine she'd ever been forced to swallow. It did warm her up, however, although she felt her throat to be on fire.

It didn't stop the shaking inside though, for that wasn't due just to the cold, and her heart began to jump about in her chest when Arthur whispered in her ear just as she drained her glass. 'Shall we go up?'

Upstairs in the bedroom, Arthur seemed like a different being. His eyes looked heavy and his mouth rather slack and Hannah knew he was filled with desire for her. She wished she felt something for him, but he stirred her not at all.

But, she reminded herself, she'd married him. Because a priest spoke words over them and they had a paper proving they were man and wife, Arthur had a perfect right to do as he pleased and she had to submit to him. She'd never felt she'd submitted to Mike. She'd wanted sex as much as he had. And now, though she didn't love Arthur, she liked him well enough and in a way longed for fulfilment, so why was she shaking and afraid? She at least knew what it was about, though she'd have to hide that fact from Arthur, so there was no need at all for her to feel nervous. It was perfectly normal and natural and she told herself to get a grip.

She undressed hastily and slid under the covers, hiding her nakedness. 'Put out the light, Arthur,' she begged, and Arthur did before getting into bed beside her. Hannah felt Arthur trembling and knowing he was as nervous as she was, she put her arms around him. 'You are a very beautiful girl, Hannah, do you know that?' he said and without waiting for a reply went on, 'I feel a very fortunate man tonight.'

'Oh Arthur . . .' Embarrassed, Hannah began to protest. However, she got no further for Arthur kissed her, but not the tender, tentative kiss she'd been expecting and would have welcomed. Arthur's kiss was like a stamp of ownership and Hannah felt her lips pushed against her teeth. And then Arthur parted her lips and pushed his tongue into her mouth till she felt she would choke and she began to thrash her head backwards and forwards.

This seemed to excite Arthur further. Panting heavily, he released Hannah and then he sat astride her, kneading her breasts savagely with his fingers, squeezing her nipples until she cried out in pain.

Arthur smiled, taking Hannah's cries to be born of desire, and slipped one hand between her legs while the other trailed over her body.

Hannah opened her eyes that she'd kept closed in pain and saw Arthur's face contorted with desire and she felt excitement building inside her. And yet, she felt no hardening of Arthur's penis against her and looking down, she saw it between her legs, as soft and flaccid as when he'd begun.

Arthur caught Hannah's eyes on him and his face flushed crimson with shame. He threw back the covers from them both and sat on the bed, his head in his hands, and began to sob.

Hannah dampened down her own frustration, for she felt sorry for Arthur and she knelt up in bed and gently put her arms around him. He raised his eyes, hardly able to believe what Hannah was doing. He felt inadequate and very ashamed. 'I'm sorry.'

'Ssh, it doesn't matter.'

'You . . . You don't mind. You don't despise me?'

'No. No, of course I don't despise you. The very idea!' Hannah said.

'But . . . But it's our wedding day . . . Our wedding night.'

'And such a lot of nonsense spoken about it,' Hannah

said fiercely. 'It would put a lot of stress and strain on anyone. It's a wonder any couple does it the first night. Maybe they don't indeed. No one would ever know. Don't worry, Arthur. Haven't we the rest of our lives to get it right?'

Arthur felt relief flood over him. He'd been aware of this problem all his adult life, though it had never bothered him, but he'd thought and hoped that with Hannah, whom he admired and respected, it might resolve itself.

And yet Hannah proved to be so understanding, so sympathetic, so special, that Arthur began to feel better about himself. He allowed her to coax him back to bed where she snuggled down under the covers, and curled her body around his. She lay awake long after Arthur slept and vowed to herself that she'd never make Arthur feel bad about that night.

The next morning, Arthur seemed fully recovered and was his usual attentive self and Hannah knew that that was how he was going to deal with it – pretend it had never happened.

She took her lead from him. That day, they strode out after breakfast up to the front. Hannah had never seen the sea, except for the grey expanse of water she'd crossed on her way to Ireland.

She'd never heard the roar of it, or seen a long beach of dull, beige-coloured sand and large grey and black boulders. She'd never seen the rising swells of it and the white-fringed rollers that came crashing down on to the rocks in a sea of swirling foam. Despite the biting wind, Hannah was fascinated and stood watching it until Arthur drew her away and put his arms around her shivering body. 'Come on, you'll get your death of cold,' he said.

'Oh, but, Arthur, it's so beautiful. Majestic, somehow.'

'And free,' Arthur added.

Hannah wished he hadn't said that. It spoilt the moment. After a while though, Hannah was chilled through and she looked longingly at the numerous cafés around them. 'I'd love a cup of tea or coffee, Arthur,' she said. 'It would thaw me out.'

'Nonsense, my dear, it's not cold, just bracing,' Arthur said. 'And really it's pointless wasting our money in such places. You'll spoil your appetite for dinner at the lodgings and after all, that is paid for. We'll just walk a little further and then turn back and be in good time for it. Hold my arm and you'll feel warmer.'

Hannah felt no warmer, but held on to Arthur's arm anyway, unable to think of anything further to say. Anyhow, she was interested in seeing Blackpool Tower, which Arthur told her was modelled on the Eiffel Tower in Paris, France, and she gazed at it in awe. There was an entrance fee to climb it with delights promised on every floor, but Arthur declared it to be a total waste of money. 'What would you want to climb up there for, my dear?' he asked Hannah incredulously, when she expressed a desire to go. 'You're complaining of the cold now. Don't you think you'll be blown to pieces and colder than ever on the top of that?'

'Yes, but I'd still like to go. It's just the experience, isn't it?'

'A costly experience.'

'It's not so much.'

'Maybe not to you,' Arthur said, turning away as he spoke. 'Come along, we'll be late for dinner if we're not careful.'

Hannah followed glumly behind him, feeling sure the dinner they'd ordered at the hotel would be little improvement on the one they had served to them the previous night. Or indeed the breakfast that morning – lumps of tepid scrambled egg served on old, soggy toast with barely a scrape of butter on it.

Most of the other residents were much older than Hannah and Arthur and not inclined to make conversation and Hannah felt the dining room to be a dismal unfriendly place. The food was no help in dispelling this feeling and yet Arthur didn't seem to find it a problem. It's probably cheap, that's why, Hannah thought later that day, as she chewed her way through sausages burned on the outside and still pink inside and tasting like sawdust. Cheapness seemed to be the only thing Arthur cared about.

It was the next day after another, fraught night when Hannah had to say similar consoling words to Arthur that Hannah finally lost her temper. It happened because Arthur declared the Winter Gardens too expensive a place to go inside.

'All I've heard you say since we arrived is that this, that and the other is too dear or a waste of money,' she cried. 'This is our honeymoon! It's supposed to be enjoyable. Much as I like the sea, I don't want to remember that on my honeymoon all I did was wander up and down looking at it.'

Arthur looked affronted. 'Hannah, if I may say so, you do not understand the cost of things,' he said stiffly.

'Yes I do!' Hannah retorted. 'I'm not a child. But if money is a problem, I'd rather not have had a honeymoon here at all. It would have been easier not showing me a host of delights I cannot enjoy or take part in.'

'Please, Hannah, keep your voice down,' Arthur hissed, looking around at the people in the street anxiously. 'People are looking.'

'Well, let them look,' Hannah snapped. Her eyes were flashing fire and her face bright with temper as she went on. 'I'm not putting up with this penny-pinching attitude any longer.'

What she was about to do to change it she hardly knew, but before she was able to make another retort, Arthur glared at her, horrified, and then turned from her and began walking away. Hannah realised she had two choices; either to turn after him berating him like a fishwife, or leave him to sulk and go about on her own.

She still felt too angry with Arthur to run after him and despite her spirited retort, she had a horror of showing herself up in public and so she stood for a moment, watching Arthur's stiff back get further away from her before turning her head and walking the other way.

All in all she had a good afternoon. She had a little money of her own and she intended to use it. She'd never seen slot machines and one-armed bandits that Blackpool had in abundance and normally would have been more careful with her money, but that day she threw caution to the wind and, though she lost every penny she spent, she decided it was good fun. She then tried unsuccessfully to get the arm of a crane that was encased in a glass box to lift a watch up for her, and she put money in the laughing policeman, which put a smile not only on her face, but anyone's in earshot.

She had little left after that, but enough to pay to climb the Tower. She stood on the top, buffeted by the wind as Arthur had prophesised, and unable to see much because of the leaden grey sky. But, she was still glad she did it. What was the point of coming to Blackpool and not climbing its most famous landmark?

Once more on the ground, she wished she didn't have to return to the dismal lodging house for the awful stuff they put in front of you under the guise of food. She looked longingly at the succulent fish and chips she saw people tucking into in the cafés and the smell of it made her stomach rumble. But she was nearly out of money and only had enough for one small cup of coffee before making her way back.

Arthur greeted her coldly, which was only what she expected, and they ate the badly cooked lump of doughy, grisly, indeterminate meat covered in brown, tasteless gravy, that the lodging house described as steak and kidney pudding, in silence.

It was as they started on the roly-poly pudding, which was made with the same dough as the dinner, but this time smeared with jam and covered with over-sweet yellow custard, that Hannah leaned towards Arthur. 'Come on,' she coaxed. 'We can't go on like this. I did have a point this morning, say what you like, but I did. You don't like spending money on anything.'

'Someone has to look after the pennies.'

'I'm not expecting you to take me to expensive places or spend every penny,' Hannah protested. 'But just to relax now and then and not go all stiff and starchy if I suggest we have a few goes on the fair, or stop for a drink of coffee.'

Begrudgingly, though never acknowledging that Hannah was right, Arthur did go to the fair later that day. It was not a success. It seemed to give Arthur actual pain to spend money and he showed such little emotion on any ride he went on that he dampened Hannah's enthusiasm. The thrill of fear that rippled down Hannah's back as the Big Wheel thrust them into the air made her want to scream, but the look on Arthur's face stifled it in her throat, as it did her shout of exhilaration on the Carousel or the Big Dipper. As for the Ghost Train, Arthur was no earthly use to her. The long moans and sudden appearance of a skeleton looming up in the blackness and the spidery things that brushed her face and trailed in her hair caused her to start suddenly and give little yelps of terror. But no comforting arm came around her.

Even the candyfloss was a disappointment; though she pulled large lumps off, as soon as she put it in her mouth it seemed to disappear and she got incredibly sticky. But she didn't complain to Arthur and didn't bother asking for a toffee apple, or an ice cream.

That night Arthur made no attempt to touch Hannah and she was relieved to be able to sleep unmolested, though she tried hard not to show it.

The following morning, Hannah lay and listened to the rain hammering on the windows and she got out of bed and padded across the floor to see heavy, relentless rain, the sort that sets in for the day, falling like steel stair rods from a blackened sky. They were to go home that day and really she was glad. Maybe Arthur would relax in his own house more and she was sure if he could relax, let himself go, the problem he had with arousal would be solved. It wasn't that she longed for the sexual act itself, knowing with Arthur it would probably be a disappointment, but she knew it was important to him, like it would be for any man. It was also necessary if Hannah was to ever have the child she longed for. She gave a sigh, turned from the window and began to dress.

The breakfast bacon was nearly raw, and the eggs scrambled and just as tasteless as those the previous day, but it hardly mattered anymore. They were going home. Hannah would be mistress of her own house and then any meals would be cooked by her. She'd been a fairly indifferent cook when she'd first come to Gloria's, but she'd learnt quickly and now good food properly cooked and presented was important to her.

She was looking forward to seeing both Gloria and Josie again, surprised how much she'd missed them. She turned to say something about it to Arthur on the train going home, but he forestalled her. 'This business of the child, my dear.'

'Josie?'

'Yes, Josie. She gets on very well with Mrs Emmerson, wouldn't you say?'

'Well, yes. Sure the devil himself would get on with Gloria.'

'Quite,' Arthur said. 'So then, if Josie were to stay with Mrs Emmerson . . .'

'Arthur, we've been through this,' Hannah said with a sigh. 'My sister entrusted Josie to me. It was almost the last lucid thing she said. I promised to look after her and she died peacefully because of it. I cannot and will not go back on that promise.'

'These deathbed promises are all very well, but to tie yourself to a child . . .'

'I'm sorry, Arthur, but that's how it is. We had this out months ago. You said you would make her welcome.'

'Have you considered the cost of rearing her?' Arthur snapped. 'At least we should have a contribution from her family for that.'

'Who from, Arthur?' Hannah said. 'One brother is a priest and one sister a nun, another in Connemara hasn't two half pennies to bless herself with. Ellen's just recently married, while Sam just makes enough to keep himself and his grandparents, and two more are making their way in America.'

'What of the house? There should be money there?'

'Yes, there will be,' Hannah agreed. 'But split between all of them it would not amount to that much. It goes to auction next week, for there wasn't enough interest in it, so Sam said. The money for the beasts is already banked and any farm equipment that Sam had no use for.'

'Well, however much it is, or isn't, when it's all settled that money should come to us,' Arthur said. 'In fact, you should have a share in it. You grew up with them.'

'But I'm not part of the family,' Hannah said. 'I don't want their money and I won't let you spend Josie's share.'

Arthur's mouth dropped open in amazement. 'That money is ours by right.'

'I'm not talking right or wrong in this,' Hannah said.

'One day the child may need money of her own.'

Arthur was furious. 'I can't be expected to bear the total cost of that child's care until she is adult without the least financial contribution.'

Hannah knew with Arthur's true aversion to spending money, Josie would never be truly welcome there if it was affecting his pocket and in a way, he had a point. Martin had said he would send something for her when he was settled and she'd never known him let anyone down before. But nothing had come yet, and she didn't want Arthur to hold any antagonism towards the child. She'd feel it, even if nothing was said, and that was the very thing she wanted to avoid.

'Then let me go back to Gloria's to work,' Hannah said. 'You know she wants me to. I'd get your breakfast first and leave the evening meal ready.'

'I didn't want you to work,' Arthur said mulishly. 'Not now we're married.'

'I know you didn't,' Hannah said placatingly. 'But think about it, Arthur. What would I do at home all day anyway?'

'What if you should have a child of our own?'

Hannah bit back the retort that something would have to be resolved in the sexual area before that could be achieved. Instead, she said, 'Then I should imagine I'd have plenty to do. But just for now, Arthur?' She felt his resolve weakening and so she played her trump card. 'And then Josie living with us wouldn't cost you anything, I'd be able to see to her myself.'

Arthur considered the proposal. He had no desire for Hannah to work. Really he had no desire for her to go anywhere and have men look at her now she was married. She was his wife and as such his needs should be paramount in her life. But he knew children were expensive, he'd heard colleagues talking about it at work, the amount they ate and the clothes and shoes they needed.

Maybe, he thought, this would be a solution to the problem for the moment. When the farm was sold, he'd have that money, whatever Hannah thought. He was the head of the house and as such he'd insist Josie's inheritance be passed over to him. No need though to upset Hannah by telling her that, not yet anyway. He nodded sagely. 'Let's try it for three months or so,' he said. 'See how it goes.'

'Okay, Arthur,' Hannah said, trying to hide her pleasure. She hadn't thought that marrying Arthur would mean a total cessation of work from the beginning, though she'd known that her hours would have to definitely change in some way. But at first, Arthur had been adamant that he wanted her at home full-time.

After three months, things might be different, but then again they might not. 'Gloria will be so pleased,' Hannah said. She gave a sudden shiver of excitement. 'I can't wait to see her again,' she went on. 'Josie, too, of course.'

Arthur gave a grunt, but said nothing further, never a man for small chat. Now that the matter had been resolved satisfactorily, he retreated behind the paper he'd bought at the station.

Hannah didn't mind. She lay back in the seat and watched the miles being eaten away. She wished she had a little gift for the two of them, but she hadn't even a stick of rock for Josie. Guiltily, she remembered her reckless spending on the slot machines that had swallowed up so much money.

Still what was gone was gone. No use crying over spilt milk was one of Gloria's sayings and an apt one, Hannah always felt. And that, thought Hannah, is true about my less than satisfactory marriage too.

Despite supposed to be helping Gloria, Josie had run to peep out of the visitors' lounge window at the front of the house half a dozen times before she saw the taxi turn into the road. 'They're here,' she screamed.

'All right, all right, I'm not deaf,' Gloria said, emerging from the kitchen as she spoke, drying her large red hands on a towel. But though her words were sharp, her eyes twinkled, and Josie knew she was pleased Hannah was home too.

Josie barely heard her anyway. She already had the door wrenched open and was halfway down the path.

Arthur and Hannah had emerged from the taxi and were standing with the cases around them when Josie threw herself at Hannah. Hannah felt a sudden rush of love for the child she'd not wanted originally and held her close in a tight hug.

Behind her, Gloria was urging them in. 'Come in and get a meal inside you. Josie has had her things packed up since just after breakfast. The house is all ready for you. I've been over and seen to it. Bought you some basics to give you a start at least, if you're determined to go there tonight. Lit the fires as well today and yesterday and aired the beds. Can't be too careful, I say. A house not lived in can easy get damp and September can be a treacherous month.'

Hannah let her talk. It was her way and she was kindness itself. She smiled at her and the beam Gloria gave in reply nearly split her face in two.

Oh, Hannah thought, I'm glad to be back home.

Chapter Five

If Hannah could have confided in Gloria she could have told her that her contentment in marriage had lasted just six weeks, until the end of October. It hadn't been a bed of roses until then of course, for the problems in the bedroom, which Arthur had never managed to control, had caused him great distress.

Added to that, his meanness, which had reared its ugly head on honeymoon, continued into their married life. He doled out meagre amounts of housekeeping every Friday evening, examined the shopping lists meticulously and quizzed Hannah for hours if she asked for more.

Apart from that, Hannah disliked his treatment of Josie. Despite his promise of trying his best to get on with her Hannah couldn't help feeling that if that was his best, she'd hate to see his worst, for he'd never really taken to the child. Sometimes he was so open in showing his dislike and resentment, that Hannah became frustrated and angry with him.

Then one day, towards the very end of October, Arthur came home from work in a foul mood. He'd been odd for a few days, morose and snappy, but Hannah, thinking he maybe had a problem at work that he didn't want to talk about, didn't worry too much about it. But Arthur had no problem at work; his problem was his marriage and that meant Hannah.

Despite inheriting the house and hints the boss was dropping about dependable married men, he doubted he'd have been swayed to marry anyone if Mrs Emmerson hadn't urged him to ask Hannah. And he had to admit that he'd been flattered when she'd accepted his proposal.

He'd been aware he had a sexual problem. He knew his penis didn't go hard, but then he thought he'd never given it occasion to. Before Hannah, he'd never had any encounter of that type, knowing his mother wouldn't have liked it. And not having discussed the matter of a hardened penis with anyone, he didn't know how normal it was and what to do about it. In fact, he was so hazy about the sexual act that eventually, and with great embarrassment, he'd entered a shop in one of the seedier areas of Birmingham and bought himself a book on the matter.

However, it hadn't touched on his problems at all. The book seemed to take it for granted that the desire and love the man had for his partner would make the penis erect naturally. It wasn't something you could ask anyone about, not even a doctor and Arthur had no idea what to do.

In his heart he knew he shouldn't have married, but he had and that was that. Initially, his abortive attempts caused him shame and embarrassment, then utter humiliation and eventually, anger.

And this anger he turned on Hannah, pushing away her arms when she sought to comfort him that night.

'Get off me! It's all your bloody fault,' he shouted at her when he'd again tried and failed.

'What is? What is it?'

'You know what! A bloody temptress that's what you are!'

Still Hannah felt sorry for him. She was as confused as Arthur over his sexual problem. Like him, she could never bring herself to speak about it, but she understood how it must make him feel. 'I told you it doesn't matter,' she said consolingly.

'Of course it bloody matters. Are you some sodding imbecile that can't understand that?'

Hannah gave a small gasp. This was the side of Arthur she'd never seen before. The face he turned towards her was almost puce, he was so angry, and his eyes were wild, his hair standing in spikes where he'd run his hands through it.

Still she persisted. 'Look, Arthur, I know it's important, but there's plenty of time. Shall I pop down and make us both a cup of tea?'

'Tea! Tea! You bloody stupid bugger, you,' Arthur cried, pushing at her so that she fell on the bed where he straddled her, holding down her arms while he spat out a stream of abuse, vile words, some Hannah had never heard before.

She thrashed on the bed to free herself, but Arthur held her fast, tightening his grip on her arms while he continued to yell obscenities at her. She closed her eyes for the light was still on and she couldn't bear the look in his eyes, nor his thin lips, rimmed with spittle.

Eventually, the violent tirade was over and Arthur

rolled away from her. Through anger, he'd felt a stirring inside him that any desire he'd felt for Hannah had never achieved, but still he was ashamed of his behaviour.

As for Hannah, she felt abused. If Arthur had had sex with her, which would have been his right after all, she'd have felt it at least showed normal behaviour. But this filthy, vitriolic abuse he threw at her was hard to bear and she hurt and ached all over, too, from his rough handling. Every time she closed her eyes she relived the scene and it was the early hours of the morning before she finally slept.

In the morning, she lay and tried to analyse the situation. Arthur was not naturally a violent man. Obviously, his frustrations had spilled over, that was all. Maybe she should battle to overcome her reticence and try and convince him to seek help. Perhaps there were things he could do, drugs he could take. They could do wonderful things these days.

Arthur, coming into the bedroom from the bathroom after a shave, saw that Hannah was awake and knelt down by her side of the bed. 'I'm sorry about last night,' he said, 'really sorry. I don't know what came over me.'

Hannah smiled at him. Hadn't she just told herself that that was the way of it? A one-off occurrence that would never happen again and so didn't have to be referred to at all. 'It's all right,' she told him. 'I understand.'

'You are a wonderful wife,' Arthur said earnestly, giving Hannah's cheek a kiss. 'The most wonderful wife in all the world.'

It was a little harder for Hannah to face Josie, who

showed by her plain embarrassment and downcast eyes that she'd heard every word of the confrontation in the bedroom the previous night. Still, it wasn't something Hannah felt she had to explain and certainly not to a child of nine, so she busied herself making breakfast.

Later, Hannah made her way to the guesthouse where she would help Gloria clear up after the breakfast, tidy and clean the rooms and prepare the evening meals for her paying guests.

It was only when the guesthouse was particularly full that Hannah would be required to wait on in the evenings now. Most times, Gloria said she could manage and Hannah was home in time to eat with Arthur and Josie.

Normally, she enjoyed the work and the company although that morning she wished she didn't have to go, for she was tired. She knew too she didn't look her best and that Gloria would be sure to remark on it. And she did, after a swift look at Hannah's face as she entered the kitchen. 'You all right?' she asked 'You don't look at all well.'

'No, I'm all right,' Hannah said. 'I . . . I didn't get much sleep.'

'Oh yes,' Gloria said with a knowing wink and when Hannah flushed crimson she went on, 'I mean it's natural and you are married.'

'There is nothing natural in our marriage,' Hannah wanted to cry. But this was something she could not share, not with anyone, so she forced herself to smile at Gloria as she exchanged her outdoor coat for an overall and began her work for the day.

* * *

For the next week things went on as normal and on 5th November, Hannah, Arthur and Josie went to a bonfire and fireworks party, which a friend of Gloria's was having in their garden. 'There will be soup and sausages and things to eat,' Hannah told Arthur. 'Do say it's all right?'

Arthur had no desire after a day at work to strike out again into the cold streets to watch a fire and a few paltry fireworks, but he went for Hannah's sake. She intimated that it was for Josie, but really she was as excited as the child.

He knew because Hannah had told him that they'd not had bonfire nights in Ireland, but Hannah had gone to her first one with friends from the hotel the first year she was in England. By the second year it was 1939, war had been declared, and bonfires and fireworks had been banned.

He wanted to please Hannah, because he still felt incredibly guilty about his behaviour and it wasn't as if it would actually cost anything. That made the decision as far as Arthur was concerned.

'Well,' he said, 'I consider it an utter waste of money buying fireworks to light up the sky and can never understand people wanting to do it, but if you want to go so much, we will look in for an hour or so.'

Hannah and Josie had a wonderful time. Josie's eyes were wide with astonishment at the fireworks. Roman candles, Golden Rain and Catherine wheels. Even the names were exciting and the bright colours of them sparking into the black night brought oohs and ahhs from more than Josie who'd eaten so many sausages, Hannah said she'd never sleep.

But she did, they all did, and the next morning Hannah got up in a buoyant mood. Life wasn't so bad, she thought, and Arthur could be handled easily with a little care and attention. Her good mood lasted all that day and even Gloria commented on it.

But Arthur came home again that evening in a foul mood. All day he'd fought his conscience because he knew he wanted to make love to Hannah and he knew not only would he fail, but also that it would probably turn out the same as last time, and he would be ashamed of himself because of it.

Hannah was unprepared for the assault that night, relaxed and at ease. She was pulling her nightie over her head when Arthur entered the room. In two strides he was behind her, wrapping one arm vice-like around her waist while pulling the nightie from her with the other.

Hannah gave a yelp and hearing the material tear, she cried out sharply, 'Arthur, stop! What's got into you?'

'Shut up! Shut your mouth!' Arthur cried, as he flicked the light out and kicked the door closed.

Hannah was nervous of the man she barely knew in this mood, but she didn't struggle. She had the feeling that he'd enjoyed her futile attempts to free herself the last time. This time she lay passive and felt his breath on her face as he screamed obscenities at her. She was conscious of Josie lying the other side of a stud wall and knew every syllable from Arthur's lips would be audible to her.

And it was audible, even when she buried her head beneath the blankets and wrapped her pillow around her ears. It was filthy talk, dirty words that she'd never heard from any man in her family. Some she didn't know the meaning of, but knew they weren't nice by the way Arthur said them. She wondered what he was doing to Hannah while he was saying such things, she'd been very quiet since the one short shout. What if he'd hurt her, killed her even? No, if he'd killed her there'd be no point in going on shouting at her. But all the same, she trembled in fear both for herself and Hannah.

Hannah wasn't dead, but petrified with loathing for the stranger her husband had turned into. His apologies the next morning were as sincere as ever, but when he assured her it wouldn't happen again, she didn't believe him.

It was as well she didn't for the same thing happened the next week and the next and the next. Sometimes only two or three days would pass, sometimes a week. Arthur always apologised and said how ashamed he was, but he refused to discuss his problem or seek help.

'My God, girl, you look peaky,' Gloria remarked one day. 'Mind you, you've not looked yourself for days. You're not . . . you know, expecting?'

'No,' Hannah said tersely, thinking 'fat chance'. Gloria looked offended at Hannah's tone and eventually she said, 'Sorry, Gloria, I'm tired, I'm not getting much sleep.'

'Well, I must say I'm surprised at Arthur,' Gloria said. 'Didn't think he had it in him.'

Hannah's mind was befuddled because of lack of sleep. 'Had what in him?'

'Don't act the innocent with me,' Gloria said quite

sharply. 'You know what's what as well as I do. Some men are the very devil, want to be at it morning, noon and night. You need to put your foot down.'

Hannah knew now what Gloria had been hinting at and hid a wry smile at Arthur being thought of as a sex-crazed Casanova.

Just before Christmas, a letter with an airmail stamp from America arrived and Hannah snatched it up eagerly, glad that Arthur always left for work before the post came. It hadn't been the first letter Hannah had had because Martin in particular wrote often and kept her up to date with the news.

This letter was no exception and in it Martin wrote of the impending marriage in March the following year of Siobhan to a wealthy New York banker.

He wrote,

Her future is assured now and so is mine for I've obtained a good job in a factory belonging to one of Aunt Norah's friends.

The farm business is now completed and Josie's share will be a little under three hundred pounds. We all also feel that while it was very good of you to take Josie into your home, you shouldn't suffer financially because of it. I will be sending twenty dollars a month for her and Siobhan and her husband another twenty dollars. We hope that this will help towards her upkeep.

Hannah was filled with relief at the offer of financial assistance, for Arthur had made it clear almost from the beginning that he was not clothing the child. Feeding her was bad enough, he'd said, and Hannah would have to apply to the family if she needed more money.

She'd never done this, but knew if Josie grew much more, nothing she had would fit her. Added to that, the black patent shoes she'd bought her for the wedding were not strong enough, nor warm enough, to wear through the winter, which was prophesised to be a bad one with much rain and snow.

So while the monthly allowance was a lifeline and one Hannah decided to use as needed, the three hundred pounds was Josie's security. The future payment for a wedding and honeymoon perhaps, for Hannah knew that Arthur would not contribute to either when the time came.

No luxuries were affordable on the money Arthur gave Hannah and she was finding more and more of her wages were being used to supplement the household budget.

But Hannah seldom complained and tried hard to keep the house peaceful, knowing that if she annoyed Arthur in any way she'd pay for it later. But somehow, she had to safeguard Josie's money for she knew Arthur would have it off her faster than the speed of light and she'd never see a penny of it again.

She wrote to Martin, thanking him for his and Siobhan's offer of financial help for Josie. She accepted gratefully on her behalf, but Josie's share of the sale, she said, she'd rather he kept and tied up in some fund or another to mature when she reached twenty-one, and in a way that no one else could touch it.

Josie was delighted that Hannah was eventually being

paid something for her keep, for she'd felt bad about living on her and knew Arthur resented it, but Hannah's handling of her inheritance worried her. 'Won't Arthur really be cross?'

'He may indeed,' Hannah said. 'Sure isn't that why I've asked Martin to have it tied up in trust for you?'

'Doesn't it . . . Isn't it a bit sneaky?'

'With Arthur, you have to be sneaky,' Hannah told Josie. 'He'd have the money off you before you'd had the chance to see the colour of it and that can't be right either. Your mammy wouldn't want that. She'd want the money to benefit you in some way, wouldn't she? I'll tell Arthur that Martin decided it that way, then he can't blame either of us, can he?' But Hannah knew Arthur would be furious when he discovered that he was unable to touch Josie's inheritance.

Josie chewed her thumbnail. 'I suppose,' she said at last. 'But what if you need it? I mean what if you had a baby of your own or something?'

'That won't happen, Josie,' Hannah said grimly. 'Believe me, that just won't happen.'

She felt suddenly very sorry for herself. She'd married a man she didn't love in order to have a child. And that was the one thing he couldn't give her. And because he couldn't give her a child, he hurled obscenities at her and abused her whenever the notion took him. It seemed to her she'd dealt herself a very bad fist indeed. It was a kind of justice, some would say.

Josie was looking at her with concern. She knew she'd said something to upset Hannah, but had no idea what it was. Hannah caught sight of the woebegone face. Whatever was wrong in her marriage at least they'd both had a choice in the matter, she told herself sternly. Josie had had none, it was nearly Christmas and she was still but a child.

She tried to push despondency aside and get into the festive mood. She extracted the dollar bills from the envelope – the first month's payment, and said, 'Now that you've broken up from school and I'm not needed at the guesthouse till after New Year, what do you say to having a day in town, just the two of us, and buying in some goodies and maybe a few presents for people?'

'Grand!' Josie said, glad that her aunt's good humour seemed to have returned. 'And,' she went on, anxious not to be a drain on resources, 'I do know all about Santa Claus and that, you know. A girl at school told me.'

'That's all right then,' Hannah said with a mock sigh of relief. She was glad she'd used some of her wages to buy things for Josie for weeks now to make sure her first Christmas without her mother and family around her wouldn't be a total disappointment. Santa Claus-believer or not, she would get a stocking to open on Christmas Day morning, before setting off for Gloria's where it had been arranged they would spend the day.

And the day wouldn't have been so bad at all, despite the lack of festive cheer in the Bradley household, if Arthur hadn't seen fit to launch one of his verbal attacks on Hannah in the early hours of Christmas morning.

He'd been moody since he'd come home that afternoon and Hannah couldn't understand why. He should have been in good spirits; they'd had a little party in the office at lunchtime, a few drinks with his colleagues and his boss, and he'd come home with a sizeable bonus, and a large box of chocolates for Hannah, the same as all the company wives had.

Hannah at least was delighted for, with the sweet ration still in place, chocolates were like gold dust, and yet nothing seemed to cheer Arthur.

Hannah wasn't too worried. She knew her husband's passion for hoarding money and for spending as little as possible and she thought it had probably upset him to have to increase her housekeeping in order to supply the few extras that even he saw they needed at Christmas time.

She took it as a hopeful sign that he agreed to go with her and Josie to the Abbey for Midnight Mass, certain the beautifully clear night with the stars twinkling and the moon shining down, lighting up the earlier fall of snow that crackled under people's feet, would be enough to lift anyone's spirits. 'Very Christmassy, a bit of snow,' she said, slipping her arm through Arthur's.

He just grunted a response, but Josie squeezed Hannah's other hand and said, 'I love snow too.'

Neither of them knew of the long hard winter to come when they'd be heartily sick of snow, but that night, it had a sense of rightness about it. The world was a beautiful place, Hannah decided, and it was almost Christmas Day. What could be better?

She couldn't believe it when she felt Arthur's weight upon her later that night. She'd been almost asleep, the carols still running in her head when he launched his attack as he came in from the bathroom. She tried to twist away from his grasp and felt her nightie rip open as it was torn from her. 'For pity's sake, Arthur, will you leave me be?' she cried.

But it was if she hadn't spoken and somehow the obscene words that Arthur spat out that night seemed to defile all that had gone before.

Afterwards, aching everywhere, Hannah cried herself to sleep and was in no great humour for Arthur's abject apology the next day. 'Don't say you're sorry,' she cried. 'Just don't. If you were sorry, you'd not do such things to me. Leave me be, Arthur. It's not right the things you do. Surely you can see that?'

Arthur got to his feet, avoiding her eyes, and began to dress. 'Look me full in the face and tell me what you do is normal behaviour,' she demanded shrilly.

And then Arthur faced her, his own face expressionless and his voice cold. 'If you've quite finished your tantrum,' he said, 'it's time to get up.' He paused at the door and said, 'By the way, my dear – Happy Christmas.'

If Hannah had anything to hand she would have hurled it after Arthur. Instead she punched the life out of the pillow and imagined it to be his face. She knew that Arthur would never in a million years believe that he might be in the wrong. In a way, she wished that she wasn't going to Gloria's house that day. Gloria was too astute by half and Hannah knew that feeling and looking as she did, she'd not be able to convince her that her life was hunky-dory.

Hannah was right; Gloria was not fooled. She sensed the tension in every line of Hannah's face and the smile that seemed to have been nailed there. Only Arthur seemed normal, for Josie was far too quiet, especially as it was Christmas Day.

I'll pop over and see her one day soon, she promised herself, and have a chat. See what's what. But she couldn't, for the bad weather put paid to any plans she had.

At first, most people had been quite philosophical about the snow. After all, that's what happened in winter and Birmingham only really got a sprinkling of it that didn't last long. The children loved it through the Christmas holidays, making snowmen, hurling snowballs at the unsuspecting and making slides that were a danger to life and limb for the unwary.

The adults struggled to maintain some semblance of order to their lives, going to work and shopping and later, when the schools reopened, taking children to school. But gradually things slowed down and ground to a halt altogether in some cases. The snow was relentless and blown into drifts by the gusting winds. This then froze solid at night and was covered by more snow the next day. The skies were leaden grey and not a glimmer of sun penetrated them and so lights were kept on most of the day and fires stoked up.

This caused a further problem in the increase in power used and so power cuts began and coal was rationed. Trams and trains were very late, or cancelled altogether. They couldn't run on rails filled with frozen ice, while buses and other vehicles couldn't operate on roads cut off by snow. As fast as the emergency services cleared them, they were soon as bad as ever.

1947 was the first year Gloria had not gone to the January Sales in the city centre stores. Normally, she stocked up on things for the guesthouse, as well as finding a few choice bargains for herself.

Even collecting the weekly rations was a chore. Not

indeed that there was much in the shops to be had, for many supplies were just not getting through. One woman that very day in the grocer's had commented to anyone interested, 'Looks like the bloke upstairs thinks Hitler d'aint kill enough of us already with his bloody bombs, he's now trying to starve us to death.'

She wasn't so far wrong either, Gloria remarked to Amy later. 'I mean, I don't say it's got much to do with God, like, but some of the shelves are near empty. And it's no joke with half the stuff on ration anyhow. I mean, if they haven't got one thing in, then you've got hardly much choice to get anything else. Must be a nightmare for women with families to feed.'

Gloria was glad she had Amy to talk to, glad their back doors were not that far away and that Tom always cleared the path so they could pop into one another's houses. She often thought she'd have gone mad in that big rambling house without Amy. Of course, normally she would have been kept busy. She was usually quieter through December, but once the New Year was over, the commercial travellers were on the road again, trying to make up the money spent out in the festive season.

But not this year. In a way, she was pleased she didn't have to heat the whole place as well as finding coal for the residents' dining room and lounge for there was a desperate shortage of it. As it was, she'd shut off all the house, but her own rooms, and even then she often went to bed early to save fuel.

She wasn't in trouble yet with money. She was canny with it and had plenty saved and yet she knew she couldn't go on with the situation indefinitely without any income.

She wasn't the only one. Many people either couldn't get to work, or got there and found there was no heating and often no light either. She'd seen pictures in the *Evening Mail* of people in shops wearing overcoats and trying to serve customers by candlelight.

But thinking of families brought Hannah to mind and how odd she'd been at Christmas. If she'd have been able to see her since, she'd have felt better. Amy knew what her friend was fretting over.

'You can't do anything about Hannah,' she said. 'She's a married woman now.'

'I know that, Amy, but you must admit she was peculiar over Christmas, they all were.'

Amy knew they were. She and Tom had come over in the evening for a bit of tea and you could have cut the atmosphere between Hannah and Arthur with a knife. But it wouldn't help Gloria to tell her that. She was a proper old worryguts about the girl as it was, but she was no fool either. 'Maybe she was a bit strained,' she admitted. 'They'd probably had a tiff.'

'Do you think that's all it was, a bit of a row?' Gloria asked anxiously.

'Bound to be,' Amy said confidently. 'Newlywed, see. Still getting to know one another.'

'If only I could see her, check that everything is all right.'

'Why shouldn't it be?' Amy said. 'She's better off than us, only yards from the High Street in Erdington and Tom says they try and keep that clear. Doesn't always work of course, but I bet Hannah can get out to shop and get coal delivered.'

'You're right there,' Gloria said. 'I thought that last coal lorry was going to overturn.'

'Or go ploughing through someone's garden and into their front rooms,' Amy said with a grim smile, remembering the coal man's valiant efforts to control his lorry that had skidded the last time he'd tried to deliver coal to them. 'Tom says this road's a bugger,' Amy went on. 'You should see him slithering and sliding over it to reach the main drag. Mind you, the kids make it worse. Them and their flipping slides. Something should be done about it before someone breaks their neck.'

'They're bored with the schools all closed,' Gloria said wearily. 'We'll just have to put up with it. God knows, it can't go on forever.' She gave a sigh and said, 'Put a few pieces of coal on that fire, Amy, before it dies out altogether and I'll make us some tea.'

Chapter Six

'What's happened?' Gloria asked, staring at Hannah in shock. Even in the gloomy half-light of Hannah's breakfast room, for the February day was dark and overcast, she could see the blue-black bruise on her left cheek and the split lip on the same side. The rest of Hannah's face was bleached white and her hair, once her crowning glory, was lank and tied back from her face with an elastic band. 'I walked into a door,' Hannah replied.

Even Josie, sitting on the chair in the room watching silently, couldn't have stilled the retort from Gloria's lips. 'Walked into a door, my Aunt Fanny. This is me you're talking to and I wasn't born yesterday. I know what manner of door it was.'

Gloria glanced at the child. There was nowhere else she could go, for the rest of the house was like an icebox and Gloria supposed Hannah could only get coal enough to heat one room. In front of Josie she could take this no further. But she'd not let it rest there. No, by God, she wouldn't. She'd encouraged Hannah to marry Arthur, she felt responsible. She never thought he'd be the kind to hit her, to hit anyone in fact.

But this would never do – this uncomfortable ominous silence. She must find something to break it. 'Did you have a nice birthday?' she asked Josie, knowing it had been two days before. 'I sent a card, did you get it?'

To her surprise, a shudder passed through Josie's slight frame before she said, almost expressionless, 'Yes, yes thank you, Mrs Emmerson.'

Gloria felt decidedly uncomfortable, but she soldiered on. 'I couldn't get out to the shops to buy you anything with the weather, you know, but I found this in my jewellery box and thought you might like it,' and handed Josie a tissue-wrapped little parcel.

'Oh,' Josie cried, pushing the tissue paper aside and taking the delicate silver chain with its sparkling sapphire pendant from the velvet box. It was the loveliest thing she'd ever owned and she was almost overcome with pleasure. 'Oh, it's beautiful.'

Hannah came forward to examine the necklace. 'Gloria,' she said. 'It's lovely, but isn't it a little valuable to give to a child?'

'Not at all,' Gloria said. 'Josie is ten now, a fine age. Double figures at last and I know she'll look after the necklace. I haven't worn it for years. It'll do it good to be worn by someone who values it.'

'You're very kind,' Hannah said and she smiled at Josie. 'Take it up to your room, pet, and put it safe,' she said gently.

There was a look exchanged between them, but Josie left the room without another word. Barely had the door closed when Gloria asked, 'Hannah, what is it?'

Hannah sighed, a resigned and weary sigh. 'It's many things,' she said. 'Too much to tell. Josie will be back in a minute, the upstairs is no place to linger. The whole house is freezing apart from this room.'

Josie would have loved to linger, to have snuggled down under the covers of her bed and pretended what had happened two nights before, the night of her birthday, hadn't happened.

She felt particularly guilty because she knew it had been partly her fault or at least that's what had annoyed Arthur to begin with.

Hannah had said she could invite three friends to a birthday tea, but with the bad weather it would be best to choose three who lived close so they wouldn't have so far to come. But that was all right for Mary Byrne, Cassie Ryan and Belinda Crosby, the three girls she'd made friends with at the Abbey school, all lived near her. 'It's a party,' Josie had told them.

She'd never had a party before in her life and neither had the others. The war years had put an end to that, rationing not allowing much in the line of party fare, and when Josie saw the table filled with delicacies and the beautiful cake in the middle with 'Happy Birthday' written on it in icing and ten candles, she felt tears prickle her eyes.

The children had gone by the time Arthur came in from work, Hannah had seen to that, and she was in the kitchen cooking his tea when he came through the door. But his eyes alighted straight away on the remains of the cake. 'What's this?'

Hannah turned down the stove. 'A cake I got for Josie,' she said and closed the door so that Josie had to strain her ears to hear. 'It's her birthday today.'

'And where did you get the money for such rubbish?'

'Not from you anyway,' Hannah snapped. 'From her sister and brother in New York, that's where I got it.'

'I should say that's for necessities, not frivolous nonsense.'

'It's for anything I see fit to spend it on. And a cake and a few goodies is not considered nonsense when you are just ten years old. Can't you see, Arthur, what the child has had to put up with this year?' Hannah hissed in a lower voice. 'This was her first birthday without her mother and family around her. I wanted to make it a little special for her, that's all.'

'I still say it's stuff and nonsense.'

'Then say what you like,' Hannah snapped. 'You have your opinion and I'll have mine.'

Josie, in the other room, sitting on a cracket pulled up before the fire, had been trying to read *The Railway Children*, one of the books Hannah had given her, but the voices distracted her. It was a shame, really, because she'd been enjoying the story. She'd never had a book bought for her before – not one to read just for itself. She'd had school books with extracts from stories in and poetry that you had to read and then answer questions about, but never a whole book for pleasure. And now she had two, for as well as *The Railway Children*, she had *Black Beauty*.

Arthur came into the room, rustling his evening paper impatiently, and Josie leapt to her feet. She wished the house wasn't so cold and she could run upstairs to escape the hateful glare Arthur turned on her. Hannah saw the look, too, and her heart sank for she knew she was in for it later that night as soon as the bedroom door was closed.

Suddenly she was angry. Why should she put up with it just when Arthur had the notion, the mean-spirited man she'd married who begrudged a child a birthday cake? He wasn't normal and she knew that as well as anyone.

She'd almost asked the priest about Arthur's verbal attacks on her in confession, for she felt sure honouring and obeying wouldn't include holding his wife forcibly on the bed while he spat obscenities at her. But how could she tell the priest that and explain why Arthur felt the need to do it in the first place? Nice Father Fitzgerald would be so embarrassed if she asked, while Father Milligan would probably say whatever a man did was just fine. He seemed to believe in the divine right of men to do exactly what they pleased to their wives.

So it was no good appealing to the priests for help, but she was determined if he started his obnoxious bullying behaviour that night he'd not have it all his own way. She remembered with a wry smile the old lady in Ireland who said she kept a hat pin under her pillow at night. She hadn't understood at the time, but by God, she did now. She thought a hat pin would have been a very comforting thing to have by her side.

But Hannah had no hat pin to hand later when Arthur came into the bedroom. She was in bed, clothes pulled up to her neck, and she saw Arthur smile maliciously as he began to peel his clothes off.

Hannah would not allow herself to be intimidated by Arthur's attitude and she spoke quickly before she lost her courage and louder than she had intended. 'Arthur, I need to talk to you.'

'You've had all evening to talk,' Arthur almost growled.

'I need to talk to you now,' Hannah persisted. 'About your behaviour. I can't have you going on the way you do. It's humiliating.'

Arthur, now naked, turned off the light and climbed onto the bed where he knelt and looked at her. 'You promised to obey me,' he said. 'Before a priest and a full congregation.'

'Not in this sort of thing.'

'It didn't stipulate. You just promised to obey.'

'Arthur, the things you say, some of them are pure filth, dirty, disgusting words. You'd need to confess them so it can't be right.'

'What I say in confession is not your business, you nosy bitch,' Arthur snapped. 'You're my wife and you'll do as I say,' and with a shot, he was upon her.

But Hannah, tensed, was ready for him and she rolled away and in a second had thrown the covers from her and was on her feet. 'You sodding bitch,' he said and added sneeringly, 'You want to play games, eh? Okay, I'll play games.' He reached her side as he spoke and as she tried to twist away, he grabbed her arms.

'Leave go of me.'

'Like hell I will, you bleeding whore!'

'I'm not! How can you say things like this?'

'All women are the same.'

Frustrated beyond endurance at her inability to get free from Arthur's vice-like grip, Hannah cried, 'Well, all men aren't the same. There's real men and half men like you.'

The blow Arthur administered knocked Hannah off

her feet. But she had no memory of falling or hitting the floor and when she came to, Arthur was bending over her. He'd been horrified that he'd hit her and then further surprised to find his penis harder and more erect than it had ever been.

Hannah, knocked dizzy by the blow, lay helpless as Arthur threw her nightie above her head and after a bit of fumbling about, entered her violently and without a word being spoken.

Hannah felt as if she had been ripped in two, for despite this not being her first time, she'd not been anywhere near ready. But she only allowed herself one little yelp of pain, remembering Josie next door, and bit her lip to stop herself crying out.

Josie had already heard the commotion in the room though, and the argument and then the skirmish and the punch and thud as Hannah's body hit the floor. Had she not been so afraid and wary of Arthur, she might have gone in then.

And then she heard the one strangled cry and gave a sigh of relief. Thank God, Hannah was all right – well, not all right, but at least alive. She'd wondered when she'd heard that thud. And then she heard the rhythmic grunts of Arthur and knew what he was doing. You can't live on a farm and not see animals mating, the stallion rising up to the mare, or the bull servicing the cows, or even the farm dogs mating with the bitches, not to know, but she didn't want to hear it and she buried her head under her pillow to muffle the sounds.

Arthur's grunts eventually stopped and he lay across Hannah, spent for the moment. So that was it, he thought, the thing talked about, that he'd wondered about, for so long. The sexual act and he'd done it. True, he'd had to hit Hannah, had to knock her down to enable him to do so and that had been regrettable. She'd asked for it in a way, but he'd never ever intended hurting her.

But now at least he'd achieved what seemed to come naturally to most people and he couldn't see what the fuss had been about. It had given him no great pleasure and he was in no hurry to repeat the process, especially if it entailed hurting Hannah to achieve it.

He eased himself from her and slowly and painfully she got to her feet and made her way to the bathroom. Arthur let her go, for something was tugging at his memory from the books on sex he had read. He switched on the light and surveyed the floor with a slight frown on his face. There was no blood and he suddenly knew he wasn't the first person to have sex with Hannah.

He was waiting for her when she came back. She avoided looking at him. She'd taken stock in the bathroom, looking at her bruised and swollen face and bottom lip oozing blood. In the past, Arthur had raised bruises on her arms from holding her too tight and across the top of her legs from the pressure of him on top of her. But he'd never before raised his hand to her and she wondered if this was going to be a new tactic he was going to employ and how she should deal with it if it was.

She knew separation was frowned upon by the Catholic Church. Divorce, of course, not to be contemplated at all, but she wouldn't stay and be used as a punchball by any man. But where would she go and now with Josie's welfare to consider too? Even Gloria might not welcome them back, because kind though she was, she strongly believed marriage was for life. Hannah had heard her discussing the moral decline of modern society many a time with Amy. She often said that war had brought a host of hasty marriages, often followed by disillusionment and divorce, and the number of fatherless children or those born to married women whose husbands had been away for years, would appear to be legion.

She never discussed these matters with Hannah, of course, that would be considered insensitive, but Hannah was well aware of her views on the subject. So her thoughts were in turmoil when she came back into the bedroom and she wasn't prepared for the question Arthur threw at her so savagely. 'Who was it?'

She looked up, perplexed, and he went on. 'The man you shagged, or were there so many you can't remember?'

'What do you mean? What are you saying?'

'Come, come,' Arthur said, mocking politeness. 'I'm no fool and you were no virgin.'

Hannah wondered for a fleeting moment if it was worth telling Arthur about the bittersweet love between her and Mike. She wondered if he'd understand how much she'd loved him and in the stolen moments they had during his short leaves how she'd ached to be kissed, held tightly, caressed and loved, and the one time when they'd both lost control. It hadn't seemed wrong. They were engaged and due to be married and it had been just one more expression of that love.

But she knew with one glance at Arthur with his

nostrils pinched tight in disapproval, his thin lips curled in disdain, and the manic light shining in his cold, brown eyes that he wouldn't understand how it had been in a million years. She must deny it. At all costs, she must deny it. But it was too late, for her slight hesitation had been noticed and it told Arthur that he'd been right in his assumption and her spluttered denial and even indignation that he should think such a thing didn't move him a jot.

'You can deny that you've slept with another before me till you're blue in the face,' Arthur said. 'But I know what I know. Incidentally, I didn't mean to strike you tonight. I regret that and I'm sorry. It will not happen again, for although you are my wife and will be given full respect in public where we will appear as a devoted couple, the sexual side of our marriage is over. I will never touch you again. I don't sleep with whores.'

What sexual side? Hannah was tempted to ask, but didn't for she was just relieved that there'd be no more of it. The only deep disappointment she had was that in the travesty of a marriage she was in, there would be no child. Maybe that was the punishment she had to bear, she thought, and she thanked God for Josie.

But how could she begin telling any of this to Gloria looking at her in that kind concerned way, especially as she knew Josie would be back any moment. 'Look at it,' she said, 'not two o'clock and almost as black as night. You shouldn't have come out, not in this.'

'Tom brought me,' Gloria said. 'He was coming to Erdington Village anyway, he had business in the bank, and I wanted to see you were all right.'

'And now you see I am,' Hannah said in a tight high

voice and Gloria noticed her eyes shining with unshed tears. And because of Josie, who'd come back into the room, Gloria said, 'Yes, I see you're fine.'

Later that same evening she said something completely different to Amy. 'Are you sure he'd hit her?' Amy asked.

'Certain and with a fist, I'd say,' Gloria said. 'She said she walked into a door. I ask you!'

'Did she say how it happened, or why?'

'She couldn't say much at all with the child in the room.'

'Oh no, of course not.'

'I'll get to the bottom of it, never you fear,' Gloria said.

A few days later, Gloria got her wish, the snow stopped and the winds, and weeks and weeks of snows on roads and pavements that had blown into drifts began to melt. With a roar like an approaching express train, thawing snow slid from roofs to lie in sodden lumps.

It was just as hard to get around with the pavements reduced to icy sludge and many of the houses that had been just cold became damp as well. There were constant reports in *The Despatch* and *Evening Mail* about the flooding in various parts of the city.

You couldn't wonder at it, Gloria thought, as they watched the streets turn into rivers of water and the lumps of ice or snow mingle with the rushing water. But despite the problems of the thaw, most people were glad the icy grip of that terrible winter, that did its best to paralyse the country, was coming to an end.

By the middle of March, people were on the move

again, the guesthouse began to fill up, and Tom Parry went to tell Hannah she could come back to work. 'How did she look?' Amy quizzed Tom on his return.

He shrugged. 'All right, I suppose.'

'She didn't have any marks on her?'

'Marks?'

'You know, marks, cuts, grazes. As if she'd had a bit of a knocking about?'

'Oh no. Nothing like that.'

'Well, did she look happy?'

'Christ, Amy,' Tom said, exasperated. 'I only exchanged a few words with her. We didn't touch on whether she was happy or sad.'

'He's useless,' Amy complained to Gloria later.

'No, he's just a man,' Gloria said. 'Don't worry, I'll get it all out of Hannah when she comes back to work.'

And she did. But she hadn't any winkling to do, for Hannah told her; she felt she'd go mad if she didn't tell someone. She told her everything from the honeymoon to what happened the night in February when Arthur knocked her senseless and was eventually able to copulate. 'I think power and violence work him up,' she said. 'I mean, it was just like he wasn't turned on by me or anything.'

'Well then, girl, he needs his head looking at,' Gloria said grimly.

'One thing, though, Gloria,' Hannah said. 'He knew I wasn't a virgin.'

'God Almighty! Didn't you deny it?'

'Of course I did, but he didn't believe me.'

'I wouldn't have thought he was that sexually experienced,' Gloria said thoughtfully.

'Well he isn't,' Hannah said. 'Couldn't be could he, even if he wanted to? No, I think he read about it. He had a book on the sexual act, I saw it when I was tidying his room.'

'So he's moved out of the bedroom then?'

'Oh, aye. That next day he did that, bought a new bed and a wardrobe and tallboy, all utility of course. They couldn't deliver them till the thaw began, so he slept on an old palliasse he found in the loft. Like I told you, he said he doesn't sleep with whores.'

'He doesn't know about the baby you had?'

'No, and he'll never need to know either,' Hannah said. She gave a shudder of apprehension at the thought of Arthur finding out about the illegitimate baby she'd been forced to give away years earlier. But even as she thought back to that painful time she felt a thrill of excitement run through her. She had news for Gloria. It was too early to be sure, but oh God, if it should be true! Anyway, early or not, she couldn't keep it to herself a minute longer. She turned to face Gloria and said, 'Oh Gloria, do you know what else? My period is late, only five days, but usually they are as regular as clockwork.'

'God, if you are, how do you think Arthur will take it?'

'I don't know,' Hannah said, 'and I don't care either. I'm so happy I don't know whether I'm on my head or my heels.' She grasped Gloria's hands and said, 'Don't you see this is one baby that won't be taken from me, one baby I can hold in my arms and one I'll see grow up. I can put up with anything to have that,' and she spun the older woman around the room. Gloria shared in Hannah's excitement and happiness. She looked at the light shining in Hannah's eyes and thanked God that sexual problems or no sexual problems, Arthur was able to perform once and that that was hopefully enough.

Arthur was more than delighted, he was ecstatic. He'd never had much time for children before; he'd accepted he wouldn't marry, so he never envisaged himself as a family man. But now, to think in that one attempt at proper sex, he had developed a little person, a baby growing in Hannah's womb, was to his mind almost magical.

That was the only jarring note, that Hannah with her loose morals might have any input into this child, this innocent baby. Well, he'd do his best to see she had as little as possible to do with it when he or she was born.

Reg Banks was delighted to hear that Arthur was going to become a father. It certainly cleared up some of the lingering doubts he had about the man which were obviously unfounded. Now Reg put it to his wife that he take Arthur into a managerial position. After all, Arthur did make it to work almost every day of that awful winter, walking the whole way more than once. Loyalty like that should be rewarded.

Elizabeth thought of Arthur's beautiful wife that she'd so taken to and agreed. 'We'll ask them to dinner and you can tell them then,' she said. 'There will have to be a hefty rise, too. Babies need so many things.'

So Arthur and Hannah, who barely spoke at home, went to dinner with the Banks. 'Can we bring Josie?' Hannah had asked Arthur when he'd come home with the news. 'I hate to leave her here by herself.'

'Of course you can't bring her. Reg Banks just asked you and me.'

'Well, they probably don't know Josie's here.'

'She's not going and that's final,' Arthur snapped. 'Ask old Emmerson to have her.'

Hannah did and Josie was glad for she didn't really like going anywhere with Arthur, he was so cross all the time. He didn't seem to like Gloria any more either, but then he didn't like a lot of people.

Arthur was resentful about Gloria because he assumed she knew all about Hannah's past, and had been laughing up her sleeve when she pushed her at him and he took the bait. He'd have liked to have gone up to her house and throttled the names of Hannah's lovers out of her.

At the Banks' house that night, few would have guessed at such thoughts teeming around Arthur's head. His manner was almost meek and he was politeness itself, solicitous of his wife's welfare to the extent that Hannah wanted to hammer him with her handbag.

'Are you well, my dear?' Elizabeth asked when the men had adjourned to the study to discuss business.

'Very well, thank you.'

'And are you excited about the baby?'

'Very,' Hannah said. 'Arthur is on at me to give up work, but I don't want to yet. It's early days and I would be bored at home. I mean Gloria won't let me do anything heavy and babies are so expensive.'

'I don't think you need worry about that, my dear,' Elizabeth said. 'Reg has a very inviting proposal to put to your husband.'

And at that moment, Arthur was staring at his boss, his mouth actually agape. Reg explained his new duties, the office he would have of his own and the secretary he would share, the expense account and the Ford

Prefect car that would be at his disposal, plus the hefty rise and bonus scheme.

'I'm . . . I must admit I'm staggered, sir.'

'You're a good conscientious worker, Arthur, and I'd like to see you get on. A family man needs a car and babies, children, are expensive little devils.'

'Yes,' Arthur said. 'And the money will be useful. I was hoping to engage a nurse when the baby is born, just until Hannah is on her feet.'

Reg looking at him thought again how he'd misjudged the fellow. Really, he was a husband to be proud of, cock-a-hoop at the thought of becoming a father and considerate and loving towards his wife. 'You'll need a first class nursing home too,' he said. 'People say the National Health System will be in next year where no one will have to pay for any damn thing, but it won't be in time for this child's birth.'

'No, indeed.'

'Book up a good place,' Reg urged. 'Early mind, for they fill up quickly. I'll pick up the tab on that.'

'Oh no, sir,' Arthur protested. 'You do enough.'

'Nonsense! Tell you the truth, Elizabeth has really taken to your wife. She would like to think of her being looked after properly. You must let us do this for you,' Reg said, offering Arthur a cigar.

Arthur allowed Reg to light the cigar before he spoke. 'Very well, sir. If that's what you and Mrs Banks wish to do. But it's very kind of you and Hannah and I will never forget it.'

He was aware that though he did work hard, he hadn't climbed so far or fast in the firm until he brought Hannah to meet his employers. He imagined Elizabeth

Banks had great influence over her husband and she'd really taken to Hannah. Not a hint of scandal about the state of their marriage must ever reach their ears and Hannah must realise that. If ever she felt the need to unburden herself to Elizabeth Banks, she would be cutting off her nose to spite her face for they'd all suffer.

But Arthur needn't have worried. Hannah was quite embarrassed at the amount she'd told Elizabeth the last time they met and steered the conversation into safer waters. She did tell Elizabeth, though, of her upbringing in Ireland and how she'd been raised by her sister and how she was doing the same for her young orphaned niece.

'And how old is the child?'

'Josie is ten now.'

'And is she pleased about the baby?'

'I haven't told her yet,' Hannah confessed. 'Nine months is a long time. I'll have to soon of course, pregnancy is something you can't hide.'

Elizabeth leant forward and squeezed Hannah's hand. 'I envy you, my dear,' she said. 'Your first child. You'll be entering a journey of discovery. Oh, Hannah, I predict you and Arthur have such a rosy future ahead of you.'

Ah yes, Hannah thought, but was wise enough not to say, 'But my path is strewn with thorns.' In fact, she was wise enough to say nothing at all; Elizabeth was quite satisfied with the smile she gave. 'Come on,' she said. 'They'll be out in a minute and Reg will start roaring for coffee,' and Hannah followed Elizabeth into the kitchen.

Chapter Seven

The first months of Hannah's pregnancy brought to mind the last time she'd been pregnant and how different it had been. For a start, she'd loved Mike, loved him with all her heart and soul. She had met him in the spring of 1941 at the Hippodrome in Leeds where she'd gone dancing with Tilly, the young northern girl who shared her bedroom. He told her he joined up when he was nineteen and had been one of the lucky ones rescued from the beaches of Dunkirk. But that was the last evening of a very short leave and though Hannah liked the young soldier very much, she wasn't sure what he thought of her, yet the fact that he was Catholic and of Irish descent like herself had drawn them together. And the man was so handsome, with his blond hair and startling blue eyes. He had full lips and a determined chin and skin slightly tanned from the outdoor life and Hannah readily agreed to write to him.

However, the letters, which started off in friendship, grew more ardent as Mike and Hannah got to know each other better and when they met, over a year later, Hannah was sure she loved him. But it wasn't until the summer of 1943, when he was invalided home, that Hannah realised the full strength of her feelings and she knew then that Mike Murphy was the man she wanted to spend the rest of her life with.

Mike's injuries were serious enough to keep him out of the army for a while, although not life-threatening, and Hannah spent every spare minute that the hotel and hospital would allow, sitting by his side and later at his house, helping him recuperate.

She'd cried when he'd been declared fit enough to rejoin his unit but was pleased and relieved that he was at a training camp for a few months. Mike told her that he felt they were training for something specific and Hannah declared she didn't care if he did that till the end of the war. It would suit her fine.

Then one evening in late January 1944, he held her tight and told her he didn't think it would be long before his unit's training would be over and then God alone knew where they'd be sent. Fear clutched at Hannah and Mike comforted her and as their passions took over, neither of them could have stopped the inevitable happening.

He'd been worried about repercussions of their passion, she remembered, but it was the last day of his leave and they could do nothing about it, but he clutched her tightly before he left and said, 'Let's get married, Hannah.'

'Why, yes. We always said . . .'

'No, no I mean on my next leave,' he'd urged insistently. 'I want to keep you safe. What if anything should happen to me? I mean what if you were to become pregnant?'

Hannah couldn't bear the look of anxiety on Mike's face. He had enough to worry about without adding her to his list. 'It'll be all right,' she said confidently. 'It never happens the first time.'

'Maybe not, but what about the next time, the time after that?'

'Perhaps there won't be a next time,' Hannah said with a smile. 'Do you think I'm some sort of sex maniac?'

'No, but I do know if you love me just half as much as I love you, you'll be unable to help yourself. No,' Mike said firmly. 'I've decided. Before I leave, I'll buy you a ring, not the engagement ring I would want for you, that will come later, but one to sort of mark our decision. We won't tell anyone just yet, because the marriage will have to be done in the registry office.'

'Registry office!' Hannah repeated and her heart plummeted. She knew that the Catholic Church would consider it no marriage at all.

'I know what you're thinking,' Mike said. 'Really I do. My parents won't like it either and that's why we must keep it secret, but things are up in the air at the moment. I sometimes don't hear till the last moment that I've got leave. We couldn't do a big church thing. We'll have to leave that till after the war. This is just to safeguard you.'

'Mike, it's all right.'

'No, Hannah, it's not all right,' Mike replied firmly. He took her in his arms and held her tight against him. He wished they could stay like that. That he could marry her that day, that instant. If anything should happen to his beloved Hannah because of that night and he was not there to protect her . . . It didn't bear thinking about. No, she would have his ring on her finger at the earliest possible moment.

Hannah saw Mike's face furrow as the thoughts raced through his mind and she held his face between her hands and kissed his lips. 'All right, Mike, we'll get married whenever and wherever you want,' she said. 'But please stop worrying about me.'

'Look,' he said, 'when I know when my next spot of leave is, I'll phone the hotel and tell you. You book the registry office for the next day, I'll bring Luke with me if he can get off too, and you bring a friend along as a witness and with the deed done, we'll go and see my parents.'

'They'll go mad.'

'If they do, it will be me they blame,' Mike said. 'But they'd get over it and they do like you.'

'I like them,' Hannah said, and she did like Mike's parents, Colm and Bridie, who obviously doted on Mike, their only child. 'When I think of some of the girls Mike could have chosen,' his mother had confided quite early on in their courtship, 'I'm glad he's fallen for someone like you, a nice Catholic girl from a respectable family.'

'I love Mike,' Hannah had said simply. 'And I will spend my life making him happy.'

'I know you will,' Bridie had said. 'And perhaps in time and if God wills it, you'll have a fine family. We wanted a host of children you know, but we only had Mike. Ah, but then he's been a son in a million.'

However cross or disappointed they might be over the clandestine marriage, Hannah knew they would not risk alienating their only child. Mike was right, they'd get over it. Not so her sister Frances who would be mortified and would never countenance such a marriage. But then, she was miles away, there was no need at all for her to be told anything. Mike had no need to tell her to keep it a secret, she'd keep it to herself all right.

There was one person she did tell though; her friend, Tilly. She showed her the ring that Mike had bought her, hanging on a silver chain around her neck, and told her what she and Mike intended to do on his next leave.

'Will you come, Tilly, and be a witness?'

''Course I will,' Tilly said. 'I'd be honoured. When will it be? Has he any idea?'

Hannah shook her head. 'He's phoning me here when he knows,' she said. 'I've had a word with the girls who man the desk and they are quite prepared to take a message.'

Mike's letters came regularly and as February 1944 drew to a close, Mike mentioned that he might get a longer leave than he thought.

'Embarkation then,' Tilly said. 'They always give them a long leave before shipping them out. People say there's summat brewing on the south coast.'

Hannah hoped it was just a rumour. In her opinion, Mike had done enough.

One morning in the middle of March, Hannah felt sick as she got out of bed and had to run to the lavatory on the landing that all the indoor female staff shared. 'What was that all about?' Tilly asked on her return.

Hannah shrugged. 'Must have eaten something that disagreed with me. I still don't feel too hot. I'll not be wanting breakfast this morning.'

The sickness had passed by lunchtime and Hannah was glad of it. But the next morning it happened again. Tilly was waiting for her when she returned the third morning, wiping her mouth on her handkerchief, her face drawn and pale so that her eyes looked even bigger. 'Don't bite me head off, Hannah,' Tilly said. 'But you couldn't be pregnant, could you?'

She saw from Hannah's face that she could indeed, but also that the thought hadn't crossed her mind till now. 'Have you and Mike . . . you know. Have you done owt?'

Hannah gave a brief reply. 'Only the once.'

'Only needs the once though, don't it?' Tilly said. 'When was your monthlies?'

Hannah had never taken much notice, but now forced to remember, she realised with horror, 'New Year's Eve. Don't you remember we were up to our eyes serving that big dinner and I had to go running to my room?'

'That's right,' Tilly said. 'God, Hannah. Ain't you seen anything since then?'

'No,' Hannah's voice was a mere whisper.

'Then I'd say you're expecting all right, girl. Best write and tell him.'

'No,' Hannah said. 'He'll be home soon. I don't want to write that in a letter for the censor to see. He's due a leave soon.'

'Someone will notice and they'll throw you out,' Tilly warned. 'It's happened afore. Oh, you needn't think I'd ever tell on you, Hannah,' she said, seeing the aghast look on Hannah's face. 'I'll cover for you, but if they should guess like.'

Hannah pressed her nightie across her stomach. 'No one will know. I'm not showing yet.'

'It isn't that,' Tilly said. 'They'll hear you being sick every morning and put two and two together.'

But she could do nothing about it and each morning would find her galloping for the lavatory and feeling washed out for the rest of the morning.

She noticed the kitchen staff and the cook looking at her askance a few times, so when eventually she got the news that Mike would be home in late April for two days and she could go ahead and book the registry office, she was ecstatic. 'So he's coming back, is he?' the cook remarked on hearing the news. And with a pointed look at Hannah's stomach, she added, 'And not afore time, I'd say.'

'We're going to be married.'

'Not afore time there and all.'

'They knew,' she said to Tilly.

'Well, they're not saying owt,' she told Hannah. 'That's good of them. If you hadn't been so well liked, you'd have had your cards by now.'

She couldn't wait to be married, to become Mrs Michael Murphy. She loved the sound of it and hugged herself with excitement as the day drew near.

She'd bought a full dress that would hide her slightly thickening waist. It was a shimmering blue and made of silk that cost her a fortnight's wages and all her clothing coupons for a month, as well as some of Tilly's, but she told Tilly she only intended to marry the once. Tilly went with her to choose her hat, shoes and handbag, the excitement mounting with each purchase.

'Every time I think about it, I feel all jittery,' she confessed to Tilly.

'You better calm down,' Tilly warned. 'You'll be a bag of nerves when the day arrives and won't be able to say "I do".'

'Oh yes, I will,' Hannah said with a laugh. 'I'm practising already.'

Two days before the wedding, a letter came from Mike. He was distraught, even his writing was scrawling and disjointed, and Hannah's heart fell as she read it.

Darling Hannah

I'm getting one of the kitchen staff to post this in the hope of getting it past the censors. All leave has been suspended or cancelled, no one is sure which. The camp is being dismantled so we're on the move somewhere. Some say south. No one really knows. I'll write more when I know. I love you, darling, but you'd be better to cancel the registry office.

'Write and tell him about the baby,' Tilly advised.

'What can he do?'

'Damned all maybe, but he has a right to know.'

So Hannah wrote and Mike's frantic reply came by return of post.

Oh Hannah, my darling. I'm so sorry. What you've had to cope with all alone! I'll see my commanding officer, plead extenuating circumstances, tell him all about you. Oh darling, something must be done. Even if I have just a twenty-four hour pass, I'll make it and we'll find a priest. It will be all right.

But Hannah and Mike's problem did not move the commanding officer one jot. They were planning an invasion on a scale never before imagined. What was one soldier and his pregnant girlfriend in the great scheme of things?

Mike Murphy and his unit were shipped south.

'It's the big push everyone was talking about, isn't it?' Hannah asked fearfully. 'Oh God, Tilly, what will I do?'

'Go and see his parents. You get on with them all right.'

'They don't even know we were to be married. The ring Mike gave me is not an engagement ring.'

'But they like you. You've always said that.'

'They did like me. What if they think I'm trying to trap Mike?'

Tilly said nothing. She knew that parents of sons, especially only sons, often behaved in an irrational way towards girlfriends and to pregnant ones they could be even worse. But something had to be done.

'Could you go home?' Tilly asked.

'To Ireland?' Hannah gave a shudder. 'You don't know what you're asking me. God, it would be awful!' She shook her head. 'I couldn't bring that shame, that disgrace, on my sister and her family.'

'Then where?'

'God, I don't know.'

Hannah sat with her head in her hands, sobs shook

her body, and Tilly's arms went around her and she held her tight. But she couldn't tell her not to cry, not to worry, because by God, she had reason to do both.

Hannah didn't expect Mike home. He could say nothing, but rumours flew about; army camps were emptying all over the country and almost the entire force of the United Kingdom and its allies were all assembled on the south coast for the make or break invasion.

Mike wrote again in mid May:

I'll write to my parents and explain, I'll tell them the child is mine and you are to go to them until I come back and then we'll be married. It's all right, my darling. You will be fine and I'll be home before you know it.

'He's writing to his mother and father,' Hannah told Tilly. 'They'll believe him.'

'Will you go to them?'

'No. I'll wait until they send for me. I don't know how long letters take these days.'

Mike's letter did take time to reach his parents. It took him a while to even find time to write it for the whole camp was in an uproar. He'd never seen so many people concentrated in one relatively small area, nor so many tanks, jeeps, army trucks, cars and motorcycles littering the roads.

The whole area was a no-go area for civilians and those in the small farms and villages were trapped there too. Orders were given by one officer, only to be quickly rescinded by another. It was mayhem. Everyone was in a state of flux and rumours abounded.

There was little time for letter writing and certainly not for writing the type of letter he had to write to his parents. They had to help Hannah and to hell with the neighbours. His mind was constantly filled with Hannah and the child – his child – and worry about her filled his mind through the day and invaded his sleep at night.

The letter did arrive at Colm and Bridie's home eventually towards the end of May. Bridie and Colm were shocked. They'd thought Hannah such a respectable girl for such a thing to happen. They'd got to know her so well, especially when Mike hadn't been so well. 'Mind,' Colm said, trying to be fair. 'Our Mike must have had a hand in it.'

'Aye,' Bridie agreed. 'But he's a man. Everyone knows that it's the girl's place to keep feelings in check.'

'Aye,' Colm agreed with emotion, remembering his own frustrated courtship days. 'But still we'll have to help the girl. It's what Mike wants and after all, the child she's carrying is our grandchild.'

Bridie agreed with her husband, but with reservations. She had a horror of the girl coming here with her belly sticking out and the neighbours knowing that there wasn't even an understanding between her and their son – not that they were aware of, anyway. It would somehow besmirch their son to allow it. And yet Mike had asked them to take the girl in so they had no choice. The damage was done now.

'Shall I go and see her?' Bridie said. 'Or write? I don't know which would be best.'

But in the end she did neither, for in the early hours of 6th June, Mike was housed in a troopcarrier on the choppy waters of the Channel heading for Normandy. The short summer night was fully over; the sky was grey and the light dusky. It was cold too, the wind damp and chilly and the men shivered.

Mike was as frightened and nervous as the next, his stomach turning over at what lay ahead, but above everything else he worried about Hannah and how she was coping and hoped she was now safe with his parents. When he was out of this damned carrier and set up in camp somewhere, he'd write to Hannah, stressing his love and concern for her and their baby. Oh God, he wished he was there with her, supporting her.

'All right?' said Luke's voice low in his ear.

'Not bad.'

'Still worrying about your bird?'

'Wouldn't you?'

'I'm the love them and leave them variety, me,' Luke said. 'Though I have to say your Hannah's a canny lass. Don't worry, we'll soon knock this lot into touch. I'm sure your folks will do the decent thing and take care of Hannah till she has the kid. You can still get married if you're determined on it, just be a bit later, that's all, and I'll still stand you the meal I promised you.'

'Thanks, Luke,' Mike said warmly. 'I'm really glad we've been in this together from the beginning.'

'And we'll stay together, mate, and one day soon we'll be drinking a pint back in dear old Blighty, you'll see,' Luke said and Mike grasped his extended hand and shook it. 'It's a deal,' he replied.

'Stand ready!' came the order from a young and nervous corporal and Mike looked about him. Some of the faces were apprehensive, some plain scared, and some of the raw recruits, who didn't yet know what it was about, were excited. Christ!

The light had brightened a little, the dawn hidden by the clouds a pearly grey as the carrier got near and nearer to the sandy shore and the men stood tense and ready.

Above them, they could see and hear the German fighter planes. The constant tattoo from their automatic guns beat against their heads and was mixed with the shouts and screams as they found their mark. Mike saw soldiers wading forward suddenly jerk and then lie still, face down in the scummy sea. God, it was carnage! Another bloody Dunkirk. He was gutwrenchingly scared and he saw from the look on Luke's face that he felt the same.

And then the carrier stuck in the sand, the sides lowered and the men were out. Waist-deep in freezing water, their rifles held above their heads, they tried to hurry for the beaches and dodge the planes trying to prevent them.

Soldiers ahead of them on the beaches had already set up anti-aircraft guns. The noise was tremendous, the roar of planes, the whine of bullets being answered by the rat-tat-tat of anti-aircraft fire, the shouts and the cries and screams of the men masking the noise of the approaching bombers.

Mike staggered to the shore, which he saw was littered with bodies. He exchanged a glance with Luke who was beside him, but before he was able to speak, a bomb blew Mike Murphy to kingdom come and blasted his friend into a hole beside him.

* * *

When Bridie Murphy went into the hall and found her husband lying still on the floor with the opened telegram in his hand, her own heart nearly stopped beating. She prised the telegram from her husband's fingers and on reading it, knew that she'd lost her husband as well as her son. The bad heart the doctor had warned him about had finally given up.

She phoned her older sister, Christine, from the telephone box down the road, before she rang the doctor, knowing that Colm was way past a doctor's help and her sister would know what to do.

Christine, unmarried and older than Bridie by five years, did know. It was a good job she was there to arrange a funeral for after the initial shock, Bridie had been so overwhelmed with grief she'd been under sedation ever since, unable to give any thought or concern to Hannah and her plight.

Christine was determined, despite Bridie's condition, that the old man at least would have the dignity of being laid to rest in a proper grave and with a full Requiem Mass. Mike's remains were probably left on the beach, like many more.

She was worried though about her sister. She had totally gone to pieces and she knew she couldn't be left alone and decided to take her back to Wiltshire to live with her. She could decide what to do about the house later. Houses would, she guessed, be at a premium after the war and she wouldn't advise her to sell it yet awhile. But she could let it out. She didn't have to concern herself about the details of it. She'd instruct her solicitor to find a reputable agent as soon as possible. Unoccupied houses ran quickly to rack and ruin and anyway, with so many being bombed out of their homes, empty houses were in danger of being invaded by squatters.

She came upon Mike's letter on the mantelpiece as she began packing some of her sister's things and read it dispassionately.

Mike wrote that this girl, Hannah Delaney, was carrying his child. How did he know that? It could have been anyone's bastard she was carrying, but she'd picked him to carry the can for it. Christine had heard there were plenty of girls doing that these days.

There'd obviously been no talk of the engagement, or a wedding before the girl became pregnant, because Bridie would have written to tell her. Well, Mike was no longer able to defend himself and her sister she knew was in no fit state to look after this girl, whoever she was. She was in no state to look after anyone or anything, and she screwed up the letter into a ball and threw it into the fire.

'God, Hannah, when would he have time to write?' Tilly said sternly to her tearful friend when there had been no letters for over a week.

By then the whole country knew that Operation Overlord, or D-Day, had begun on 6th June 1944 and was deemed a success. 'They're advancing in enemy-held territory,' Tilly went on. 'He can hardly say, "Hold on a minute," and get the whole company to stop while he writes a note to you. Even if he managed to write, where the hell would he post it? It's not like at the camp where there's a handy military pillar box nearby.'

Hannah knew all Tilly said was true and she tried

to make herself believe that any day there would be a letter, maybe a clutch of them, and she'd know he was safe. She wondered if he'd ever even had time to write to his parents. She'd expected to hear from them by now too. Something would have to be decided and soon about her pregnancy, but worry about Mike seemed to loom over everything.

There had been an absence of letters for almost three weeks when Hannah was summoned to the supervisor Miss Henderson's office. She'd been expecting it for some time for she was five months pregnant and had had to let out her work and leisure clothes to their fullest extent and that morning she'd seen the supervisor's eyes on her as she served breakfasts.

The supervisor looked at her over the top of the glasses people said she just wore for effect. Hannah had had little dealings with her since the day she'd been interviewed for the job. She hadn't liked her manner then and she didn't like it any better now.

Miss Henderson was thin, not just slim, stick thin, and she wore suits with fitted jackets to emphasise her shape. Everything about her was thin; her long face, her nose, her lips, even her voice had a thin snap to it.

Beside her, Hannah felt big and ungainly. But she raised her head when Miss Henderson said disdainfully, 'You've been putting on weight lately, Miss Delaney?'

'Yes, Miss Henderson.'

'Are you expecting a child?'

There was no point denying it. 'Yes, Miss Henderson.'

'And how long, pray, did you intend to keep this information to yourself?'

'I don't know, Miss Henderson.'

'You don't know, I see. Who is the father of the child?'

Hannah thought of telling Miss Henderson to mind her own business. She shrugged, what did it matter now? 'A soldier, Miss Henderson. Name of Mike . . . Michael Murphy.'

'Married?' Miss Henderson snapped in a voice full of scorn.

Hannah was shocked. 'No, Miss Henderson.'

'So he can marry you?'

'We were to be married, Miss Henderson. Everything was booked. But then he got shipped south and then overseas.'

'So now what will you do, for you realise you can't stay here?' Miss Henderson said. 'You'll upset and embarrass our guests, so when I tell you to pack your things, where will you go?'

Hannah chewed on her bottom lip. There was only one place. 'To Michael's parents,' she said. 'Mike told me to go to them and wait there for him. On his first leave we are going to be married.'

'I'm glad someone is prepared to offer you a place to stay,' Miss Henderson said. 'I suggest you go straight up and pack. We will have the cards and any wages due ready for you in one hour. I want you away from here by noon at the latest.'

The news flew around the kitchen and Tilly went pounding up the back stairs into the room to see Hannah stuffing her case with things she was taking from the wardrobes and small chest. She was crying. She'd done a lot of that lately and Tilly put her arms around her. 'The old cow. It's true then?'

Dumbly Hannah nodded.

'What will you do?'

'What can I do?' Hannah said through her tears. 'I'll go to Mike's parents. At least there I might get some news of Mike. They'll be informed officially if anything has happened, you know, if . . . If he was injured or something.'

'He won't be injured,' Tilly said confidently. 'Didn't they say D-Day was all a big success?'

'Aye, they did, but the Germans hardly held a welcoming committee on the French beaches.'

Tilly didn't want to go down that road, so she said, 'D'you think they'll take you in?'

'I think so,' Hannah said, with more confidence than she was actually feeling. 'I'm carrying Mike's child, their grandchild. They'll not turn me away.'

'Keep in touch. Let me know where you are,' Tilly said.

'That's where I'll be, with Mike's parents,' Hannah said firmly, 'and you have that address.'

Hannah clearly remembered the despair and panic she went through when she alighted from the taxi she'd taken from the railway station and stood on the pavement with her case and holdall beside her. The house was boarded up, the garden overgrown and neglected, and a 'To Let' board was stuck in the garden and creaked as it moved slowly in the wind. She was so horror-struck, she was almost rooted to the ground, and the taxi driver had to remind her of his fare.

She knew then that Mike was dead. Nothing but a disaster of that magnitude would cause Mike's parents to leave the house they'd loved.

This was confirmed by a neighbour. 'Don't know where the old girl's gone,' she said in answer to Hannah's question. 'Heard she weren't right in the head either. Not to be wondered at. I mean it weren't only the son . . .'

'The son?'

'Mike. The son. The old man got the telegram saying that he'd been killed and he dropped dead too. Just like that. In the hall, I heard. Bridie's sister came and took over. Never liked her much myself, but someone had to see to things and she wasn't capable. Bridie, I mean. She was out of it most of the time.'

'She left no message for me?' Hannah asked desperately.

The woman regarded the swell of her stomach and said gently, 'No, love, she didn't. But ask at the estate agent's who's trying to let the house out. His address is on the board. She might have left some word with him.'

But no one had left a message for her and the estate agent knew nothing of Bridie Murphy's whereabouts. Everything was handled through a solicitor, he said, and he wasn't at liberty to disclose which one it was.

Hannah dragged her case and holdall to a nearby park and sat on the bench and tried to think what to do. Mike was dead and later she would grieve for him and cry for the future denied them, but for now worry filled her mind. Her one possible bolt hole had been irrevocably closed with Mike's father dead, his mother disappeared. What the hell was she to do?

The day was hot and trickles of sweat ran down the sides of Hannah's cheeks and she felt it dribbling down her back and between her swollen breasts. She took off the coat that wouldn't fit in either the case or holdall, but still she sat and thought of what she must do.

Eventually, she got to her feet. She'd make her way to her parish church, she decided, and pray for guidance. She could think of nothing else. But she could afford no more taxis or trams and the rattly uncomfortable bus seemed to take ages and when she alighted from it, there was still a hefty walk before her. When she arrived at the church, she was hotter than ever and very tired and light-headed with hunger.

Inside it was dim and cool and she was glad of it. She genuflected in front of the altar and went into a pew, intending to pray for guidance. When she knelt down, she was suddenly overwhelmed by all that had happened and wept.

She'd thought herself alone, but Father Benedict was in the sacristy and came out when he heard her. He knew Hannah by sight, knew her to be a good Catholic who seldom missed Mass and went to Communion often, and he wondered what had distressed her so much.

Going closer, he took in other things, the luggage she had with her and the fact that with her coat removed it was obvious the girl was pregnant, and his heart sank. She'd been dismissed from her job, that much he was certain of, and if she was here, then she'd been let down in some way by the father of the child she carried.

She would be another candidate for the unmarried mothers' home in Leeds, run by the Sisters of Charity. Mind, Father Benedict thought, that name didn't suit them at all. 'Judgemental Sisters of Bullying and Intimidation' would be better.

He knew the girls had sinned, but he thought it wasn't helpful to ram that fact down their throats every mortal minute. Still, if the home hadn't been there, what would happen to the unfortunate girls? Society hadn't made much provision for them and not all of them had families, or at any rate, families that would accept them and bear the shame.

He put a hand on Hannah's shoulder and she turned a tear-stained face to look up in alarm at the priest. 'Come, come, my dear,' he said gently. 'Don't upset yourself like this. Come and sit up on the pew and tell me all about it.'

In the ensuing miserable months afterwards, Hannah remembered the priest's kindness as she told him her tale, explaining her panic and shame, and his concern for her when she admitted she had nowhere to go and she didn't know which way to turn. He took her arm gently and when she stumbled leaving the pew, he prevented her from falling and then sat her down again. 'When did you last eat, my dear?' he asked.

'Breakfast,' Hannah muttered and she saw the priest consult his watch. 'And now it is after five,' he said. 'My housekeeper will have my evening meal ready for me shortly. I suggest you come home with me and share it.'

Hannah felt far too weak to argue with the priest, but just as if she had, he went on, 'You need a meal inside you and a good night's sleep,' he said. 'Tomorrow, I will take you to a place I know that cares for girls in trouble.'

'Oh Father,' Hannah cried. 'Are there such places?'

'Oh, yes. Yes indeed there are, my dear,' the priest

told her reassuringly. 'But if we don't go home this instant and eat the marvellous meal that my housekeeper has undoubtedly prepared, neither of us will reach it, for she'll lash the pair of us to death with her tongue.'

Hannah smiled at him because he was being so kind, but it was a watery smile, and she made no attempt to speak for she knew the tears would have begun again. The priest, however, seemed to understand and he helped her to her feet and led her from the church.

Chapter Eight

By June 1947, three years on from that fear-ridden first pregnancy, Hannah was four months pregnant. The nausea she'd suffered was quite gone and she felt well. Doctor Humphries, to whom she'd gone to have her pregnancy confirmed, was quite young, despite the beard he was sporting, and Hannah was glad he was, because she felt she had to tell him that this wasn't her first pregnancy. He wasn't at all shocked. He said such things happened, especially in wartime, and she wasn't to worry about it.

His voice was gentle and reassuring and his kind brown eyes full of understanding. 'You're not an old woman, you're young and healthy,' he told her. 'And you have signs of having an easy labour and birth. Was your other one trouble free?'

Immediately, there was a flashback in Hannah's mind to the birth of her first baby, a little boy, in the stark room in the home. You were not allowed to have problems there. Those that did and necessitated a doctor's attention were considered worse than nuisances. They were treated as if they'd done it on purpose.

There had been no attempt at pain relief and no

sympathy for those suffering. Hannah had heard one of them tell one girl, who screamed out in pain and fear as she writhed on the bed, that pain would help purge her soul, while another told her sternly to stop making such a fuss.

Hannah, stunned by the nuns' attitude, prayed devoutly that the birth of her child would go smoothly. Her prayers were answered and she had bitten her lip to prevent any cry escaping from her. No doctor had had to attend her, she was left to the ministrations of Sister Celia who'd learnt a smattering of nursing and did duty as a midwife and had sewn the large tear that the baby's birth had caused, crudely and unfeelingly.

'Yes,' Hannah told the doctor. 'The birth was fine.'

'Excellent!' the doctor smiled at her. 'I know it's early days yet, but have you decided where you will have the child?' He checked her medical notes. 'You have a fine house of your own, I believe?'

'Yes, yes, I have, but my husband insists on a proper nursing home,' Hannah said. 'He's keen on Oaklands in Sutton Coldfield.'

'My, my, what a fortunate young woman you are. I wish all my pregnant ladies had such consideration and care,' Doctor Humphries said. 'Oaklands has a good reputation, I believe. Well, Mrs Bradley, there is little more to be said. Come and see me next month.'

As Hannah made her way home, she thought about Arthur's changed attitude towards her. She knew he still considered her as soiled goods that he'd been inveigled into marrying, spoke to her as little as possible and often looked at her as if she'd crawled out from under a stone, but just lately she'd sensed a softening in him. The previous evening, he'd passed her a bundle of notes. 'Get yourself some decent clothes to cover you up,' he'd said. 'I won't have the neighbours say I keep you in rags.'

Though the gesture was done for the neighbours' sake rather than Hannah's, Hannah was pleased. She now had trouble finding things she could wear every day, for the slight increase in her girth had caused her to fasten her skirts, which she could no longer zip, with a safety pin.

'Why thank you, Arthur,' she said. 'That is very generous of you.'

Arthur made no comment on that. Instead, he said, 'I'm increasing your housekeeping as well. I want you to eat as much fruit and vegetables as you can get and drink plenty of milk.'

Hannah was surprised that Arthur seemed to know so much about the needs of a growing baby, but Arthur had read up on it. This baby, the only one he'd ever have, was going to be his and his alone and he wanted a healthy child. To ensure this, the mother had to be cared for while she was carrying the child, but he didn't tell Hannah any of this.

He'd also insisted she give up the job at Gloria's in July and though Hannah was disappointed, she complied, as keen as Arthur was to produce a healthy infant.

She did balk a bit, though, when he said that in future the groceries were to be delivered. 'Arthur, we're only a step away from the village.'

'I know that, but I'll not have you carrying heavy bags,' Arthur said firmly. 'And get Josie to help you more. She can fill the coal scuttles in the morning and help you with the washing and any heavy work.'

'She has school, Arthur.'

'She could do more than she does,' Arthur snapped. 'She should do something to earn her keep.'

'Oh, Arthur, you know her brother and sister send money every month.'

'Oh yes, I know they do,' Arthur said. 'But they tied up her share of the farm effectively, didn't they? No one can touch it until Josie is twenty-one. By rights, that money should have come to me.'

'I don't agree, Arthur,' Hannah said wearily, for this was a recurring theme that Arthur constantly harked back to. 'That money is to secure Josie's future,' she went on. 'She'll probably marry one day. She wouldn't expect you to foot the bill then.'

'No indeed!' Arthur said heatedly. 'I should hope not. After all, I will have my own child to see to by then and I shall see my child will lack for nothing.'

Arthur said a similar thing to Mr and Mrs Banks who'd invited Arthur and Hannah to dinner the following month. 'Oh my dear, how exciting for you,' Elizabeth said, giving Hannah's arm a squeeze.

She sincerely hoped the baby would take away the inner sadness that still lingered in Hannah's eyes that she thought was because Hannah still grieved for the young soldier who'd died. She was convinced a child would help her get over it. 'There's nothing to beat holding your own child in your arms,' she said confidently and was surprised at the look that came over Hannah's face at her words. It spoke of deep sorrow. 'She looked bereft,' Elizabeth was to say later to Reg.

But she wasn't able to ask Hannah what she'd said

to upset her so much, for Arthur was holding the floor. 'Oh, there is a lot of expense, certainly enough,' he was saying to Reg. 'But I have money saved. I can assure you my child will lack nothing. Only the best will be good enough. I thought a Silver Cross pram and a rocking cradle. Later, there will be a cot to buy and a highchair.'

'My goodness!' Elizabeth exclaimed. 'Hannah, you have a husband in a thousand. Reg wouldn't know one make of pram from another. Buying the nursery equipment was my job alone, he wouldn't have been interested.'

Hannah hadn't known that Arthur would have been interested either. It wasn't something they'd discussed together, but then when did they ever discuss things? Arthur made a declaration or issued a command and Hannah obeyed him and that was that. It would be the same with things for the baby. Arthur would decide.

Maybe, she thought, she should feel pleased that he was so involved, but she wasn't, not at all. She also didn't like the way he'd referred to the baby as 'his' baby. She felt as if it was hers. She didn't even want to share it with him because it meant remembering the horrid night it had been conceived, but she knew that if Arthur wanted to claim the child he would, and there would be nothing she could do about it.

Despite Hannah's misgivings, her pregnancy passed peacefully. Josie had been delighted to be able to help Hannah more and was very excited about the baby.

Now, Josie couldn't remember why she made such a fuss about coming to Birmingham. She remembered her sense of loss and sadness at her mother's death and then having to leave Ireland, but it was becoming shadowy, almost as if it had happened to someone else. Her letters to Eileen had petered out. It was frustrating to write to someone who wrote terse notes in reply and eventually Josie stopped trying. Given the choice, she wouldn't leave Hannah now, not for anything. Hannah had asked her when she'd been there about a year if she wanted to live elsewhere, as she'd promised she would, but Josie had said firmly that she didn't and she knew that Hannah had been pleased at her decision. She felt Hannah needed and wanted her there and of course would do so even more when the baby was born.

She neither liked nor disliked Arthur. She had disliked him intensely, hated him even, when he'd shouted horrible things at Hannah in the dead of night. But, since the night after her birthday, it had not happened anymore. Arthur had moved out of the bedroom then and into the small room beside the bathroom.

She didn't even mind moving in with Hannah so that the baby could have her bedroom, which Arthur wanted decorated as a nursery. She wouldn't leave now if someone had offered her a hundred pounds and she couldn't wait to hold Hannah's baby in her arms.

Hannah had never had such an easy life. She had little to do. She wandered up to Erdington High Street and placed her order for grocery, greengrocery or meat, which would be delivered later that day. Often, she went on to Gloria's. She and Amy had begun to knit for the baby as soon as they'd been told the news and Hannah had taken to it as well.

Many afternoons, the three women could be found

sitting in Gloria's sitting room, talking together, their needles clicking, turning out cardigans, matinée coats, bootees, mittens and bonnets for the baby soon to be born.

Hannah often thought it was a far cry from her previous pregnancy three years before when she remembered waking up in the spare bedroom of the presbytery after a fitful, fear-filled sleep, despite the comfortable bed.

She'd been apprehensive of the place the priest would take her to that day, even while she was relieved. She wanted no breakfast, but Father Benedict insisted she ate. 'We'll leave straight afterwards,' he said. 'But you must eat. You need to keep up your strength.'

When she saw the grim, grey building looming before her later that same morning, she realised what he'd meant. It had taken a long time to reach it, a train journey, followed on by bus and even then a long walk for the home was stuck out in the back of beyond.

The door was opened by a nun with a stiff, disapproving face, which widened into the grimace of a smile as she saw who was there. 'Father Benedict,' she said. 'What a nice surprise.' And then she cast a baleful look at Hannah, who blushed at her close scrutiny, and went on, 'You'll be wanting to see Mother Superior?'

Father Benedict nodded. 'If it is convenient, Sister Carmel?'

'She'd always make time for you, Father,' the nun told the priest and she led the two of them into the large house.

Hannah let her eyes slide around the large and draughty hall the nun had invited them into, while the priest talked quietly to Sister Carmel. It had once been a grand house, she thought, and big, wrought-iron gates had once led to the gravel path that approached the house. She'd known because the stumps of metal were still in the ground, the gates themselves carted off long ago, like every other bit of available metal for the Spitfire appeal.

Now, though, the home was unloved, the front lawn unkempt and untended, though she was to learn the grounds at the back were well cultivated. Her begrimed nails and aching back would eventually bear evidence to that.

The hall led to a short corridor with doors leading off each side and another door at the far end. Two girls were scrubbing the floor on hands and knees. They were both dressed in shapeless smocks, one in dark green, the other grey, their distended stomachs hanging down before them, evidence of their advanced pregnancy. Hannah was shocked and she knew she was seeing a foretaste of her life there and followed the priest reluctantly as they were ushered into a small room.

The nun behind the desk was small and old and had thick brown spectacles on her small nose. 'Father Benedict,' she said, rising to her feet to shake his hand. 'So nice to see you again.'

So, I'm not the first girl he's brought here, Hannah thought, but the priest was introducing her. 'This is Hannah Delaney.'

Hannah put out her hand, but the nun ignored it. Instead, she turned away and indicated they sit the other side of the desk with a wave of her hand. Then she faced them again, pulled a form for the file and looked at Hannah. 'Age,' she rapped out.

'I'm . . . I'm twenty-four.'

'Twenty-four? Not a young girl then. Old enough to know better. No father, I presume? No visible means of support?'

'No!' Hannah willed her voice not to tremble. 'The baby's father is dead, in France somewhere.' And then, because she didn't want the nun to think she was a bad girl, she burst out, 'We were engaged. Due to be married.'

It didn't impress the nun one jot. She looked at her with scorn. 'How far on are you?'

'Five months.'

'Right,' the nun said, leaning forward. 'Let's put a few rules before you. Firstly, my name is Sister Theresa and I'm in charge of this home. You're in luck; three of our girls left us last week, so we have space to take you. But it will not be a rest cure. In exchange for housing and clothing you, you will work for your keep. We employ no help. The cleaning of this house, preparation of meals, washing, ironing and tending the vegetable garden are done by the girls here. You will not wear your own clothes, but smocks, underclothes and shoes, which we will supply. Do you understand all this?'

'Yes, Sister.'

'In addition to your duties, you will attend chapel. You will rise at half-past four in the morning and must be in the chapel, washed and suitably attired by five-o'clock matins. Vespers are at five o'clock in the evening and prayers before bed at eight-thirty. Each Saturday a priest will come to hear confession and the same priest will say Mass every Sunday morning in the chapel. You will not leave here until your child is born, when it will be taken from you and given to one of the good Catholic families we have waiting.'

That brought a response from Hannah. 'Taken from me!' she repeated.

'Surely you knew that?' Sister Theresa said, her face puckering in a frown. 'Didn't Father Benedict . . .?'

'I told Hannah nothing about that.' Hannah turned to look at him and knew that the priest was embarrassed, that he hadn't wanted to tell her. His face was brick-red and there was sweat glistening on his brow. But Hannah was too distraught to care about the priest's discomfort. 'You can't take my baby from me,' she cried. 'Please don't do that. It's all I'll have of Mike.'

'Then how will you keep it?'

Wild plans leapt into Hannah's mind, all of them to be swiftly rejected. She realised she was totally alone. She hadn't really thought of what she would do once she'd given birth to the baby. And the nun was right. There wasn't one job she could think of which she could keep and look after her baby and anyway, there was her family in Ireland to consider.

The nun watched her dispassionately. This same scene had been enacted many times in that room and the same decision always reached. When Hannah eventually looked from Father Benedict to the nun, the priest had to turn his head away from the look of resigned sadness on her face. Sister Theresa said, 'You see, my dear, there is no other solution. We will give your child to a couple who are usually childless and are willing to adopt who will love your baby very much. They will give the child a better life than you could offer it.'

'It's a brave thing to do, Hannah,' Father Benedict put in gently. 'And you'll bring joy to a childless couple.'

'But what about me?'

'You,' said Sister Theresa sternly, 'will get over it eventually and get on with your life.' Her tone implied that it was more than Hannah deserved and Hannah, looking from one to the other, knew she was powerless before these people.

Over the next months, Hannah was to know true misery and tiredness such as she'd never felt before. There were times every bone in her body ached when the bell to rouse them was sounded in the morning, but no one was allowed to slack.

Before matins, they had to wash, dress and make their beds and after matins, some cleaned the dormitories, while others made and served the breakfasts. After breakfast, the washing-up began and preparation of the midday meal, the whole house had to be cleaned and others were sent into the garden to work or to the laundry. After the midday meal, the whole process began again as the evening meal had to be prepared before vespers.

But it wasn't the work alone Hannah felt the most tiring, it was the way many of the nuns spoke to them. Some seemed to use every means possible to provoke and annoy them and remind them of their disgrace in bringing an illegitimate child into the world.

Hannah found settling in difficult and though she wasn't unfriendly, she tended to keep herself to herself, but after working in a bustling hotel and being a good friend of Tilly's, she often felt immeasurably lonely. In the end, she decided to write to Tilly, who wouldn't have a clue where she was, and ask her to visit if it was allowed. It was, but few of the girls had visitors. Most girls there had been disowned by their families, though from the talk around her, Hannah learnt that some would accept their daughters back home when the 'problem' had been resolved, when they could pretend it hadn't happened.

Tilly came, as Hannah knew she would, complaining of the place being out in the sticks as soon as Hannah was ushered into the visitors' room to see her. 'Bloody haul, this is. Took me all bloody morning to get here.'

'Ssh,' Hannah cautioned, checking the door had been shut properly. 'They'll have your tongue cut out for saying less than that.'

'I believe you,' Tilly said, then surveying Hannah's swollen frame she said, 'What the dickens have you got on?'

'Oh, everyone wears these smock things,' Hannah said dismissively. 'You should see what I have underneath – convent issue underwear.'

'Oh God! Let me guess, passion-killer bloomers and a chastity belt?'

'More or less,' Hannah agreed with a smile.

'That's better,' Tilly said. 'I thought you'd gone and had your smile amputated.'

'There's not been much to smile about here, Tilly, just lately.'

'Listen, you,' Tilly said, gripping Hannah's hands tight. 'Don't lose your sense of humour. It helps you survive. Honest to God, it does.'

'Tilly, you don't understand,' Hannah said. 'Let me tell you all that's happened to me since I was evicted from the hotel and see if you can find a joke in it at all.' And Hannah told Tilly about finding Mike's house locked up and about the double tragedy that had affected his mother.

'I know, love,' Tilly said when she'd finished. 'I went looking for you when I heard nothing from you for a bit. I went on my first day off. God, I was worried. You'd disappeared into thin air and I was scared to death you'd done something daft, like throwing yourself in a river, or under a flipping train.'

'It might have come to that if it hadn't been for the priest,' Hannah said seriously. 'He was so kind, Tilly, and I know this place isn't The Ritz, but it's better than the streets.'

Tilly looked at Hannah's strained face, with the blue smudges underneath her eyes, her beautiful hair, now dull and lank and pulled back from her face in a band. She looked like a different person to the young vibrant girl she'd shared a bedroom with for some years. Mind, she thought, the clothes didn't help, those terrible tent-like dresses and her feet thrust into Godawful, clod-hopping shoes she'd not be seen dead in. It was as if the nuns went out of their way to make the girls as unattractive as possible.

'You might be right, but it's only just,' Tilly said. 'It's a bloody awful place, this. You know what's the matter with them holy Joes, don't you?' she went on confidingly. 'Bloody jealous. Every girl here has done something they'd like to have a go at themselves, given half a chance.'

'Tilly!'

'Tilly what? It's right. Everyone knows it. Married to God! Huh! That would keep you warm in bed, I don't think.'

'Tilly, you're dreadful,' Hannah said, realising suddenly how much she'd missed her.

'I know,' Tilly said, unabashed. 'Can't do a blooming thing with me.' She was very glad to see Hannah less despondent than when she'd arrived, for she had bad news for her. But first she said, 'Have you thought what to do after? Are you keeping the baby or what?'

'There's no choice here,' Hannah said. 'The babies are taken and given to a couple who want to adopt. My baby's parents might have already been chosen.'

There was a catch in her voice and Tilly said, 'Don't get upset, Hannah. You can take up your life again. You can . . .'

'Forget it ever happened,' Hannah burst out. 'Forget Mike who I loved with my heart and soul and the baby he would have adored. I'll just rub him out of my life as if he didn't exist.'

'You know I didn't mean it like that,' Tilly said. 'But if you kept the baby, what could you do? How would you manage?'

'Oh, I've been through that more times than enough,' Hannah said. 'And how could I keep a thing like that from my family, my sister?'

'Maybe you should write and tell her anyway?' Tilly suggested.

'You don't know what you're asking.'

'She'd get over it in time.'

Hannah shook her head. 'She might,' she said, 'because she loves me. But the shame of it, everyone would blame her and say she hadn't brought me up properly. Some would even say she shouldn't let me come back home at all. I'd be away from it over here, but she'd have to live with it every day.'

'Well, you'll have to write something to her,' Tilly said.

'Why?'

'Look, Hannah, I don't want you to get scared or anything, but a telegram came for you the day before yesterday. I signed for it, because just two days before that I got your letter telling me where you were. I opened it, Hannah, because I didn't know how urgent it was. It's from your sister.'

The roof of Hannah's mouth was suddenly very dry. All through the war people dreaded the sight of the telegraph boy trundling up the road, the harbinger of death. Sometimes it wasn't death, but the news was never good, and the one Tilly handed Hannah was no exception.

PADDY VERY ILL STOP HASN'T GOT LONG STOP
ASKING FOR YOU STOP LOVE FRANCES.

'I can't go to him,' Hannah said, looking at Tilly with eyes full of anguish. 'I'm letting down the man I love . . . far, far more than my own true father. Paddy was patient and kind. And when I wanted to go to England, it's him I went to. He understood and in the end he talked Frances round.' Her eyes spoke her misery. 'He's asking for me and I can't go, even though he's dying.'

Hannah hid her face in her hands and Tilly watched her, knowing the terrible dilemma she was in. 'I'll write to Frances and say I'm ill,' Hannah said. 'It's all I can do. Later, when it's over and I'm out of this place, I'll go and see them all. I'll have to ask the Sisters if I can go out to get a card, or a sheet of writing paper. I must write straight away, the telegram came two days ago, she'll be wondering why I haven't written.'

The nuns were surprisingly sympathetic to Hannah's plight, but she found it the hardest letter in the world to write, the one to tell Frances that she would not be there to bid farewell to Paddy Mullen.

Just a month later, Tilly, who now made the long journey to see Hannah once a week, brought another telegram. 'Came this morning,' she said. 'I opened it like you said to and then I changed my day off so I could come straight round.'

PADDY DIED 31 AUGUST STOP FUNERAL AT 11 O'CLOCK STOP MAMMY EXPECTS YOU STOP LOVE MARTIN.

Hannah, the telegram crushed in her hand, put her hands to her heart and wept and Tilly, putting her arms around her in an attempt to comfort her, found herself crying too.

Much later, Tilly sent a telegram in reply that Hannah had written out for her, in which she'd expressed her regret that she couldn't be with the family at this tragic time.

Most of the girls were aware of the bad news Hannah had received, but didn't know her well enough to show her much support. The nuns assured Hannah that her brother-in-law, if he was the good, God-fearing man she said he was, would be in Heaven now.

Neither response helped Hannah. Nor, she imagined, would it help Frances, or the family who didn't want Paddy in Heaven, but back at home, working the farm in Wicklow.

Feeling isolated and unsupported in her grief, Hannah was glad to go to bed, where she tried to muffle her sobs, lest they disturb the other girls in the dormitory. When she was woken in the early hours of the morning with griping pains in her stomach, she knew she was about to give birth to the child she couldn't keep and she almost welcomed the pain, feeling she deserved it. She knew, too, that the baby was a month early and hoped he or she would be all right. But it was out of her hands now. Soon it would be all over.

She lay in a stark white-tiled room, her smock rolled up to her middle and a towel tied to the bedhead. 'That's for you to pull on when the pains get strong,' Sister Celia said.

God, thought Hannah. Can they get stronger than this?

The nun caught her train of thought. 'Oh yes, my girl,' she said with a smile – a satisfied, 'serve you right' sort of smile. 'This is nothing. They'll be worse than this, bye and bye. You'll be glad of the towel then.'

And she was glad of it, mighty glad. She nearly pulled the bed on top of herself, she tugged it so hard. Now she understood those who roared and screamed and called for their mothers. But because of the nun's smile and because she'd seen what happened to people who did make a fuss, Hannah would not utter one sound. She was terribly frightened, though, and threshed on the bed to try and get rid of the wild beast trying to tear her in two.

It went on for hour after weary hour, until Hannah felt she could bear no more, could push no more. She had no strength left, but Sister Celia wouldn't let her give up, urging and shouting at her, 'One more push. And another. You can do it! Come on – push and again, and one more. Come on, you can do it!' Hannah wished the damned nun would shut her mouth and if she could have got breath enough, she'd have told her.

'I can see the head,' the nun cried, but Hannah just wanted to die. Then, as the pain threatened to totally overwhelm her, with one almighty push, which seemed to sap the energy from every part of Hannah's body, the head was out and Hannah felt the baby's body slither after it and the plaintive cries of a newborn filled the room.

'Didn't need a smack this one,' Sister Celia said.

'What is it? Let me see!'

'You're building heartache for yourself,' the nun said, her lips pursed.

Hannah felt anger pulsating through her. 'At least I've got a heart,' she yelled at the startled nun. 'Not like you, you heartless cow. I've just given birth. At least let me hold my own baby one time.'

'I'll ignore your remarks and put it down to stress,' the nun said haughtily. 'And if you want to hold your baby, you shall. You'll regret it, for it will be harder for you in the end. I know what I'm talking about.'

Hannah barely heard her, for as she put the baby into Hannah's arms, she became entranced. He was very, very tiny, and wrinkled, but then he was a month early. She checked that he had the right number of fingers and toes and she searched for any likeness to his father but found none. He had an apple-shaped birthmark on his left arm and Hannah lifted him up and kissed it. The blemish didn't detract from his beauty, for he was beautiful, Hannah thought, totally unprepared for the rush of maternal love for the little scrap that suddenly coursed through her body. 'Michael,' she whispered to him. 'That's your name, Michael, after your daddy.'

The baby was rooting at her, his mouth open and searching and Hannah pulled down the gown and put Michael to her breast as if it was the most natural thing in the world. She saw the baby's eyes flutter shut in contentment and his tiny hands knead her breast that his small mouth tugged upon and felt so at peace she could have cried with happiness.

And then, the door crashed open and Sister Theresa, an angry Sister Theresa, was glaring at her. 'What possible good have you done, holding your baby and now feeding him?' she demanded. 'You'd have been better letting Sister Celia take him away without even looking at him. Give the child to me!'

'Please, please,' pleaded Hannah, not even sure what she was asking. She didn't know how she'd bear it if they took Michael away now.

'Come, come. This is just prolonging the agony,' Sister Theresa said, taking hold of the child. At her slight tug, Hannah's nipple popped out of the baby's mouth and his eyes opened in surprise and his little face screwed up as if he was about to cry. But he was forestalled by Hannah, who let out an animal-like howl, and another, and another. Sister Theresa carried the baby away and Hannah felt as if her heart had been torn from her. 'Pull yourself together!' Sister Celia snapped. 'You knew it had to be done. Stop this nonsense and cover yourself up. You're a disgrace!'

Hannah stopped howling, but the hurt buried itself deep, deep inside of her. She didn't know how she'd ever overcome this despair. She'd felt this way when she heard Mike had died, but he was dead and gone, his son was alive and well and she'd given him away. Somehow, the thought that some other mother would love him, feed him, play with him and watch him grow up, made the pain worse.

The next day in the room, she said to the young nun, Sister Monica, who didn't seem as bad as some of the others, 'I called my baby Michael. Can you tell them that, whoever has him? It's after his father.'

'I'm sorry, my dear,' the nun said gently. 'I'm afraid you'll have no say in any of this. His new parents will probably have their own choice of name.'

Somehow, it seemed the final blow and Hannah sunk into depression. Tilly came to see her, but there was no baby to admire and Hannah barely spoke. 'This came for you,' Tilly said, handing Hannah a letter with a Southampton postmark.

Hannah opened it with trembling fingers to find it was from Mike's friend, Luke, who explained when and how Mike had died and said he was sorry for the delay in writing, but he'd been injured himself in the explosion that killed Mike. He also said his mother had told him that Mike's parents had just disappeared, and no one seemed to know where. It was the last straw for Hannah. She'd held on to the dream that Mike's mother would come back home and Hannah could go to live with her and they'd get her baby back and take pleasure and consolation in raising Mike's son. She'd known it was only a dream, but it had helped sustain her, and now the dream was blown wide apart and she knew her child was gone from her. She also knew that she'd never see him again and she wept great gasping sobs of pure grief that she could barely cope with and that even frightened Tilly with their intensity.

'Ah, Hannah, don't. Don't upset yourself like this,' she begged, her arms tight around Hannah's shaking body. She held her until the sobs had eased to snuffles and then because she'd like to have Hannah near her where she could keep an eye on her, she said coaxingly, 'Shall I ask about you getting a job back at the hotel?' 'Be a laugh if we worked together again, wouldn't it?'

Hannah suppressed a shudder. She couldn't go back there with everyone knowing and nudging one another, smirking and sniggering. But it did bring to her mind the idea of employment. She couldn't live on fresh air, but she wanted work far away from Yorkshire.

At her insistence, Father Benedict came to see her when her lying-in period was coming to an end. 'Do you think it a good idea to look for employment miles away?' he said. 'Surely you have friends here?'

'Oh yes, fair-weather friends,' Hannah said bitterly. 'Apart from Tilly, did you see anyone breaking the door down to see how I was? No, Father, let it go. This place holds sad memories for me and I don't know what a good thing is anymore.' She looked steadily at the priest and went on, 'I'm very unhappy, Father. I can't remember ever being this unhappy before.'

'It will pass, Hannah.'

'Will it? I'm not so sure,' Hannah said. 'I think this may be with me always. But I know it will be harder trying to put it behind me here where I am surrounded by memories.'

Seeing that Hannah was adamant, Sister Monica wrote to her second cousin, Gloria Emmerson, who ran a guesthouse in Birmingham and who had helped girls in similar circumstances in her own parish in Erdington, asking if she could find lodgings and employment for Hannah. The woman wrote back by return of post, offering Hannah a job and a home with herself until she was settled with digs and employment.

Sister Theresa wrote to Gloria Emmerson, outlining Hannah's travel plans and urging her to take good care of the girl and to try and get her respectably married to a good, God-fearing, Catholic man. Hannah, knowing nothing of the letter, or the charge laid upon Gloria Emmerson, turned her back on Yorkshire, her past life and her memories, and set off for Birmingham without a backward glance.

Chapter Nine

Hannah arrived in Birmingham on a day in late October when the sun shone as if it were high summer but inside she felt as if her heart was dead and cold. She didn't care where she went, or what happened to her. She felt her life was over, taken with the child she'd given birth to and lost forever.

Gloria saw the girl, the truly lovely-looking girl, emerge from the taxi and thought she seldom felt such sorrow as there was reflected in Hannah's startlingly green eyes. There was beauty there, in her face and her figure, but masked in sadness and sadness so deep that it affected Gloria like a hammer blow to her heart.

Hannah was an ideal guest and that's how Gloria thought of her at first, a transient visitor like the other girls had been. But this girl, Hannah Delaney, got under her skin in a way none of the others had.

She was aware of her suffering and knew she had need of a job and a place to live, and she'd promised the nuns to look after her and yet couldn't find any suitable employment in that area, let alone a place to live in a city ravaged by war. On the other hand, she had a thriving guesthouse and though she'd managed without help for years, she wasn't getting any younger and the doctor had warned her for years to slow down. 'Would you like to work here, for me, I mean?' she asked Hannah one day.

In Hannah's deadened eyes there was a flicker of interest. 'Yes,' she said.

Gloria was confused. Was she really keen or was she just being polite? 'You don't have to agree,' she said. 'I need to know what you want.'

For so long, Hannah's wants had not been considered and she was confused. 'I really don't care what happens to me now,' she said.

It was that acceptance that finally caused Gloria to feel such pity for the girl that she enfolded Hannah in her arms. 'Ah, pet,' she said, and she felt her heart melt as she held the shuddering girl close. Hannah gratefully accepted the love Gloria offered and in those arms of a woman she knew little of, she cried out all the hurt and pain she'd suffered.

'Do you want to work here for me?' Gloria was able to ask again at last and Hannah was unable to speak for fear she would begin to cry again, but she gave an emphatic nod. And later, when the nightmares began, it was Gloria who held her tight until it was over and sat by her bed talking to her and holding her hand.

During this time, a deep friendship developed between the two women and Hannah knew she'd always be grateful to Gloria. In the dark recesses of the night, the dimness hiding her shame, Hannah told Gloria of Mike Murphy and the love she had for him. She told of what had happened to him and later how that had affected his parents who she was sure would have taken her in. And when she cried during the telling, Gloria cried too, and she resolved to do everything in her power to help the girl.

How different, Hannah thought, her pregnancy and birth experience would be three years on. The nursing home was a comfortable place. There was a bright day room for patients and visitors and all the rooms were private. No communal wards here.

'We encourage our patients to walk around if they are able to, even once labour starts,' the sister-in-charge, Sister Prescott, told Hannah and Arthur on their first visit.

'Is that wise?' Arthur asked.

The nurse smiled. 'I assure you, Mr Bradley, many of the mothers prefer it. Only in the early stages, you understand. They are of course at liberty to retire to their bed whenever they want and of course they are never left alone.'

'I see.'

Sister Prescott turned to Hannah with a smile. 'There is nothing to be afraid of in the actual birth itself, Mrs Bradley,' she said. 'The days of women screaming in agony for days are a thing of the past, I'm glad to say. We have gas and air to help our mothers now. And if it gets too much or baby is uncooperative there is of course always a doctor at hand when a birth is imminent.'

'What do you think?' Arthur asked Hannah on their way back home.

'It's lovely, almost luxurious,' Hannah enthused. 'But isn't it very expensive?'

'You don't need to worry about that,' Arthur said.

'I had a bit put by for it anyway, but then Reg Banks insisted on paying for it. Like me, he thinks nothing is too good for my baby.'

There it was again, the reference to 'his baby'. At home, they had an enormous Silver Cross pram and a beautifully crafted rocking cradle complete with drapes that Arthur had bought, pooh-poohing Gloria saying it was unlucky to bring the pram home before the child. 'What does she know,' he said. 'She has neither chick nor child belonging to her.'

Hannah didn't argue. There was no point, Arthur would go his own way.

But even she'd been surprised when, just the previous day, he'd come home with a complete layette. Hannah looked at the bundle in amazement.

'Two dozen terry nappies and a dozen muslin,' Arthur announced proudly, 'and little vests and nighties and tiny mittens and bootees and two complete pram sets.'

'How did you know what to buy?' Hannah asked in astonishment.

'I asked the lady in the shop,' Arthur said. 'She said she'd never seen a father so involved.'

Neither had Hannah, only it wasn't involved. It was more like obsessed. 'I would have liked to have gone with you to choose the things and I would have liked some choice in the pram and cradle,' she said quietly.

'Hannah, you don't understand,' Arthur said. 'The child is mine. You are giving birth to it, that is all. You will have little to do with it once it is born.'

'Arthur, what are you saying?'

'I'm saying that I will not allow you to sully and taint my child.'

'Arthur, this is silly,' Hannah said. 'All right, so I wasn't a virgin when I married you. But it was only the once with one man. I know Gloria told you about Mike Murphy. We were engaged to be married and yes once, just once, we got carried away and then Mike was killed before we could marry.'

'It makes no difference, once or many times, one man or several,' Arthur said sternly. 'It was wrong and I want my child to grow up pure and unsoiled, which he or she will.'

There was no reasoning with Arthur, but Gloria told her not to worry. 'Every child loves their mother, never fret,' she said. 'You'll have the child all day. Hasn't Arthur a job to go to?'

Of course he had. She'd have care of the child all day, with help from Josie before and after school, she was sure. She'd let Arthur have his little fancy. It wasn't worth arguing over.

Doctor Humphries said her medical notes relating to her pregnancy and general health would be sent to the nursing home. 'Will they have to know . . . you know, about the other pregnancy?' Hannah enquired anxiously.

'Yes,' Doctor Humphries told her. 'But please don't get agitated over it. They will be discreet. Please believe me, Mrs Bradley, you were not the only one that such a thing happened to. They won't sit in judgement on you.'

'Or tell my husband. You see he doesn't . . . I couldn't tell him.'

'Your notes are yours, Mrs Bradley. They are not for anyone else but medical staff to see. But I'll have a word with the doctor there if it will put your mind at rest.'

And Hannah liked and trusted the doctor she saw at the nursing home. His manner was efficient, yet reassuring, and his voice surprisingly gentle and she wasn't filled with dread as she'd been the last time.

As the autumn drew to a close, November dawned, wet, miserable and blustery, but Hannah just felt contented, knowing that before too long, she'd have her beloved baby in her arms. She was glad now, because of her size and the awful weather, that she hadn't to carry shopping home. Josie was more than willing to run up to the shops with a list and the ration books after she'd finished school for the day and Hannah was glad to be able to sit by the fire with her knitting and daydream.

Arthur was openly impatient for her to give birth and asked every day if she felt all right and if she'd visited the doctor, she had to give a blow-by-blow account to him. All in all, despite Arthur's references to 'his baby', which Hannah refused to rise to, life was peaceful and uneventful.

The baby was due on 4th November, but the day came and went and nothing happened. On the 5th, Josie was asked to a bonfire party at Mary Byrne's house. Hannah and Arthur had been invited, too, but Arthur refused for the two of them. Hannah didn't mind; everything was becoming an effort for her and the night was chilly and the wind fierce and she had no desire to venture out in it.

Josie, though anxious to go to the party, was worried about leaving Hannah. 'Don't be silly,' Hannah said.

'It could be days yet. You go off and enjoy yourself. You're hardly a million miles away.'

But the door had barely closed on Josie, when Hannah got her first pain. It wasn't bad so she said nothing to Arthur, but carried on knitting.

Two hours later, the pains had settled into a pattern and were coming every twenty minutes and Hannah thought she'd better alert Arthur. 'Arthur, I think I've started.'

Arthur leapt to his feet, the paper he'd been reading cascading in crumpled sheets at his feet. 'I'll go and ring the nursing home,' he said, struggling into his shoes.

'Yes,' Hannah said. 'And call round to Mrs Byrne and ask her if she'll keep Josie tonight. I've already asked if she could look after her when I'm in the nursing home and she won't mind.'

'Yes, yes,' said Arthur, looking flustered. 'Thank God we have the car. But, we should have a phone installed. I must see about it.'

Hannah wished they had a phone, too, when a sudden intense pain gripped her stomach so that she doubled over with it. 'Hurry, Arthur,' she gasped when she had breath to do so. 'I think this one is in a rush to be born.'

In the car, Arthur was full of consideration for her comfort. Hannah wondered if the baby could possibly cement the large cracks in their marriage. She could exist without sex and had been happier since Arthur had moved into the spare room and she shared the large bedroom with Josie. She was sure if they tried, they could live amicably together.

She knew he was nervous for he talked nonstop. 'You'll be fine, you'll see. We'll be there in no time. You just hold tight.' On and on he went as Hannah rode the waves of pain.

At the nursing home, they chided her gently for leaving it so long, but Hannah remembered the hour upon agonising hour she'd lain in labour in the other home. There had been no one to comfort her and no information and she'd been terribly frightened. She'd been alone most of the time, except for the young girl in the far bed who'd screamed and cried for her mother constantly. She depressed Hannah greatly, but much as she wished the girl would shut up, she'd been shocked to the core by the vicious slap one of the nuns gave her. It stopped her screams but the gasping sobs she reverted to instead were just as bad.

This experience was so different. There was no time for a bath; a brief examination showed that the actual birth wasn't too far away and so Hannah was helped into bed in a small room on her own and a pretty young Irish nurse called Nurse McIntosh attended her. Her accent was soothing and her hands were gentle, yet she seemed efficient and Hannah felt she could relax. She knew Arthur would be pacing the day room, probably smoking cigarette after cigarette in his anxiety, and she hoped for both their sakes that the predictions were right and the baby would soon be born.

'How much longer?' Arthur demanded of Sister Prescott. 'She came in over three hours ago. It's now past midnight. You said the birth was close.'

'Calm yourself, Mr Bradley,' the nurse said, and

added with a smile, 'Babies can be remarkably contrary creatures and yours is no different. The point is, the baby is anxious to be born, but just can't seem to give that final push and your wife is tiring fast.'

'So what's to be done?'

'I've sent for the doctor. He'll probably advise forceps.'

But he didn't advise forceps. He could scarcely believe that Hannah had given birth without help before for her hips were very narrow, but then of course she'd told him her first baby had been a month premature and she had torn badly. He'd known that of course. He'd seen the evidence of it the first time he'd examined her and had thought then, that whoever had stitched her needed shooting. But this full-term baby would need more help than a forceps' delivery and a proper episiotomy, for it was showing signs of distress and so was the mother. She'll have to go for a Caesarean, he thought, but first he'd have to talk to that husband of hers. By, the man was anxious. He'd seen some agitated fathers in his day, but this one seemed beside himself. If he didn't calm down, he'd give himself a heart attack.

Arthur was very concerned about the operation planned and asked many questions, but Hannah just nodded when the doctor explained it to her. She was past caring about anything by then and just wanted the pain to end.

Hannah opened her eyes, blinking because of the brightness, and saw Nurse McIntosh's face above her. 'Hello, Mrs Bradley,' she said cheerfully. 'You have a beautiful daughter. But no wonder you had trouble bringing her. She was nine pounds!'

'Nine pounds!' Hannah remembered her tiny first baby. She didn't know how much he'd weighed, or how long he was – that wasn't information they would share with the mothers – but nine pounds sounded big.

She opened her mouth to speak and was immediately assailed by a feeling of nausea. Nurse McIntosh had been expecting that and held the bowl expertly and when it was over, she brought Hannah a drink of water and wiped her face. 'It's the effects of the anaesthetic,' she said. 'It's to be expected.'

'Can I . . . can I see my baby?'

'Not yet, in a wee while. She's in the nursery,' the nurse said. 'Now, she's fine and you're not to worry. She was just a little distressed over the birth.'

'Distressed! What do you mean distressed?'

'It's quite common, believe me,' the nurse said. 'She'll be fine in a day or two.'

'A day or two?'

'Maybe sooner.'

'Maybe sooner,' Hannah repeated and wondered what was the matter with her that she seemed only able to repeat the nurse's words. She felt suddenly incredibly weary, but she must demand to see her baby. If the child couldn't be taken out of the nursery, then she would go to see her. She struggled up in the bed and felt pains shooting through her stomach.

'Come, Mrs Bradley,' the nurse chided. 'You'll do yourself an injury and pull your stitches into the bargain. Settle yourself for a little sleep. Don't worry about your baby. Your husband has seen her and held her. In fact, he's been very helpful. He's given her her first bottle.'

'Her first bottle.' There she went again. 'I . . . I was going to feed her.'

'You were in no fit state then. Perhaps we'll see later, but don't you worry about it for now.'

But Hannah remembered Arthur's words. 'This is my baby. You'll have little to do with it once he or she is born.' It was coming true, she thought in panic, and tears trickled down her cheeks. 'There there,' Nurse McIntosh said gently. 'Don't upset yourself. You're tired, that's what it is. You settle down now.'

'I'm not sleepy,' Hannah tried to say, but her eyes closed in spite of herself and she slept again.

As the day wore on, she opened her eyes only to be sick, and in her dreams she was back in the home, begging to be allowed to see, hold and keep her baby, while the nuns laughed at her as they receded further and further away. The nightmares she'd had for years were happening again.

Eventually, she woke in the dusk of evening and Arthur was sitting beside her, a huge satisfied smile on his face. 'The baby?' she said.

'She's fine, beautiful. I've just seen her,' Arthur said. 'And I've given her another bottle.'

'No!' Hannah cried. 'I want to feed her.'

'Your wants don't come into this,' said Arthur. 'I've talked it over with the doctor and he agreed that you would find it difficult to feed. National Dried Milk is just as good, I've heard, and tomorrow you will be given tablets to dry up your milk.'

Hannah said nothing. She sat stunned, looking at her husband. She'd longed to feel her baby, tugging at her breast. She felt that it would help banish the terrible feeling of desolation she still felt at times when she remembered the baby boy snatched from her.

All right then, she thought, she couldn't breast-feed, but she could give her a bottle. She could still have the closeness with her. 'Why can't I have her beside me?' she demanded. 'I can give her a bottle. She's my baby.'

'She has to stay in the nursery a little longer,' Arthur said, 'and you're not well enough to be taken down there yet.' He leaned towards Hannah and said, 'Get used to it, my dear, I told you how it would be.'

Later, Sister Prescott found Hannah in such a distressed state, she sent for the doctor who was extremely worried. By the time he came, she'd stopped thrashing around the bed, screaming and crying, and lay comatose and silent, though her eyes were open. He was unable to get any reaction from her. He sedated her and could only put her condition down to the trauma of the birth and he told Arthur this the following evening.

Arthur knew why Hannah had become so agitated, but she'd played directly into his hands. 'She's never been that strong emotionally,' he said. 'That's why I was so concerned with the birth taking so long and her eventually needing an operation and everything,' he said, mock concern on his face. 'I'm thinking of engaging a nurse to help for a while when Hannah is well enough to come home.'

The doctor remembered how anxious Hannah had been the first time she'd visited him and how her own Doctor Humphries had said how agitated she'd become at times. Then he remembered the silent figure on the bed who'd seemed locked into something in her mind and thought a nurse to help her over the first traumatic weeks when she'd have total care of the child a very good idea. 'Excellent plan,' he said to Arthur. 'That would certainly have my recommendation. I only wish half of my fathers were as considerate to their wives as you.'

The next day, the baby was wheeled into Hannah's room in her crib. Hannah struggled to sit up and looked at her baby daughter.

She lay swaddled in her blankets, so that just her down of auburn hair and her face were visible. Hannah had no desire to pick her up. As she looked at her, she felt nothing, nothing at all. This was her daughter, her own flesh and blood. What was the matter with her? Where was the rush of maternal feeling she'd felt for Michael? Whatever Arthur said, once she was home, she'd have to care for this child. Surely she could love her own child? It shouldn't be hard.

'Don't you want to pick her up?' the nurse asked, puzzled. 'She'll be awake screaming for a feed anytime soon. I'll bring you the bottle and you can wake her gently.' Her hands were in the crib as she spoke and suddenly Hannah was filled with panic. 'No,' she almost screamed, and then seeing the nurse's startled face tried to explain. 'I don't want to . . . I'm too tired. Can you take her away?'

The nurse said nothing to Hannah, after all these were private patients, but she said plenty to her fellow nurses. 'Barely looked at the poor wee thing and refused to hold her. Told me to take her back here and feed her. Like Lady Muck, she is.'

'I hear the husband's engaging a nurse,' another put in.

'Good job!' the first nurse said. 'If you ask me, that Mrs Bradley would be too idle to get off her bum and see to the poor mite anyway.'

'At least her father seems to care. Proper dotes on her, he does.'

'Oh, he's a thoroughly nice man,' said the first nurse. 'A proper gentleman and yet he's not above cuddling the baby and feeding her. We have few fathers like him. Comes in here even before he pops in to see his wife. Mind you, I can understand that. She's probably a right madam.'

'Yes,' said another. 'The baby's probably a lot more interesting and far less carping than that piece.'

Hannah was aware the nurses thought her an odd and unnatural mother when she refused to feed her baby twice more that day. Sister Prescott had never had a case like it before and summoned the doctor again. 'It sometimes happens with a difficult birth,' the doctor said. 'Especially if the mother and child are separated for a little time after the birth, unavoidable of course after a Caesarean operation.'

'What is to be done, Doctor?'

'I don't know if much is to be achieved by forcing the child on her,' the doctor said. 'I'll talk to the husband, he's a sensible chap and concerned for his wife. Maybe now that she is better and the baby recovered enough to be with her, visitors might be encouraged. Maybe showing the baby off would rekindle her maternal feelings, for they are there, but hidden.'

Arthur was surprised at what the doctor had to tell

him that night. He'd bought flowers again, the second bouquet to decorate Hannah's room, and could see as soon as he went in that Hannah was so nervous of him she actually shrank back in the bed. But she had no need. That day, Arthur had engaged a nurse, Pauline Lawson, one of the old school, hot on order and discipline.

For the first few months she would sleep in the child's bedroom, but she would have the sitting room as her own part of the house, which she could convert to a bed-sitting room later if she wished.

Pauline Lawson had never worked in such a small house. Before the war, she'd worked in a large ancestral home in the countryside in Sutton Coldfield after losing her husband at the Battle of the Somme in 1916 and her two young daughters to the Spanish 'flu in 1919.

She spent the war years in hospitals, tending wounded soldiers and afterwards, nursing the elderly. But her first love was children, for she'd not really got over the death of her daughters, and she readily agreed to care for Angela when Arthur explained his wife was not very strong. He went on to say that his wife was emotionally unstable, prone to attacks of nerves, and for some reason hadn't taken to the baby. Pauline's face didn't change, but she couldn't understand an attitude like that. Unnatural, she thought, that was.

Arthur said he didn't want Hannah bothered about nursery matters. He would deal with anything when he came home. Did she think she could cope? Pauline was longing to cope. He needn't worry, she told him, his small daughter would get all the mothering she would need from her.

It fell into place nicely. Pauline had to work out a week's notice with the family she was with and she could move in the day before Arthur was due to fetch Hannah and baby home.

So Arthur, pleased with himself, could afford to be pleasant with his wife. The nurse exclaimed over the beautiful bouquet and noted the fact that Hannah said nothing. 'I'll leave you two alone,' she said, 'and put these in some water,' and she went out to report on the ungratefulness of Hannah Bradley.

'How are you, my dear?' Arthur said, giving Hannah a peck on the cheek.

'Stop this, Arthur.'

'Stop what?'

'This . . . this play-acting. You don't care for me.'

'I married you,' Arthur said.

'Married people sleep together,' Hannah snapped. 'Married people make love.'

'We made love,' Arthur said. 'And the evidence of that is lying in the nursery down the corridor. Then I found out I'd married a whore.'

'Arthur, I'm not. It wasn't like that.'

'I don't care what it was like,' Arthur snapped. 'This child is the only child I will ever have and I will claim her. It hardly matters to you. I'm told you can hardly bear to look at her. The nurses can't understand you at all. They think you're unnatural.'

Hannah had a sneaky feeling they were right. She'd felt that herself and she lowered her head in shame.

'So, my dear, I'm hardly displacing your maternal feelings,' Arthur said. 'Now I've decided on a name for her. Angela Maria. Angela, because she looks like an angel, and Maria after my mother. Do you like my choice?'

'I seem to have no say in it. Call her what you like,' Hannah said, her voice weary and sad.

'You're learning, my dear,' Arthur said, smiling at her as if she'd performed some amazing feat. 'Now,' he went on, 'the doctor thinks visitors might help you in your relationship with your daughter. I doubt it myself, but Mrs Emmerson and her friend are desperate to come. So is Josie, but children under twelve aren't allowed. Even Mrs Banks asked if she could see you.'

Hannah wanted visitors. She wanted to see people other than the disapproving nurses who thought Arthur such a grand fellow and Arthur himself, who frightened her and never failed to make her feel a failure. Gloria and Amy and Elizabeth Banks would be a welcome change.

So they came, Gloria and Amy bringing more flowers and even sweets and chocolates for Hannah, and for the baby, they'd bought warm dresses and little jackets and pram sets. They were both enchanted by Angela, who Hannah asked the nurse to bring in from the nursery, but both were surprised she wasn't by Hannah's bed. 'She disturbs me,' Hannah said. 'And I've needed rest at first. It seemed easier.'

'Can I . . . Can I pick her up?' Gloria asked tentatively, knowing some mothers were possessive about newborn babies.

'Of course.'

Gloria lifted the baby tenderly and peeling back the layers of blanket, exclaimed about her tiny hands and chubby little feet and minute nails but Hannah, who had not really examined her daughter at all, watched and felt nothing. The baby was handed from Gloria to Amy and she too was full of praise. 'You must be very proud of yourself,' Gloria said and her words had a wealth of meaning in them, known only to her and Hannah.

'Oh, yes,' Hannah said and Gloria was surprised at the tone of her voice.

'Do you want her?' Amy said, holding the child out to her.

'No, put her back in the cot,' Hannah said. 'The nurse will be along to take her back to the nursery and give her a bottle.'

Gloria and Amy exchanged glances. They knew Hannah couldn't feed the baby herself. Arthur had explained about the operation, but Gloria would have thought she'd have still taken the opportunity to cuddle the baby and give her a bottle.

'It was too tiring for me,' Hannah told them tersely. 'Arthur agreed with me that as I can't actually feed her myself, it might as well be left to the nurses.'

On the way home, Gloria said to Amy, 'There's something the matter with Hannah.'

'It's from the difficult birth, I've heard it before. Like a sort of depression.'

'Well, she'll have to snap out of it,' Gloria said. 'For she's got to see to that babby when she goes home.'

That very thing was playing on Hannah's mind. She didn't know how she'd cope when she went home with Angela. Oh, she could feed her and change her, she supposed, but she couldn't seem to love her, feel anything for her at all and then she was so tired all the time.

It was Elizabeth Banks who put her mind at rest. She came with the largest basket of every fruit imaginable. In that world of shortages, Hannah couldn't imagine where she'd got it from. 'I'm so glad that Arthur has engaged a nurse to give you a hand for the first few weeks at least,' she said. 'You look quite washed out.'

'A nurse?'

'Oh dear. Didn't he tell you? Me and my big mouth,' Elizabeth said. 'It was probably meant to be a surprise.'

'Well, it's a surprise all right.'

'I worried that he wouldn't be able to afford it, but Reg has given him a sizeable increase and of course the house is all paid for. He's become a different man since his marriage, you know, my dear, more dynamic and forceful. Reg has come to rely on him a great deal. Arthur has a great future ahead of him. He's determined that his child will want for nothing and you can understand it for she's quite the sweetest thing.'

Hannah asked Arthur about the nurse that evening. He was surprised she knew, but not unduly worried, and he sat and told her what he knew about Mrs Lawson. For the first time, Hannah looked forward to going home where someone else was at hand to care for her daughter.

Chapter Ten

Pauline Lawson saw straight away that she'd have no trouble with Hannah. She wasn't at one with the child and it was apparent in one glance. The baby was in a basket and Hannah couldn't seem to wait to hand it over to the nanny, as soon as introductions were over. 'Go and get the child settled and come down to the kitchen where you can have a proper chat,' Arthur advised Pauline.

But when Pauline took Angela upstairs, she didn't put her straight in the cot, but held her instead to her breast. She felt strangely drawn to this child. 'I'm going to love you like you were my own flesh and blood,' she told the baby who looked at her with baby blue eyes. 'In fact, I'm going to love you so much, you won't even miss your mother,' and she kissed Angela's chubby little cheek.

Josie galloped home from school, ecstatic that Hannah and baby Angela were coming home that day. Arthur hadn't let her get back before Hannah did, so she knew nothing about the nurse installed in the house. She ran down the entry and in through the kitchen door to see

Hannah at the sink, peeling vegetables, and Arthur sitting at the table, reading a paper. 'Can't you ever learn to come in through the door properly?' he said irritably, but Josie ignored him. 'Where is she?' she demanded of Hannah.

Hannah didn't even turn around to greet her and it was Arthur who answered, 'In the nursery, with the nanny we've engaged for her care.'

'A nanny?' Josie repeated. 'What do we need a nanny for?'

'We need a nanny because I say so,' Arthur answered. 'Her name is Mrs Lawson and her word is law in all matters regarding the child. You may not go and see Angela unless she says so.'

Josie felt suddenly deflated. She'd carried pictures around in her head of how it would be. Her and Hannah tending Angela, feeding her, bathing her, loving her and playing with her. And now this! Hannah continued peeling vegetables as if her life depended on it, taking no part in the conversation. In fact, she carried on as if she'd not even heard it.

Arthur had gone up to help this Mrs Lawson bath the baby, when Josie had been in about half an hour. She thought that very odd. She would have thought Hannah would have gone, but she'd made no comment when Arthur said where he was going, but just carried on setting the table.

Josie was terribly confused. Was she not to get a glimpse of this baby at all that night? 'Hannah, why have we the need of a nurse for just one wee baby?'

Hannah's eyes were expressionless. 'Arthur wanted it that way.'

'But why?'

'It's best, Josie, believe me,' Hannah said. 'I . . . I was ill after having the baby.'

'I know that,' Josie said. 'But you're all right now, aren't you?'

'No, Josie, not really,' Hannah said. 'It's best Mrs Lawson takes over till I'm on my feet again.'

Hannah could see that Josie was still confused and unhappy, but she couldn't think of anything to say to help the situation. She was tired, so terribly tired.

'When can I see the baby?' Josie asked, her voice mutinous, but Hannah heard the tremble and knew her to be upset.

'Ask Mrs Lawson,' Hannah suggested. 'She'll be eating with us when she gets Angela settled.'

'Oh.' That information took Josie's breath away. She hadn't expected that.

'She'll eat with us all the time,' explained Hannah. 'We're not a large household.'

Josie was all set to heartily dislike the nanny. She felt she had taken Hannah's place – pushing her out and in doing so, pushing Josie out too. She hoped no one expected her to be nice to this woman who she just knew would be awful.

So when Pauline came into the room, Josie scowled at her. She disliked everything about her; the grey hair she had scooped into a bun, the lines on her plump face, the high old-fashioned dress she had fastened to the neck, her thick, dumpy shoes and her woollen stockings.

But Pauline Lawson had had years of caring for children and she was instinctively drawn to Josie because she resembled her elder daughter who'd died years before. And so, as she took her place at the table, she said, 'You must be Josie?'

Josie just nodded. 'And how old are you, Josie?'

'Ten,' she answered briefly.

'A fine age,' Pauline pronounced. 'I bet you'll be a great help to me in the nursery.'

'You do?' Josie cried, incredulous and interested in spite of herself.

'Certainly I do,' Pauline said. 'We'll go and have a little peep at the baby after tea and then tomorrow, when you come home from school, you can help bath her if you like.'

Like! Of course Josie would like, but she wondered whether it was being disloyal to Hannah. She glanced at her, but though she was picking at her dinner, it was if she was someplace else, as if she'd erected a glass wall and she was behind it. 'Would you mind, Hannah?' Josie asked.

Hannah looked at her vaguely as if she could scarcely remember who she was. 'Mind what?'

'Me helping with the baby?'

'Why should I mind?' Hannah said and her tone indicated that the child was nothing to do with her. 'If Mrs Lawson said it's all right and your uncle, then I won't object.'

Arthur was irritated, in fact, at Pauline's suggestion for he felt that it was his place to help bath the baby in the evening and yet he had no wish to argue with her so soon and so said, 'If you wish to and you don't get in Mrs Lawson's way, I don't see the harm.'

And over the next couple of days, Josie enjoyed

helping Pauline and she adored the baby. Pauline was patient and kind, showing her how to bath Angela safely and put a nappy on and dress her in her little flannelette nightgowns before tucking her snugly into her cot.

Despite herself, Josie felt herself thawing towards the woman. In fact, she was glad to have someone to talk to for there was little conversation or anything else to be got from Hannah. Josie didn't know what was wrong with her, but she was unnerved by the change and was relieved that she had the nursery to escape to.

The neighbours came bearing gifts, some of whom Hannah had barely spoken to. It was overwhelming and wearying for Hannah and she could see their puzzled looks when she directed them to the nursery, where they viewed the baby under the watchful eye of Pauline Lawson.

The general consensus amongst them later was that Hannah Bradley was getting above herself. 'After all, she's only an ordinary person like us,' said one. 'First, it was a private nursing home, I ask you, when she had a perfectly good home for a baby to be born in and now a nurse.'

'I think it's her doing though,' another put in. 'I mean her husband is such a pleasant man, always passes the time of day. You can barely get a word out her, though. Sat there today like a stook.'

There was a murmur of agreement. Even Mrs Byrne, Mary's mother, who'd looked after Josie while Hannah had been having Angela, had had something to say about it. 'Hannah's certainly nothing like Josie,' she said to her husband one evening. 'Josie's a pleasant wee thing, even if she is a trifle plain. Her aunt now is beautiful to look at, but she has no personality, no spark somehow. I've noticed it before with beautiful people. They don't feel they have to make an effort. I mean, I tried to make conversation today. I thought I'd make the effort, you know, with Josie and Mary being such good friends. She obviously doesn't do much with that poor wee baby with that nurse there so I asked what she thought of the Royal Wedding and you won't believe it! Do you know she asked me which wedding I meant?'

John Byrne smiled at his wife who'd been agog, like most of the country, at the impending wedding of Princess Elizabeth to Philip Mountbatten, on 20th November, which had been just three days before. 'Not everyone is as ardent a royalist as you, my dear,' he said, but even he thought it odd that not only had Hannah expressed no opinion whatsoever, but that she didn't even seem to be aware that it had taken place.

Gloria saw another example of Hannah's strange behaviour at Angela's christening a couple of days later and it annoyed her. 'What's up with you, girl?' she demanded of Hannah. 'Go up now and tell that bloody woman to sling her hook and take charge of your own baby and look after the guests in your own house."

'Oh, Gloria, I can't. I feel so tired all the time.'

'Tired! At your age! Stuff and bloody nonsense! You're run down, that's all. It's natural enough after having a baby. Get yourself down the doctor and get a tonic. That'll fix you.'

Gloria, Amy and Tom Parry nearly didn't get an invitation to the christening party at all. Arthur had arranged it all and though Hannah was aware of it, it didn't seem to matter. Everything seemed to float over her head.

As soon as Josie found out that Gloria, Amy and Tom had been left off the list however, she enlisted the help of Pauline after getting no joy from Hannah, who could not summon the energy to fight with Arthur over anything anymore. 'Hannah doesn't seem to care,' she said. 'Yet she knows that Gloria will be destroyed if she's not asked. You talk to Arthur, Pauline, he'll listen to you.'

And Pauline did ask him, pointing out how important they were to Hannah and then because she knew he cared about the neighbours' opinion, said people would think him very mean-spirited if he didn't ask them. Arthur knew what Pauline said was right and reluctantly an invitation was issued.

Arthur would have liked Reg and Elizabeth to be godparents, but they were non-Catholics, so he asked a colleague from work to be the godfather and, after much prompting by Pauline, he chose Josie to be Angela's godmother, a duty the child took very seriously indeed. Arthur took it seriously, too, and had engaged caterers to provide a stupendous buffet for all the friends, neighbours and people from work that he'd invited after the ceremony.

Hannah knew she was cutting a poor figure and Arthur a magnificent one, the beam of pride plastered to his face as he cuddled his baby daughter dressed in the long silk christening robe he'd bought for her. Everyone commented on the fine father he made and Hannah knew it would be noted and discussed that she hardly glanced at the child and never held her. Nobody but Gloria ever said anything to Hannah openly, but she knew that she'd be the subject of gossip again, but was too weary to care.

Hannah never went near the doctor's as Gloria had advised; she'd have felt ashamed. But she viewed Christmas approaching fast with dread. She wanted none of it and was thrown into panic when Pauline said she wanted a week off over the festive season. Arthur said of course she must, it was only fair, and Hannah knew it was. Pauline was supposed to have her weekends free, but in practice it seldom happened, for she said she had nowhere to go just for the weekend, so she was on hand most of the time.

So it was more than fair but, 'How will we manage?' she asked that night, when she, Arthur and Josie were alone in the breakfast room. Arthur looked up from his paper, a frown puckering his brow at being disturbed. 'What are you talking about?'

'When Mrs Lawson . . . I mean, Pauline goes away for a week?'

'Well, I'm off for most of it,' Arthur said. 'And Josie will be here too.'

At first, Arthur had resented Josie's incursions into the nursery, but Pauline was not a woman to be trifled with, nor one easily bullied. 'Don't be silly, Mr Bradley. It doesn't become you being jealous of a child,' she'd said. 'Josie is a great help to me and we've become friends, and it will do the girl good to know how to look after children. With God's help, she'll have her own to see to one day.'

So Arthur had been put in his place and now he

knew he would be glad of Josie's help in caring for his daughter, for he knew he'd get little help from his wife. Half the time, Hannah didn't seem totally with it and he wondered if she was losing her mind.

Well, whatever it was, he felt it had to be kept within the family. That was why he'd refused a dinner invitation to the Banks', claiming that Hannah's nerves were bad after Angela's birth, and he gave the same reason for refusing the tickets for the New Year's Ball.

Pauline took on the bulk of the shopping. Armed with a list and pushing the pram, she'd put the order and ration books in at the regular shopkeepers' for delivering later and gone on into Erdington Village to shop for presents and more Christmas goodies.

She'd also decorated the house and tree with Josie's help – more lavishly than Hannah would ever have done, while Hannah slept the afternoon away. And that evening, over dinner, far from grumbling at the waste of money, Arthur was expansive in his praise. 'We have a baby in the house,' he said, explaining his change of heart. 'We must get in the mood.'

Before Pauline left for her holiday, she did much of the seasonal cooking, including the cake, the pudding and mince pies, and left instructions for Josie to do much of the rest. She also suggested Josie write the Christmas cards she'd bought, for she knew Hannah wasn't up to it.

In fact, Hannah wasn't up to much and Pauline thought if she hadn't snapped out of it by the New Year, she'd have to talk her into seeing a doctor.

Hannah viewed her life like a vast void, where she stood alone in a sea of nothingness and those around her carried on with their life, unable to touch her, or affect her in any way. She was convinced she was going mad and afraid of betraying this in her speech, so spoke less than ever, not indeed that there was much opportunity for her to speak at all for she was incredibly lonely. The neighbours had been so put off with her manner when they'd called in to admire the baby, and later at the christening, that they never came again.

Even Josie seemed to have deserted her; from the minute she was home from school, she spent her time in the nursery and often Hannah heard her and Pauline laughing together. Hannah couldn't blame the child for seeking more cheerful company. There was precious little humour, or even conversation, in her.

Arthur also spent most of his spare time in the nursery. What was wrong with her, she asked herself, that she had to steel herself before walking into that room to see her baby? And what was wrong with her that the slightest thing tired her so much that she dropped off in the chair, or gave in to the fatigue and flung herself on the bed and slept for hours?

When Pauline returned in the New Year, Hannah was still no better and she mentioned to Arthur that perhaps she should see a doctor. He was hesitant to encourage this, because he thought Hannah was suffering some form of mental illness and if she was, he wanted that shameful fact kept hidden. He wanted no doctors involved.

Pauline decided not to push it. As it was, she had a free hand in the nursery and though Arthur was more involved than any father she'd ever met, he was out every weekday from morning until night. She didn't want Hannah coming up each day finding fault, disrupting her routine and perhaps upsetting the child. In her heart of hearts, she faced the fact that she wanted to be the most important person in little Angela's life after her father. She thought Hannah unnatural anyway to show no interest in the child at all and someone had to love the little mite. So far, during the day, that person had been her and really she wanted the status quo to remain.

Day after day, week after week passed and Hannah felt more despondent than ever and even more certain it was all her own fault. She wasn't a proper person, she decided one day, not lovable, or even likeable. If she had been, her father would not have rejected her. The nuns had recognised this fact straight away. They knew she didn't deserve to be a mother and that's why they'd taken her baby from her. Michael, at least, would have a chance of a normal life in a proper family, better than he would have done with her – a mad woman.

In early March, Hannah visited Gloria, desperate to confess to the negative feelings that she had about Angela to someone. Somehow, it all seemed mixed up with her past and it was driving her crazy. She honestly felt that if she wasn't able to unload some of her problems she would explode.

'Listen to me,' Hannah begged her friend. 'I've come to tell you this terrible thing, this shameful thing, because if I don't speak of it to someone, I feel as if I will go out of my mind.'

'What is it?' Gloria asked, watching Hannah biting her bottom lip in agitation.

'I . . . I don't love her, Angela, I mean,' Hannah confessed. 'I feel nothing for her.'

Whatever Gloria had expected it wasn't that. One of the reasons she'd been so happy about Hannah's pregnancy was that it might help ease the ache of loss she knew she still felt for her first child. But here Hannah was saying that she couldn't love her own baby. Gloria had known there had been something wrong right from the beginning.

'Do you think me awful? Wicked?' Hannah asked. 'I feel it myself.'

'No, of course not,' Gloria said confidently. 'You've had a difficult time. It does happen, I've heard of it.'

'I never have,' Hannah said emphatically. 'I feel a failure, Gloria. I couldn't have had a worse experience than that first time, worked half to death, constantly berated and told how sinful we were and knowing we were to give birth to a child we couldn't keep. And yet, when I held Michael in my arms for such a short time, I knew I loved him, oh so, so much. I would have laid down my life for him. For Angela, I feel nothing.'

'Oh my dear!' Gloria said in sympathy. 'Why don't you tell the doctor?'

'I couldn't. He'd think me a monster.'

'No, I'm sure he wouldn't,' Gloria said, putting her arms around Hannah. 'Maybe it's linked to that first time. You know, perhaps you won't let yourself love because of what happened?'

'Can you turn love off just like that?' Hannah said, shaking her head. 'I don't think so.'

'The mind's a strange thing,' Gloria said. 'You do things sometimes without being aware of why and how.'

'Oh, Gloria,' Hannah cried. 'I'm so scared.' Gloria held Hannah's shivering body in her arms. She knew the girl was suffering terribly and yet she didn't know what to do to help her. She realised this was a demon she'd have to fight on her own and all she could do was be there for her whenever she needed support.

All in all, Hannah thought it would be easier to stay in bed all day, and each morning she had to force herself to her feet. As soon as everyone had gone their separate ways, she often returned to bed and stayed there for the rest of the day, until everyone came home in the evening. Pauline was the only one aware of this, but she didn't tell Arthur. She thought he would hardly be interested anyway, because he didn't seem to know or care what Hannah did.

Angela learned to recognise Pauline, Arthur and Josie and smile at them and kick her legs and wave her arms in excitement when she heard them approach or when they leant over her. She was a sunny baby, but then she was never let cry, her wishes were attended to immediately and there was always someone to play with her and amuse her.

Arthur was captivated by his beautiful daughter. His creation! He bought a camera and recorded almost daily photographs of the baby. Certain she was the most beautiful and cleverest child that had ever been born, he was forever showing pictures of her around the office. 'God, the man's besotted,' Reg told Elizabeth one evening. 'The baby is all he talks about. It's nice that he so enjoys being a father, but I hope he soon shuts up about it, it gets incredibly boring after a while.'

'I'm glad he likes being a father, too,' Elizabeth said. 'For I'm sure Hannah doesn't like being a mother. In fact, I'm desperately worried about her.'

'Oh?'

'I called in to see her the other day,' Elizabeth said, 'and she looked dreadful, Reg. Really ill.'

'Must be these wretched nerves Arthur says she's had since the baby was born,' Reg replied. 'Do you remember we asked them to dinner that time and that's what he said?'

'Yes, and they didn't go to the New Year do either,' Elizabeth said. 'I hope it is just nerves, though heaven knows they can be disabling enough, but I have a horrible suspicion it could be something more sinister.'

'I certainly hope not,' Reg said. 'Hannah is such a pretty young woman. And Arthur is besotted by her, that's obvious enough, and little wonder. It's always such a pleasure to see them together.'

Someone else besides the Banks was desperately worried about Hannah too and that was Doctor Humphries. Not that he'd been summoned to see Hannah, but to see her daughter Angela. She was five months old when Pauline went to lift her from the cot one morning in early April. She'd been fretful all night and was grizzling again, but apart from that she was also limp and so hot Pauline believed she was running a temperature.

Arthur had already left for work and Pauline knew there would be no point in asking Hannah's advice. She had to do what she thought best, although she did tell Hannah she was sending for the doctor and mentioned her concern for the child she held in her arms. Hannah made no response and Pauline sighed. The woman was definitely not right.

She took the baby upstairs and mindful of convulsions in babies with high temperatures, bathed Angela with tepid water before phoning the doctor, grateful that Arthur had at last got the phone installed and she hadn't had to leave Angela in Hannah's care while she ran to the phone box.

Doctor Humphries, when he arrived, didn't like the set-up in the house at all. Knowing Hannah's history, he'd expected her to be a doting mother. He knew Doctor Marshall at the hospital had recommended she have a nurse for a few weeks after her discharge, his letter had been included in her notes. He would have probably suggested the same after her emergency Caesarean section, but the child was five months old now, and the nurse obviously well installed and no sign of Hannah.

He recalled now the health visitor saying they'd never seen little Angela Bradley's mother, but some nanny or some such. But that had been in the early days. He had no idea it was still going on months down the line.

Angela had measles. 'Don't ask me where she got them,' the doctor told Pauline, 'because I don't know. But got them she has. I'm sure you know what to do. Bathing her down with tepid water was a good idea for lowering the temperature, but I'll give you something to help keep that down. Keep the light shaded and the blinds drawn, plenty of fluids, and keep an eye out for secondary infection on her chest or in her ears.'

'Thank you, Doctor. I'll see to it.'

'Now where is her mother?'

Pauline hesitated. Often she'd gone back to bed, not long after breakfast, but she hadn't heard her come up the stairs that day. 'She could be in the breakfast room.'

'Does she know the child's sick, that you sent for me?'

'I told her I was concerned and that I'd sent for you,' Pauline said. 'But honestly, Doctor, Hannah isn't right and hasn't been all the time I've known her. I'd never met her before she had the child but . . . well, you'll soon see what I mean.'

When the doctor saw Hannah sitting in the breakfast room he knew she was far from right. Her face had no vestige of colour in it and her hair was tangled around her face, but it was her deadened eyes and expressionless face that told Doctor Humphries that Hannah was very sick indeed, and he felt his stomach contract in sympathy. He sat down beside her at the table. 'My dear Mrs Bradley,' he said gently. 'Have you been ill?'

Hannah smiled a sad little smile. 'Not ill, Doctor, but bad. Shameful!'

'Come, come. That isn't true.'

'It is, Doctor. Oh yes, it is,' Hannah cried. 'I'll tell you why and you'll be shocked. You see, I don't love my baby, not a bit, not at all. Pauline Lawson cares for her and Josie helps and even Arthur, but not me.'

'Listen to me, Mrs Bradley,' Doctor Humphries said, covering Hannah's agitated hands that she was wringing together, with his own. 'I think you have an illness that some people have after childbirth. A sort of depression.'

He remembered as he spoke that some fellow doctors would refute such an illness existed at all, but he'd seen a fair number of cases, more certainly than could be put down to coincidence. It was made harder by the fact that many women could not face the fact that they felt nothing for their child. They felt it an unnatural reaction and certainly not something to confess to their doctors.

'I am depressed all right, and disgusted altogether with myself,' Hannah said. 'And I'm always so tired. Sometimes I'm too tired to make an evening meal and if Josie didn't help me with the washing on Saturday, it wouldn't get done.'

'Tiredness is a classic symptom,' the doctor said. 'I've glanced over your notes from Oaklands and you had an emergency caesarean operation and then were separated from your baby for a few days. Bonding didn't take place between you.'

'Will I always feel like this?'

'No, no, not at all,' the doctor said. 'Will you come down to the surgery tomorrow morning? I want to give you a thorough examination.'

'And then will I learn to love my baby?'

'I'm sure you will. Of course you will.'

Although the doctor was soothing and reassuring with Hannah, he was worried and angry that her condition hadn't been brought to his attention before. Surely, no one could think she was behaving normally? Why didn't her husband spot it? Usually the last person to recognise he or she is ill is the depressive themself. That has to be brought home to them. Now he feared it would be a long drawn-out course of treatment before any significant improvement would be seen.

* * *

And it did take a long time for Hannah to pull herself out of the dark abyss she'd fallen into. At first, the improvements were almost unnoticed. She'd felt she was surrounded by a deep, dark fog and that everyone else was on the other side of it and she couldn't reach them. Everything was such an effort anyway that, in the end, she'd stopped trying.

But, gradually, with the doctor's encouragement and the tablets he prescribed, she grew a little stronger. She began to notice that some days the fog would lift slightly before swirling about her once more and it gave her hope and she began to fight the black despair that swept over her at times. She knew, as she began to improve, how near she'd come to true insanity and she also knew that she still walked on the knife edge of it.

'When will I get out of this?' she asked the doctor one day.

'You are getting better all the time, you must see it for yourself?' Doctor Humphries reassured her. 'Your mind has been badly hurt. It takes time to heal. If you'd broken your leg, you wouldn't expect to be skipping down the road the next week, now would you?'

Hannah smiled at the thought and realised that the smile felt strange. She put up her hand and touched her mouth. She couldn't remember the last time she'd smiled.

The doctor took it as a good sign too. 'That's nice to see,' he said. 'A beautiful smile.'

Hannah liked and trusted her doctor and thought him a kind man and one never too busy to talk to her, to listen and reassure. And so, though she longed to return to the old Hannah immediately, the one on the other side of the fog, she did as the doctor advised and took one day at a time.

The spring drew to a close. In June, Josie made her confirmation and Hannah strived for her sake to be more alert, more able to cope. It fooled no one, however, and when Hannah looked back on that day, she found she could remember so little about it, it was as if it had happened to someone else.

In July, Elizabeth Banks paid a call. By that time, Hannah was rising every morning and finding it easier to do. Threads of mist still clung to her mind at times, though, making her forgetful and unsure of herself. Elizabeth saw this, but she also saw that Hannah was much improved from her previous visit.

'I thought there was something wrong the last time I came around,' she told Hannah. 'I said as much to Reg, but I never imagined . . . I should have done, I suppose, because I had a touch of bad nerves after I'd had my second.'

'I'm almost recovered now,' Hannah said.

'Oh my dear, I can see that,' Elizabeth replied. 'The doctor has prescribed something for you, I suppose?'

'Oh yes,' Hannah said. 'He's very good. And the tablets help me cope.'

'That's what you need,' Elizabeth said. 'A sympathetic doctor. They can do wonders these days.'

Hannah continued visiting her doctor, taking the tablets religiously, and slowly but surely her recovery continued.

By the end of August, she was much better, well enough in fact to regret missing so much of Angela's babyhood. The baby, now turned nine months, was fully recovered with no aftereffects from the measles. She was a happy child who laughed and chuckled at anyone and pulled herself up to stand on anything to hand. She could drink from a cup and clap her hands and say Dada, Po, her name for Pauline, and Jo for Josie.

However, she didn't know Hannah when she popped into the nursery and her smile was tentative and unsure. Hannah bent down to her haunches and held out her arms, but Angela, who'd been standing holding on to a toddler truck, dropped to all fours and began backing away. Pauline scooped her up. 'Here's your mommy,' she said. 'Say Mommy.'

Angela said nothing till she was placed in Hannah's arms and then she began to scream and writhe and struggle and hold her arms out for Pauline to take her.

'Every time I go into the nursery, she does the same thing and each time it's like a knife twisting in my heart,' Hannah told Gloria who'd come on a fleeting visit a fortnight later. 'It hurts like mad to know my daughter can't stand the sight of me.'

'It's bound to take time, pet,' Gloria said. 'The child hardly knows you.'

'I know, but oh, Gloria, look at what I've missed already.'

'I know. You'll never get those moments back, you'll have to face that and move on.'

'I know that,' Hannah said. 'Oh, don't I know it.'

'Maybe you should think of getting rid of the nanny?' Gloria suggested.

Hannah shook her head. 'Arthur would never allow it,' she said. 'Anyway, the child would fret, she truly loves Pauline, and I couldn't do that to Angela. After all, none of this is her fault. I know none of it is Pauline's fault either, but I can't help being jealous of her. But then what would have become of Angela without her? To tell you the truth, I wasn't much help to Josie either those past times. She's admitted now that she was frightened of me.

'God, that child has not been dealt a good hand in life. All those she loves either die or disappear from her life and I drag her here to a place she doesn't want to come to, with a person she doesn't want to live with, and then produce a child of my own and go doo-lally-tap.'

'Stop it,' Gloria said firmly and added, 'and you were never doo-lally-tap.'

'Oh my God, but I was, Gloria,' Hannah said fervently. 'You weren't in there with me. It was like visiting the gates of Hell.'

'All right, so I wasn't there,' Gloria conceded. 'But it was the birth brought it on, hormones or some such. And you're as right as rain again now.'

Hannah said nothing; she knew she wasn't, although she was a lot better than she had been. She knew it would take time to completely recover, the doctor had explained it all to her. And she also knew every time Angela rejected her, it knocked her self-esteem again. And yet, she knew she couldn't just give up. She had to keep trying with the child she was longing to be able to love like any other mother. She was determined that Arthur wouldn't have it all his own way and push her out of the child's life altogether.

'Come on,' she said to Gloria. 'Let's go up to the nursery and you can see the set-up for yourself.'

Chapter Eleven

Pauline felt bad that Hannah had been so ill and that she'd not insisted Arthur get the doctor earlier. She had to admit that she'd not tried that hard and when Hannah began to get better and she saw what a lovely person she was when the depression was lifted from her, she felt worse than ever.

Then there was the child's attitude to her and the cold way Arthur spoke. She knew Arthur didn't like Hannah having much to do with the child and though she couldn't understand it, she knew that he was the boss in the house and Hannah had little or no influence.

However, she still did her best to help forge links between Hannah and her child, encouraging them to go out on their own sometimes. She knew Arthur wouldn't have approved, but he'd not actually said that Hannah wasn't to take her out.

The outings were rarely a success, though, for Angela constantly showed Hannah up in public and when she remonstrated with her or attempted to stop her doing something, her tantrums had to be seen to be believed. It did nothing for Hannah's self-esteem. She knew other people besides Arthur thought her a useless mother when she seemed to have no control over one small toddler.

She took Angela to Gloria's one day and the older woman had gone to great lengths to make the child welcome, getting in the cakes and drinks she particularly liked and buying her a colouring book and crayons, a couple of jigsaws and a book of nursery rhymes to amuse her.

However, Angela squashed the cakes between her fingers and smeared the resultant mess over Gloria's sofa and then deliberately tipped her drink over the coffee table. When Hannah scolded her, she stuck out her tongue and ground the crayons into the carpet while she ripped pages from the book. Hannah didn't know what to do. She hesitated to smack her because she knew Angela, who'd never been smacked in her life, would be sure to tell Arthur and she'd be afraid of his reaction, not just for herself alone, but also for Pauline for encouraging the visits.

Somehow, young as she was, Angela knew her mother could do little with her and she laughed gleefully as she flung the jigsaw across the room. It caught the teapot which fell over, shattering a cup and saucer before spinning on to the floor, pouring tea leaves and hot water on to the carpet.

Exhausted and embarrassed beyond measure, Hannah took Angela home and the next time she visited Gloria, she went alone. She could see Gloria was relieved and didn't blame her. 'Between the lot of you, you have the child ruined,' she told Hannah plainly. 'That child needs to know who's boss and she needs to know how to behave and have her bottom smacked soundly when she's naughty.'

'I know,' Hannah agreed. 'She's two years old and she rules the house. But,' she was honest enough to admit, 'she isn't so badly behaved for any of the others.'

And she wasn't. Pauline only had to say, 'Your daddy wouldn't like you to do that now, would he?' for Angela to conform. As for Josie, she had only to say, 'I won't play with you, or take you out if you are naughty,' for her to be good as gold.

Hannah could use none of these ploys, for if she said she would tell her daddy, Angela would toss her mop of auburn curls and say, 'Don't care,' and she didn't. Even at her tender age, she knew Arthur never bothered to listen to anything Hannah said. As for playing with her, Angela wouldn't usually let her play. If Hannah offered to read to her, she'd shake her head. Pauline could, or Josie, or her daddy, but not her mother. If she got down on the floor to help her with a jigsaw or play a game, Angela would be quite direct. 'Go away, I don't want you.'

Pauline, sympathetic to Hannah's plight now, would chide her and try and make her apologise, but she seldom succeeded. Angela knew who ruled the house, it was her daddy, her wonderful daddy, and he never cared what she said to her mommy. He hardly ever talked to her at all himself.

Every evening, she'd wait for his car to turn into the end of the road and she'd run shouting for Pauline or Josie to open the door for her. Arthur would catch her up in his arms at the door and swing her up on to his shoulders.

Hannah, watching them, used to feel a stab of envy. If only Angela had just once been so pleased to see her, but she didn't seem to care if Hannah was in or out. Reluctantly, she would go out with Hannah now, but Hannah was always on edge. When she showed her up in the street, Hannah would grow hot with embarrassment. How could a grown woman let herself be controlled by a child only two and a half feet high?

Yet, they were all controlled. She only had to say she wanted something for Pauline, Josie or Arthur to rush to get it for her. 'She's seldom corrected and never punished,' Hannah said to Gloria. 'Pauline plays war about it, of course. She says to spare the rod is to spoil the child and I think if she had a free hand in rearing Angela, the child would be better for it. I get on better with her now and she does try to include me in things she is doing with Angela and she does tell her off, but Angela just says her daddy lets her say what she likes to me.

'Arthur and Pauline had some heated words over it one day, until Arthur reminded her that she was employed by him and he made the rules. He virtually said if she didn't like it, she knew what she could do.'

'I'm surprised she stayed then.'

Hannah shrugged. 'She loves the child,' she said. 'Everyone loves the child and she knows it; the only one she hates is me.'

'Don't be silly, Hannah!' Gloria said. 'She's only two years old. They take fancies at this age.'

Hannah shook her head. 'Believe me, Gloria. This is no passing fancy. She tolerates me on occasions, but on others pushes me away. It breaks my heart and yet I know I deserve it.'

'Now what rubbish are you spouting?'

'I'm an unlovable person,' Hannah said. 'Even my father couldn't stand the sight of me. Mike might have stopped loving me had he lived. His parents that I supposedly got on so well with never gave me a thought. I mean, I know his father died, but his mother never wrote me so much as a scribe of a letter. Not then, not straight after the telegram, but anytime in those miserable months in the home she could have written to me. She knew I was carrying her grandchild because Mike wrote to tell her. It was part of Mike, for God's sake. Maybe it was better to have little Michael adopted. At least he'd be part of a loving home and have a proper mother to love him.'

'Hannah, this is rubbish!'

'Is it? What about Arthur then?' Hannah demanded. 'He's seldom given me a kind word, never mind a loving one. He told me I'd be a useless mother and I was. I couldn't even love Angela. Maybe it's justice that she can't take to me now. It's what I deserve.'

'Oh for God's sake, Hannah.' But Gloria knew that Hannah's feelings of inadequacy went deep, initiated first by the father who never sent her a Christmas or birthday card and wouldn't even come over to give his daughter away at her wedding. Hannah seldom spoke of it, but Gloria knew it was there, lodged tight inside her, and now this rejection of Angela was the last straw.

The child was a madam, all right, and made worse by Arthur. She did adore him, but she understood many fathers doted on their daughters and vice-versa. If he'd have wanted her to, the child would have come to love Hannah, too, if only to please her father initially.

Angela was spoilt and because they'd never have any

other children, she'd continue to be spoilt. It was one more child removed from Hannah, not physically perhaps, but removed none the less.

'Of course we don't see much of Angela or Arthur either on dry and bright weekends,' Hannah went on, 'because Arthur takes her out.'

'Where do they go?'

'All over,' Hannah said. 'I expect it depends on how much of the petrol ration he has left. He never tells me, but he often tells Pauline and I overhear. They've been to Sutton Park, Drayton Manor, Cannon Hill and the Lickey Hills.'

'Goodness! Just the two of them?'

'Mostly. He has taken Pauline the odd time.'

'But not you?'

'No, nor Josie,' Hannah said. 'Mind you, he's softened a bit towards Josie now, because Angela likes her so much and so does Pauline.'

'And what does Josie think of the situation? She was always so fond of you.'

'She still is. She was frightened of me when I was changed that time you know, but now . . . I think she feels sorry for me. But still, she's besotted by Angela. She loves little ones. She'd make a good nursery or infant teacher.'

'Is that what she wants too?'

'Josie is wise enough not to want what she can't have,' Hannah said. 'Arthur wouldn't let her sit the eleven-plus. He said we couldn't afford the uniform and he wasn't keeping her on at school past the age when she could be out working. To be honest, he had a point about the uniform. In fact,' she went on, 'I don't know what we would have done if Siobhan hadn't sent the confirmation dress for Josie. She must have told them how difficult it was to get things over here and all about clothing coupons when she wrote their cards at Christmas. I was out of it at that time and still not really myself when Josie made her confirmation in June.'

'What will she do then when she leaves school?'

'I'd like her to go to secretarial college somewhere,' Hannah said. 'But if Arthur kicks up a fuss, she'll have to try for a job in Dunlop's or similar where they send you to college a couple of days a week. I'm determined on finding her a decent job. She's anything but stupid. Arthur won't pay out a penny more than he has to on anything but Angela, and I have no money of my own.'

'What about housekeeping?'

'What about it?' Hannah said. 'Pauline sees to the house and has the housekeeping. Every penny he gives me has to be accounted for. I haven't had my hair cut for ages, for example, nor had any new clothes and my shoes are near dropping off my feet. Yet, he has Angela dressed to the nines, especially now that clothes rationing has ended.

'Mind you, he used to get hold of things before, too,' Hannah said. 'Elizabeth Banks let the cat out of the bag one day. They used to have these spivs touring the offices offering things on the black market. It was mainly ladies' things, but I suppose some of the mothers asked about children's wear. Anyway Elizabeth said it amused everyone no end, because Arthur was the only man seen poring over little dresses. And some of the stuff was lovely.'

'Yes, and a lot cheaper than in the shops,' Gloria

replied. 'They sometimes came around the doors here and I bought things a time or two. You really can't blame people. The damned clothing coupons went on long enough.'

'I don't blame anyone,' Hannah said. 'I'd probably have bought things myself if I'd had any money to spend.'

'It's terrible you not having any money of your own,' Gloria said. 'Have you considered taking a job?'

'Arthur wouldn't allow it.'

'Why wouldn't he?' Gloria said. 'It wouldn't affect him. Haven't you that Pauline to see to things and look after the child? Maybe if Angela saw less of you, she might be glad to see you when you did come home.'

'She wouldn't care,' Hannah said. 'She doesn't even seem to notice, but hanging about the house all day, waiting for a smile from my own child is no good either. I try so hard. I often think she senses it. But I'm sure Arthur wouldn't agree to me taking a job.'

That same evening Arthur came home in a jubilant mood. This usually boded ill for Hannah, but she knew if Arthur needed to tell her anything, it never amounted to any sort of discussion between them and he would do so in his own time.

He waited till they were alone, Angela and Josie in bed and Pauline out at the pictures, before he said, 'Make a cup of tea, I need to talk to you about the child.'

Hannah made the tea and brought it in apprehensively, watching Arthur as he spread leaflets he'd drawn from his pocket out on the table before them. 'I've decided on Angela's school,' he said.

'School! The child's only two years old.'

'Three in November,' Arthur reminded her, 'and this place in Sutton Coldfield, Haselhurst's, has a preparatory section. She will begin in January.'

Hannah picked up the leaflets and thumbed through them. There was the history of the school and the supposedly fine reputation it had. Another leaflet was full of pictures of the nursery department, classrooms throughout the school, the language and science laboratories and the gymnasium.

Yet another leaflet outlined a list of the uniform required. Hannah gazed at the little girl in the picture in her cream shirt and tie, topped with a green pleated pinafore and blazer, and a green velour hat on her head. The child was about five, but Angela was little more than a baby. It seemed all wrong to her.

'She isn't a baby,' Arthur said, when Hannah voiced her concern. 'And she is going to get a first-rate education.'

'Will we need to keep Pauline on then if Angela goes to school?'

'Of course we'll keep Pauline on,' Arthur snapped. 'How do you suggest Angela gets there? Do you suggest we put her in a taxi by herself?'

'I could take her.'

'You still don't get it, do you?' Arthur said with a slight sneer. 'You are still my wife, but Angela's mother only because you gave birth to her. After that you wanted nothing to do with her. You made your choice.'

'I was ill, Arthur, I couldn't help it. The doctor explained it all to you.'

'Ah yes, he explained it,' Arthur said. 'But you see,

Angela hasn't forgotten that. Be honest, Hannah, the child can't stand you.'

'You encourage her.'

'I don't, I don't have to.'

'Well, you don't discourage her. She is allowed to behave towards me as she pleases.'

Hannah badly wanted to slap the supercilious smile from Arthur's face, which stayed in place as he said, 'But you must ask yourself why does she behave as she does? Pauline has no trouble, nor does Josie, and she is as good as gold for me. No, my dear, you must face it, as a mother you would win no medals.'

Hannah felt her face flame crimson with embarrassment and tears sprang to her eyes, but she brushed them away with her hand impatiently. This wasn't the time to cry. 'Arthur, there is no need for you to be so cruel.'

'Cruel, my dear? The truth hurts, so they say. Honestly now, would Angela prefer you or Pauline to take her to school in the morning?' Hannah knew who she'd prefer and it wouldn't be her and that fact hurt. It hurt like hell.

'Why do you treat me like this?'

'Like what?'

'Like . . . Oh, I don't know,' Hannah said. 'As if I'm of no account. You seldom talk to me. I'm never given a penny piece for myself. I feel worthless.'

'I told you I would treat you with respect in public and I hold to that,' Arthur said. 'Reg and Elizabeth think we're a devoted couple. If you were to dispel that myth, you would jeopardise our entire future.'

'Future! What future have I got with you?'

'Better than you'd have without me,' Arthur said. 'You'd really be cast adrift then. You and Josie turned out. I doubt Josie would be in favour of cutting all contact with Angela, nor you either.'

'She wouldn't have to. Angela would come with me.'

'I don't think so,' Arthur said. 'For a start, as you commented earlier, Angela doesn't like you and no court in the land would give custody to you when they hear how indifferent you were to her in the early months when she needed your care. You were also in an unstable emotional state, so bad, in fact, that I had to engage a nurse to ensure the baby was given adequate care – facts that can be verified by the medical staff at the nursing home.'

'But . . .'

'And then of course, you'd have no means of support,' Arthur went on. 'This house was gifted to me and I therefore couldn't be forced to sell it. Why would they take a child from a fine house, when I have a job that pays enough to employ a nurse for the child and a private education, and give her to an unstable mother with no job or place to live? If you broke this marriage apart, Hannah, you'd never see Angela again.'

Hannah knew what Arthur was capable of and that he meant every word he said. 'Is that whole vendetta just because I slept with my fiancé once before he sailed to France?'

'This vendetta, as you call it, is because I was duped into marriage. Soiled goods is what I had.'

'You were duped into marriage?' Hannah echoed incredulously. 'What about me? Look how you used to abuse me for your sexual inadequacies and yet Angela was conceived and to this day I don't know how. You should never have married. To get aroused you have to be violent, I know that now. You say as a mother I'd get no medals, well as a lover you are worse than useless.'

Arthur was angry; she could feel the heat of his rage coming off him and she wondered for one moment if he would hit her. He didn't, but pinched her chin between his fingers and said, 'Say what you like, Hannah, I hold all the winning cards.'

As much as she wanted to, Hannah could say nothing, for she knew Arthur was right.

The following evening he pulled some notes from the wad in his wallet and threw them across the table. 'You look a mess,' he said. 'Get something done with yourself, a new hairdo and something decent to wear, we're going to the Banks' for dinner on Friday.'

'Hannah, you look exquisite,' Elizabeth said. Hannah knew she did. She'd spent all the money Arthur had given her. Her hair had had a good cut, and the silk dress fitted where it touched, patterned in swirls of different shades of green from pastel to olive. Her handbag and shoes were of a darker green, like the soft mohair shawl she had around her shoulders.

Even Angela's mouth had dropped open when she caught sight of her before she left. 'Do you like it?' she'd asked and Angela's head had nodded slowly.

Josie gave Hannah a hug. 'You look wonderful, amazing,' she said. 'Haven't you got a pretty mommy, Angela?'

Angela nodded again and stroked the dress gently. Hannah lifted her into her arms and she didn't kick or squirm or demand to get down and she submitted to the kiss Hannah planted on her plump, pink cheek. As Hannah let the child down, she felt tears behind her eyes. It was such a little thing to hold and kiss your own child, but one that, up until now, Angela had shown plainly she didn't like, not from her. She knew if Arthur had been on her side, eventually Angela could be won over. But he was afraid that she might taint his darling daughter.

Arthur said nothing about her outfit until he was in the car and then he said, 'You look very fine, Hannah.'

'Thank you,' Hannah said sarcastically. 'I'll pass muster then? You think it money well spent?'

Arthur didn't answer Hannah's question. Instead, he said, 'Remember our conversation of a few days ago, my dear. We are to all intents and purposes a devoted couple once we are outside our own four walls.'

Hannah wasn't such a good actress – or was it a liar – as Arthur was. She found it hard to throw off the feeling of resentment and unease Arthur evoked in her. This often wrong-footed her, making her seem surly and ungrateful in public.

But for the Banks she tried harder, knowing Arthur would have no hesitation in throwing her and Josie from the house if she should bring disgrace upon him. But it was difficult to act naturally when Arthur came up behind her, hearing Elizabeth's comment. He slid an arm around her shoulders and pressed her to his side while he said, 'I couldn't agree with you more, Elizabeth. I consider myself a very fortunate man.'

'You are that,' Reg said. 'A regular sight for sore eyes is Hannah.'

After that, over dinner, the talk was all about Angela and the school Arthur had enrolled her in with her third birthday two months away.

Hannah contributed little to the conversation and it hadn't gone unnoticed by Elizabeth. She waited until they were making coffee in the kitchen before she said, 'Are you not happy about the school, Hannah? It does have a marvellous reputation.'

'She's still so little.'

'They grow so quickly,' Elizabeth said. 'Before you know it, they're grown up and it's too late. From the little I've seen of Angela, she is a bright little spark. I'm sure she'll benefit from such an education. She will only be in the nursery section as yet.'

Hannah still looked unsure and Elizabeth asked, 'Have you seen the school yourself?'

'No, only leaflets Arthur brought home.'

'Oh, I think you should look around the place,' Elizabeth said. 'It will set your mind at rest, I'm sure. Let's see, Monday afternoon would suit me very well. I could collect you and we could go together.'

'It's very kind of you . . .'

'Not at all. It will be a nice run out and I don't want you worrying. You needn't, you know. I've seldom seen a father quite so besotted as Arthur and he'd do nothing detrimental for the child.'

'Yes, I know,' Hannah said, fighting to keep criticism from her voice as she continued. 'He is exceptional in the amount of time he spends with her.'

'I can imagine. And look at the lavish party he has planned for her third birthday. He's organised that church hall and invited half the street and work colleagues with children and has a conjurer hired to entertain them. He is a man in a million.'

'Yes,' Hannah had to agree, though she'd known nothing about the details for the party until that minute.

She resolved to tell him nothing about her proposed visit to Haselhurst School, knowing he wouldn't approve at all, and hoped Elizabeth wouldn't let the cat out of the bag. But when they rejoined the men there was no chance, for they were talking about politics and the election planned the next year and whether a Labour or Conservative government would be better for business.

Then, they went on to talk about the new televisions they were developing alongside wirelesses and whether they would really take off. Elizabeth glanced at Hannah and raised her eyes to the ceiling, for she hated it when the men talked business all night, but Hannah didn't mind and she sat and planned the outing she was going on with Elizabeth Banks.

'This is the nursery unit, Mrs Bradley,' the rather stern-faced headteacher said. She'd introduced herself as the principal, Miss Halliday, and readily agreed to show Mrs Bradley and Mrs Banks around the school.

Hannah followed her down the corridor and thought the woman with her sharp features and grey hair scraped severely back from her face would frighten the living daylights out of her.

But any doubts about the suitability of the school for Angela vanished as they entered the nursery unit. She was open-mouthed at the array of toys, the home corner where two earnest little girls were cooking on a pretend stove, and another area where water in a large container was offered for the children to play with and one small boy was painting in lurid colours at an easel. Children's art work covered the walls of the bright and airy rooms and Miss Halliday explained that the mornings were given up to the more academic work with the older age group.

There was a yard outside where wooden tricycles and prams were for the children's use and other trolleys that the children pushed one another about in. On the grassy area was a slide, climbing apparatus and a swing and the children were making use of the outside equipment, as the afternoon was dry and quite warm.

'My daughter is coming here in January,' Hannah said, looking about her.

'And you were anxious, feeling her a trifle young?' Miss Halliday enquired. 'Many mothers feel the same. Have we allayed some of your doubts?'

'You certainly have,' Hannah said. 'I'm sure she'll be very happy here.'

'At least she'll have the benefit of other children to play with,' Hannah told Gloria, just a few days before Angela was due to start her posh new school.

'Yes, and she may learn to share.'

'And not think she's the most important person in the world like she did at that ridiculous birthday party,' Hannah put in.

Angela had been awful, wanting to be first in everything, pushing others out of the way and screaming if thwarted in anything. Arthur had proudly looked on in amused tolerance while Hannah had writhed in embarrassment. She knew it was no good her trying to control the child, it would only lead to worse behaviour, but she appealed to Arthur, but he refused to intervene. 'It's her birthday,' he said. 'She's excited. What do you expect?'

Hannah expected better behaviour from a child of hers. She'd grown up in a family of children where no one ever thought to push themselves forward like that and behaviour only half as bad as Angela's would assure them a sharp slap on the legs and better manners in future.

Hannah saw the mothers looking askance at her tolerating such bad behaviour. She knew they didn't blame Arthur. Disciplining children was a woman's job and everyone knew that. Hannah knew it was another black mark against her, but by that time she didn't care, she just wanted the whole fiasco to be over.

Gloria had shaken her head over her when she'd come to tell her about it later. 'Exert your authority over her before it's too late,' she told her sternly.

'It is too late. Gloria, you have no idea,' Hannah said. 'Arthur's laid it on the line. I either accept it, or I go and if I go, so does Josie, and I have her welfare to consider and he'll bring any pressure to bear – medical or otherwise – to prove that I am an unfit mother, to prevent me from possibly ever seeing Angela.'

'He couldn't.'

'He could, Gloria. In the hospital, the nurses thought me cold and unnatural and even the doctor doubted my emotional state of mind. Arthur and Pauline, even neighbours, could testify I cared nothing for Angela after her birth.'

'But you were ill.'

'Do you think that would matter?' Hannah cried. 'The clever lawyers Arthur could afford would make mincemeat of me. They'd think me a candidate for the funny farm by the time they were through.'

'Oh Hannah. I feel so responsible,' Gloria said. 'I pushed you and Arthur together.'

'I could have said no,' Hannah said with a shrug. 'I married him for a child and that's no reason to marry anyone. But I'll tell you this, Gloria, I know what I have isn't ideal, but if another child was taken from me again, which in effect is what Arthur is threatening, I really don't think I could bear it.'

Gloria remembered the state Hannah had been in when she came to her and she doubted she could either. She squeezed her hand tight. 'You know the answer then,' she said, 'if you can't change the situation, you'll have to live with it, at least till the child is grown.'

And Hannah didn't say anything, for there was nothing to say.

On 6th January 1951, Angela stood before Hannah, dressed head to foot in the Haselhurst school uniform; the green gabardine coat covered the cream blouse with the tie on elastic, the pleated pinafore, the cardigan and barathea blazer. Thick green stockings covered her legs and stout black winter shoes her feet, while the green velour hat with the Haselhurst band tried to tame the unruly mop of auburn curls.

It failed miserably and tendrils of hair poked from beneath the hat and framed Angela's lovely little face, the green of the uniform making her green eyes look larger and more beautiful than ever. Hannah choked back a sob. Angela's babyhood was almost gone already. 'You look lovely, darling, so you do. You're absolutely beautiful.'

Angela was happy that morning, happy and excited, not a bit apprehensive, but then why should she be. All her experiences so far had been good and pleasant ones and her daddy said she would enjoy this place and he never told her lies, so she was anxious to be gone and couldn't understand why her mommy should look so sad. 'Will you miss me today?' she asked.

'More than you'll ever, ever know.'

'Well,' she said. 'You can hug me if you like,' and Hannah lifted her into her arms and hugged her daughter and if someone had told her she'd just won a million pounds she couldn't have looked happier.

It only took a matter of weeks to determine that Angela adored her nursery and would have gone Saturday and Sunday too if it had been open. It took the same amount of time to establish that Hannah was bored out of her brain with nothing to do all day, for the house wasn't big enough to occupy the two women.

'Gloria suggested me getting a job,' she confided in Josie one night.

'Well? Why don't you?'

'Arthur wouldn't allow it. He was bad enough before.'

'Does he have to know?'

'Pauline will tell him if I don't.'

'No she won't. Not if you ask her not to,' Josie said. 'She'd probably welcome it, because she knows you're getting under one another's feet here.'

'Has she said?'

Josie shrugged. 'Not in so many words,' she said, 'but I know.' Then she looked at Hannah and said, 'What kind of work were you thinking of anyway? Will you go back to Mrs Emmerson's?'

'No,' Hannah said. 'She has someone in my place anyway. I was thinking of something different. Office work maybe, or work in a shop. Oh, I don't know. Anyway, like I said, Arthur would never stand it, so that's that.'

But Josie kept the conversation in her head. She knew how unhappy Hannah was, both in her marriage and in her relationship with Angela. Really she had very little to look forward to each day.

Maybe a job would give her more self-esteem. At least it would get her out of the house. And then, she might have people to talk to who didn't make fun of her like Arthur, or reject her like Angela. She decided to put her thinking cap on. There must be a job somewhere that Hannah could do and if Arthur didn't like it he could bloody well lump it, she decided.

Chapter Twelve

Josie didn't exactly forget about Hannah and her decision to get her a job, but she was taken up with excitement as were many more with the preparations for the 'Festival of Britain'. It was beginning in May and it was to show the world how far Britain had come on since the war. Many thought it was premature. Conscription had been re-introduced for men aged eighteen to twenty-six since 1948 and with the increase in hostilities between North and South Korea, many of these conscripts were out there fighting in yet another strange land. It seemed wrong for some then to celebrate.

'Don't they think this country's done more than its fair share?' Gloria said to Hannah one day when she popped up to visit. 'And another thing, they say this festival is going to cost eleven million. Think how many that would house that are living in slums now.'

Hannah knew she was right; many people were living in substandard housing and not everyone had a job and yet she couldn't help feeling that maybe this festival was the boost everyone needed.

The Labour government had done some good things, powering through welfare reforms, but those reforms, in the wake of the expense of a World War, had put the country even more in debt to America. They'd also nationalised the steel works, coal mines, the docks, railroads and electricity in order to try and rationalise employment to peacetime.

But still, Hannah felt people had to have something to look forward to after the grim and austere post-war years. The festival was supposed to be going some way to put the Great back into Great Britain and give the people something to be proud of again.

It promised to be spectacular. The bulk of the festival's activities were to be in London as expected, though smaller events were planned all over the country, and special trains were being laid on for those who wanted to travel to London. Josie came home in a fit of excitement in April. Mary Byrne and her family were travelling down the first weekend and wondered if Josie would like to go with them.

Hannah looked lovingly at her excited niece. She was very dear to her. She'd been fourteen in February and in the ordinary way of things would be leaving school in July, but in 1947 the school leaving age had been raised to fifteen. She saw the girl was growing up fast, her dress straining over her budding breasts – new clothes needed there. Well, that's what the money from America was for, and also for treats, like going along to this festival in London. Something she would remember for ever.

Hannah, however, was not prepared for Arthur dropping his bombshell a week later as they sat around the table for their evening meal. 'Take Angela to London to the Festival?' she repeated incredulously, looking at

Arthur as if she couldn't believe her ears. 'Arthur, she's only three years old!'

'Three and a half,' Arthur corrected, and he beamed across the table at Angela who was looking from one parent to another. 'You'd like to go with Daddy to London, wouldn't you, pet?'

'Yeah! Yeah! I wanna go, I wanna go,' said Angela, banging her fork on the table. She had no idea what a festival was and she didn't care as long as she went with her daddy. She glared at Hannah and said, 'Nasty Mommy!'

Arthur smiled. 'And who would you like to come with us, darling, Mommy or Pauline?'

'Arthur . . .' Hannah began, but Angela shouted above her. 'Po! Po! Po!' she cried, for she'd retained her baby word for Pauline. 'I love Po,' Angela continued. 'I don't love Mommy.'

Pauline and Josie saw the colour drain from Hannah's face and Pauline said sharply, 'Angela, that was very unkind and very rude.'

Angela's eyes slid to her father's and he said, 'Unkind? Rude? Nonsense! Angela speaks the truth, but it is unpalatable to some.'

Hannah could bear no more. 'Excuse me,' she muttered, jumping up from the table and making her way from the room. Josie gave a sigh and her eyes met those of Pauline, who she now knew felt deeply, deeply sorry for Hannah.

Hannah sat on the bed, rocking herself, her hands gripped between her knees to stop them shaking so much, and she moaned, but quietly, so no one could hear. She felt as if she was crumbling away inside, dying, falling apart. She was hurting all over. She knew her child didn't like her, she'd accepted it, or thought she had, but to hear her say it like that at the table and then for Arthur to applaud it. How in God's name could he be so cruel?

Much later, when a form of numbness had taken over her body, Josie came looking for her. 'Hannah?'

'I'm all right,' Hannah said shakily. 'I feel nothing now.'

'Angela is going to bed. Pauline wants to know if . . .'

'No. Whatever it is, the answer is no. I couldn't cope with a second rejection tonight.'

'She doesn't mean it. She's only wee yet. She doesn't know what she's saying.'

Hannah lifted her face to Josie and said, her voice steady, 'She does mean what she says, however small she is. Maybe because of what happened after her birth, but certainly compounded by Arthur, the child doesn't like me. One day, when you're fully grown up, I may tell you why that hurts me so much.'

'Oh Hannah, I feel for you,' Josie said. 'Pauline and I both do. Pauline feels guilty. She says you should be the one going with Arthur and Angela, not her.'

'There's no need for Pauline to feel that way.'

'Maybe not,' Josie said. 'But I can see her point too. Anyway, this has decided me, I'll tell Mary tomorrow at school that I can't go with them. They'll soon sell my train ticket, there were hundreds after it.'

'You will do no such thing!'

'Hannah, I can't go off to London and leave you on your own.'

'You can.'

'But what will you do with yourself?'

'God, girl, there's hundreds of things I can do,' Hannah said. 'I may go and see Gloria, or give the house a good clean when I've got everyone out of it, or spend the day in bed with a book. That's my business, but if you pass up this chance, I will be cross with you.'

But for all Hannah's spirited response for Josie's benefit, it was hard to see them all set off that Saturday morning. Josie had already gone, as she was spending the night with the Byrnes, and as the door closed behind Arthur, Pauline and an excited dancing Angela, the house seemed incredibly empty. For a little while, she was overcome with self-pity. Here I am, a married woman, mother of a three-year-old, aunt to a young woman of fourteen and I'm here alone while the whole household is out enjoying themselves. She decided to take a grip on herself. She wouldn't stay in the house, she decided. She would go out. She'd visit Gloria, talk to people and stop feeling sorry for herself.

Gloria was delighted to see her. 'I hoped you'd come,' she said. 'I've bought one of those new televisions. It's in the residents' lounge and much of that Festival in London is being televised, they say. When young Josie comes home, you'll be able to tell her you've seen everything.'

Gloria knew about Josie going to London, but not Arthur and Angela, and when Hannah told her, she exclaimed, 'And he took that nanny instead of you? God, but he's a mean bugger! Well, this isn't the same as being there, duck, but it's the next best thing. And one thing, eh, we don't have to push our way through the crowds. We can sit in comfort and have a cup of tea with it as well. So I'll put the kettle on, shall I?'

Most of the televising began in the afternoon and no one could fail to be impressed. Hannah saw the long series of pavilions alongside the Thames and displays telling the story of Britain and the British people. A thing called a Skylon, a thin pencil of aluminium and steel, seemed to hover in the air, while a huge Dome of Discovery was perched on stilts. Two and a half miles down river, the muted sound of the fair in the Festival Gardens in Battersea reached them and put Hannah in mind of her disastrous honeymoon at Blackpool.

In the pavilions, architects and designers were out in force. For years, any furniture made had been utility-stamped and styleless, but now Hannah saw beautiful tables and chairs to match with spindly legs, and modern comfortable armchairs and sofas and wished she could change some of the heavy furniture she'd inherited and now seemed stuck with.

'Against the background of the grime and ruins of a battered, battle-scarred London, the South Bank is an enclave of colour and light,' said the announcer and Hannah was caught up by his enthusiasm.

They were holding up a new way of living, one that had no place in the grim and dreary 1940s, and Hannah and Gloria looked with awe at the piazzas and brightly coloured restaurants and the accent on youth and fashion and the good times to come. Hannah hoped with all her heart that they were right and the world would be a better and safer place for the youngsters to inherit.

* * *

Only a couple of weeks after Josie had been to London, she sought Hannah out one evening, because she'd heard news that day at school that might benefit both of them and help them get employment. In September of that year, Josie was to begin her last year at school and the school were offering the boys the chance to do woodwork and the girls a commercial course.

'Do you think it would be useful?' she asked Hannah.

'What does it entail?'

'It sort of prepares you for office work; accounts, shorthand and typing.'

Hannah was delighted. 'That's just what I wanted for you,' she said. 'It's great that you can do it at school. I wish I'd had the chance. You go for it!'

'Aye, but this is it, Hannah,' Josie said. 'What if I was to show you what I learn in the day and you practise it at home? It would make me concentrate more and it would help you get a better job, too. We'll have to get a typewriter, though.'

'Will it cost much?' Hannah said. 'I have no money of my own. There is a tidy sum in the account I opened for you, but I'd feel bad using that.'

'Come on, Hannah. This is to help both of us,' Josie said. 'It's better than asking Martin and Siobhan for more money.'

'Okay then,' Hannah said suddenly. 'We'll do it.'

And so it began from that September. They purchased a Remington typewriter, which they had up in the room they shared. Hannah used Josie's notes and exercises and practised typing, the hieroglyphics called shorthand, and accounts in her room for hours on end, through the day and often into the evening after Angela had been put to bed.

At first, she thought Arthur might be alerted enough to investigate what was keeping her upstairs, but Arthur had found other interests which took him out of the house three or four times a week. Hannah didn't know what these interests were, nor did she care, and used those nights to polish up her shorthand and accounts work as well as the typing, until Josie complained she was getting on faster than she was.

But Hannah had a goal. She wanted a good job that might command more than adequate wages. In her heart of hearts, she didn't know how long she'd be able to stomach this sham of a marriage. In the back of her mind as she worked in the bedroom was the realisation that one day, this might be for real.

Pauline knew what was going on of course, though she said nothing of it to Arthur, but rather applauded what Hannah was doing and often came up and helped by dictating letters for Hannah to take down in shorthand and then type up. She had begun to feel sorry a while ago for the way the child treated her, that Arthur condoned by not correcting her, and also for the way Arthur treated her. It bothered Pauline when he told her things concerning the child that she found out later Hannah knew nothing about. If she wanted to better herself, well good luck to her. Now if only the child could take to her, it would mean everything.

Mind you, she had to admit the school had been good for Angela. She no longer screamed in temper, nor snatched at food or anything else. She ate daintily and said, 'Please' and 'Thank you' without being reminded. But once through the door of her home, she was still once more the kingpin, the one everyone kowtowed to, the one everyone rushed to satisfy when she issued orders in her imperious little voice.

She'd been taught a veneer of politeness, so she no longer showed her dislike of her mother quite so obviously, and Hannah was grateful even for that small improvement and tried, like the others, to please her. But still, when her father stepped through the door, it was as if everyone else had ceased to exist. It was to him she brought the news of the day at school, showing him her paintings and models.

Hannah knew the paintings adorned his bedroom and the crude constructions Angela had made lined his tallboy for she'd seen them when she'd tidied and she felt sad that she hadn't been shown these things. Pauline advised her to have patience and really Hannah hadn't any alternative; she could only hope and pray that she would be able to build something worthwhile with the child before she was much older.

Angela was now rising four and did academic work for part of the morning at the nursery and Hannah was explaining this to Gloria one afternoon in late autumn. 'Arthur tests her every day on what she's learned,' Hannah said. 'She never seems to mind anything her daddy suggests. The rest of us might as well not exist if Arthur is around, but then you know that, I've told you before. I can never seem to amuse or satisfy the child. Whatever I do, she moans that she's bored and wants her daddy.'

'If you ask me, you're making a rod for your back

giving the child all your attention the way you are,' Gloria remarked. 'You would be prepared to turn cartwheels so that that child would throw you a few crumbs of affection and she senses that.'

'Aye,' Hannah said. 'And I know you think that daft and I know too that crumbs might be all I ever get, but without those crumbs, life wouldn't be worth living.'

'I know, lass,' Gloria said gently. 'But it's no good for the child the way you have her, particularly Arthur, because he's raising a wayward child with no thought for any but herself. It will come home to roost eventually, mark my words!'

'Well, there's no sign of it so far,' Hannah said.

'You need to stand back from it a bit. Get something else to fill your life. Have you thought any more about getting a job?'

'Aye, but the point is, though I know accounts, shorthand and my typing speed is fast, I've no certificates to prove it. Josie has got on really well, but she'll be taking exams in May. She says I'm as good as she is, but I don't know.'

'Well, I don't know how good or bad you are,' Gloria said, 'but I do know employers won't be beating a path to your door and you'd be better fixing your mind on something other than Miss Angela Bradley.'

Hannah knew Gloria was right, but she couldn't seem to pluck up courage to go anywhere. Anyway, where did she go? The employment exchange, she supposed. She hadn't looked for a job since coming off the boat in Liverpool and travelling to Leeds in 1938, thirteen years before, and even then Molly had already spoken for her and had a job lined up at The Hibernian.

Christmas was nearly upon them again. Angela's birthday had been as lavish as ever and had included a sumptuous tea, organised games and a puppet show. Almost the entire nursery school had been invited and Angela showed off on her father's present to her, a large three-wheeler bike in bright red and silver, with a huge bread-box on the back between the back wheels, that she'd allow no one else to touch, let alone ride.

For Christmas, Hannah knew that Angela was having a majestic rocking horse and a doll's house that would almost take up one wall of her bedroom. She only had to say she wanted something for her father to buy it. But there was nothing Hannah could do about that.

She had her head down against the wind as she made her way up Erdington High Street, and she almost careered into someone. 'Hey, steady!'

'Oh, Doctor Humphries, I'm so sorry.'

'It's all right,' the doctor said, looking Hannah up and down. 'This wind is pretty fierce. How are you now? You must be all right for I never see you in the surgery.'

'Oh, I'm fine.'

'How's Angela? How old is she now?'

'She's fine,' Hannah said. 'She was four in November and is at nursery full-time, leaving me and Pauline falling over one another in the house. I'm thinking of getting a job for myself in the New Year.'

'Oh? Doing what?'

'Well, I've been practising secretarial skills,' Hannah said. 'Josie's learning at school and she teaches me and I practise at home.'

'Are you any good?'

'I don't know. Josie says I am, but I'm not sure myself.'

'Do you know shorthand and typing?'

'Yes, and accounts.'

Vic Humphries scrutinised the woman in front of him who had been so ill in the weeks and months following her baby's birth that she'd almost tipped over into the abyss of true mental illness. She certainly looked better than she'd looked then, but there was still something in her manner, something not right.

She certainly, on the face of it, didn't appear to have problems. Her husband was in full-time, obviously well-paid employment, she had help in the house and the child was full-time at a private school. Certainly, that was the view of the neighbours – many of them he'd treated had given him their opinion of Hannah Bradley. He'd gathered they thought her uppity and above herself and far too good for the likes of them.

Doctor Humphries had never got that impression in the weeks she'd been going to the surgery for treatment over three years ago when she'd been so ill after Angela's birth. In fact, he'd felt then that Hannah was lacking in self-esteem and certainly not totally happy. He applauded her decision to teach herself skills to enable her to better herself, though he knew most employers would need vital pieces of paper as proof that she could do what she claimed.

He was in a bit of a hole himself, but if he was to

offer a position to Hannah, was he doing it totally because he felt sorry for her? She might be useless. But then he dismissed that. He thought her an honest person and he was sure she would not say she was any good if she wasn't. He decided to take the risk.

'You wouldn't care to give me a hand, would you?'

'Work for you?'

'Yes, don't sound so shocked,' Doctor Humphries said. 'The point is, my secretary went down to London in a rush when her father died suddenly four days ago. I held the post for her. But just this morning, I got a phone call to say that she can't leave her mother and that she'll be looking for a job down there to be nearer to her.'

'But you don't know if I'm any good,' Hannah said.

'I know you've got to be better than me,' Doctor Humphries said. 'I jab at the typewriter with two fingers. I was on my way to put a card in at the employment exchange, but I'm rushed off my feet now what with the colds and flu and similar infections of winter and such, and I haven't time for the rigmarole of interviewing. If you could just help me for a few weeks, I would be grateful.'

Hannah accepted the opportunity the doctor was offering her and when Arthur kicked up when she told him about it she hit back. 'You never give me a penny piece for myself, unless you want to impress the Banks. Well, I'm fed up with it and that's the truth. Anyway, I thought you'd be pleased that I was out more and probably will see less of my daughter. That always seems to please you.'

'It seems to please you equally, my dear. You've never

had time for her. Angela's always been just a nuisance to you.'

It wasn't true, but Hannah, weary with arguing with Arthur, didn't bother denying it. She turned her head impatiently and then bitterly wished she had challenged Arthur, because standing in the doorway, where she'd heard every word, was Angela. She cast her mother a baleful look and ran.

Hannah saw Arthur's curled lip and the satisfied look on his face and she cried, 'You're a fiend! An unnatural fiend!' She went off to find Angela, but she was already upstairs, buried in Pauline's arms. Pauline hadn't known what had sent Angela flying up the stairs sobbing and she'd comforted her without knowing what had brought it about for Angela had been too upset to tell her.

When Hannah came into the room, Pauline had tried to coax Angela to speak to her mother, but to no avail. 'No,' she declared, her voice muffled as she spoke into Pauline's shoulder. 'She doesn't like me and I don't care because I don't like her either and I wish she'd go right away.'

Defeated, Hannah turned, left the room and went downstairs where she sat alone in the kitchen. 'She's but a child,' Pauline said later. 'She was hurt and lashed out. It meant nothing.'

'Pauline, she's only ever just tolerated me.'

'Oh, Hannah, you take too much notice of her childish outbursts.'

'So would you if it was you they were directed towards.'

Pauline had to agree. Her initial feelings of wishing

to usurp Hannah's place in the child's heart had disappeared in the sympathy she'd developed for Hannah's position. She'd lost her two young daughters to influenza, but at least she thought they'd died loving her. She didn't know how she'd have coped if they constantly rejected her and pushed her away as Angela did her mother. And sometimes guilt niggled at her that she hadn't helped the situation. But she did think it might help Hannah's self-confidence that Angela was unwittingly battering away at to take the job the doctor offered and she said so.

'You don't see it as another admission of failure?'

'No, not at all, quite the opposite.'

'Angela heard me agree with Arthur that I always thought her a nuisance,' Hannah said suddenly.

Pauline shook her head. 'I can't see you saying that.'

'No,' Hannah said with a sigh. 'I didn't say it, Arthur did, but I didn't bother arguing. He often says similar things and I just let it go. I didn't know, but Arthur did, that Angela was right behind me. That's why she was so upset and that's why she said what she did to me.'

Pauline had wondered why the child had been upset. But she thought the situation had been Arthur's fault, not Hannah's. He'd hurt the child he purported to love to gain a point over his wife. 'I'll talk to her,' she promised. 'Try and get her to see that . . .'

'Don't bother, Pauline,' Hannah said with a sigh. 'She'd not believe anyone over her father. If he told her hell would freeze over, she'd believe him. Let it go. But this has decided me, I'm taking that job. Maybe I'll make a better fist of being a secretary than I have a mother.'

'Don't degrade yourself.'

'I'm not, Pauline. Really I'm not,' Hannah said. 'I'm just facing facts.'

Chapter Thirteen

Doctor Humphries, or Vic as he insisted Hannah call him out of the patients' earshot, seemed delighted with Hannah's decision and the day she began it was easy for Hannah to see why. The whole place was in a terrible muddle; patients' files dumped on any available surface, unanswered letters scattering the desk and bills and accounts stuck haphazardly on to a spike.

Added to that, the whole place was grubby and a queue of people were outside waiting for the doors to open. 'As you can see, it's a bit of a mess,' Vic Humphries said.

'Aye, I see that,' said Hannah, but she was thinking to herself that the place couldn't have got so bad in a few days. His last secretary, she decided, must have been bone idle.

'I'll tidy it up after surgery,' she promised. 'You'll have to open the doors up now. It would cut you in two out there and you'll have them all go down with double pneumonia if you're not careful.'

Hannah was kept busy after that. Taking the names and addresses was easy, but finding their files, with no obvious system in place, was a nightmare and one she resolved to remedy as soon as she could.

Christmas came and went and by the New Year, Hannah and Vic had a routine going. The National Health Service was well underway by then and the waiting room was often packed, but now that it was better organised, it was easy for her to find files and patients' notes and have them ready for Vic as he called each patient in.

Hannah soon understood the patients, those who needed sympathy, especially the elderly, and those that needed a no-nonsense approach. She recognised those who were apprehensive, the children trying not to cry and their worried mothers, the men who thought illness was a weakness and would rather be anywhere but there, and the workshy who came for another panel note from the doctor.

With them all she was polite but friendly. She remembered former ailments and asked about other members of the family and many would sing Hannah's praises to the doctor in the surgery.

When surgery was over, Hannah would make her and the doctor a cup of coffee and go in with her shorthand pad, while Vic dictated letters he needed to write. Lunch was cooked and eaten in Vic's kitchen upstairs. It hadn't been the case at first. Then Hannah had arrived with a sandwich and flask of tea until Vic said it was ridiculous to bring a cold sandwich when there was a kitchen upstairs where she could cook herself something warm, so now Hannah heated up soup or something.

Vic was seldom there. He was usually out on his rounds and she often didn't see him again till afternoon or evening surgery. She had plenty to occupy her, for as well as the letters to write, she had the accounts to bring up to date. Vic was remarkably lackadaisical about money matters, but the Government paid the doctor for each patient treated. Then there were the accounts for those who insisted on staying on as private patients and the bills for their home visits and drugs or treatment prescribed for them.

But still Hannah doubted her ability. She'd only agreed to help Vic out for a few weeks initially and felt sure when things settled down, perhaps in the spring, he would look around for a proper secretary with certificates and qualifications, and she didn't want him to feel guilty about asking her to leave.

But as January gave way to February, every day the waiting room was filled with people with streaming eyes and hacking coughs and Vic was rushed off his feet visiting those unable to get out of bed altogether.

Even the King succumbed to the lung disease he'd been suffering from for years and on 6th February, he gave up the fight. The patients in the waiting room were voracious over it. Princess Elizabeth would be the new Queen, the first Queen since Victoria. She wasn't even in the country at the time, but in Kenya, and most remembered how frail the King had looked in the photographs in the newspapers as he'd waved his daughter off only a week earlier.

'Don't envy the task of being Queen, now any road,' one old man said, and there was a murmur of agreement. 'I mean, we're supposed to be at peace, but we ain't. We've got soldiers fighting in Malaya and Egypt, as well as bloody Korea, and now these bloody Mau-Maus in Africa rising up against one another.'

'Yes,' commented an old lady. 'I thought Churchill would sort it when the Conservatives got in last October. Didn't you? I mean he was good in the war.'

'Good in the war!' spluttered the first man. 'Never even fired a gun. Only thing he was good at was shouting his mouth off.'

That seemed to be the consensus at home too. 'Of course,' Pauline said. 'He's an old man. I mean, to vote a man of seventy-six to lead the country, it's madness. He's living in the past.'

'Yes, and it's amazing how people who excelled in the war can't revert to peacetime,' Hannah put in. 'I mean we've had ex-servicemen in the surgery suffering from stress and bad nerves and all sorts. First-rate soldiers and they can't hold down a job in civvy street.'

'War does dreadful things to people,' Pauline said. 'But let's all cheer up. We can do nothing about the Government, at least not for a few years, nor nothing about the skirmishes, but we can prepare for a coronation.'

'What do you mean, prepare?' Josie asked.

'A party,' Pauline said. 'Bound to be a party, isn't there, for a coronation? I remember the coronation of this King in 1937. I was working at the big house then and they had a huge marquee and invited everyone from the village. The kitchen staff were working morning, noon and night preparing for it and on the day, village girls were pressed into service too. They organised games for the children, and a band played and people danced on the lawns. Oh, it was a wonderful day.' But now there would be a young Queen on the throne, for Elizabeth was only twenty-six and the mother of two young children, Charles and Anne. 'A New Elizabethan Age,' the papers heralded it and though Hannah was convinced whoever was on the throne wouldn't make the slightest difference to her life, coronation fever seemed to be gripping everyone else.

But the thing uppermost in Hannah's mind was her job. She'd only agreed to help Vic out for a few weeks and he'd only agreed to employ her at all because he'd been in a bit of a hole. By April, the weather was better and the frenetic pace of work had slowed down a little and Hannah thought it was the time to broach the subject of Vic getting a proper secretary.

It wasn't that she wanted to leave, far from it, for she loved her job. Apart from that, she thought it a novel experience to work with someone who seemed genuinely pleased to see her and valued what she did, but she'd only agreed to help Vic out for a little while. With daily use, her office skills had improved drastically, but she hadn't got the important bits of paper to say so, which she imagined doctors would demand.

But Vic's mouth dropped open when she mentioned the prospect of her leaving one day as she brought in the coffee. 'Leave!' he repeated incredulously. 'You want to leave?'

'No,' said Hannah earnestly. 'And I'd never leave you in the lurch don't think it. I just thought you might need a proper secretary. I wouldn't want you to . . .'

'Proper secretary! What are you talking about, Hannah?'

'One like Josie. One with typing and shorthand certificates?'

'I don't need things like that,' Vic said. 'You do just fine. Anyway, your job is more than just typing.'

'I know, but . . .'

Hannah had regained the spring in her step since coming to work and the sparkle had returned to her beautiful green eyes, and her auburn hair, tied loosely back from her face with a ribbon, caught the lights of the surgery when she'd come in to talk to him. He realised with a shock so sudden that it was like a kick in the stomach, that if Hannah left, the light would go out of his life, for she was like a breath of fresh air.

'Hannah, Hannah,' he said, reaching over the desk and catching up her hands. 'Listen to me. You are the best secretary, the very best that I've ever had. I don't know what I'd do without you and I don't know what I did before you came.'

Vic's touch was sending tremors through Hannah's whole body and she could hear and feel her heart thudding against her ribs as she tried to free her hands, but Vic hung on fast. 'You're such a lovely, generous person, Hannah, such a joy to work with and what's more, the patients like you.'

Hannah knew that was true. Even some of the neighbours who'd once had such a bad opinion of her had revised it. She'd seen it in their eyes and their friendly greetings. She knew they couldn't understand why an ordinary woman, living in an ordinary house, who employed a nanny to look after one small baby now worked in the doctor's as if she needed the money, but that apart, they had to agree she was pleasant enough.

But what was going through Hannah's mind was not what the patients thought of her, but what Vic had said in his soothing doctor's voice. He'd called her a lovely person, a generous person, and someone who was a joy to work with. Heat flowed through her body and she wondered if it were sinful to accept such compliments from a man who was not her husband.

Maybe, maybe not, but oh how good it felt! For years she'd been made to feel bad and useless. Even Arthur, in their courtship and early weeks of their marriage, had used few endearments and she'd never felt cherished or special.

Now this man, this good, kind man, had said things that made tears spring to her eyes. She told herself she mustn't cry; it was silly and Vic would think her stupid, but unbidden, the tears seeped under her eyelids and trickled down her cheeks. 'Oh, my dear, don't cry,' Vic said, and had the insane notion of pulling her into his arms. For comfort only? Comfort be damned! He knew what he wanted, he'd sensed the same need in Hannah, but to take it further would be madness.

He released Hannah's hands and reaching into his pocket, pulled out a snow-white handkerchief and handing it to her, he busied himself tidying his desk to give Hannah time to compose herself. 'I'm sorry,' she said at last.

'No need to be sorry. Sometimes tears are the best thing,' Vic said. 'But please – no more thought, or talk, of leaving.'

'No, no, of course not, if you don't want me to.'

She thought as she returned home that evening what a difference the job had made to her life. Not just financially, but in all sorts of ways. It had raised her confidence, for it's always a boost to self-esteem to know people like you. How funny, tragically funny, that her own child couldn't seem to. She'd come to accept the fact now that she might never have the deep relationship she craved with Angela with so many forces against her; she knew there was little she could do to remedy the situation at least for the moment.

She saw less of Arthur too, for he was still often out in the evening. She didn't ask where he went. If she had done, he'd probably not have answered and anyway, she didn't care. She felt her body slump in relief when the door slammed shut behind him for he made her feel such a failure and often cut her to ribbons with his tongue.

Josie was well aware of this and hated to see Hannah beaten down emotionally, but was helpless to do anything about it, and Pauline was an employee and couldn't openly oppose Arthur's behaviour towards his wife, though she often felt immense sympathy for her, and was very glad she enjoyed her job so much.

Pauline wasn't the only one to be thankful. Gloria was too, for she saw a new Hannah emerging, like a caterpillar who had turned into a butterfly. She saw a Hannah she'd never seen before, for the cowed and shameful girl who came to her years before, with an aching yearning for a child she'd never rear, bore no resemblance to the new Hannah.

There had been flashes over the years that led Gloria to think that underneath there was a vivacious and happy young woman and it was an attempt to regain that happiness that she was sure Hannah would find in children, as well as ensuring financial independence, that had encouraged her to ensnare Arthur Bradley on Hannah's behalf. That had gone badly pear-shaped, but Hannah had found her own solution and like Gloria's own, it had been work – different work, but still work – that had saved her.

Elizabeth Banks hadn't the same understanding and indeed knowledge of the state of the Bradleys' marriage and so found Hannah's decision to return to work slightly puzzling. She knew the salary Arthur was paid and even allowing for the private school for his daughter and the nanny he claimed was retained to give Hannah a hand, there would be plenty over. Arthur was always well-dressed and so was Hannah, for when a business function with wives invited or dinner with the Banks was in the offing, money was no object to Arthur. So Elizabeth couldn't see the need for Hannah to earn money.

But even she could see the change in Hannah, which Hannah openly attributed to her new job. 'It gives me independence, having my own money, that I've earned and can spend as I want, and self-confidence that I can do something worthwhile,' Hannah said. 'And I enjoy the work and feel I'm doing some good.'

'Well, my dear,' Elizabeth said. 'I can see that it's doing you good at any rate. You're positively glowing. I didn't even know you knew shorthand and typing.' They'd left the men to their cigars and port, otherwise Elizabeth would have remained ignorant of how she'd learnt, but with Arthur out of the way, Hannah told her of Josie and the commerce course and how she'd begun to learn alongside her and practised at home for hours.

'I think it's marvellous,' Elizabeth said. 'How old is Josie now?'

'Fifteen.'

'Is she due to leave school in the summer or is she stopping on?'

'Leaving,' Hannah said, and wondered what would happen if she was to tell this kind woman that the chance of a scholarship to enable her to go on to higher education had been denied her by Arthur, because of the cost of the uniform. But then, she knew in a flash, she'd not believe it. Arthur had inveigled his way into their life very well, proving himself invaluable to Reg Banks. They'd think Hannah was being emotional, unstable even, and she couldn't risk anyone thinking that of her. She didn't know, and was frightened of, what use Arthur would make of such information.

'What line of work is she looking for?' Elizabeth asked and Hannah, startled out of her reverie, wasn't at first at all sure what Elizabeth was talking about.

'What?'

'Your niece.'

'Oh, Josie,' Hannah said. 'Like I told you, she's been learning secretarial skills in her last year at school and so she'll be looking for clerical work.'

'Has she anywhere in mind?'

'No, not yet.'

'First jobs can be hard to find,' Elizabeth said. 'Most people want experience and how is a youngster to get that? I've said to Reg often, I don't know how they manage. I might have an opening for your niece though, if she doesn't care where she goes,' and then with a short laugh she said, 'Within reason of course.'

Hannah knew Josie had no preference. She was just desperate to leave school and earn money. 'No,' she said.

'Reg has a cousin in the insurance business,' Elizabeth said. 'I'm sure he could use another girl in the office.'

'Oh, Elizabeth, that is kind of you!'

'Think nothing of it, my dear,' Elizabeth said. 'I like to see youngsters getting on.'

Hannah thought of Josie's face when she told her she might have secured a job for her that evening and knew she'd be delighted. Elizabeth, she decided, was totally ignorant of her life and generally naive about life in general, but she was essentially kind, her heart was certainly in the right place. 'I know Josie would be very grateful for that,' she said. 'So I will say it for her,' and Elizabeth smiled, replying, 'It's the least I can do. I'm just glad I can be of some help.'

Chapter Fourteen

Elizabeth Banks was true to her word and Josie began work in Blakeway and Battersby Insurance Company in July 1952 and from the start, she hit it off with fun-loving Cynthia Scanlon. She was a year older than Josie and had already been there nine months, so was able to put her right about things.

She had, too, all the attributes Josie envied. She was more than just pretty; she was vivacious and striking. She appeared extremely self-confident for one so young and never seemed to care a fig for anyone's opinions.

As the two youngest in the office, the dull and mundane jobs came their way and the first thing they had to do each morning was open the post and put it in the relevant baskets in front of them for the assessors to deal with later. It was boring work, though Cynthia said, much better now there were the two of them to share it, because although talking wasn't allowed as such, it was tolerated if it wasn't loud enough to disturb others.

So very soon, Hannah and Cynthia learned quite a lot about each other.

Josie heard a lot about Cynthia's older brother, Peter,

five years her senior and her mentor. It was his words that had coloured Cynthia's attitude to life. 'He told me that the only people's opinions I should bother about are those that I care for, the rest don't matter,' Cynthia said.

'Oh, Peter's the fount of all knowledge,' said a young man passing by, who'd already shown himself in Josie's eyes to be a braggart and a know-all. 'Always right is our Peter Scanlon.'

Cynthia's face flamed and Josie wished she had the authority to tell the man to shut up and go away. Instead, she said, 'Don't you bother about the likes of him, Cynthia.'

'In a way, I maybe asked for it,' Cynthia said. 'I know I go on a bit. It's just that he's such a great big brother.'

Josie felt her stomach lurch. If only she could have said that about one of her brothers, or even one of her sisters. If only one of them cared about her welfare. Again, there was that lurch in Josie's stomach. Even the loss of her parents she could have coped with if she'd had the unconditional love of just one of her siblings, she thought.

Why had none written to her, asked how she was doing? Why hadn't Ellen asked her over for a short visit? Did she think she never thought of the home she was taken from six years before? She was settled here in Birmingham now and wouldn't have left Hannah for the world, but she'd grown up in a large, and she'd have said, happy family, but it seemed after her mother's death that it was as if she'd ceased to exist for everyone.

She had Hannah and was glad she did and loved her dearly, but it wasn't quite the same for Hannah hadn't come into her life until she was nine years old. What about her own brothers and sisters? They were all too busy and too concerned with their own lives to bother about hers. Oh yes, Martin and Siobhan sent money to help with her upkeep and it had been a help to Hannah, struggling with a mean husband, but to Josie it had been like conscience money, as if they'd actually said, 'We can't bring you to America with us and we don't want to. You'd cramp our style, so we'll give you this money to stop us feeling guilty about it.'

They'd never said those words and didn't have to, the dollar notes said it for them. Once she'd got the job and began paying keep to Hannah, she'd asked her to write to Martin and Siobhan and say she needed no more money. She'd stand on her own two feet from now on.

Hannah did as she asked, knowing that it was important to Josie, but Martin and Siobhan's reply had come back by return of post. They were so grateful to Hannah. Words couldn't express their gratitude and they knew what it had cost her to take Josie on. If she no longer needed the money, that was fine, but they would continue putting it into her account and she could do anything she wanted with it. Hannah agreed without saying a word to Josie, knowing she might have need of it some day.

It had become obvious to Josie as she'd listened to her new friend talk about her brother that though her love was based on hero worship, it was plain that Peter cared deeply for his young sister. That fact had made her feel sad that she'd never experienced such devotion from a sibling. In the beginning, she'd missed her brothers and sisters very much. It was mixed up with her homesickness. She'd been used to the noise and bustle of the farmhouse and though her siblings were a lot older than she was, she'd known them all her life. But never in any shape or form did she tell, or show, Hannah how she was feeling as she might have felt she was second-best and Josie would have hated that. So she kept her feelings locked away inside her and it was only when Cynthia began talking about her brother that they rose to the fore again.

However, Josie was too kind-hearted to begrudge Cynthia her brother and she gave her arm a squeeze and said, 'You talk about him as much as you like. If I had a brother or sister half as good to me as your Peter seems to be, I'd bore the pants off you rabbiting on about them all the time.'

Over the next few weeks, Josie learned that Peter was the clever one in the family, the one who got in to King Edward's High School and from there won a scholarship to Oxford. But for all the pride Cynthia had in her brother, Josie sensed a sadness in her and she imagined there would be little attention in the house left for a mere mortal like Cynthia. It would all have gone on their brilliant first-born and only son.

This suspicion was verified one day when Cynthia was explaining that her brother was twenty-one now and would be starting his final year in September.

'Then what? What does he want to do?'

'Oh, he's not leaving yet,' Cynthia said. 'At least not if he gets the degree they say he'll get. He wants to go on to do a doctorate.'

'Be a doctor?'

'Not a medical doctor. It's just what they call it.'

'Right.'

'He won't be finished until he's about twenty-four or -five.'

'Right,' Josie said again. This Peter sounded a little selfish to her, she thought, but she knew better than to say that to her new friend. She chose her words carefully. 'Don't you think . . . I mean, wouldn't it be better if he got a job now,' she said, 'next year when he finishes his degree, I mean, and pay your parents something back? Make life a little easier for them?'

'Easier for them? You don't know what you're saying,' Cynthia cried. 'Their whole lives revolve around Peter. It wouldn't be worth them living if he didn't go on. It makes all the sacrifices worth it.'

'What about you?'

'What about me? I don't need anything, not like Peter has,' Cynthia said. 'And he does appreciate it. We talk for hours sometimes when he comes home. I can't ever remember a time when I didn't love him and look up to him. And he really is kind to me and always has been. He always looked after me when he was at home and even now, nothing is too much trouble for him.'

But soon the talk in the office, as in the country as a whole, was of the coronation planned for June the following year.

As Hannah had prophesised, the new Elizabethan age had brought little change in her life. The only boost for the nation had been the news that Edmund Hillary had climbed Everest just four days before the young

Queen was to be crowned and given it, he said, as a gift to his new Queen.

The Bradley household watched the entire coronation on the television set that Arthur had bought for the occasion and had installed in the parlour. Hannah would have preferred it put up in the breakfast room, the room they used most, but she didn't bother saying so – it would have made no difference and Arthur probably would have made some scathing comment.

She seldom spoke to Arthur, except about everyday matters, because she only needed to do the slightest thing for him to sneer at her, an attitude immediately copied by Angela. Hannah had learned to accept it, hoping that when Angela had grown up a little, she would make her own mind up. She was capable of affection, not only for her father whom she openly adored, but also for Pauline and Josie, and was very popular at school.

On Coronation Day, she looked angelic. She was five and a half and Arthur had bought her a dress based on one of those worn by Shirley Temple. It was of white satin, trimmed in blue, reminiscent of a sailor suit. Stiff petticoats pushed the skirt of the dress out and she wore white sandals and socks, but because of the temperature of the day, Arthur had bought a pure white cardigan in fluffy angora to wear over the dress.

She accepted the acclamations of delight as if it was her right and stood docilely enough for Pauline to brush her hair. It had been in rags all night and framed her face and bobbed on her shoulders in perfect auburn ringlets.

She stood out amongst all the other children, however

well-dressed they were, and Hannah would have felt proud of her if she'd had any hand in the child's upbringing at all, but she was Angela's mother in name only.

However, she refused to be downhearted and settled down to enjoy the coronation and she watched the Queen arrive at Westminster in a golden coach through flower-decked streets. The announcer described the diadem of precious stones upon her head and the robe of crimson velvet, trimmed with ermine and bordered with golden lace around her shoulders, the train carried by six maids of honour adorned in white and gold.

Everyone could hear the music resounding and the Queen's scholars of Westminster singing 'Vivat Regina Elizabeth, Vivat, Vivat, Vivat'. The pomp and ceremony of it rendered everyone, even Angela, speechless as Elizabeth began the slow walk up the aisle to the Chair of Estate.

After the blessing and anointing, Elizabeth was dressed in ceremonial robes. She held out her slim wrists for the armillas to be fastened around them, bracelets of sincerity and wisdom. And then the heavy crown was taken from the altar and placed on her head.

Philip, resplendent in his Navy uniform of blue and gold, knelt before his wife and now his Queen and promised allegiance to her. He rose and touched her crown and kissed her left cheek and all the women in the room sighed and dabbed at their eyes as the cries of 'Long Live the Queen!' resounded in the Abbey.

The street party for the children had to reconvene to the church hall from the road, due to the drizzling cold rain, but the children didn't mind and tucked into the food with gusto. Then each child under fifteen got a coronation mug and a golden coach to remind them of the occasion and after the children's activities were over, there was a coronation dance.

The place was familiar enough to Josie and Mary Byrne for they'd been going to the youth club there since they'd been fourteen. Cynthia had laughed when Josie had described it to her one day while opening the post. 'Let's get this right,' she said. 'You stand one side of the room and boys stand the other and you never meet?'

'Sometimes we do, but not often,' Josie said. 'There's a table tennis table and snooker down one side, you see, and the boys play there. The girls go the other side near the music and dance together around their handbags. Some of the boys pluck up courage to come over now and again. Mary, my friend, has been asked up to dance, but not me. She's pretty, see.'

Cynthia looked Josie up and down and said, 'So could you be if you set your mind to it.'

'Oh get off, Cynthia,' Josie said. 'I know what I am. Don't be codding me.'

'I'm not,' Cynthia said. 'Your hair is fabulous, a lovely colour and so shiny and thick with those natural waves and curls. Don't you know people spend a fortune having a Marcel permanent wave put in their hair? My mom has her hair shampooed and set each week and it never looks like yours. No, Josie, all you need is a good cut.'

'A cut?' Josie cried. She'd done nothing to her hair but brush it since she was a child and she started work with it just tied back as she'd worn it at school. 'I don't know whether I want it cut.'

''Course you do. Be adventurous,' Cynthia encouraged.

'I have mine chopped off. It will always grow back if you don't like it.'

Cynthia had had her hair cut into a pageboy like many girls, but she knew that style wouldn't suit everyone and certainly not Josie. 'Look, Josie, let's just go and find out,' she said. 'Will Hannah go mad with you if you have your hair cut or what?'

Josie thought about that. 'No,' she said at last, 'I don't think so. Hannah never seems to get mad.'

'So what d'you think she'd say if you had your hair cut short?'

'I really don't know,' Josie said. 'But at the end of the day, it is my hair.'

Hannah did have a shock, though, seeing a shorn Josie, and yet when she was used to it, she had to agree it suited her. So did Pauline and Gloria when she popped in on a visit and so Josie didn't care that Arthur said she looked a sight or that Angela, taking the lead from her father, said it looked horrible.

'You should use a bit of make-up too,' Cynthia suggested when Josie had got over the shock of her hair. 'It would highlight your good points.'

'What good points?' Josie asked sarcastically.

'For God's sake,' Cynthia exploded. 'To hear you talk, Josie, anyone would think you looked like one of those gargoyle things outside some old churches.'

Josie grinned at her friend. 'Okay. So, say I don't frighten the children to death and send old ladies running for the smelling salts, I still say, what good points?'

'God, you're aggravating!' Cynthia cried. 'Your eyes for one thing.'

'They're too big.'

'Eyes can't be too big. You just need to emphasise them. They're so dark and people would die for lashes like yours.'

'I bet. How do you know all this?'

'It's all in the *Woman* magazine my mom gets. She keeps all the recipes and I cut out the beauty tips and fashion, of course. After all,' she went on with a toss of her light brown hair, 'a girl has to have all the help she can get.'

Josie burst out laughing for Cynthia was a very pretty girl. 'And that's not all,' Cynthia went on with a grin. 'There are your cheekbones.'

'What about them?'

'They're lovely but would be better with a bit of rouge rubbed into them.'

Josie had never heard anyone talk about nice cheekbones before. 'Are you having me on?'

'No, I'm not!' Cynthia said firmly. 'If you did define your cheekbones a bit, it would draw attention from your mouth which is, I'll admit, a bit on the big side.'

'Mine will be nothing to the size of yours if you don't stop this nonsense,' Josie cried, her voice high with indignation.

'Girls! Girls! Stop this chattering!' came the supervisor's sharp words. The girls bent industriously over the envelopes, but when the supervisor's attention had drifted from them, Cynthia whispered, 'Come over to our house and I'll show you. Come to tea. Our Mom won't mind and after we'll try all my make-up. If you don't like it, you can wash it all off and I'll not say another word about it.'

But when Josie looked in the mirror in Cynthia's bedroom that evening, she barely recognised herself. She'd become used to her hair, but now long, black, curled eyelashes framed large eyes dusted with brown powder and underlined in black, while a delicate peach-pink colour was brushed over her high cheekbones. 'No bright colours of lipstick,' Cynthia said authoritatively, applying a pale brownish red colour to her lips. 'There,' she said. 'Don't you look a treat?'

Josie could only stare at her reflection as if she couldn't believe it. 'Now for the clothes,' Cynthia said, rummaging about in the wardrobe. 'Get your frock and cardigan off.'

'What?'

'You heard,' Cynthia said, taking a dress in different shades of pastel blue from the wardrobe. 'This is the new look this year,' Cynthia said, holding it out. 'It has a dropped waist and a full skirt. Come on, slip it over your head and then get those thick stockings off and put these nylons on, but carefully, because I've only got the one pair, and then slip your feet into my high heels.'

What a transformation!

She remembered that Hannah had suggested that she take the money she had saved for her over the years and get herself a couple of rigouts for work and things to wear in the evenings, especially as clothes rationing was over, but she had pooh-poohed the idea. Now she saw how silly she'd been and she looked disparagingly at her discarded clothes.

'Clothes maketh the man,' Cynthia said, catching her look. 'Women, too, if you ask me. You want to get yourself down the Bull Ring. If you know where to go you can pick up bargains there for next to nothing.'

'I wouldn't know what to buy, or where to start.'

Cynthia thought she probably didn't. She'd have to take her in hand. 'Tell you what,' she said. 'I'll go with you. We'll go Saturday. By the time I'm finished with you, my girl, the boys will be lining up to dance with you and your friend will be green with envy.'

Josie had been to the Bull Ring before of course, but she found going with Cynthia an illuminating business. As the two girls pushed their way through the seething mass of people thronging the cobbled streets of the Bull Ring, Josie remembered how frightened she'd been on her first visit when she'd been in Birmingham just a few short weeks. Now she loved the place as most Brummies did.

There was a special buzz, an excitement in the air made up of many things. There was a clamorous noise from people talking, shouting, arguing, laughing, the costers yelling out their wares and prices, entertaining the shoppers with their patter, and above it all, a blind old lady, who'd been at the Bull Ring as long as Josie could remember, who called out constantly, 'Andy Carriers, Andy Carriers.'

The barrows stretched from Bell Street, past Woolworth's, downhill as far as Edgbaston Street. Fruit and vegetable stalls mixed with those selling meat and fish and other stalls with rolls of curtain material or bedding, or baskets of cheap crockery and kitchen utensils. The different smells of the goods rose in the air, sweetened by the different scents from the flower sellers who ringed Nelson's Column and the front of the church, St Martin-in-the-Field, which towered over everything.

There was always so much to see. Woolworth's, where nothing cost more than sixpence, Peacocks, which sold an array of things and where the toy department had been a particular favourite of Josie's when she was younger. Then there were the hobbies shop, the Army and Navy Stores and the Market Hall, roofless since 1940, courtesy of the Luftwaffe, but where bargains could still be had.

But Cynthia would not allow Josie to dawdle around other shops or stand and daydream, for Cynthia was a serious shopper and on a mission to dress Josie in more suitable clothes than those she had. She led the way to the Rag Market. It still held a slight reek of fish, for it was only on a Saturday that it was used as a general market, the other days it sold fish, but it was, Cynthia declared, the best place for bargains.

And there were bargains and Josie nearly died of embarrassment when even those prices Cynthia refused to pay and she bartered as Josie squirmed with discomfort, her face flushed. 'They expect it,' Cynthia said, and true enough no one seemed to resent Cynthia for pressing for a lower price and the banter between them, Josie saw, had entertained many of the other shoppers.

And so for far less money than she'd anticipated, Josie acquired some fashionable, but serviceable work clothes and a few classier things for evening wear, including stiletto-heeled shoes and a fashionable blue coat.

Mary had been unaware of Josie's total transformation, though she seemed to disapprove of the new hairdo. But that night, when Josie called for her to go to the coronation dance, Mary was astounded when she opened the door.

Josie had always been the plain and dowdy one. In fact, that had been one of the main reasons Mary had gone around with her, for her plainness emphasised her own prettiness. This Josie with new clothes and the carefully made-up face seemed like a different being. 'What you all dolled up for?' she asked cattily. 'We're only going to the flipping youth club.'

Had Cynthia not warned Josie about Mary's possible reaction, for she could guess the type of girl she was both from what Josie said and what she didn't say, then Josie's fragile confidence would have crumbled at that moment. Instead, remembering Cynthia's words, she said, 'Well, I got some new things, have to wear them sometime. Anyway, it isn't a normal youth club night tonight.'

And of course it wasn't. A proper bar was set up in the corner. 'No home-made cakes and orange juice here tonight,' one of the girls remarked in the hall before they went in.

'Maybe they'll pass on the cakes all right,' another retorted. 'But I'd like to bet you'll get nothing stronger than orange juice from those behind the bar.'

Josie didn't care about that. She just cared about the band and hoped they weren't a fuddy-duddy lot that played the old-fashioned stuff alone. 'Haven't they done it up nicely?' she said to Mary, for it was unrecognisable as the youth club.

For a start, there was no sign of a snooker table, or table tennis equipment. Instead, there were tables arranged around the whole room covered with table-cloths of red, white or blue, leaving a largish dance floor in the middle. The lighting was dimmed and the room festooned with banners of red, white and blue, while a large flag hung above the stage, where the band sat.

Mary hadn't answered, for she was watching as Josie took off her coat to reveal a dress of shimmering red satin, that rustled and swirled as she moved, and nylon stockings with black patent stiletto-heeled shoes. Mary was consumed by envy and she'd never have imagined in a million years being envious of Josie.

For Josie the evening was a wonderful success. The band alternated between the Big Band sound, the music of Duke Ellington and Tommy Dorsey that the young liked to jive to, and the music of Frank Sinatra, Bing Crosby and Doris Day for the older people.

The highlight of the night came early on for Josie. A boy Mary had fancied for ages came across to the girls as they danced in a circle around their handbags. Mary smiled as he approached, certain he was going to ask her to dance. Josie thought so too; such an occurrence had never happened to her. She'd been as surprised as Mary when she realised the boy was talking to her.

And he wasn't the only one. She jived with the best of them and learnt the rudiments of the quickstep, the foxtrot and the waltz and won a spot prize of a coronation box of chocolates.

Each time she returned to the table, Mary had a face on her that would sour cream, until in the end, after Josie won the spot prize, she couldn't be found at all and was discovered in the ladies', having a major sulk.

Josie danced on air all the way home for she'd seldom had such attention, but Mary was cool and distant.

'You can't do anything about that,' Cynthia told Josie the next day. 'The green-eyed monster has got hold of your friend.'

'Jealous of me?' Josie echoed, for never in her life had she thought anyone would be jealous of her. But she remembered Mary's behaviour at the dance and realised Cynthia could be right. It was a shame, she thought, especially as she and Mary had been friends for years. But Josie, having tasted popularity and the attention of boys for the first time, had no intention of reverting to the drab she had been to please anyone. She was enjoying life far too much.

Josie enjoyed herself still further when Bill Haley and the Comets released 'Rock Around the Clock' the following year. It was the theme music to a film called *The Blackboard Jungle* that was for adults only. Josie and Cynthia were tempted to find a way into a cinema until they heard of the teenagers rioting in places, ripping up seats and generally trashing the place.

'I don't think it's ordinary teenagers,' Hannah said to Gloria. 'I think it's these teddy boy types.' She, like many more, had been alarmed when gangs of them appeared in the streets with their heavily Brylcreemed, slicked-back hair with sideburns, wearing long Edwardian frock coats, drainpipe trousers and thick suede shoes.

Josie, at first, had thought the teddy boys fine and the clothes just a bit of fun, but she soon changed her mind. They were so objectionable and menacing to members of the public and committed such heinous deeds that teddy boys became synonymous with troublemakers. Hannah went up to see Gloria and their conversation came around to the teddy boys' latest atrocities that had been reported in the *Evening Mail*.

'This is all the fault of that damned war,' Gloria said. 'Lack of control, see. Mothers in munitions or God knows what till all hours, fathers away and kids running wild in the street. Then for many, of course, fathers didn't come back. Children need fathers for discipline.'

'Ah Gloria, will you listen to yourself,' Hannah burst out. 'Christ, you know there's a child not a million miles from here that I think would have a chance of growing up to be a decent human being if she *hadn't* a father.'

'He's no father,' Gloria said dismissively. 'Not a proper father. He dresses her up like some doll, buys her everything she wants, treats her like a princess and resents anyone else she shows a spark of affection for. The man's not normal.'

'I know that all right,' Hannah said with feeling, 'and it isn't just the way he is with Angela I'm talking about.'

'I know, I know,' Gloria said. 'But his time will come. As you sow, so shall you reap. He's bringing up a wilful child there who expects her own way in everything.'

'Well, I hope this teddy boy thing is over by then,' Hannah said. 'For I hear there are girls caught up in it now. Teddy girls! I ask you? Mind you, if I was Mary's mother, I'd be worried. I've seen the girl myself hanging around the coffee bar in the High Street where the teddy boys hang out.'

'Why doesn't her mother stop her?'

'I don't think she knows,' Hannah said. 'I would say something, but we've never really hit it off and she might think I'm just out to make mischief. I've an idea Mary tells her mother she's coming to our house, but her and Josie don't get on that well now, not since Josie met that girl Cynthia at work and she started taking an interest in her appearance.'

'Well, your Angela will be another one if you don't watch out.'

'I have no authority there, you know that,' Hannah said with asperity then added thoughtfully, 'Do you know, I don't know how Arthur would react. He's put her on a pedestal and if she stumbled or fell off, it would humiliate him. I don't know that he'd stand it.'

'He'd have to stand it.'

'No listen, Gloria,' Hannah said. 'He did it to me. Put me on a pedestal and I fell off it totally when he realised I'd had sex with another man. The fact that I was engaged to the man and it happened only once made no difference. I was defiled, soiled. Angela he has created and moulded and will continue to mould, but she will grow up, have relationships, boyfriends, sex.' She shook her head and a long shudder of apprehension about the future ran down her spine.

Chapter Fifteen

Angela made her first Holy Communion in June 1955. Hannah didn't know where Arthur had got the dress, but it was the most exquisite thing she'd ever seen, though far too elaborate for a child. As Gloria said, 'You'd think he had her decked up for a bride.'

Angela's satin and silk dress, bedecked with ribbons, bows, seed pearls, little rosebuds and lace, fell over many starched petticoats like a dainty white flower. Her snow-white veil hung down her back and the diadem, holding it in place, flashed with stones and on her feet were white patent leather shoes. She made every other girl there seem dull in comparison.

Josie couldn't help contrasting it with her first Communion, in a dress worn by all her sisters. Her mother had done her best, but her heart hadn't been in it for her father was dangerously ill. But, all in all, many of the other girls' dresses were as bad or worse than hers and given the choice she'd prefer to look like everyone else and not stick out like Angela did.

Not that Angela seemed to care. She paraded and flounced about the house, accepting praise as her due. Her daddy said she was the most beautiful girl in the world, prettier than any princess, and she believed him, like she believed everything he said.

The rosary he presented her with was mother-of-pearl and her Bible bound with white leather. Hannah told her daughter, who was fishing for compliments, that she looked lovely, which was true, but Angela, used to more lavish praise, pulled a face.

But then her daddy was there scooping her up. 'Do you love me, Angela?'

''Course I do, Daddy. I love you millions and I'll love you forever.'

'I'll always be your best man, the one you love the most?'

'Always. You're the bestest in the world.'

Hannah shivered at the interchange between them. Forever was a long time for a child of seven.

The party Arthur planned for Angela's first Communion was the most lavish to date. Hannah wondered if he had a hint of shame for what he was doing to the child, but no. Pride alone shone in his eyes as he beamed at her while Hannah squirmed at the malevolent looks the mothers shot her way. They'd assume, all of them, that Hannah had bought the dress, because it was a job mothers usually did.

They would think she'd done it just to show every other little girl in the parish up. She could almost hear them condemning her.

And this is what she told Vic when he asked how it had gone. 'Why can't you tell them the truth?'

'How can I?' Hannah said. 'Nothing was said, do you see, I just read the looks. Anyway, do you think I really want to admit that I am such a useless mother that I don't even choose my own daughter's Communion dress?' She sighed. 'That's what Arthur banks on, you see. He reads me like a book at times. He knows what I'm fearful of and plays on that.'

God, Vic thought, what a marriage.

Hannah gave a sigh. 'And there's something else.'

'What?'

'I don't know, but Arthur has something planned.'

'To do with your daughter?'

'Of course. Every thought in his head concerns Angela,' Hannah said. 'It won't be good, not for me that is, not when he has this stupid sneering smile on his face.'

'Why don't you ask him? Face it?'

'Because he'd not tell me,' Hannah said. 'You don't know how it is in our house. We seldom speak, Arthur and I. He talks at me when he wants to. We don't ever discuss anything. He tells me and I have to do it, or put up with it. He's told me my needs are unimportant and I seldom ask him questions, you lose the habit of it when you get no answers.'

'Hannah, how do you stand it?'

Hannah shrugged. 'I stand it because I must,' she said wearily. 'I tell myself people cope with worse. He doesn't drink or gamble the housekeeping. I'll find out in the end.'

But it took a further fortnight before Hannah found out what Arthur had planned. During the fortnight, Arthur had been out a lot and stayed out all night on more than one occasion but Hannah had just been glad of his absence. But now, one evening, as they were finishing their meal, he licked his lips and with a grin of satisfaction, like a cat that's had the cream, spoke directly to Hannah. 'After the child is in bed, I wish to talk to you,' he said. 'Go into the breakfast room and wait for me.'

Hannah's eyes met those of Pauline and Josie. She had told them already that she thought something was afoot and now they knew that this was it, the moment when she'd be told.

Later, she gazed at Arthur as if she couldn't believe her ears. 'A boarding school! Arthur, she's but a baby.'

'She is no baby,' Arthur snapped. 'She will be eight in November.'

'But why?'

'Why? Because I want her to mix with the right society, that's why. You saw the performance at her Communion. She outshone every other child there because they're common. Little more than guttersnipes some of them. I want her removed, I want her companions to be more her equals and I want her husband to be the right sort.'

Hannah stared at Arthur. Where in God's name did he think he came from? A jumped-up travelling salesman when she met him. Fortune had shone on him, that was all. True, he'd risen in the firm, but surely not far or fast enough to make him forget his roots, or where he came from?

And these people, she told herself, that he's just called common and degraded in such a way, think him a grand fellow. It's me they think of as Lady Muck, me they pull to pieces and snigger at behind their hands and me they'll blame for this last outrage.

For that's what it was, an outrage to send a little girl

away from a more than adequate home, because their neighbours, who were fine, upstanding people in the main, could not be considered good enough for her to mix with.

But worse was to come. 'It's a Catholic school of course,' Arthur said. 'A convent school in Leeds called St Anne's.'

'In Leeds?' Hannah's voice echoed in a shriek. She felt herself going alternately hot and cold and the room began to tilt away from her. 'You can't,' she begged. 'Please, please, don't send her so far away.'

'Can't? What is this, my dear?' Arthur said. 'You know I can do as I please with my own child. The school is highly recommended. It's right out in the countryside in its own grounds. Hannah, are you all right? Hannah!'

Hannah was far from all right; she'd fainted clean away and in the dark recess of the night, after she'd been helped to bed, she woke screaming and thrashing in the bed. It was the nightmare she'd had many times – a nun taking her baby further and further away and her trying to run after him, but with each step getting further away.

This time, though, Josie was there to comfort her. 'Hush, Hannah. It was just a dream, that's all. Hush. It's all right now.'

But it wasn't all right. As Hannah jerked into full consciousness, she remembered it all. Was she never to forget the past? Gloria always said, 'As you sow, so shall you reap.' Well, she'd sowed well, hadn't she? Dear God, was she to pay for it till the day she died?

'Hannah, what is it? What's upsetting you so much?'

Josie cried, holding Hannah's shivering frame in her arms.

When Pauline and Josie had been called in by Arthur earlier and seen Hannah crumpled before the fire, Josie had thought Arthur had hit her. 'What have you done?'

'Nothing.'

Josie, on her knees before her aunt, looked up at him. 'You must have done something.'

'Nothing, I tell you. She fainted.'

'Well what did you say to make her faint?'

'It was nothing to do with what I was saying. I was telling her about the school I've chosen for Angela.'

Neither Josie nor Pauline, not even after they'd roused Hannah and helped her to bed and got the full story from Arthur, could believe that what Arthur had said had anything to do with Hannah passing out. 'Granted, she might have been upset,' Pauline said. 'I was myself, learning of a child of seven being sent from home. It's what the gentry always did to their sons and I never held with it then either. If she'd cried I could have understood it. I mean she's never passed out before, has she?'

'Not that I've known.'

If it had been a different household, Pauline might have thought Hannah was pregnant, but she knew that to be an impossibility.

Josie knew that too and she urged again, 'What is it, Hannah?'

And Hannah for the first time told Josie the whole story from her meeting with Mike Murphy until she came to live with Gloria. Sometimes Hannah cried and so did Josie, but Josie never let go of her aunt, nor did she speak and the short summer night was ended and the sky lightening before Hannah finished her tale. 'Are you shocked, Josie?' she finally asked.

'No, Hannah. Just so incredibly sad for you,' Josie said.

'You see now why I couldn't come to your father's funeral?'

'Oh yes, perfectly.'

'When it was over, the birth and everything, I told myself I'd go, see how you were. But I was so ill, distraught, you know, and so ashamed. I just wanted to hide myself away,' Hannah said.

'And why did you marry Arthur?'

'To have children, that was the main thing, and also to have someone special to love and cherish me,' Hannah said. 'I suppose really I've never got over my father rejecting me.'

There was a moment's silence, then Josie said, 'You didn't make a good bargain of either, did you?'

'No, Josie, I failed on both counts,' Hannah said. 'But the nightmare I had tonight and the reason I fainted and was upset was because of where the school is that Arthur's chosen to send Angela.'

'Leeds?' Josie said. 'Pauline and I couldn't understand that. I mean, neither of us could think why she had to board anywhere, but that apart, did it have to be so far away?'

'No, it's not that, or not totally that,' Hannah said. 'It's the place – Leeds. I've never been back since. I'm afraid of the memories it might evoke.'

'Maybe it's time to lay the ghosts,' Josie said gently. 'What you did with a man you loved and were engaged to be married to wasn't such a terrible thing. I think you were more sinned against than a sinner. Perhaps it's time to face that.'

'I don't know if I'm ready to face it,' Hannah admitted. 'And if Arthur was to ever find out . . .'

'He doesn't know about the baby then?'

'No,' Hannah said with a slight shudder. 'He knows I wasn't a virgin when I married him. I was what he called "soiled". That's why he moved out of the bedroom.'

'I was glad he did,' Josie said. 'When you shared a room he used to yell at you, terrible things, obscene words, I used to try not to hear, but he was too loud.'

Hannah said, 'I think you need to know the kind of man Arthur is, Josie. You're not a child anymore and it's good to know,' and she told Josie all about Arthur's sexual problems and how he became aroused and how they'd managed to make love just the once, resulting in Angela.

'Does anyone else know this?'

'Just Gloria. Do you remember her coming around that dreadful winter and she saw the bruises and my split lip?'

'Yes, after my tenth birthday,' Josie said. 'She gave me that lovely pendant that I wear all the time.'

'Yes, that's right. After that, I told her.'

'What about the baby? Who knows about him?'

'Again just Gloria,' Hannah said. 'The nuns arranged that I stay with her, so she had to know. Vic also had to know of course, when I was having Angela, but he doesn't know everything.'

'You've not told Pauline?'

'No,' Hannah said. 'Once, when she first came here,

I viewed her as the enemy. She looked after my baby better than I ever could. I thought she was on Arthur's side.'

'She might have been,' Josie agreed, 'but she isn't any more, I know that. Can I tell her? It's best for her to know.'

'All right,' Hannah said, 'but no one else. Whatever you say, I am ashamed and don't want it broadcast.'

'I won't say a word to anyone else,' Josie promised. 'I'll nip down and make us both a cup of tea.'

Hannah nodded, but when Josie returned a few moments later, Hannah was in a deep sleep such as she hadn't enjoyed for some time, for her heart was eased now that she'd told Josie everything.

'Won't you miss her dreadfully?' Elizabeth asked both Hannah and Arthur when they'd gone round to the Banks' for the evening.

'Of course,' Arthur said.

'Our two boarded,' Elizabeth went on. 'But not until they were eleven and then I cried for a week, didn't I, Reg?'

Reg affirmed that she did and then asked, 'Why Leeds, Arthur? Isn't there a place nearer?'

'Maybe,' Arthur said. 'But this place is highly recommended. I went to the priests at the Abbey and this is the one they suggested. First-rate education, they said. However much it will hurt us, we must make sure that Angela has the best chance in life. Of course we'll see her, we'll go up weekends and check that she is all right.'

'Oh Hannah,' Elizabeth said later when they were alone. 'You are so brave.'

Hannah wanted to say she wasn't at all brave, that it would break her heart when the child walked out the door and that when she began in September, she'd not see a bit of her till the Christmas holidays. 'How does Angela feel about it?' Elizabeth asked.

Angela was fine. Arthur had make it all sound so exciting for the child and she believed every word from her father's lips was the gospel truth. 'She . . . She's looking forward to it,' Hannah answered truthfully. 'She's not a bit nervous, not so far anyway.'

Arthur reiterated what Hannah said later as Elizabeth poured out their after dinner coffee. 'I've told her all about it,' he went on. 'And shown her the pictures. We're off to look around the place next week.'

'Oh, I always think it sets your mind at rest when you see where they'll be,' Elizabeth said to Hannah. 'Somehow you are able to picture them afterwards, like the time we went to see her nursery school. It helps settle any anxieties you might have.'

Hannah saw Arthur's eyes widen in surprise for he'd never known Hannah had visited Angela's nursery school with Elizabeth. And now the bloody woman had put him in a quandary, for he'd had no intention of taking Hannah with him on his trip to Leeds, but if he didn't now, the Banks, particularly Elizabeth, would think it odd.

Hannah saw the set of Arthur's jaw and his eyes harden as he looked across the table to her. She hadn't known until the moment before that Arthur planned to visit the school the following week, but knew with piercing clarity that he had had no intention on God's earth of taking her with him until Elizabeth had spoken.

The smile didn't reach Arthur's eyes as he said, 'Yes. It will be a nice run out if the weather stays fine. We're quite looking forward to it aren't we, my dear?'

Hannah would have liked to have thrown the hot coffee in Arthur's face and told the cold-hearted, cruel man exactly what she thought of him, but his reaction if she did that didn't bear thinking about. She gripped the cup so tight in her hand, her knuckles turned white, and she fought to control her voice as she said, 'Yes, and like you say, Elizabeth, it will ease the parting if I feel happy with the school.'

'You did well, my dear,' Arthur said as they drove home. 'You probably know I had no intention of taking you with me?'

'Oh, I knew all right,' Hannah said. 'But now you must because if you don't, Elizabeth Banks will take a very dim view of it altogether. And take it from me, she'll get to know about it if you change your mind at all. It would never do for them to lose their good impression of you, now would it?'

'Be careful, my dear,' Arthur said and his voice was clipped and as cold as steel. 'You are in no position to threaten.'

'Maybe not, but you take care, too,' Hannah retorted angrily. 'Don't push me too far. I might feel I've got little more to lose. Even a worm can turn, you know.'

Gloria said she couldn't see the point of folks having kids if they were going to send them away just as soon as they could and what was the matter with Hannah that she couldn't put her foot down.

'Where Angela is concerned, I have no say.'

'What's the matter with you?' Gloria snapped. 'You're the child's mother.'

'I might as well not be,' Hannah said glumly.

'Give up that bloody job and learn to be a mother.'

'You wanted me to work,' Hannah said. 'And you were right. It's restored my self-respect. But with Angela it's too late. She adores her father and what he wants, she wants. To be honest, she just about tolerates me, because she sees little of me. If she saw more of me, she'd soon show her true colours and probably put me in my place.'

Gloria shook her head. 'You've been a fool to let it go so far.'

'You don't understand,' Hannah said. 'It hurts to know your child dislikes you so much and it hurts when she says so and is never even corrected for it and sometimes even applauded. I have had two children, Gloria, and one doesn't even know I exist and the other doesn't care if I do or not. It's hard to take.'

The break in Hannah's voice betrayed her distress. Gloria didn't argue further, but patted her shoulder as she got to her feet. 'I'm really sorry for you,' she said. 'And as guilty as hell that it was me that pushed you into that man's arms, for the sake of a house and a well-paid job. They can be cold comfort if the man's wrong and maybe money and material possessions aren't everything.'

'Will you be able to go back to Leeds?' Pauline asked Hannah when she told her she'd be going with Arthur to see Angela's new school. Josie had told Pauline Hannah's story and she'd been horrified by it. 'Won't it bring back awful memories for you?'

'Maybe,' Hannah said truthfully. 'But I must go and see the sort of place Arthur has chosen for her.'

But Hannah had to fight down the rising tide of panic the following day for the convent school was the very place where she'd been incarcerated for months in 1944. In Hannah's time there, there had been no gates, just the evidence of where they'd been, but now large wrought-iron gates framed the entrance with 'St Anne's Convent School' written across it on a board in letters of gold.

She'd known where they were heading with a dread certainty as soon as Arthur had turned and headed north before they'd reached the centre of Leeds and she'd been sick with fear. At first, she wondered if it was Arthur's idea of a joke, if he'd found out about Michael and was going to throw it in her face in the very place she'd given birth. She knew Arthur would be capable of it, but doubted that he would involve Angela in any plan like that. But still, when Arthur stopped the car, she had the desire to leap out and run and she fought to control the urge, sitting on her hands so that Angela wouldn't see them trembling.

Arthur opened the gates and Hannah saw the familiar gravel drive. But there the similarity stopped. The lawns before the house had been turned into a rounders pitch, where a cluster of little girls, who all looked much bigger than Angela, had begun to play.

Angela studied them intently and they were just as interested in her. They stopped their game and stared back until the teacher, clapping her hands, broke the spell.

Hannah had time to have a good look herself when Arthur stopped the car again to close the gates and she had to admit the children looked very smart. They all had smart white Aertex shirts with a maroon trim and little maroon games skirts, their white socks had a purple trim and they had white plimsolls on their feet.

'What are they playing?' Angela asked.

'Rounders,' Hannah answered.

'It looks fun,' Angela said.

Arthur slid back into the car as she spoke and heard the remark. 'Of course it's fun, darling, and that's just the start. You'll enjoy yourself so much here, you won't have time to miss me at all in the week and at weekends, I'll be along to visit you.'

She didn't ask if her mother would come too but Hannah hadn't really expected her to. To prevent herself getting emotional, she studied the house before her and wondered if she'd ever have the courage to go inside.

However, gone was the grey forbidding fortress. In front of Hannah was a beautiful building with a cream coloured facia. Each sparkling window had a window box in front of it, arrayed with beautiful colourful flowers, and a set of white steps led to the front door. It was no longer like the door of a prison with a huge clanging bell and reinforced with metal bands, but far more modern, light oak in colour.

But still, as Hannah stood before it, her limbs began to tremble. She'd been mad to come. What if she was wrong? What if the very nuns who'd tormented her years before were still here? Should she have taken the risk to have her ultimate shame denounced before her husband and child?

She would have turned back to the car, but the door was opened at that moment by a smiling young nun, as far removed from Sister Carmel as if they'd lived on separate planets. 'Mr and Mrs Bradley and Angela?' she enquired. They were most welcome, she said, the headmistress, Sister Beatrice, was expecting them and did they require a nice cup of tea after their journey?

They stepped into a hall that seemed bathed in light. The floors, a light walnut colour, gleamed and Hannah remembered the pregnant girls scrubbing the same hall on her first visit as she herself had done many times after it. But those floors had been dark and dull, not this honey-like colour, which matched the panels of the door.

Hannah had no time to see more than this before they were ushered through the door marked 'Headmistress'. A nun sat the other side of a large desk with sheaves of paper before her. At their entrance, she rose to meet them and came forward, her hand outstretched in welcome, a smile on her face, and Hannah realised with a slight jolt that she never remembered a nun smiling at her before and now two had done just that.

Sister Beatrice was, as far as any nun's age can be judged, middle-aged and kindly-looking. Hannah saw she was very taken with her daughter and little wonder, for she looked very pretty. She was dressed in a flowery summer dress and the green colour in the dress and that of the ribbons holding back her beautiful auburn hair picked out the green of her eyes. Sister Beatrice smiled. 'I can see at one glance who you take after,' she said, looking from Angela to Hannah, who to mark this occasion was wearing one of the outfits bought for dinner at the Banks' and so was looking very beautiful herself.

'Like mother, like daughter,' the nun went on and if she didn't understand the frown on Angela's face, she put it down to the strangeness of the situation and the quite natural apprehension of the child.

'Approximately half of our girls are boarders,' Sister Beatrice said, beaming at them. 'We have only four to a room, more homely, we thought. All the girls have a personal tutor, though for the younger girls this is often more of a substitute mother, who deals with their emotional needs. They also have access to the priest from our local church, St Anne's, that the convent is affiliated to and where we attend Mass and so on.'

'Where is Father Benedict?'

For a moment, Hannah thought she had spoken aloud but then from everyone's unchanged demeanour, she realised she hadn't. She'd often thought of the priest's intervention that night and knew it was kindly meant, even if what happened to her afterwards at the home wasn't. There had been no alternative open to her anyway, none but suicide. The workhouses, bad though they were, had been rightly closed down, but nothing had been put in their place and because of their community's lack of charity, many girls had been left destitute and desperate as she had been herself.

But these feelings were not ones she could share and she pushed them to the back of her mind and concentrated on what the nun was saying because her daughter was going to spend her formative years in this school, whether she liked it or not.

Hannah soon realised that here, Angela had every

opportunity to do what she most wanted in life. They were shown the classrooms and the prep room and the language and science labs, the music room and art room, the magnificent gymnasiums, showers and changing rooms.

The vegetable plot which Hannah had spent back-breaking months tending in 1944 had been covered in Tarmac and some of it marked out for netball. There was no sign of any garden now, although she had noticed the large conservatory attached to the main building with girls moving around inside. To the right behind them were the tennis courts and stretching away from the school yard were the extensive grounds.

These grounds had been her salvation when she'd been resident there. You were allowed to walk around them in your free time. It was getting free time that had been the problem. 'The devil makes work for idle hands,' was one of the nuns' favourite sayings. But whenever Hannah could escape, she did and imagined there was no home, no baby, no shame and that she was back in Wicklow amongst her family.

But she wasn't in Wicklow, not then, not now and she'd shaken off her daydreaming and gone after Arthur and Angela who were following Sister Beatrice to the stables to see the ponies.

Back once again in the Headmistress's office, she again extolled what the school had to offer. The girls, they were told, were encouraged to take up a hobby, to participate in sport, learn at least one foreign language, learn to play an instrument. The list of opportunities was endless. They inspected the cosy dormitories with their matching candlewick bedspreads, fluffy blankets and snow-white sheets, and the bathroom shared between the four occupants.

'How long have you been established?' Arthur asked.

'Not long,' Sister Beatrice said. 'The house, of course, has been here for years. It was used as a home for unmarried mothers in the war years. Morality then, I'm afraid to say, was very lax,' she said, looking from Arthur to Hannah with a disapproving air.

'Oh. Quite,' Arthur said, but Hannah stayed silent.

'Then after the war, there were fewer girls coming forward and more families wanting a better education for their girls,' Sister Beatrice said. 'Before the war, many thought it was senseless educating girls who'd just marry and raise families. The war changed that conception of women forever. They had to do what formerly had been seen as men's jobs and, I believe, did them very well indeed in the main.

'Then of course many young women were left widowed, or with a disabled husband, and often with a family to bring up. Many parents came round to thinking it might be a good thing to educate their daughters as well as their sons. Fathers, in particular, wanted a school with a strict moral framework for their daughters. A convent school fitted that criteria.'

'So not all the girls are from Catholic homes?'

'Ah no, alas, though the great majority are,' Sister Beatrice said. 'But most families have no objection to their daughters having religious instruction and attending Mass. Who knows, perhaps some of these girls will be tomorrow's converts – more souls saved.'

'Indeed,' Arthur said.

He seemed wholly and completely satisfied, smug,

and Hannah wondered what he would do if she was to leap to her feet and shout that she'd been one of those girls with lax morals and that she'd given birth to a bastard son in this very building. That would wipe the smile off his face all right. But she knew she couldn't do such a thing and so she shook hands with the nun and meekly followed Arthur and Angela to the car.

Chapter Sixteen

'So, what d'you think?' Arthur asked Angela as they drove away from the convent.

'I like it, Daddy.'

'I like it, Daddy,' parroted Hannah in her head and wondered what was the matter with her. Of course the child would like it. Even she, who'd been totally against Angela boarding anywhere, had been impressed with the place. The whole atmosphere of the school was good. There was no danger of any ghostly reminders of humbled, pregnant girls there, or those in labour screaming for their mothers as the pains became almost unbearable.

'Won't you miss your home at all?' Hannah asked.

Angela appeared to give it some thought and then, 'No,' she said. 'Not really. I mean I'll see Daddy every weekend. He promised.'

And she'd be completely satisfied. Angela needed only her father, Hannah knew that, she'd accepted it, so why had she laid herself wide open to further hurt by asking her about it?

Arthur smiled the sort of smile that made Hannah want to poke out his eyes or pull the remaining hair from his head in large clumps. He turned to Angela and said, 'That's right, darling, I promised. Now shall we find a little hotel and stop for lunch?'

'Ooh, yes.'

Hotel! Hannah told herself not to panic. There were many, many hotels in Leeds. Why would he go into the hotel she once worked in? It was just chance that her daughter was going to go to school in the same building as the one where she'd given birth to her half-brother. Coincidences weren't going to dog her all day.

But, it appeared, they were, for Arthur turned away from the city centre. He seemed to know his way around the area and although Hannah didn't comment on this, he said in explanation, 'Used to stay in Leeds and around the North a fair bit in the early days of travelling. Reg wanted to break into Yorkshire. Funny people, I thought, stick in the muds, many of them, and blunt isn't in it. 'Course, I stayed in dingy boarding houses then, but I always promised myself that one day I'd eat at The Hibernian and as today's a celebration . . .'

Hannah felt faint. For a moment, Arthur's voice seemed to come from a great distance away and she forced herself back to full consciousness as she said, 'Why don't we find a nice café somewhere?'

'Because I've just said I always promised myself I'd eat there,' Arthur said and he turned to Angela beside him, patted her knee and said, 'It's the best and biggest hotel in Leeds and nothing is too good for my girl.'

Hannah could have told him that and she began to tremble all over and was glad that Arthur had insisted she sit in the back of the car and let Angela ride in the front, for Arthur would have known there was something wrong with her if she'd been beside him.

She told herself it was years since she'd been thrown out of The Hibernian. She looked totally different, she was no longer a young girl, or even a young woman. Anyway, hotels were notorious for the high turnover of staff. She was worrying about nothing.

But the worry was affecting her bladder and she mentioned to Arthur as they went in that she needed to find a ladies'. 'I'll see if I can book us a table,' he said brusquely. 'Don't take all day.'

'Do you need the toilet?' Hannah asked Angela and how glad she was just moments later for the mute shake of her head, for when she came out of the toilet she came face to face with Tilly.

Tilly was, if anything, more shocked than Hannah. Her mouth dropped agape, her eyes widened and her eyebrows nearly disappeared under her fringe. 'Oh my God, you're a sight for sore eyes, you bloody well are,' she said, giving Hannah a hug. 'You old bugger! Just disappearing like that. God, Hannah, what you put me through. If them nuns and that priest knew where you'd gone, they weren't for saying. I searched all over the bleeding place. Where did you end up?'

'Birmingham.'

'Why Birmingham, in God's name?'

'There isn't a logical reason,' Hannah said. 'I wasn't thinking straight. I had to get away. One of the nuns was related to someone in Birmingham who'd helped girls like me in the past, finding them jobs and things like that. She had quite a busy guesthouse and she offered me a job with her and a place to stay. She didn't know what she'd taken on at first, because I wasn't easy in the beginning and used to have dreadful nightmares and flashbacks.'

'But what are you doing here now?'

'My daughter. She's starting at . . .'

'A daughter. You have a daughter? I am glad. It's got to help.'

A shadow flitted across Hannah's face, but all she said was, 'And you?'

'Oh, I'm married too. Married the year after you left. Two kids now, but we want our own place. We live with Ted's mother, see? Houses are like gold dust up here and pricey too, so I help out waiting on. I do two evenings and two lunchtimes when the nippers are at school. It all helps. But tell me about your daughter?'

'I'd love to, Tilly, but not now,' Hannah said. 'My husband knows nothing about my past and that's the way I want it to stay. We're here for a spot of lunch. If I can, I'll slip away later and we'll have a chat, if I can't, I'll leave my address behind the bar. At least we'll be able to write then. But if I don't go now, he'll come looking for me and that's all I need.'

As it was, Arthur grumbled all through the meal about the time she'd taken leaving the two of them sitting there like lemons, not even able to order till she came back. Hannah was tempted to say she was surprised either noticed her absence, but she wanted to do nothing to spoil the day for Angela and nothing either to further Arthur's antagonism.

Tilly served at their table. Hannah had been surprised at that, but she told her later that a couple of the waiters who were there in her time still worked at the hotel and might have recognised her and not have been as discreet as she was. She betrayed nothing. There was no sly wink or nudge. She served Hannah, Arthur and Angela as if they were strangers who'd walked in off the street.

After the meal and coffee, Arthur said, 'I rather fancy a walk around Leeds, Angela. We'll look at the places we can go to and things we can do when I come up weekends. What do you say?'

Angela was very agreeable. Although she'd enjoyed the meal, she was becoming bored with sitting. But as she got to her feet, she looked towards Hannah. Arthur caught the look and said quickly, 'Mommy won't want to come with us, darling. It will be just me and you.'

That should have been the point when Hannah protested that of course she wanted to come. Prove to Angela that she was as interested as Arthur.

But Arthur was glowering at her and she remembered Tilly saying she'd be free at three o'clock and it was past two already. She'd love a chat with Tilly and she felt she owed her something after disappearing the way she did years before. So she said to Angela, 'Daddy's right, darling. I'll sit in the hotel and wait for you.'

She nodded her head, as if she'd almost expected that answer, and turned away from her to hold her father's hand.

Hannah watched them go with fists clenched by her sides and then walked into the hotel bar and ordered a large gin and tonic. She'd never tasted it in her life, but she'd heard people talking about it. Amy swore it gave her a lift and Hannah badly needed one and seeing how much it cost, hoped it worked.

She did find the drink pleasant, much more palatable

than the brandy Arthur had bought her on honeymoon, or the sips of beer she'd tried, or even the sickly sweet sherry she drank to please Gloria.

She was still nursing the dregs in the glass when Tilly found her. 'Let me off early,' she said. 'There weren't many in today and he's a good sort, the head waiter. He knows too I'll work over if they're short-handed. What you drinking – G & T?'

'Yes, I've never had it before.'

' "Mother's ruin", they call it. Like another?'

'Oh, I don't know.'

'Look here, Hannah, we got years to catch up on, haven't we? We can't sit at a table in a bar without a drink.'

'I usually have an orange juice.'

'Orange juice be damned!' Tilly cried. 'This isn't what you'd call a usual meeting and we need a couple of large G & T's to help it along.'

Hannah laughed. She'd forgotten how Tilly had often made her laugh and when the laughter had ended, what a staunch friend she'd proved to be and how shamefully she'd treated her.

Tilly returned with the drinks. 'That's better,' she said, 'seeing you with a smile on your face. God, you looked as if you'd lost a pound and found sixpence.'

'That's your influence,' Hannah said. 'Believe me, my life hasn't been a bundle of laughs.'

'Whose has?' Tilly said. 'Got to make the best of it, I say. Look at me. I met Ted not long after you disappeared into the blue yonder. He'd been in the army, but was invalided out early because of a leg wound. Still got a limp now. But, in the army, he'd learnt mechanics for cars, lorries and that and he got taken on in a garage and before the other fellows were out, see. But we couldn't get no house, council lists are like a roll of wallpaper and we're stuck way at the bottom and houses to buy are going for silly prices.

'We married in January 1946 and Colin was born in April 1947 and Louise two years later. Ted's mom's all right for babysitting and watching the nippers in the holidays when I'm at work, but she's an interfering sod. I'm too soft on the kids or too hard. I give them too much attention or not enough. I feed them too much or not enough, or not the right kind of things. God, there's times I could brain the bloody woman.

'Then Ted comes home and we're going at it hammer and tongs. I think he should support me because he married me and his mother thinks he should support her because she's his mother. Poor Ted can't do right for doing wrong and usually ducks out of it altogether by going to the pub.'

'But you don't let it get you down,' Hannah said because all during Tilly's relation of the tale, her eyes had danced and there had been a quirk to her mouth.

' 'Course it bloody gets me down at the time,' Tilly said. 'I said to Ted one of these days he'll come home to find his mom cut into pieces that I'm feeding into the mincer. Huh. Thought I was joking. No, the point is, Hannah, I don't dwell on it after. You can't. It don't do to look back either. And now you've got summat to live for, because your daughter is beautiful, and she's the spitting image of you.'

'Yes, in looks,' Hannah said. 'That's as far as it goes. She is her father's child.'

Tilly was surprised. She'd been stunned by Angela's resemblance to her mother. It was like seeing Hannah as a small child and she estimated Angela to be much the same age as her Colin. But she hadn't thought much of Hannah's choice of husband. He had no flair about him, no zest for life as Hannah once had, no sex appeal – nothing. And Hannah – Hannah who could have had the pick of anyone, who could have been dressed in a paper bag and look better than most women – chose him and now said the child preferred him to her.

But when Hannah began her story from the time she left Yorkshire, Tilly's eyes grew wide with sympathy. She told her how ill she'd been after Michael's birth and how she'd eventually agreed to marry Arthur to secure her own future and to have a family. Then she told her about the letter from Ireland and going home to her dying sister, the child she'd agreed to care for, and then on to the wedding and disastrous honeymoon.

Tilly bought another drink, sensing Hannah needed it. 'Here, take a swig of that to give you courage,' she said, pushing the drink across the table.

Hannah did as she suggested and then with the glass clasped between her hands, she went on in a rush. She told of the abuse that began on their honeymoon and the one violent sexual act that had resulted in Angela.

'He'd read books on it and knew I wasn't a virgin,' Hannah said. 'He never slept with me again, not even in the same room. He thinks me a harlot, a whore, and when he knew I'd become pregnant, he said he'd keep the child away from me, lest I taint it.'

'He can't.'

'He could and he did. He's bought everything for

Angela and I mean everything, the pram, the cot, her toys, her clothes.'

'Yes, but you're her mother.'

'Yes, that's one thing he can't dispute,' said Hannah, with a grim laugh. 'But I had to have an emergency Caesarean, and was out of it for ages and even when I woke up, I was in no state to see Angela and she was in distress anyway and had to be kept in the nursery. I couldn't feed her, Arthur gave her her first bottle and every evening after that he fed her when he came to visit. He was lovely to me when there were people there, flowers and chocolates, you know the sort. He charmed the nurses. But when we were alone he kept telling me I was useless.

'When I eventually saw Angela, I felt nothing. No rush of love – nothing. It was nothing like I felt when I had Michael. Then I was ill because he'd been taken from me and this time my baby was there and I didn't want her. I didn't even like her very much. Arthur hired a nanny to look after her and she's still there. Her name is Pauline.

'Vic said it's something to do with being separated from my baby for those first few days. You don't bond or something and you have depression. I think it was Arthur telling me I'd be useless too. Maybe part of me thought if I don't try, I can't fail. I don't know if I thought that, but I might have. Vic talks a lot about the mind and subconscious thoughts, planting an idea in someone's head, especially if that person is vulnerable and has low self-esteem.'

'And who's this Vic?'

'The doctor. I work for him now,' Hannah said and

went to on to describe her job and how much good it had done her and how kind and generous Vic was. She explained her relationship with Pauline and how it had begun to change over the years until Pauline was now more of a friend than a foe.

'Is your old man wealthy?' Tilly asked, as she set two more drinks on the table before them. 'All this hiring a nanny and private schools, I mean it's not what ordinary people do.'

'He's not wealthy,' Hannah said, 'but he is comfortable. He's risen in the firm and I imagine has a good salary. I don't see a penny piece of it, unless we are going to dine at the Banks' and he gives me money to get my hair done and buy clothes. He wants them to think that we are a devoted couple.'

'And you?'

'I play along.'

'Why?'

'Why! I've had one child taken from me already and now Angela doesn't care that much for me, though I hope that when she gets older, maybe as a teenager or young woman, she'll turn to me more. Pauline won't be with us much longer. She's going on for sixty-five now and has very bad legs and really with Angela boarding, she has no need of a nanny. There will only be me and Angela through the holidays.'

'But if you want to get along with her so much, why are you sending her to boarding school in the first place?'

'Again that wasn't my choice,' Hannah said. 'As I told you, I have very little say in anything that concerns Angela. Personally, I think she's too young and I believe it's another ploy to keep her away from me. Arthur has already told her that he will be up to see her every weekend and I know I won't be invited. That's where they are now, checking on the haunts that they can visit in and around the town. But Tilly,' Hannah said fiercely, 'even if I was sold on the idea of a boarding school then I wouldn't have sent her where she will be going. Not even if it was the only school on the planet.'

'Why? Where is it?'

'You'll never guess, not in a million years. Do you remember that grim building out in the sticks run by the Sisters of Charity?'

'You're not sending her there?' Tilly said, horrified.

'I'm sending her nowhere. This is all Arthur's doing. But the place is so changed you wouldn't recognise it. It's bright and airy and full of children's chatter and laughter. It's a Catholic convent school and still run by nuns, but they are teaching Sisters. It has a very good name and in theory, Angela will have every advantage there.

'Personally, I think it's a big mistake. Private day school was bad enough, but when she mixes with real moneyed people, she won't think much of our ordinary little terraced house. Arthur can't, or won't, see a problem and despite my telling you the convent is changed from the place where I gave birth to my baby Michael, I know I'll still get tremors of anxiety at her going there.'

'I can well understand that.'

'Everyone else can see my point of view,' Hannah said.

Tilly felt sorry for Hannah, but as she said, she couldn't do anything about the situation. She went to the bar and came back with two more drinks and Hannah said not a word about it, for the gin was making her feel better than she had in ages. Tilly decided to change the subject. 'And how's your niece that you took to live with you? Josie, is it?'

'Oh, she's great,' Hannah said. 'She goes about with a girl from work called Cynthia and Josie says Cynthia'd love her to take up with her brother, Peter. Josie likes him, but not that way. She prefers his friend, Phil. At the moment though, they're both complaining about national service. They date a boy a few times and then off he goes for eighteen months. They get a few letters if they're lucky and then nothing.'

'Eighteen months, huh. We had six years of it.'

'I know and look at us,' Hannah said and they both laughed. 'Oh Tilly,' Hannah went on earnestly. 'It's good to see you.'

'It's the gin talking.'

'No it isn't,' Hannah said, 'but I could well develop a taste for it.'

'Well, you better have no more of it. You can't meet your old man legless.'

'I think it's too late,' Hannah said. 'I haven't tried standing up, but my head is decidedly not right and you know what?'

'What?'

'I don't care.'

'Oh Lord, you are tipsy,' Tilly said. 'I'll order us some coffee and you can tell me about the doctor.'

'About the doctor?'

She repeated the question when Tilly came back and Tilly replied, 'Yes, the doctor. Maybe you don't know how your eyes go all soft when you talk about him, but I've noticed. Is he dishy? Do you fancy him?'

Hannah considered the questions. 'Is he dishy? I don't know. He's lovely, so kind and thoughtful. His mouth is full, not like Arthur's thin lips, and his teeth are pure white, his skin sort of tanned and his eyes deep, deep brown and so is his mop of untidy hair and the beard he grew to make himself look older when he started in practice.'

'Oh, you have got it bad,' Tilly said and waited till the tray of coffee was before them before she spoke again. 'You definitely fancy him. How does he feel about you?'

'I do not fancy him, Tilly. Don't be ridiculous. He's my boss, that's all.'

'So what? You can fancy your boss you know.'

'Well, I don't. I'm married and a Catholic, Tilly.'

'Oh, and that puts a block on your feelings, does it?'

'It means you can't act on them, even if you are attracted to someone because marriage is for life. And before you say a word, I do not fancy Vic. This is all a figment of your vivid imagination.'

'Oh yeah!' Tilly said, with a sardonic grin. 'You just believe that if you like. Will you struggle along in your loveless marriage for ever and a day then?'

'Yes I will, for Angela's sake if not my own. It's like a form of punishment.'

'Punishment! For what? For loving a man who was blown to kingdom come? God, Hannah, you've got some horrible idea of God if you think you deserve punishment for that. And if you're right, you can keep your God, I'd want no part of him.'

'Oh Tilly,' said Hannah with a smile. 'It's been worth coming to see you. You're like a tonic. There is no one like you for making me laugh.'

'Huh, Ted's mother wouldn't agree with you,' Tilly said and then catching sight of her watch went on, 'And talking of Ted's mother, I'm going to bloody well catch it when I get home. Our Louise will be home. She's only in the Infants'.'

'Will you get into trouble?'

'When do I not?' Tilly said with a cheerful grin. She scribbled her address on a piece of paper and passed it to Hannah, downed her coffee in one swallow, and said, 'Write to me and for God's sake, be good to yourself. Grab a chance to be happy for once in your life. But for now, help yourself to the coffee, there's usually two each in one of those pots, so there will be a fair bit left. Okay?'

'Yes, yes, I'm fine. Never better.'

'You're bloody pissed, that's why,' Tilly said and then suddenly she knelt down and put her arms around Hannah and gave her a hug, before hurrying from the room. Hannah watched her go with her eyes misted with tears.

And Tilly, even knowing her mother-in-law would surely harangue her and her Ted would probably take himself off to the pub and they were no nearer getting a house than ever, knew she wouldn't swap her life for Hannah's – no way. No bloody way.

Hannah finished the coffee, but thought that honestly it hadn't done much good. She still felt terribly woozy and yet worryingly, wasn't bothered about it at all. She wondered if she would be able to stand or walk, but didn't care if she couldn't. She didn't seem to care about anything.

Why hadn't she thought of taking a drink earlier to help her cope with Arthur? Ah, but that was the start of the slippery slope, wasn't it? 'Mother's ruin', that's what Tilly had said. She could quite see how it could be that. Oh, she was glad she'd bumped into Tilly. She made her feel better. She thought if Tilly fell in a dung hill, she'd come up smelling of roses.

And yet she's wrong about me and Vic, she thought. Trust her to see romance in everything when Vic and I are just friends, good friends maybe, but definitely no more than that.

'I've been searching everywhere for you,' Arthur's peevish and angry voice broke in on Hannah's thoughts.

'Well, now you've found me.'

'I didn't expect you to be in the bar.'

'Well, where did you expect me to be?'

Arthur didn't answer. Instead, he eyed the glasses on the table beside the tray of coffee. 'Have you been drinking?'

'Yes. It's usually what people do in a bar,' Hannah said, 'and it may have escaped your notice, but I am over eighteen.'

'You've been sitting here drinking alone since I left?'

'What did you expect me to do, Arthur?' Hannah barked. 'Sit twiddling my thumbs and counting the flowers on the wallpaper?'

Arthur was surprised at Hannah's tone and his eyes narrowed. 'Are you drunk?'

'Very possibly.'

'You're disgusting!'

'I know. You've told me often, like you've told me I'm a harlot and a whore.'

'Keep your voice down,' Arthur hissed. 'People are looking. Come on, Angela is waiting in the foyer.'

Now to see if I can walk, Hannah thought, and got to her feet slowly. She would have fallen then, but for Arthur's arm and he grasped her firmly and almost marched her out of the room while she laughed at the expression of stern disapproval on his face.

'What's the matter with Mommy?' Angela asked, who couldn't remember a time when she'd ever heard or seen her mother laughing.

'Nothing. Mommy's very tired.'

'She doesn't look tired. She looks as if she's been having fun,' Angela said. She liked the sight of her cheerful mother.

'We'll sit in the back on the way home,' Hannah told her daughter. 'And we'll sing all the songs we can remember. What do you say?'

Angela's eyes widened. She'd never heard her mother sing before, but it sounded more entertaining than just watching the road and the traffic and concentrating on not being sick. She looked automatically at her father for approval, but too many people had heard what Hannah had said and were looking towards the handsome woman and the child who was a carbon copy of herself for Arthur to say what he really thought.

'Come along.'

They sang all the songs of the day. 'Singing in the Rain', 'Charmaine', 'Singing the Blues', and songs from Walt Disney's film *Dumbo* and *South Pacific*, both of which Angela had seen with her father. They went on to a medley of war songs and then any hymns Hannah could remember, finishing up with 'Rock Around the Clock', and all the time, Hannah was aware of the stiffness of Arthur before them in the driving seat, anger and resentment apparent from the back of his head and even the nape of his neck which he held rigid. Arthur's face, which she saw in profile, was drawn and tight, his nostrils pinched in and his mouth a thin line. She knew he was seething with anger, yet found she couldn't give a damn; in fact, she was pleased.

'You were drunk!' Gloria cried with glee when Hannah told her about it. 'Good on you, girl! God, I'd have gone on the bottle before this if I'd been married to Arthur Bradley.'

'It's the first time I remember having fun, real fun with my daughter,' said Hannah. 'I think that's what bothered him more than anything.'

'It would.'

'It was worth the headache that developed later,' Hannah said, 'and the silent treatment I got from Arthur, because that night Angela wound her arms around my neck without being pressured and gave me a kiss. If Arthur had been a different man, then I'm sure I could have built a relationship with my daughter.'

'You can still build one. The child is only seven.'

'She'll be at school after September and I'll only see her for a few weeks a year. It will not be enough to build on the shaky start we've had and the annoying fact is that that is how Arthur wants it.'

Gloria said nothing for she knew Hannah was right. Instead, she changed the subject slightly. 'I'm glad at any rate you met your friend. Did you know Tilly well?'

'Very well,' Hannah said. 'We shared a bedroom, you see. I'd only been in Leeds a matter of months when Molly, the one who got me the job at The Hibernian, married and went to live down south and then Tilly came in her place. She was to be my witness, you know, at the registry office when I was going to marry Mike. Tilly knows everything. She's the one person I don't have to pretend with and the only one who came to visit me in that Godawful prison.'

'I can't believe he's sending the child to board at all, but to think he picked the very place,' Gloria said. 'Monica told me they were leaving the convent, but they were all being split up into other places and she is based in Ireland now, Dublin. She didn't tell me what their house was being used for.'

'It wouldn't have done any good if I'd known anyway,' Hannah said. 'I could never influence Arthur in anything, you know that. And I could hardly tell him the real reason I didn't want Angela going there.'

'Good God, no,' Gloria agreed.

'No one seeing it now would guess the horrors that once went on there,' Hannah told her. 'It's even had a facelift outside. Inside, it's totally transformed, but still . . . Yes, I felt quite weird when I went in there.'

'But you did it.'

'Of course. You must know, Gloria, I'd do anything for Angela. She is all I have.' And Gloria knew she spoke the truth.

Chapter Seventeen

Hannah hadn't realised how everyone would miss Angela so much. She'd been the pivot they'd all spun round and now Pauline's life at least seemed without purpose.

So, when in the spring of 1957, Pauline sought Hannah out and said she wanted to give in her notice, Hannah wasn't surprised. She'd been with the family nine and a half years and said she'd be sorry to go but added that, 'Angela will be ten in November. She hardly needs a nanny now.'

Angela seemed to need very few people now, for each holiday she was changing as Hannah had prophesised. At first it was hardly noticeable, but it was there. Angela was pulling away from all of them, except her father. Her friends had names like Vanessa and Belinda and Hillary and seemed to have more importance than any family member. 'They're bound to,' Vic said when Hannah talked to him about it. 'She sees more of them than she does of anyone else. They've become her family.'

'Arthur often takes one or two of them out with Angela when he goes up at the weekend,' Hannah told Vic.

'Does he go every weekend?'

'Yes.'

'And never takes you?'

'No, never.'

'Do you mind?'

'Of course I mind, but don't suggest I tell Arthur how I feel, he wouldn't care.'

'Hannah, why do you put up with such old-fashioned attitudes?'

'Vic, listen,' Hannah said. 'This is how it is. Arthur is an old-fashioned man and so I didn't dare tell him about the baby I had in Leeds. But he worked out I wasn't a virgin. For him, that was it. I was a fallen woman, "tainted", used. But by then I was pregnant with Angela. He swore he'd keep the baby as far away from me as possible so I'd not taint it. He's kept his word and I played right into his hands by becoming ill after Angela's birth and then not wanting anything to do with her for months.'

'It was hardly your fault.'

'Fault doesn't come into this,' Hannah said with a sigh. 'This boarding school is all part of his plan; separating me from my daughter, driving a wedge between us and it's working very well.'

'This is monstrous! Would it help if I spoke to him?'

'Vic, it would do no good at all. It might make things worse if Arthur thought I'd talked to other people about any problems.'

'I wish I could do something.'

'You do,' Hannah said firmly. 'You listen. You're a friend.'

'I'll always be your friend, you know that,' Vic said,

his voice soft and gentle and the look in his eyes which sent a shiver down Hannah's spine. 'Don't, Vic!'

'Don't what?'

'You know what,' Hannah cried. 'For God's sake, I'm married.'

'I know. That's why I said I'd be your friend. I know I can be nothing else.'

Hannah put her head in her hands. She had to shut out the sight of Vic's face and his eyes before she weakened and asked him to hold her close. Heaven alone knew where that would lead.

That night, for the first time, she admitted her feelings for Vic in a letter to Tilly. Each week she wrote to Tilly and because she hadn't to face her, she was able to write of things she couldn't have said, not to her, or anybody else either. When Tilly read the letter, she smiled to herself. Her reply was swift and to the point:

For God's sake, Hannah, you have one life. Grab a chance of happiness while you can.

But Hannah knew happiness would be eroded away by guilt if by having Vic, she lost Angela, and she knew Arthur would make sure she lost her. And she could never be married again, not truly married anyway. Divorce was not recognised in the Catholic Church. There were insurmountable obstacles, things that Tilly wouldn't understand, and she knew however she felt and however Vic felt, there was no future for them together.

After Pauline left, Josie was loath to leave Hannah alone in the evenings, for Arthur was seldom in, but

Hannah insisted, saying Josie had a life of her own. She never went out with Mary Byrne now. Months before, she'd come to their door distraught and pregnant and Josie had accompanied her back home, where Mary broke the news to her mother.

Mary was married to the baby's father, Seamus McAllister, speedily. Josie confided to Hannah that she wouldn't have had him as a gift for he was lazy and work-shy and liked his beer too much. But Hannah knew that Mary's mother would think any man better than none to clothe her daughter with respectability and take the shame away from her parents.

Six months later, Mary gave birth to a baby son and Hannah and Josie went round to see the child. They admired the healthy eight pound baby and neither batted an eyelid when Mary's mother said the child was delicate with him being so premature.

Not everyone was so circumspect. 'Big bonny baby and she says it's premature,' one woman was heard to say in the waiting room one day. 'I ask you. Thinks we was born yesterday.'

Hannah took no part in the conversation or derision of Mary's mother and just hoped it would work out for the girl who was still living at home with Seamus.

Josie used to go along and see her because she felt sorry for her, but they had less in common than ever. 'Mary's days for gadding about are over, I fear,' Hannah told Gloria, 'while Josie is taken with the skiffle sound and goes to a skiffle club in town with Cynthia. Her brother goes too sometimes and his friend Phil who Josie likes so much.'

'Skiffle,' Gloria said. 'What's that when it's at home?'

'Oh, it's the new thing,' Hannah said. 'They use washboards to make music.'

'You're kidding?'

'No, I'm not,' Hannah assured Gloria. 'It was all to do with this Lonnie Donegan, who sang a song called "Rock Island Line", and this year followed it with "Cumberland Gap". Now it's Tommy Steel with "Singing the Blues" and someone else too called Buddy Holly who does a type of music called "rock and roll".'

'How come you know the names of them all?'

'Names! I know all the words,' Hannah said. 'It would be hard for me not to know them, serenaded as I am morning, noon and night whenever Josie's at home.'

Gloria chuckled. 'And what about the man with the funny hips that everyone in America was so worried about?'

'Elvis Presley. He's still around,' Hannah said. 'Elizabeth was so concerned she came round to talk to me about him. Apparently, he comes from Memphis, Tennessee and his songs seem innocuous enough, until he begins to shake and wiggle his hips. Elizabeth was very alarmed about it, but it seems the girls enjoy it well enough. The man appears to drive them mad no less.'

'Are you worried at all?' Gloria asked. 'I read a bit about him in the paper.'

'I read it too,' Hannah said. 'But Josie is a sensible girl. She just likes the music.'

'Ah, but that's where it starts,' Gloria said. 'In the *Evening Mail* it said this Elvis had been on television in the States, but they only televised him from the waist up because of his suggestive hips.'

'I don't know that that is such a good idea,' Hannah said. 'Denying people things only makes them more attractive.'

'That's a novel approach,' said Gloria. 'You could be right.'

'It's just this rock and roll they are all mad about,' Hannah said. 'And I honestly don't see any harm in it.'

'Well,' Gloria agreed. 'Josie's a good girl and very sensible. You never saw her head turned with those teddy boys and now these beatnik types from America.'

'She wants a record player now,' Hannah said. 'They're not like the old gramophones, you know; the records are really small and bendy and Josie tells me the needle is now called a stylus if you like. Cynthia has one her brother bought her and they buy records for it at Woolworth's. Phil has said he'll buy Josie one for Christmas.'

'Is it serious then between them?'

'It could well be,' Hannah said. 'Of course Josie's young yet but Phil is six years older and he has a good steady job lecturing at the university. Maybe he thinks it's time to settle down.'

'Does the age gap worry you?'

'Not at all. Josie is older than her years, always has been, and Phil is lovely. Peter, Cynthia's brother, is probably the more handsome with his jet black hair and dark eyes and he's a nice boy. But somehow Phil is a kinder, more genuine person. I have a very soft spot for him. Mind you, I like all the young people, they're so vibrant and alive somehow. Josie is mad about Phil, but she told me she doesn't know how he feels about her. I know, though. You just have to see them together,

Gloria, and see the way he looks at her. They'd be good together, for Phil has a terrific sense of fun that matches Josie's. I think and hope he's just biding his time because of Josie's age.'

'Well, they do say the course of true love never runs smooth,' Gloria said.

'I hope for Josie's sake it runs a damned sight smoother than mine,' Hannah remarked with a wry smile. 'Still there's no point worrying about it.'

Gloria gave a sigh. 'No good worrying about anything if you ask me. I think the world is a dreadful place just now.'

Hannah glanced at Gloria. This attitude wasn't at all like her. She could see her skin seemed taut across her cheekbones, which had not a vestige of colour on them. 'Are you all right, Gloria?'

'Of course I'm all right,' Gloria snapped. 'I'm tired that's all. I'm getting on you know. Been here a long time. Maybe too long.'

'Don't say that!'

'Face it, Hannah, I am getting on,' Gloria said. 'And I'm weary of the things happening. There's been unrest everywhere since the war ended. I mean look at Suez last year and our lads in there bombing and invading and that Nasser one lording it over everyone and then those Ruskies marching in on Hungary. Criminal, that was. But we didn't rush to help them out did we? Seems we please ourselves where we stick up for people. Fact is, Hannah, since I've had that telly, I've been amazed at what I've seen and heard. Been upset as well as angry too, I don't mind telling you. Somehow it seems more real when you actually see it.'

Hannah knew what Gloria meant. She like many others had been horrified by the news from Hungary of the bloodshed and massacre of hundreds of Hungarians to bring the rebellion under control. She watched the footage smuggled out of the country and transmitted to the television with a sense of shock and horror.

'And now those same Russians are shooting Sputniks into the air for no apparent reason,' Gloria said. 'As for us, what do we do but fill the country up with black people.'

The remark was so unlike Gloria, who'd always been of the opinion that everyone was equal whatever their colour and creed, that Hannah was shocked and a little dismayed.

'Come on, Gloria,' Hannah said. 'Be fair. You must have seen black Americans in the war?'

'Yeah, I did, but they were soldiers,' explained Gloria. 'These . . . Well, Amy went to town one day and the conductor was black and there were another two walking around the Bull Ring and those white boys called them "niggers" and there was a fight. The police had to be called. It will lead to problems, you mark my words.'

But Hannah, who'd seen the devastating effects of civil unrest in her own country, replied, 'I hope not. Everyone can get along with everyone else with a bit of compromise.'

'I wish you could go and see Gloria,' Hannah said to Vic a few weeks later, after she'd paid another couple of worrying visits to her friend.

'I can't. She's not registered with me. She sees Doctor Simmonds in Holly Lane. I can't tread on his toes.'

'You couldn't just pop in as a friend?'

'You know I couldn't,' Vic said. 'Anyway, she'd soon send me away with a flea in my ear. You're probably worrying unnecessarily. She's a good age now and people do slow down and things become more of an effort.'

Hannah wasn't totally convinced that was all it was and resolved to talk it over with Josie that night when they'd have the house to themselves. But when Josie came in it was to break news of her own that drove Hannah's concern for Gloria out of her mind for a time. Josie's face was shining and her eyes sparkling with happiness. Phil had asked her to marry him. Hannah was pleased, but not surprised. So, she thought, I was right, he was just biding his time.

'I said yes,' Josie went on, 'but really I'll need Arthur's approval, won't I?'

'For the next few months only,' Hannah said. 'And Phil is a lovely young man and well able to look after you, I can't see Arthur raising much objection. When were you thinking of marrying anyway?'

'Not till I'm twenty-one,' Josie said. 'I'll have money from the farm sale then, so if it's all right with you I'll write and tell Martin I'm getting married. I want him to give me away. Do you think he will?'

Hannah hesitated, remembering her own wedding when not a soul belonging to her, bar Josie, was there. She'd hate the girl to be disappointed. But then Martin and Siobhan had been more than decent over the years and the American dollars came regularly. Even Josie seemed to have lost any animosity she might have felt towards them recently and Hannah knew it was important for her to have some of her family about her on her special day and resolved to write to Martin, stressing the importance of it if he should refuse.

So she replied, 'I'm sure Martin would be honoured. Where are you going to live?'

'Phil thinks we should look for a place in Moseley Village,' Josie said. 'It's close to the university where Phil works and closer to the city centre than here for mine and the houses are cheapish because lots of students live there.'

'Moseley,' Hannah repeated, sorry that Josie would be so far away, for Moseley was the other side of the city. 'I'll miss you.'

Josie put her arms around Hannah. 'And I'll miss you,' she said. 'But I'm not going yet a while and there's lots to do over the next months. And another thing, I don't want you paying for any of it.'

'I have a surprise for you,' Hannah said. 'Though you asked me to write explaining to Martin and Siobhan you wanted no more money from them after you began work, they continued to send it and I opened a post office account for you. It's quite a bit now, forty dollars a month for five years. It will pay for your reception, your honeymoon and still leave change, I expect.'

Josie's mouth dropped open. She had never in a million years expected that. 'Oh God, Hannah. Thank you. Thank you for just being you and thinking so much of others.'

'There's not that many others to think of,' Hannah said. 'And you are very special to me. I'll tell you something, this wedding is going to be a real celebration.'

* * *

And it was. Martin and Siobhan needed no persuading to come to their young sister's wedding and both came with their respective partners, though they'd left their children behind. They stayed at Gloria's guesthouse and when Hannah got over their American accents, she got on with them all, particularly Martin, whom she'd been close to growing up together in Wicklow.

Martin was delighted with the turn-out his little sister had made which he attributed to Hannah's upbringing. 'She'd value a letter from you and Siobhan now and again,' Hannah told him. 'She sometimes feels as if she's been forgotten, you know, as if she hasn't any brothers and sisters.'

'I know, she told us both off about it,' Martin said with a grin. 'The point is I still thought of her as the nine-year-old child I left behind. But she's hardly that anymore and I promise things will be different now. I like Phil, the chap she's marrying. He's a fine man and I think he'll be good to her.'

'He'd better be,' Hannah warned, 'or he'll have me to deal with.' But she wasn't worried really for she knew Josie and Phil truly loved each other.

There had been a letter of congratulations from Miriam, though Hannah wondered if she still thought marriage worthy of congratulation, for she now had twelve children and Hannah, much as she'd longed for a family, always felt sorry for her. Ellen also wrote with regret that she wouldn't be there. She had two children of her own now and said springtime was a hard time to leave a farm.

'Seems like every time is a bad time to leave a farm,'

Gloria said to Hannah. 'You had some of the same when you married in the autumn. And isn't there a fine family of them back there to look after her children for a few days so she can see her wee sister married?'

There was and Hannah also felt it to be an excuse. Peter said he wouldn't be able to get time off at the moment and Sam wrote that he couldn't leave his grandfather, being the only one left, and from Margaret in Africa there was no word at all.

Despite these letters of regret, the day was almost perfect. Although it was only March, the sun shone from a pale blue sky all morning and both Hannah and Gloria had tears in their eyes as they watched Josie, her face so radiant with happiness that it was truly beautiful, walk down the aisle of the Abbey on the arm of her brother. Martin looked distinguished in his grey pinstriped suit and shining black shoes, his dark hair slicked back with Brylcreem.

Not for Josie the wartime restrictions and the practical costume. She had more money at her disposal than Hannah had ever had and anyway, this marriage wasn't one of mutual convenience, but one of true love that Hannah had seen developing between them for months.

The wedding dress was a work of art and so too was Angela's bridesmaid's dress of apricot satin. But there was no danger that Angela would upstage the bride, for Josie's beauty shone from within her and Hannah wished for her and Phil all the happiness in the world.

Now that Josie was an adult and soon to be a married woman, the relationship between the two women had changed. But the love they'd always had for each other hadn't diminished at all, but deepened if anything, and

Hannah knew she'd miss Josie more than she'd missed her own daughter.

Lent was forgotten in the reception that went on in the Lyndhurst pub, just next to the Abbey, even by Father Fitzgerald, who'd accepted the invitation to attend.

Father Fitzgerald had always had a soft spot for Josie. He'd never forgotten the day Arthur had sought out his advice about the child before he'd married Hannah and he was glad to know the advice he'd given him that night had been heeded. Strange man, Arthur – he'd always felt it. Still, the man had taken the child in. Pity he hadn't let her take the eleven-plus, the teachers said she had a good brain.

But all in all, Josie had made good, coming top in her exams for typing, shorthand and book-keeping, he'd heard, and had got a good job in an insurance firm and now this marriage to a lecturer at the university no less and what's more a good Catholic like herself. And as for the wedding – well! He'd heard tell Arthur Bradley was inclined to be mean. The things people say. There was nothing mean about this wedding. Lavish would be a better word to describe it. It must have been just a rumour about his meanness, Father Fitzgerald thought, and accepted a glass of sherry from the silver tray that the waitress offered him and beamed at everyone around him.

Hannah was glad to talk to Pauline again and Tilly too. Josie had insisted on inviting her once she knew the whole story of Mike Murphy and the child Hannah had had by him and how supportive Tilly had been. Gloria also said she'd like to meet another one who'd had Hannah's interests at heart.

Tilly came alone although the invitation had been for the whole family.

Bring the old man? Not likely. Nor the kids either. His mother can have them for a few days and see how she likes it then. As for Ted, well, we couldn't talk properly in front of him. This isn't part of his life and he'll know no one. He's best stopping here, but I wouldn't miss it for the world. I didn't see your wedding and you didn't come to mine neither, but these people, Josie and Gloria and even Pauline, you write so much about, I feel as if I know them already. And I can't wait to see your daughter again.

There was another one Tilly couldn't wait to see too, but thought it better not to put that in a letter. Letters could be read by others.

All in all, Tilly got on well with Gloria, Josie and even Pauline, who she was all set to resent slightly. She hadn't revised her opinion of Arthur though. When she'd first seen him in Leeds, she'd marked him out as a nondescript nowt with narrow, cold eyes, and at the wedding she found he got worse the more she saw of him. She saw quite plainly that Josie and Hannah's American relations hadn't taken to him either. She couldn't begin to understand why Hannah had married the thin man with spectacles perched on his nose, an exaggerated idea of his own importance and no charm whatsoever, unlike Reg and Elizabeth Banks, who she thought lovely people.

Angela was beautiful, her manners perfect before her

father and her American relations. But Tilly had seen how offhand she was, even downright rude and defiant to her mother and how used she was, within the family at least, to having the lion's share of attention and getting her own way in everything. Hannah had often expressed her concern at these traits in Angela and Tilly thought her right to be bothered about it.

Tilly was used to observing people. It was a habit she'd picked up waiting on and she wondered if anyone had noticed that Gloria was anything but well. Make-up carefully applied can hide many things, but sometimes the colour would drain from Gloria's face altogether and it would look quite grey, while her eyes would glaze over and she'd nip her lips together. She was obviously in pain and Tilly also noticed she ate little of the meal, though she drank plenty of the wine.

She would have mentioned it to Hannah, but a wedding wasn't really the time and anyway, she told herself, she probably knew. It wasn't something one broadcasted. So later when she got close to Hannah, she said nothing about Gloria, but asked eagerly, 'Is the delicious doctor here?'

'Of course not,' Hannah hissed. 'Why should he be?'

'Well, isn't he your boss?'

'Yes.'

'He's not any more than that yet then?'

'Tilly, keep your voice down,' Hannah said, looking around to see if anyone was in earshot before she went on. In an undertone, she continued, 'No, he's not my lover, but my special friend, and that's how he will remain.'

* * *

Josie and Phil had only time for a few days' honeymoon because of Phil's lectures and they intended to take a proper honeymoon at Easter. Josie was glad of this because she really wanted to spend time with her brother and sister who were staying on for a week after the wedding.

Hannah was glad too and after Angela returned to school, she spent as much time as possible in their company. Vic was very understanding about her having time off and she showed them the city she'd brought Josie to live in, a task made easier by the car they hired. They visited the city centre and Josie's beloved Bull Ring one day and another day went to Sutton Park, marvelling at the lakes in some parts and woodland and meadows in another and the miles and miles of open space at such a premium in New York.

When Josie returned, they toured the art galleries and museums and visited the Botanical Gardens and Cannon Hill Park adjacent to them. And then, on their last day, as the sun with a hint of warmth in it shone from a sky of Wedgwood blue, decorated with fluffy white clouds, they drove across the city to the Lickey Hills, where they spent a very enjoyable day.

Hannah was amazed how she slipped so easily into the friendship she'd enjoyed with Martin and Siobhan as children growing up and was pleased that they had time to spend with their little sister they'd been separated from for so long. Arthur was never invited on their outings and Hannah wondered why no one mentioned it. But Martin unbeknown to Hannah had asked Josie.

'Don't ask him,' she advised. 'He and Hannah don't

get on.' Martin wasn't surprised. He had spoken to Arthur at the wedding, making an effort for he was Hannah's husband, but found the man boorish, almost objectionable, and very boring. He had no desire to spend more time in the man's company and Siobhan, who'd made similar efforts, felt the same.

Yet Arthur and Hannah were married for life, so Martin asked, 'Why don't they?'

How could Josie begin to explain? There were things she could never tell anyone. 'It's a long story,' she said. 'We haven't time to go into it now. Anyway, I'd rather not spend time talking about him.'

'I take it you're not that keen either?'

'No. No, I'm not, but let's not spoil the time we have talking about it.'

'Right enough,' Martin said. 'Not another word.'

He said nothing further to Hannah or Josie, but talked about it long into the night with his wife, Deirdre, Siobhan, and her husband, Jonathan. 'I thought it was odd her not asking us over for a meal,' Siobhan said. 'It's what I would have expected her to do. Now I understand a little more.'

Hannah would have loved to have them over to her own home, but she was never sure how Arthur would behave. He wasn't aware she was with her American relatives or even that they were still in the country and Hannah had no intention of enlightening him.

It was after she'd bid them all a tearful goodbye that she unburdened herself to Vic. 'I miss them so much,' she said. 'Josie, too, of course. The house seems so empty.'

Never was she so thankful for her job, but that only

accounted for the days, not the weekends or evenings which strung out long and terribly lonely. How she wished she had the money to fly to New York as Martin and Siobhan urged her to.

They wouldn't have any idea of her penury. Josie's wedding had been lavish enough and her own clothes and those of Arthur were classy and well-made, for Arthur would always give money to Hannah to impress. He didn't want her to appear drab for the fancy Yanks and more importantly, Reg and Elizabeth Banks.

It bore no resemblance to the man who doled out meagre amounts of housekeeping for now that Pauline had left, Hannah had charge of the housekeeping purse. She knew Pauline had had far more than Arthur allowed her, but when she complained to Arthur that it wasn't enough, he'd barked back, 'Pauline was feeding a household. You have only yourself mainly because most evenings I eat out now.'

What he said was true, but there were more expenses to running a house than food costs. She was glad she earned a decent wage as a good proportion of it now went to supplement the housekeeping, for she wouldn't beg Arthur for more money.

And so she struggled through the days and endured the evenings, missing Josie's chatter and the talks she used to enjoy with Pauline.

Josie had urged her to visit often, but she wouldn't. A young couple out working all day would value their weekends and their evenings together. Not that they seemed to have much time alone. In the four months since Josie's marriage, Hannah had visited them just twice, though they'd been to see her far more often, and both times she found the house over-run with teenagers – students of Phil's.

Hannah had never visited Moseley before and knew little about it. It was Josie who told her of the separate thriving little village of the past very like Erdington, which long ago had been sucked into the conurbation of Birmingham.

The larger houses had almost all been made into flats and a great proportion of these were occupied by students. In the smaller terraced houses, the area was multicultural with Afro-Caribbean, Asian and West Indian people happily rubbing shoulders with their white neighbours. Josie loved it and she and Phil often shopped in the ethnic shops, buying ingredients the standard British shops didn't stock and bringing them home to experiment with exotic ethnic dishes. They often tried them out on Phil's students, many of whom would pop in for a meal when their funds were low. On Hannah's two visits, she got on well with them, though she sometimes found their attire strange.

The boys' hair generally was worn as long as the girls' and held back from their face with bands of woven cloth circling their heads. They were similarly dressed in ragged jeans and tops that looked as if they'd been bought large for them 'to grow into' and on their feet, from one extreme to the other, they wore either sandals or ungainly boots.

They sat in groups, drinking coffee from earthenware mugs and smoking endless cigarettes, while they spoke of the world's problems. In particular, they were concerned about conscription, which most lads had deferred until they'd finished their university course, and the CND march planned for Birmingham in the summer.

'CND?' Hannah said questioningly to Josie.

'Campaign for Nuclear Disarmament,' Josie told her.

Hannah wasn't much the wiser and Josie went on, 'You must know that Britain, as well as America and Russia, has nuclear weapons now?'

Hannah hadn't and was surprised Josie knew. But since she'd met Cynthia and through her, Phil and Peter, and they started going about together, Josie's eyes had been opened. She'd realised she had only the very basic education, never encouraged even to ask questions, and there were great gaps in her knowledge which Phil had been happy to fill in for her.

And now she said to Hannah, 'As well as having their own atomic weapons, they've loaned out nuclear launching pads to the Americans. Tried to hide them, of course, calling them RAF bases, but they're not. I mean, what is the point of us all pointing nuclear weapons at each other? They say it's a deterrent, but really they have the potential to blow the whole world up. Not,' she added, 'that I trust the Russians anymore. I mean, look at the ballistic missile they tested last year.'

Hannah didn't know what a ballistic missile was but she acknowledged that it didn't sound a very friendly thing to have about. She knew as well as any that in a future war, nuclear weapons could be used and that very few people would survive that. She gave a sudden shiver and said, 'So there's a march about it all, is there?'

'Well, we can't just leave it, can we?' Josie said. 'Cynthia is coming too and Peter. I mean, as Phil explained it to me this is our world now, for us and our children. Older people made a bit of a mess of it one way and another. I mean two world wars! But then ordinary people didn't have much of a say in any of it. Now they are demanding more. The voice of the people.'

Hannah didn't know whether governments ever listened to ordinary people, but she understood more of Josie's concern for a safer world when she uncharacteristically called in after work one evening in September.

Hannah had barely got in from work herself. Arthur had informed her that morning that he'd be eating out, a fairly normal occurrence now, and she had no desire to cook just for herself and was wondering what she fancied when the knock on the door came. 'I wanted you to be the first to know, well, after Phil, of course,' an excited Josie exclaimed as soon as the door was opened a crack. 'Oh Hannah, I'm expecting. I'm nearly three months gone.'

'Oh!' Hannah didn't have to ask if Josie was pleased, but she was still only twenty-one. She wondered if it had been planned. Did that matter? The child was much wanted, by Josie at least.

'Is Phil pleased too?' she said, drawing Josie inside.

'Oh yes. Like a dog with two tails,' Josie said. 'It's what we both wanted. To have our family while we're young enough to enjoy them.'

'You'll give up your job then?'

'Not yet, but I will for a while at least,' Josie said. 'Later, I might go back part-time.'

Josie ate with Hannah. She hadn't intended to, but later she was to say to Phil, 'I had to. She looked so lonely somehow and it seemed cruel to land on her with that news and then just leave her.'

It was a splendid meal. At Josie's house they ate a lot of spicy food mixed usually with rice or pasta. Hannah didn't do meals like that, but the pork chops which had seemed such a burden for her to cook for herself suddenly seemed an excellent idea for them both. Together they sat down to the wonderful dinner and discussed the baby and Hannah thought that maybe Josie's baby would be her consolation for not having a family of her own. Maybe she could share in the care of Josie's baby and she began to look forward to the birth possibly as much as Josie did.

Chapter Eighteen

The following Saturday morning, Hannah made her way to Gloria's house. Gloria had eventually been unable to withstand both Hannah and Amy's nagging and had gone to the doctor's who'd sent her straight to hospital for tests.

She was expecting to get the results on Friday, and Hannah had been tempted to phone that day, but felt it would be better to see her face to face and so, armed with a bunch of flowers, she went to visit her friend.

Amy met her at the door, a grave expression on her face. 'Gloria's in bed,' she said, taking the bunch of flowers from Hannah. 'She was taken bad again. I'm seeing to things at the moment, but she's not taking any more bookings.'

'What did the doctor say?'

A cloud passed over Amy's face. 'It's not good,' she said.

A little later Hannah looked down on the figure in the bed, grey-faced and shrunken so that she seemed swamped by the bedclothes, and would have known the news was bad just by looking at her. 'A tumour in her stomach,' Amy had said. 'They can do nothing for her.'

'Has Amy told you?' Gloria asked, her voice sounding weary.

Hannah's eyes filled with tears. She gave one brief nod. Gloria reached out and took her hand and Hannah sat down by the bed. 'Now don't you be upsetting yourself,' she said. 'Lord knows, I've had a good innings and I'm in pain, Hannah. I want to go. It will be a relief.'

Hannah couldn't speak. She felt choked by the tears she fought to control, the lump in her throat so large, it hurt to swallow. 'I've sent for my solicitor,' Gloria went on. 'To put my house in order. Doctor Simmonds said I haven't long. He can't put a timescale on it, but it's best to be prepared. Father Fitzgerald's coming tomorrow.'

Hannah couldn't believe she was hearing this. That this wonderful, lovely woman would soon not be here. She wanted to stamp her feet and scream and denounce everything and everyone, God, the Saints, doctors – everyone. None of them could keep this dear woman alive.

She sat by her bedside, took hold of her hand and told her how fond she was of her and how much she would miss her. She told her how grateful she was for Gloria taking her in that time when she'd been in such a state and the friendship and love that had subsequently grown between them. Tears rolled down her face as she spoke and down Gloria's, too, tears of memories shared, and filled with sadness that the time to say any of this was running out.

It was afterwards when Hannah was outside and the door had closed behind her that the real tears came, torrents of sobs making her whole body shudder. She turned away from home, knowing she couldn't face Erdington Village packed with shoppers, nor the empty house at the end of it.

She walked the length of Grange Road and there across Chester Road was Pype Hayes Park, drawing her like a magnet.

It was as she crossed the road that Vic Humphries saw her. He was returning to his car after visiting a patient in Chester Road when he saw Hannah. He stood and watched her for a few minutes and knew she was upset. He left the car where it was and followed her.

Hannah looked about the park in dismay. On this dry warm September Saturday, it was full of people. There were mothers with prams, others getting in a late game of tennis, children flooding the playground, youths kicking a ball about and others strolling with their arms around a girl.

Hannah looked around in panic. She wanted to be away from people. The few who'd passed her on Grange Road had looked at her askance, one had even stopped to ask if she was all right, but she'd shaken her head helplessly and ran on.

She saw the stream below at the edge of the park sparkling in the sun. While children were playing in it just below her, she was certain she could find some solitary spot if she followed it because it became marshier further on as she and Josie had once found to their cost.

Vic found her sitting on a rock above the stream sobbing as if her heart was broken. She was shaken with emotion, sodden and light-headed, and Vic was stirred with pity for her. She turned her blotched, puffy face to him as he called her and gave a cry of despair.

Vic couldn't help himself. 'Oh Hannah, don't give way like this,' he cried, as he enfolded her in his arms.

Hannah gave a sigh. It was not a contented one. She was too upset for that. It was a sigh almost of relief, a sigh that she was glad there was someone who could recognise her distress and try and comfort her, for she could hardly bear the pain of the imminent loss of her dear, dear friend. 'Hannah! Hannah! What is it? What has upset you so much?'

But though Vic asked, he'd already guessed, for he'd seen Doctor Simmonds just the previous evening at a medical function. He'd known Gloria had been sent for tests and asked Doctor Simmonds if he had any news. He had and shouldn't have shared it with Vic and wouldn't have done if he hadn't been a medical man. Vic asked, 'Have you been to see Gloria?'

The nod was barely perceptible, for Hannah's head was buried in Vic's shoulder, his arms were tight around her and his lips were inches from her hair, her eyes and her lips and he whispered, 'Oh my love, my love, my darling.'

'Vic, I . . .'

'Ssh. Darling, darling Hannah,' Vic said. 'If I could take this sadness away from you I would.'

'I know,' Hannah said, her voice a mere whisper. 'And thank you. No one can help, but it's good to know that you care.'

'Of course I care. My darling, I love you so.'

Hannah felt her whole body jerk. Oh, to have the love of this good, good man. 'Oh Vic,' she said, covering her face with her hands and crying afresh.

'Darling, please,' Vic pleaded. He knelt before her and pulled her hands from her face and kissed them. He kissed the tears from her cheeks, her eyes and finally her lips. Hannah moaned yearningly and she felt the resistance she'd initially built against this man and fought to retain crumble away to nothing. She clung to Vic when he would have released her for the kiss was easing the ache in her heart somewhat.

Vic could hardly believe that he was holding and kissing his beloved Hannah and when he tentatively touched her lips with his tongue, they parted immediately and Vic knew Hannah's longing matched his own. He felt the blood pound through his body and it brought an ache to his loins and his low moan was of pure desire.

Hannah's heart quickened at the sound and she knew she wanted this man, needed him, but unless she told him in some way, she knew he would take this no further.

Suddenly, two children splashed in the water in front of them and their mother's angry voice followed them. Hannah and Vic sprang apart. 'Vic,' Hannah said. 'I need you.'

'Oh, darling,' Vic sighed. 'How I've longed to hear you say those words. I have the car not far from here if you're sure.'

Hannah just nodded.

Vic wanted to catch her hand and claim her as his and go running up the bank like a child. He was walking on air, but instead, they had to walk sedately side by side with both their hearts pounding. Hannah's stomach was turning somersaults in anticipation and her effrontery in what she was allowing to happen, was looking forward to it happening.

As Vic let them both into the surgery and they stole up the stairs to the bedroom, he remembered he was only halfway through his visiting. But, he told himself, the other house calls could wait. He was on fire for Hannah and she for him and that fire could only be quenched one way and he knew it was going to be wonderful.

And it was wonderful and afterwards Hannah cried again, but those tears were of joy. She'd been truly loved by a man again. She was naked, as Vic was, as she'd been with Mike that once and never with Arthur. But she didn't want to think of Arthur, for whatever he was, she'd cheated on him and she felt a shudder of apprehension run through her body.

'Hannah, don't feel bad about this at all,' Vic said, but Hannah suddenly did. She was disgraceful. That day, she'd found out her dear friend was dying and to console herself, she'd behaved shamelessly, first kissing and canoodling in a public park and then making love to the man she'd thought only to be a friend. But despite the guilt, she felt sated, loved and cherished by the man who continued to whisper how much he loved her, adored her, how beautiful she was, how wonderful she'd made him feel. She felt utter sadness engulf her for much as she loved Vic and he loved her, she must give him up. But she couldn't face telling Vic yet, the man was still in the throes of passion, but she must make it clear to him first thing Monday morning.

* * *

Monday morning made things no easier though. Hannah had done her best. Racked with guilt, she'd told Vic that she'd been wrong on Saturday and though she had deep and sincere feelings for him, there must be no further intimacy between them. She said she was shamed both by what she had done and the time she'd chosen, the very day she'd found out the severity of Gloria's illness. 'I should have been racked by grief, not lust,' she said.

'You were.'

'Some grief,' she said disgustedly. 'Grief that could be eased by a session in bed with a man who was not my husband.'

'Hannah, talk sense. It happened because I was comforting you.'

'Oh, is that what they call it these days, comforting me?'

'Hannah, stop this sort of talk! Let's discuss it reasonably,' Vic pleaded.

'Vic, there's nothing to discuss – I'm married.'

'For God's sake! I know that,' Vic said bitterly. 'But not happily married.'

'There's nowhere in the wedding ceremony that talks of happiness,' Hannah told him. 'Nowhere that says it has to be an ingredient of marriage. If I'm unhappy, then I'm surely not the only one.'

'So you'll deny yourself any sort of life because of the words spoken by a priest?'

Hannah's eyes glistened with tears for what might have been and yet she replied, 'Yes, I must.'

Vic, moved by the tears in Hannah's eyes, suddenly gripped her hands and a weakness so affected Hannah's limbs at his touch that she was forced to sit down. All day, she had avoided Vic, avoided looking into his eyes and any opportunity where he could touch her. Even when she took the coffee in after surgery, she'd not sat near him at all.

Vic had assumed she was embarrassed and had let it go, but now it was lunchtime and they were in the flat on their own and Hannah was feeling very strange and the more Vic talked, the stranger she became. 'Hannah, darling, don't you realise how I love you? I've loved you for years and yet didn't recognise it at first.'

'Don't!' Hannah cried, attempting to pull her hands away, but Vic held on tight.

'Tell me you love me?' he pleaded.

'I do, I do.'

'Then, darling, we must discuss the future.'

'Haven't you listened to a word I've said? There can be no future for us,' Hannah said sadly. 'Our feelings don't come into it.'

Vic released Hannah's hands and sank on to the couch. 'Oh God, Hannah! What are we to do?'

His face was such a picture of anguish that Hannah felt an actual pain in her heart. Heartache, like the pain when her baby was removed from her and she let out a cry of grief.

But when Vic's arms came around to hold her, she pushed him off. 'Vic, listen,' she said. 'This is my problem. Much as I love you we must stop this madness now. I am giving notice, so that you can get someone else to help you and forget me. You deserve a girl of your own and the chance of a family and . . .'

'Damn it, Hannah! Stop this!' Vic cried angrily. 'Do you think I can let you walk out of my life like that? I love you.'

'But I can offer you nothing.'

'Maybe not yet. But please, don't talk of leaving me, getting another job. I couldn't bear not to see you at all.'

'Don't you think it would be best? Easier?'

'Perhaps, but I don't want it, Hannah. You have me at sixes and sevens now, I couldn't cope at all without you here.'

And Hannah knew that her life wouldn't be worth living without seeing Vic either. She hadn't enough to fill her life and without Vic, it would be worthless.

'Let's go on as we are,' Vic said. 'Just for now. I'll not force you to do anything you don't want, or feel you're not ready for. Just to be near you will be enough for me. Please, please, for pity's sake, don't abandon me.'

And Hannah couldn't and agreed to stay though she didn't know whether it was a sensible decision or not. However, soon the deterioration in Gloria took her mind off herself. She was glad to be needed at Gloria's bedside, for it kept her mind away from Vic and her confused feelings for him. She went most days to see her, either straight after work or later in the evening. In the early days and even now when Gloria was having a good day, she was always pleased to see her. The burden of care had fallen on Amy, with help from district nurses, and Hannah was glad to be able to lend a hand in practical ways like doing the shopping or taking washing to do at home.

Arthur couldn't understand Hannah's concern for

the old lady, but Josie and Angela could. She wrote to them both and Josie paid her a visit straight away, while Angela sent her a 'Get Well' card with a note inside saying she would see her at Christmas. Hannah was very pleased Angela did that. It showed that despite the way Arthur had raised her, the child was still capable of feeling and showing compassion and Hannah was heartened by that.

'Christmas,' Gloria mumbled when Hannah gave her Angela's message. 'I don't think I'll still be here.'

Hannah said nothing. She knew to try and jolly her along would only annoy the woman who realised the true state of her health.

Hannah felt immense sadness whenever she thought about Gloria's impending death. She cared for her so much, owed her such a lot, and knew she'd miss her terribly. Gloria wasn't always lucid. Sometimes her mind wandered, dulled and disorientated by drugs, and it reminded Hannah of her sister Frances's death.

And then, just before Angela came home for Christmas, Hannah met Elizabeth Banks one Saturday afternoon in the city centre, where she'd gone to do some selective shopping to try and tempt Gloria's flagging appetite with some delicacies. Hannah, what with working and visiting Gloria, hadn't seen Elizabeth for some months and was pleased to meet her. Elizabeth seemed equally pleased. 'You look well, my dear,' she said, clasping her hands warmly. 'Are you quite recovered now?'

'Recovered?'

'Yes, Arthur said you had that nerve trouble back and that was the reason you couldn't come to the firm's Christmas function this year.'

Oh, did he? Rage coursed through Hannah. She'd deny it, denounce him, show him up to be the vindictive liar that he was.

But before she was able to formulate the words, Elizabeth went on. 'Reg said what a damned nuisance it was. Amazing how many women suffer from nerves now. Still, you're better now. That's the main thing.'

The moment for Hannah to tell Elizabeth the truth was gone. They went for coffee together and there Elizabeth dropped another bombshell. 'Are you excited about going to a hotel for Christmas?'

'Pardon? What?'

'Oh dear,' Elizabeth said. 'Don't say I've done it again. I always seem to be putting my foot in it with you. Arthur obviously wished to surprise you and I've blown it again. I'm so sorry, my dear.'

I bet Arthur wants to surprise me, Hannah thought. But, she assured Elizabeth, it didn't matter that she'd let the cat out of the bag as it were and though her thoughts were churning inside her head she managed to steer the conversation into more settled waters, though she was determined to have the whole thing out with Arthur at the first opportunity.

She had to wait for Arthur because he had gone up to Angela's school to fetch her home for the Christmas holidays and Hannah had no intention of spoiling her first few days at home with a hint of acrimony. Angela was no fool, though, she knew her parents didn't get on, and was probably aware by now that it was unusual for parents to have separate bedrooms.

Arthur was anxious to show Angela the improvements he'd made to the sitting room, for now that Pauline had left, he'd told Hannah he was making the room over for Angela. 'She is growing up,' he'd said. 'She needs a room where she can invite her friends in.'

And he'd made a good job of it, Hannah had to admit. Like Angela's bedroom, no expense had been spared here either. A soft and thick Wedgwood blue carpet covered the floor and matched the curtains that covered the narrow French door that opened on to the garden. A modern gas fire stood in the grate with a cream sheepskin rug before the fender, and a coffee table between the two armchairs, which were in a darker blue with cream cushions. Either side of the chimney breast were wooden bookshelves and in the corner on a table stood a Dansette record player and the whole room was lit softly by rose-coloured lamps.

It was the first time Hannah had seen it completed, for Arthur had kept the door locked and the curtains drawn and much of the furniture had been delivered while she was at work, and she felt her mouth drop open in surprise. She would have been overcome with delight if she'd had such a room at her disposal and she looked at Angela who'd not said a word and wore a strange expression on her face.

Arthur hadn't seemed to notice. 'Now this here,' he said crossing to the table, 'isn't what it seems. It opens at the front, do you see, to store records. I didn't know your taste, but we'll take a run in to town to choose some for you and Santa Claus might have a television in his sack to put in here too. Now what do you think of that? It will of course have the new commercial channel you were so keen on us having.'

'It's . . . it's lovely, Daddy,' Angela said at last. 'Who's it for?'

'Why, you of course,' Arthur said. 'And any friends you care to invite in.'

'Daddy, I haven't any friends around here.'

'I don't mean from around here,' Arthur said dismissively. 'I didn't send you to a fine school to associate with riffraff. What about your friends from school? They could come for a day or two. There's always one or two anxious to come out with us at the weekends, but you've never asked any of them home.'

Angela's face was very red and Hannah knew she was upset about something. Eventually, she said, 'Daddy, I don't want you to be angry, but I couldn't invite friends here. They all have big houses, not in little streets like this either, but in their own grounds. They have servants, my two best friends have ponies and some even have their own swimming pools. If I asked them here, they'd think I lived in a slum. I could never hold my head up again.'

Hannah's gasp was audible and she saw the tic that signalled the onset of Arthur's temper beating in his temple. 'So,' he said in a voice Hannah had never heard him use to Angela. 'So. We're not good enough for you? Is that it?'

'No, it's not,' Angela cried, as angry as her father. 'And I never said it was that. But it's no good getting cross. It was your own fault. You sent me to that school and you must have known even the way they talk when they're out with us. You must have heard them and guessed where they lived. If we even lived in a bigger house somewhere else, it might help.'

But Hannah knew Arthur would never move. He was fond of the house and besides that, it was paid for. If he had to take on a high mortgage as well as Angela's fees, he couldn't manage. She knew the fees had increased dramatically when she'd gone into senior school the previous year, because he'd let it slip one evening. She knew Arthur just didn't have the money to provide the lifestyle Angela craved and yet he insisted on keeping her at a school where such things were the norm.

She could have told him she'd been afraid that such an event might happen and Angela would have been better going to a less illustrious Birmingham day school, or a grammar school if she proved clever enough, but she knew better than to comment and draw attention upon herself with Arthur in such a mood.

Arthur left the house straight after the strained and almost silent meal, something he never usually did on Angela's first few nights home, and when the door had slammed behind him, Angela looked at Hannah and said, 'He's really angry, I think.'

Hannah was always honest. She knew Arthur had put great store in preparing that room, not to mention the cost of it. She could even in a small way feel sorry for the acute disappointment he must have felt in Angela's reception of it.

'I think he was hurt more than angry.'

'Hurt?'

'Angela, he's spent ages planning that room, buying things for it, making it nice,' Hannah said. 'You seemed very ungrateful. I mean, I never heard the words "thank you" pass your lips.'

'You don't understand.'

'Oh, yes I do,' Hannah snapped. 'I don't have to visit your school or go out with your friends to know how people of that class are. Before I worked for Gloria, I worked in a large hotel and served people like that all the time. Your father is trying to make you into something that you're not. You are, to coin a phrase, like a fish out of water, not one thing or the other. But you'll just have to cope with it, Angela, because your father will never leave here – he can't afford to.'

'What do you mean?'

'You don't understand finance, Angela, and why should you at your age?' Hannah said. 'But I'll just say this house is paid for and because of it your father can afford your school fees and to treat you at the weekends, to buy you nice presents and pretty clothes and give you a generous amount of pocket money. He probably couldn't afford to if we moved.'

'So we're stuck here?'

'Yes we are, you little snob,' Hannah burst out angrily. 'And whatever you think, it's a fine house. God, Angela, if you want real slums, I can show them to you. They're teeming all over Birmingham. Maybe such a visit would make you thankful for what you have.'

'Why is everyone so horrid to me tonight?' Angela said plaintively. 'It makes me wish I'd never come home.'

'Oh, stop feeling sorry for yourself,' Hannah said hardheartedly. 'Come on, I'll fill a hot-water bottle and you cut along to bed. Things often look better in the morning.'

But nothing could make Hannah feel better when she eventually was able to pin Arthur down about the things he'd said to the Banks. It was just three days after Angela had come home and an uneasy truce lay between Arthur and Angela and Hannah knew it was not a good time, but it was the only time there was since Angela had been taken to Josie's to spend an evening with them.

'Yes I told the Banks you had bad nerves,' Arthur said when Hannah questioned him. 'What of it?'

'But . . . but, Arthur, you can't go around just saying what you like about people,' Hannah protested. 'Things that aren't even true! Surely you can see that?'

'Rather that than say my wife is a whore and a harlot and I can't stand to be seen with her in public.'

Before Vic, before Hannah's moral slip in not only allowing Vic to make love to her, but actively encouraging him to do so, this statement would have brought a strident denial of these claims from her lips. But this time she hesitated, not totally innocent now, and Arthur noticed the hesitation and his eyes narrowed in suspicion.

Hannah tried another tack. 'Elizabeth also told me that you'd booked us into a hotel for Christmas,' she said. 'I wish you'd said or asked. You know Josie and Phil are coming to dinner on Boxing Day.'

'My dear, you are going nowhere,' Arthur said. 'I've booked the hotel for Angela and myself only. We go on Christmas Eve and return the day after Boxing Day. These arrangements should not affect your plans in any way.'

Hannah leapt to her feet. 'Arthur, this is monstrous! Inhuman! You cannot separate me from my child on Christmas Day!'

'I can do whatever the hell I like,' Arthur said.

'Angela will jump at the opportunity, you'll see. To spend Christmas in a plush hotel is far better than at home. It will be something to boast of to those posh friends of hers that she is so anxious to impress.'

Hannah knew Arthur was right. Given the choice, she knew what Angela would say.

But the point was, it left her out on a limb. Determined that this Christmas she'd make a concerted effort to save her marriage, she'd not demurred at all when Josie had suggested that she and Phil spend Christmas Day with Phil's parents and Boxing Day with her, Arthur and Angela. Should she now say she'd changed her mind and please would they come and chase the loneliness of the day away for her? Surely Phil's parents would understand? After all, he had another brother and a sister.

However, she couldn't do that. Her pride, if nothing else, wouldn't let her. Pauline, then: could she muscle in on the festivities she was sharing with her sister, or should she throw herself on the mercy of Elizabeth Banks and tell her what a vindictive and vicious sod her husband was?

She knew none of these courses were open to her. She continued to cook mince pies, ice the cake, pour brandy over the puddings, wrap presents and write cards, but her heart was as heavy as lead.

She told no one she'd be alone that day. When Angela had asked, she said Gloria was so ill she'd decided to spend the day with her, but was warmed by Angela's concern. Angela had seen Gloria by then and been shocked by her appearance and accepted Hannah's explanation.

But no way would Hannah impose on the quiet Christmas that Amy and Tom planned to spend with Gloria. She now tired easily and it was highly unlikely she'd last the day out and Hannah felt she couldn't push her way in there, using Gloria's illness an excuse to cover up her own loneliness.

You are a grown woman, she told herself sternly. You have a beautiful home decorated for the festive season, cupboards full of food and drink, a warm hearth and a television for company and you will spend the day alone like many more and not moan about it either.

Hannah stuck it out as long as she could before she rang Vic. She'd tried hard. After she waved a tearful goodbye to Angela, she'd got herself ready for Midnight Mass, calling in first on Amy and Tom, now installed in Gloria's house to be on hand for her over the festive period where there would be fewer visits from district nurses. But she didn't see Gloria who'd already gone to bed.

'Tucked up snug as a bug in a rug she is now,' Amy said. 'But don't worry, I'll see she gets your presents in the morning.'

'I could call in.'

'Oh no,' Amy said. 'She wouldn't expect that, not when you have a family to see to. We'll just have a quiet Christmas on our own. Really it's all she's fit for just now.'

Even Midnight Mass didn't soothe her battered soul that night and she strolled back through the quiet city streets with a cold, depressing drizzle seeping into her coat. At home, the silence hit her and the decorated house and tree and smell of seasonal food seemed to mock her. What was the point of cooking that lovely turkey she'd got from the butcher for herself alone? Well, she wouldn't, she decided, she didn't care what she ate. Christmas for her was cancelled that year.

But at eleven o'clock Christmas morning, Hannah phoned Vic. She knew he was on call, that much he'd told her so she knew she'd be able to contact him, but she didn't know if he'd made any further plans. She'd deliberately not asked him about Christmas, in case he should question her, but she didn't care about any of that now. She needed to hear a friendly voice.

Vic, not thinking Hannah would call, was brisk and professional at first, until he recognised her voice and then he assumed something was wrong with her, or Arthur, or Angela.

'No, no,' Hannah said. 'They're not here, none of them. That's the point.'

'What is?'

Hannah began to explain, telling Vic how Arthur had booked himself into a hotel, but her voice broke in the telling.

But she'd said enough. 'Do you mean you're there in the house all alone?'

'Yes.'

'You poor love,' Vic said and the sympathy in his voice caused tears to run down Hannah's cheeks. 'And what a swine your husband is.'

There was silence on the other end of the phone and Vic said, 'Are you crying?'

Hannah made an effort to control herself. 'A bit,' she admitted.

'Hannah, what do you want of me?'

'I need you, Vic. I didn't realise how much. Will you come?'

Vic paused. 'Do you know what you're saying, Hannah?'

'Yes. Yes, I know. Will you come?'

'I'll come and fetch you,' Vic said. 'But I must stay here because of the phone.'

'You had no plans at all?'

'None,' Vic said and elected not to tell her of the Christmas tea he was supposed to be taking with his family and the two emergency numbers printed outside the surgery that he would remove before collecting her.

He'd phone his parents, he knew they'd understand. It wouldn't be the first time he'd missed a family celebration. 'You wouldn't believe so many people were ill at Christmas,' his mother had remarked one year.

'I don't think they do it on purpose, Mother,' Vic had said with a laugh.

'No, I know that, but you know what I mean.'

And of course he knew what she meant. Vic's parents were immensely proud of their doctor son and not a word of censure would ever pass their lips about any area of his work. In a way, Vic felt bad that he was exploiting this aspect and yet for Hannah he knew he would put his whole life in jeopardy. 'Are you quite sure this is what you want?' Vic asked anxiously when they got back to his house and Hannah took off her coat and hung it up in the hall.

Hannah thought back to Arthur telling everyone she

was suffering from 'nerves' and then taking Angela away to a hotel for Christmas without her and said she was totally sure and she'd held Vic's hand tight and led the way up the stairs.

Chapter Nineteen

The following morning, Boxing Day, Hannah expected to be filled with shame, but instead she felt as if she was alive with joy as Vic drove her home. Josie, visiting later that afternoon with Phil, was puzzled about Hannah's evident happiness, especially after she was told what Arthur had done. 'Were you by yourself all day?' she asked.

Hannah didn't answer directly. 'It was all right,' she said. 'I had plenty to do.'

Her face flushed slightly as she remembered the hours spent in Vic's arms, the gentle lovemaking in his bed that left her lifted to heights of exquisite joy so that she cried out over and over and afterwards fell asleep in blissful contentment. She wished she could tell Josie all about it and might have done if Phil hadn't been with her.

Once she would have poured her heart out to Gloria, but that avenue too was closed to her. She would write to Tilly. She wouldn't be shocked, or even surprised. She'd almost been waiting for something like this to happen.

But all that was for later. Today was for Josie and

Phil. She cooked the turkey and brought out the best tablecloth, crystal glasses and a cracker beside each plate. 'I didn't bother for myself yesterday,' Hannah said, although she'd had a fairly festive meal with Vic. That had been thanks primarily to his mother, who'd brought her son a cooked chicken on Christmas Eve to ensure he didn't starve to death entirely. She wished he had a nice wife to look after him and said so often, but he seemed to take no interest in any girl his mother introduced him to.

Hannah made a more than decent meal for the pair of them, which Vic, used to scratch meals for himself, was quick to praise. Nothing marred the perfection of the first day and night they spent together, not even the two house calls he had to make which were, he said, mainly due to overindulgence.

'You did right,' Josie said. 'Let's pretend today is Christmas Day and yesterday never happened.'

Ah, as if that could be. Hannah recalled every detail of it, the delicious comfort of being held in a loved one's arms. She remembered every inch of Vic's face, the brown hair that refused to be slicked back and insisted on falling over his forehead, his deep brown eyes which crinkled with laughter, his chiselled nose and his wide, generous and very kissable mouth. She loved his smile, his sense of humour, even his smell, so essentially male, and his touch sent her wild.

She didn't know it was possible to love someone as much as she loved Vic; so much that she longed to be with him, even as she sat at the table with her beloved Josie and Phil. But she forced herself to be still and listen to their plans for the future. But even as she sat and discussed names for the baby, due in the spring, her mind was on Vic and the flat, their lovenest above the surgery.

'Did you think Hannah a bit odd tonight?' Josie asked Phil as they drove home in the car Phil had bought as soon as he realised he was to become a father.

'Hmm. Maybe,' he replied. 'Can't wonder at it really. On her own at Christmas while her husband and daughter are elsewhere. Funny do whichever way you look at it.'

'I wish she'd leave him,' Josie said vehemently. 'Living on her own would be better than living with him. He enjoys tormenting her.'

Phil glanced at her. 'Why does he? Why did he marry if he felt like that?'

'He didn't dislike her at first,' Josie explained, 'that came later, though he was never what I'd term "warm" towards her. I didn't want her to marry him in the first place. In a way, she did it for me, to provide us both with a home. I know sometimes it's been hell on earth for her.'

'But why?' Phil asked and Josie told him from the beginning.

'He punished her all her married life for that one slip,' Josie said to Phil as she finished her tale. 'But the worst punishment of all was keeping her and Angela apart, as far as he can, that is. Over the years, he's caused her terrific pain.'

'It's incredible,' Phil said. 'As far as I'm concerned Hannah was just another victim of war.'

'I agree,' Josie said. 'But that's not how Arthur sees

it and even Hannah is riven with guilt every so often.'

Phil stopped the car and helped Josie out of it. 'Don't worry so much,' he said at last when they were inside their own house and he was trying to coax life into the nearly-dead fire they'd left banked up with slack till their return. 'After all, however Hannah sees herself, she wasn't exactly unhappy or down today, was she?'

'No,' said Josie thoughtfully. 'That's what I found so strange. I would have expected her to be sad, even upset. Instead, it was as if she was lit up by some inner excitement.'

Hannah couldn't have put it better herself. Sometimes the happiness would bubble up inside her making her want to burst into song or skip around the house like a two-year-old. Arthur and Angela returned jubilant from their holiday and if either had expected Hannah to be depressed or short-tempered with them, they were disappointed. She greeted them both warmly, thrilled when Angela threw her arms around her and hugged her tight and said she'd enjoyed it all, but she wished Hannah could have come too.

More and more, as Angela grew up, she'd found the situation between her parents odd, especially when she compared with other girls' – not that she ever discussed personal matters. Many of the girls, nearing adolescence, had also drawn closer to their mothers and Angela often felt left out. She hardly knew Hannah. Yet there were things that she'd love to tell her about that she could never discuss with her father.

She'd once asked her father on a weekend visit if he could bring her mother along the next week, partly because she wanted to see her and partly because her friends thought it odd that she never came. But her words drove Arthur into a monumental rage and he'd then sulked for the entire weekend and didn't visit at all the next one.

She wouldn't risk that reaction again by mentioning her mother's name, but for all that, she was glad that she didn't seem at all upset by them leaving her all alone at Christmas time.

Josie wanted Hannah and Angela to spend New Year with her, but both refused. Angela had a letter waiting for her when she returned from the hotel inviting her to spend the rest of the holiday, including New Year's Eve, with a girl called Hillary Masters. She lived on the outskirts of York in one of the houses Angela had told her father about when she came home. Hillary's house stood in its own grounds, with access to a private lake, which her father took his yacht out on. Hillary and her brothers had their own ponies and Hillary had promised to teach Angela to ride. In the letter she said she was longing to see Angela again and Angela herself was wild to go.

Arthur was displeased with the letter and would have liked to have forbidden her to go, but he'd refused her little in her life and anyway didn't think he could cope with the tantrums and sulks if he was to put his foot down. Much to Angela's surprise, her mother seemed to know just how she felt and urged her daughter to go if she wanted to and to phone straight away and make arrangements.

Hannah felt a little guilty that she was encouraging Angela to do this in order that she could spend time with Vic. But Angela wasn't aware of this and was heartened by her mother's encouragement. Her father seemed to want her with him all the time and much as she loved him, she was changing as she grew older and sometimes wanted to meet with people her own age.

In actual fact, Hannah was dying to return to work, which she did the day after Angela left for York. She was longing to see Vic again. To hear his voice. To be near to him. And he so obviously felt the same, for barely was she through the front door than Vic had her in his arms. 'Oh, my darling. My darling. I have ached for you the last few days.'

The kiss was ardent and Hannah felt her senses reeling as she realised that the love she had for Vic was even deeper and stronger than the love she'd had for Mike Murphy. She'd loved him in the careworn days of Britain at war, when time was precious, to be snatched at and enjoyed, for any moment might be one's last.

Their love for each other had been new and tender, an awakening of emotions. But it was passionate too and they cared for one another. Had Mike survived the war, Hannah thought that their love would probably have deepened through their life together, as they brought up young Michael and maybe brothers and sisters of his.

But this feeling for Vic, that she'd denied and shied away from, was like an explosion inside her. Since the Christmas Day and night that they'd spent together, she'd known she'd never love another besides this man and if he was to walk out of her life, it wouldn't be worth living.

Hannah knew that Arthur would be out over the

rest of the holiday. In fact, unless Angela was there, he was seldom in now and when he announced that he was off to Scotland for a couple of days over the New Year, she was delighted. Even later, when she found out it had been a company thing for those in the upper ranks of management to be put up in a Scottish hotel for Hogmanay and she'd been invited too, she didn't care, for she knew she would be spending the time with Vic instead.

And she did, cuddled in his arms, and as 1958 drew to a close, Vic pulled Hannah closer to him and raised his glass. 'Let 1959 be our year,' he said.

'Oh, yes.'

But even as she spoke and their glasses chinked together, Hannah knew even for the sake of her own happiness and that of Vic, she couldn't just walk away from everything else. 'I wouldn't like anything to happen before Josie's baby is born in March,' she said. 'And then Angela is to be confirmed in June. I wouldn't want to miss that. We are getting on better than ever before now and she's started to ask my advice on things. Maybe if I was to leave Arthur and explained it to her properly, perhaps going to the school and seeing her there, I might not lose contact with her totally. After all, she's only here for the holidays now.

'Then of course there's Gloria. I couldn't go anywhere without . . .'

'She won't live much past spring,' Vic said. 'I was talking to her doctor. He's amazed she's hung on so long, but her time is really running out now.'

Gloria's imminent death was the one blot on Hannah's horizon, the one thing that could depress her. And yet sometimes Gloria seemed to be almost back to her old self, in her manner at least. These were only short bursts of energy, but then she was astute and forthright as ever.

A week into the new year, Hannah visited at such a time. 'What's got into you, girl?' Gloria demanded as she walked in.

'What do you mean?'

'You're like the cat that's got the cream,' Gloria said. 'It's like there's a light shining behind your eyes.'

Hannah was nonplussed at how to answer. 'Well, I . . . I don't . . . I'm fine.'

'I'll tell you what I think,' Gloria said, leaning forward in the bed. 'I think you are in love. That's what I think.'

She watched the blush rise in Hannah's face and smiled in satisfaction. 'Is it the doctor chap?'

Useless to deny it, Hannah thought, and nodded. 'And does he love you like you so obviously love him?'

'Oh, yes.'

'You know, Hannah, I often think of the man I rejected to marry another with money to secure my future and I wonder if I made the right choice. I've had a good life, none better, and I'm not complaining, but I was only thinking the other day that I've never been loved, truly loved, by a man. And then there were no children in the marriage. Maybe that would have satisfied me, like it satisfies many women. I never felt the lack of children till you came into my house. You weren't the only girl I'd helped, but you were the one I felt most drawn to. I wish I'd had a daughter like you, Hannah.'

'I wish that too,' Hannah said quietly.

'All I'm saying is, my life is now nearly over,' Gloria

went on. 'Don't go all sad on me now, Hannah. There are things to say and not much time left. Life is too short for regrets. One day you'll turn around and Angela will be grown and gone her own way and what will you have? A loveless marriage to a man you can hardly stand who enjoys tormenting you. That is no future for anyone. If you've found a man that loves you and that you love, go for it. Forget convention and the Catholic Church. Few know what your life is really like behind your own four walls.'

Go for it! It was Gloria's blessing for Hannah to take her stab at happiness. Oh, how she would miss that wise old lady.

And yet for the moment they had to be careful. Not by word or deed could they let people have suspicions of their association. And none did, though many had commented on Hannah's good spirits, her friendly smile and general happiness. 'Proper tonic to come here,' one old man commented. 'Makes you almost feel better to see someone so cheerful.'

'Put the doctor out of business if you're not careful,' said another with a dry laugh.

For Hannah, these dismal, dark and cold winter days were beautiful and she felt warmed from the inside because she was loved; loved and wanted.

Gloria Emmerson died on 3rd February 1959, the same day that it was announced on the wireless that Buddy Holly had died in a plane crash and also the day that Hannah first realised she might be pregnant.

Amy phoned through the news of Gloria's death. Hannah'd been in the kitchen, working things out on the calendar, and had just realised with a slight lurch of her heart that she should have had a period on the 6th January and now a month later there was still no sign. It must have been Christmas when she conceived, she thought. It had been the only time, apart from the first time, when they'd had sex without using contraceptives. Vic had insisted on that afterwards, but maybe it was a case of shutting the door after the horse had bolted.

Part of Hannah was worried, for she knew stormy waters lay ahead, and yet part of her was elated, for now the die was cast, the path set.

But for the moment, it was Gloria's death and funeral that took precedence over everything and she resolved not to tell Vic yet. She shelved her own problems for the moment to give the woman she loved the type of funeral she deserved.

Hannah gazed with stupefaction at the solicitor. 'There must be some mistake,' she said.

When she'd been asked to attend the reading of Gloria's will, she'd assumed that Gloria had left her some keepsake. She had some nice pieces of jewellery which Hannah had often admired, but never had she imagined that Gloria had left her the house.

She glanced at Josie and Amy to each side of her, who'd both been left a sizeable settlement. Angela sat slightly behind and to her, Gloria had gifted some beautiful pendants, necklaces, bracelets and rings. Josie remembered the sapphire pendant Gloria had given to her on her tenth birthday which was still one of her most prized possessions.

'No mistake I assure you, Mrs Bradley.'

'But isn't there anyone else?'

'I have no idea,' the solicitor said. 'I believe there were few, if any, close relations, but the fact remains, Mrs Emmerson wished you to have the house and that's that as I understand it.'

There was nothing more to say. Hannah knew if Arthur had been present there would have been plenty said. He'd been furious when Angela and Hannah had been invited to the reading of the will the same day that Reg had called a board meeting that he dared not miss. He had expected a small bequest to them both and intended to strip Hannah of hers fairly sharpish. Not in his wildest imaginings had he thought Hannah would be left Gloria's house. He wasn't a bit pleased about it. In fact, he was blisteringly angry and Hannah was glad that they were within their own four walls and there was no one to witness his tirade, not even Angela, for Josie's husband Phil had run her straight back to school.

'The woman was obviously not of sound mind, giving one thousand pounds to Josie and that woman next door, a house to you and a few tawdry pieces of jewellery to my daughter.'

'She was perfectly of right mind,' Hannah retorted angrily. 'And the jewellery she gave Angela is not tawdry – anything but. I should imagine Gloria thought Angela would always be provided for.'

She looked Arthur steadily in the eye as she spoke and he recoiled slightly from the look and then snapped out, 'I hope you are not insinuating anything by that remark. You are adequately clothed, fed and housed.

You have no room for complaint. I even let you continue to work, though the wives of most of my colleagues don't and many think it odd.'

'Well, I wouldn't know what they think, would I?' Hannah said testily. 'I'm never in a position to meet them anymore and yet I know we've both been invited to functions. What do they think, Arthur, that I'm some blubbering nervous wreck languishing at home? Don't any of them express surprise that someone who suffers so badly from nerves can hold down a job at all?'

'This is why I don't take you to things,' Arthur cried. 'You embarrass me with your ability to make scenes.'

'I've never embarrassed you.'

'That's surely for me to know.'

'It's your telling lies about me that would embarrass you,' Hannah said. 'That's why you won't let me go with you, it's because they'd find out what a liar you are.'

'This discussion is getting us nowhere,' Arthur said dismissively, 'and is not in any case what we began talking about. What do you intend to do with Gloria's house?'

'Do with it?'

'Yes, do with it,' Arthur repeated, accentuating every word as if Hannah was an imbecile. 'It's stupidity to keep two houses. You must sell it of course.'

'I have no intention of selling it.'

'Come, come, Hannah! You know on marriage your property became mine, so I can insist you sell it.'

Hannah wasn't sure of the legal system regarding anything she had belonging to Arthur; the situation had never arisen before. But she knew in this case the house was solely and totally hers because the solicitor had explained it to her when he pressed a sealed letter into her hand while she was still reeling from the news that she was a home-owner. 'This is from Mrs Emmerson who was most insistent that we give the letter to you after the will was read.'

Hannah hadn't opened it then. She knew the words of her friend whose loss she was still coming to terms with would reduce her to tears and she had the urge to be alone before she opened it. And her instincts had been right:

Dear Hannah

I am leaving you my house. I know you've always loved it, but I'm not leaving it to you for that reason, but because I believe many years ago, I did you a disservice in encouraging you to marry Arthur Bradley. Hannah, my dear, dear friend, you have suffered for years from rejection and betrayal and downright mental torture. I regret having any part in it. This is to try and redress the balance, Hannah, for I would hate you to be forced to stay with Arthur because you have nowhere to go.

There is only one thing you cannot do to the house, and that is to sell it. You can live in it yourself, or rent it out, but if, in the next ten years, you try to sell it, it will revert to Josie. I am determined that Arthur will not benefit from the sale of my house and that is why it is a gift to you alone.

You are still young and desirable and you deserve to be loved. Grasp life with both hands and before

it is too late, have a chance of happiness.
With all my deepest love
Gloria

The tears dropped onto the paper blurring some of the words, but it didn't matter. She knew what Gloria was saying and she intended to leave Arthur and live in her house with Vic, but not yet, not till Josie's baby was born.

Her baby, Vic's baby, she intended to keep and bring up herself and this time she would allow nothing to separate them. Her child's parents might not be married, but that wouldn't matter. He or she would be surrounded by love. She'd talk to Angela. She was too young to fully understand that she might have fallen in love with someone else, but Hannah would do her level best to explain it to her.

So, with these thoughts still running around in her head, Hannah faced Arthur and said, 'You have no claim on this house. It was given to me as a gift. I am unable to sell it anyway for ten years and if I try, it will revert to Josie.'

His outrage was frightening to see. His whole face seemed to contort. It took on a reddish, purple hue and his furrowed brow glistened with sweat, his nostrils flared out, and spittle formed around his mouth.

'You're a pair of filthy conniving bastards,' Arthur spat out. 'Don't think you'll get away with it either of you. Christ, one day I'll do for you, you stinking whore, see if I don't. As for the other old bag, it's a good job she's bloody dead, that's all I can say.'

'Arthur, there's no need for this,' Hannah protested.

'There's every need, you fucking whore!' Arthur screamed. 'What are you anyway but a pile of shit? You and her together, a couple of slimy fucking buggers trying to do me out of what is rightfully mine.'

'How in God's name can it be rightfully yours?' Hannah asked in amazement. She was becoming angry. What gave Arthur the right to act like this, spewing out his venom in obscene words?

Arthur leapt forward and grasped Hannah's arms. She struggled, but was held like a vice. Arthur really appeared to have lost control. Filthy invective was spat into her face, in a stream. 'Fucking wanker, filthy trollop. Sodding stupid tart . . .' and on and on Arthur went until Hannah could stand no more and, with an almighty heave, she freed her arms and turned from Arthur, intending to make for the door.

His grip on her arm as he yanked her back was vicious. 'Where the sodding hell do you think you're going when I'm talking to you?'

She shook his arm off. 'Don't you dare do that to me!' she cried. 'You're talking to me? Don't make me laugh. You're yelling at me and I'll stand no more of it.'

'You'll stand what I say. I'm your husband.'

'Yes, more's the pity.'

The punch took her by surprise, stunning her for a moment or two, but then she was upon him with her nails scoring his face and feet kicking out at him. When his arms went around her in a grip she knew she couldn't break, she brought her knee up sharply into his groin and he loosed her and fell to the floor with a groan.

She felt no sympathy for him and turned away, only

stopping to pick up her bag and coat before stepping into the night. She knew there was little likelihood of Arthur following her because he craved respectability and would be horrified at the neighbours knowing their business.

Hannah hurried on, her coat collar turned up, her head down, glad of the dark night that hid her battered face from view, and she let herself into Gloria's house with a sigh of relief. She drew the heavy curtains before she turned lights on, not wanting Amy to think intruders were next door and feel obliged to investigate, because she'd hate her to see what Arthur had done to her face. One eye was almost closed and her nose had bled down her face and spattered her blouse and when Hannah felt gingerly around her mouth with her tongue, some of her teeth seemed loose. She wasn't surprised because she'd tasted blood in her mouth and she bathed carefully at her cut lip, glad that the following day was Sunday and she hadn't to go to work and face Vic.

Everything ached when she woke next morning and when she had a bath to help her aching body, she was shocked by the mass of bruises. The massive black one on her arm she could remember getting, but she was covered with others. Obviously Arthur's fists had made their mark, but she'd been so involved in lashing out at him that she hadn't noticed at the time.

She spent a lazy day resting her aching limbs, watching a lot of television and bathing her face often. She thought sometime through the day that Arthur might seek her out, because he knew where she'd be, well aware she'd never travel to Josie's with her face in such a mess. She waited in some trepidation, but he never came near.

On Monday morning, still without a word or sign from Arthur, she returned to the house after she knew he'd have left for work. Then in clean clothes, she made up her face with care.

She thought she'd done a good job, but Vic was immediately shocked on seeing her. 'What happened to you?'

She sighed. 'A lot. We need to talk, Vic.'

'Did Arthur do that to your face?'

'Not now, Vic. There isn't time. There's a queue of people outside. We'll talk at lunchtime.'

And so the day began and because Hannah knew the patients would be curious and because she didn't want them to form the correct assumptions and start speculating on the reason for it, she had her story ready. She told a few selected for their ability to gossip about stupidly tripping over the hearth rug and catching her face on the hearth and accepted their sympathy.

Vic was told the truth that lunchtime and was flabbergasted at Arthur's reaction. 'Arthur loves money,' Hannah said. 'Apart from Angela, it's all he really cares about and he saw Gloria's house only in terms of how much he could sell it for. But she knew him, knew how his mind would work and outfoxed him. That's what he couldn't stand.'

'It still seems excessive, to lash out over that.'

'He probably thought I was in on the whole thing,' Hannah said. 'I wasn't at all. You could have knocked me down with a feather. I thought she might leave me a few choice bits of jewellery, but certainly not her house. You see, Vic, Gloria knew about us. I didn't tell her, she just guessed, and she virtually told me to leave Arthur. She told me to grab at happiness while I could, but she also knew I'd find it difficult to leave Arthur because I had nowhere to go. That house I live in is his alone, a gift from some long-lost uncle. I don't think he could be forced to sell it, even if we separated legally. These things take time anyway. I'd have to have somewhere to live meantime.'

'You mean . . .?'

'I mean I love you and want to marry you. We can't marry, but we can live together.'

'That'll suit me.'

'Will it suit your parents?'

'They'll be fine about it,' Vic said, knowing they wouldn't. He was the son they constantly boasted of, the one who'd got somewhere. They would like a big fancy wedding for him, with photographs of it in the paper, so that they'd be the talk of the town. And his bride – a beautiful young woman, they imagined, from a good family who entered the married state as a virgin, not a woman estranged from her husband, who'd already had children.

'As soon as Josie is over the birth of the baby and I can explain to her, I'm ready to leave,' Hannah said. 'And Vic, there's a reason for the rush.' At this she put her hands across the table and clutched at his. 'You're going to be a daddy.'

Vic felt shock waves go all through him. He wanted to be a father, yes, eventually, but not this way. It must have been that time at Christmas, he thought. What a bloody, bloody mess! He'd taken precautions since, when they'd made love sometimes at lunchtimes and sometimes when he'd visited Hannah in the evenings after Arthur had gone out on business of his own. He wondered if Hannah knew it was against the law for a doctor to have a relationship with a woman patient. Probably not. But he did. God, if he was struck off through this! It wouldn't only be the end of his life, but his parents', who'd gone through so much to put him where he was.

And yet he loved Hannah, loved her so much that just to look at her caused him to catch his breath.

At least this way she could shillyshally no longer, he thought. He felt a thrill of excitement as he realised she'd be his and soon. Whatever was to come afterwards they would face together. It wasn't the way they'd planned things, but then life didn't always go to plan.

But his silence had been noted. 'Aren't you just the tiniest bit pleased?' Hannah asked, her voice tentative, unsure and afraid.

'Of course I'm pleased, darling,' Vic said. 'I am delighted but just stunned by the news.' He left his seat and crossed to the other side of the table and put his arms around Hannah and held her tight.

'I want this baby, Vic.'

'Of course you want this baby,' Vic said vehemently. 'It will be the most loved and wanted baby in the whole world and I love you too with all my heart.'

Hannah was satisfied. As she smiled and pulled Vic towards her and kissed him long and hard, Vic knew that he'd go through any trial in the world if he was to gain Hannah at the end of it.

Chapter Twenty

Josie's baby son, called Phillip after his father, was born at home in the early hours of a mid March day that definitely thought it was springtime.

Hannah, who'd been there most of the night, heard the dawn chorus join their chirping and whistling to Phillip's cries and let a yawn escape her. And yet she didn't regret being there to help Josie, only too aware that in six more months she'd be doing the selfsame thing. Soon, once Josie was on her feet, she'd explain it all to her, visit Angela at school before they broke up for the Easter holidays and tell her and then the way would be clear for her to leave Arthur.

But for now there was a new baby to love and Josie to make a fuss of. Phil thought his wife had done something absolutely splendid. Hannah saw the look of awe on his face as he held his small son and decided to go home. The midwife would do all that was necessary to make Josie and the baby comfortable. She was, she decided, superfluous and she guessed Josie and Phil really wanted to be alone where they could gaze on the child their love had produced till their hearts were content.

Hannah felt no contentment going home. Since the night Arthur had lashed out, the two had trod an uneasy line. They'd been polite when they'd had to speak, but that was all. Arthur hadn't been sure that Hannah hadn't left for good when she'd walked out and was surprised how little he'd cared. He'd certainly not expected to see her in the kitchen cooking his tea when he arrived home on Monday evening. 'So, you're back.'

As that was evident, Hannah made no reply. 'Tantrum over now?' Arthur taunted.

'Tantrum nothing!' Hannah cried. 'I'll not be treated like a punchball for you or anyone else either.'

'That was regrettable,' Arthur conceded and added, 'but in a way, Hannah, you asked for it.'

'I asked for nothing,' Hannah spat out, 'and the whole thing was just because you couldn't get your greedy paws on Gloria's money.'

'Perhaps I had reason,' Arthur said. 'I am the man of the house, a fact you seem to have overlooked, and all money should come to me. I foolishly allowed you to keep your wages when you began that ridiculous job at the doctor's. It's given you ideas above your station.'

'Arthur, stop being so bloody pompous!'

'Oh, pompous is it to assume my rightful place as head of the household?'

'Yes, it is. We're no longer in the Victorian era. And what household? Me – that's all. Angela is never here and you certainly do exactly as you want with her when she's home.'

But Arthur had seen a change in Angela, a softening towards the mother he'd sought to teach her to ignore and scorn. As she grew up, he could imagine that she'd defer to her more and more, to ask her opinion, to talk to her. Her suggestion for her mother to travel to school to see her some weekends had shocked him to the core. She'd never made the suggestion again, but that in itself made it no easier.

Hannah, too, had noticed a difference in her daughter. She was a pre-adolescent and the pull between them was growing stronger, for all Arthur had tried to rip it asunder, and she rejoiced in it and hoped that she might be able to make Angela see why she couldn't live with her father anymore.

But to live with him even temporarily, she had to make a stand. 'I don't care who you are, or what role you want to assume,' she said heatedly. 'You lift your hand to me again and I'll go and not come back.'

It was on the tip of Arthur's tongue to say, 'Go then! See if I care.'

But what if Angela was to find out he'd virtually thrown Hannah out? And the damned woman now had a house to go to – and a better house than this one, he had to admit. What if Angela was to take sides with her mother? Even live with her in the holidays? No, he'd never tolerate that. The child was his. So he said to Hannah, 'If you do not provoke me, it will not happen again.'

Hannah took such care not to provoke Arthur that she seldom spoke to him at all and though they'd never been lively conversationalists, the strained silence between them became very wearying. She was always glad when he'd taken himself off for the night and she could ring Vic. Just to hear his voice soothed her and they'd make arrangements to meet later and Hannah lived for those moments.

Visiting Josie and seeing her with young Phillip also helped Hannah. Josie was proving to be a natural mother and Phillip a placid, easy-going baby who slept and fed well. 'I watched Pauline with Angela,' Josie explained when Hannah praised her. 'Practising on Angela has helped me a great deal.'

Hannah couldn't help feeling a pang of guilt. Josie should have learnt things from me, she couldn't help thinking. But she smiled at her, not wanting Josie to feel bad about what she'd said, and she silently fought a feeling of resentment towards Pauline that she'd not felt in years.

'I sent Pauline a card to tell her about the baby,' Josie said, 'and she sent a lovely card back with a couple of matinée jackets and romper suits.'

'That was kind of her,' Hannah said. 'I haven't seen or heard from her since your wedding. I keep meaning to write, but I never get around to it.'

But in her heart of hearts, Hannah knew why she'd not contacted Pauline. Every waking moment now she thought of Vic and sometimes he even invaded her dreams and she didn't know how she'd write to anyone without betraying herself, so she'd cut herself off from everyone for the time being. With Josie it was different. She was so besotted with her son that she didn't notice the change in Hannah and Hannah so obviously adored Phillip. Holding him brought back the bittersweet memories of baby Michael, for because of the depression following her birth, she had few memories of Angela at the same age.

With Phillip, it was totally different. He looked nothing like Michael, with the black hair he'd inherited from his father and Josie's deep brown eyes and snub nose and full mouth, but still to hold his small body close and rock him to sleep brought her immeasurable comfort. She longed for her own baby, though she was frightened of the birth, frightened she'd reject her baby as she did Angela. Vic said her fears were ridiculous. He said she'd have the best care in the world and he'd personally take on her welfare, but still she worried.

Soon, she thought, I'll tell Arthur and once it is out in the open, that's it and I'll be able to confide in Josie. 'When?' Vic asked urgently. 'This isn't something you can just leave, Hannah.'

'I know,' Hannah said. 'It's just I can't find the right moment. I mean, is there a right moment for hitting a man with that? I'm leaving you, oh and by the way, I'm having a child, not yours of course, but someone else's?'

In the end, she decided to tell Josie first. Phillip was three weeks old and she watched him tugging at Josie's breasts, his tiny hands kneading at her, and it brought that remembered ache to her own breasts. She wrapped her arms protectively around them and envied her niece.

'Are you all right?' Josie asked and misinterpreting the gesture added, 'You're not cold?'

'Oh no, my goodness, no,' Hannah assured Josie.

'Then what?' Josie said. 'Something has been the matter with you for the past few days.'

Tell her, said a little voice hammering inside Hannah's

head. What does it matter if Josie knows? It might be better. She knows you inside out. She won't judge.

'You're right,' Hannah said suddenly. 'There is something. I don't know if you'll be pleased or not. I'm pleased.'

'What?'

'I'm pregnant.'

'Oh,' Josie said awkwardly, remembering again the early years of Hannah's marriage and the obscene words Arthur had flung at her and the one awful fight on her tenth birthday that had culminated in Angela and separate rooms. 'I . . . I didn't think you and Arthur . . . well, you know, I mean . . .'

'It's not Arthur's baby, Josie.'

'Not Arthur's baby?'

'No it's Vic's.'

'Who the hell is Vic?'

'The doctor, the one I work for.'

'Oh! My God!'

'It's all right,' Hannah assured Josie. 'We love each other. I denied it for years because I was married, but it was there, smouldering under the surface. It came to a head the day I found out Gloria was dying. Vic found me in tears and comforted me and one thing led to another . . .'

'Yes,' Josie said sharply, 'I don't need the details.'

'Don't look like that, Josie, I didn't intend for this to happen. You know I've never loved Arthur.'

'But you married him,' Josie replied and at the same time wondered what was the matter with her. Hadn't she wanted Hannah to leave Arthur? Hadn't she resented the way he spoke to her, treated her? Of course she had, so why was she acting such a prude now?

'I'm sorry, Hannah,' she said. 'Tell me how it was.'

'It wasn't anything,' Hannah said. 'Not then at least. I told Vic it was wrong. He was wrong to press me. I was worse for agreeing. I knew we were sinful and though I continued to work there, nothing further happened till Christmas. I was left alone and I needed someone to be with me that day. I weakened and phoned him.' She gave a slight shrug. 'Now I'm pregnant.'

'What will you do?'

'Tell Arthur and move out,' Hannah said.

'Rather you than me,' Josie said. 'He'll go up the wall.'

'He doesn't think that much of me.'

'Not you perhaps, but respectability,' Josie said. 'Would you like me to come with you when you tell him?'

'No,' Hannah reassured her. 'Don't worry, Vic will be with me. I'll be fine.'

In the end telling Arthur about her affair with Vic didn't turn out the way that Hannah had visualised it. She still hadn't broached the subject with him by the time the Easter holidays began and because she hadn't told him, she knew there was no way she could prepare Angela. Explaining things now would have to wait until she went back to school.

But then Angela wrote to them both just before school broke up asking if she could spend the bulk of the holidays with the friend she'd stayed with over the New Year.

She says I'm a natural rider and I can have Gamble

the pony like last time and this time we can try little jumps and . . .

Hannah, though she would miss Angela, could see the child's point of view. There was little to offer her at home and things between her and Arthur were worse than ever. Arthur, however, did not see things the way Hannah did. He threw down the letter in disgust. 'She's coming home,' he declared. 'And there'll be less of this "staying with friends" nonsense from now on that you encouraged her in last time.'

'She needs company of her own age,' Hannah said in an effort to explain. 'She has it all the time at school and then in the holidays she is often bored. She won't invite friends here, you know that, and the children in this area she barely knows anymore.'

'She has no need to be bored. I will take a week's holiday added to my Easter entitlement and take her out and about. As for the rest of the holiday, well, if she enjoys riding and wants to ride, then she shall. There are riding stables in Sutton Coldfield, I'll ring up a few today.'

So Angela came home, disgruntled and surly, unused to not getting her own way. She had reacted badly to the letter her father had sent, so certain had she been of his assent that she and Hillary had planned their time together. As well as riding, Hillary's father had promised them a trip out in his yacht, which he'd teach them to sail properly. Then there were picnics planned for fine days and Hillary's two brothers would be home from school too and they were going to build a tree-house in the large oak tree in the little wood that began at the end of the lawns to the rear of the house.

How could Harrison Road, Erdington, even with riding lessons, compare with that? She told nothing of her holiday plans to her father, though, as she barely spoke to him at all that first night and answered any questions he asked in monosyllables.

Arthur was irritated and took it out on Hannah, complaining about everything she did. Hannah did not retaliate, not wishing Angela to witness an ugly scene between her and Arthur. In fact, so annoyed was Arthur that he went out after he'd eaten. Barely had the door closed on her father, when Angela said to Hannah. 'Isn't Daddy unfair? It's me he's angry with, but he took it out on you.'

Hannah chose her words with care. She knew their relationship had hit rocky ground, but knew Angela was the one person in the world Arthur loved. She was going to leave him soon and had no wish to alienate Angela from her father. 'It's natural to do that,' she said. 'Perhaps you've done it yourself at school. Maybe a teacher does something to annoy you and you take out your bad temper on a friend.'

Angela could indeed remember incidents when this had happened, but instead of citing them, she asked, 'Why are you so nice about Daddy? He never says nice things about you.'

That shook Hannah, not that Arthur said things about her, but that Angela should speak of it so bluntly. 'Oh, that falls off me like water off a duck's back,' she said, forcing a light note into her voice. 'Your father loves you very much, you know. He wanted you home because he misses you.'

'Misses me? He sees me every week. I never see you,

except holidays. Why don't you come sometimes?'

'Your father doesn't wish me to.'

'Why not?'

'He wants you to himself.'

'That's selfish.'

'Oh, Angela, people do perplexing things sometimes,' Hannah said. 'I'll explain more when you're older.'

'I'm nearly twelve now.'

'You are not!' Hannah contradicted. 'You are eleven and a half, that's all.'

'Well, it's not far off twelve.'

'Far enough,' Hannah said. 'Now what do you say to us having a cup of tea and you can tell me what your friend and her family had in line for you and we'll plan our own holiday. How's that?'

Angela's face lit up. 'Okay, Mommy,' she said and added, 'I really do miss you, you know. You will come to my confirmation in June, won't you? All the other parents will be there.'

By then, I'll have left Arthur, Hannah thought, and he'll have no right to forbid me to go anywhere, although I'll be much bigger by then. I'll have to find a coat or something to try and hide my shape for I mustn't embarrass Angela on my first visit. But none of these concerns did she show to Angela. She smiled and gave her a hug. 'Of course I will, darling. You try and keep me away.'

'Promise you'll come.'

'I promise.'

Angela's holiday, as far as Arthur was concerned, was not a success. He took her to a hotel on the North

Wales coast for a few days, but the weather was blustery and cold, and most days it rained. Angela complained to Hannah that the hotel was full of old people and that it was worse than being at home.

In contrast, Angela enjoyed her time with Hannah and was pleased to see Josie again and enchanted with baby Phillip. Arthur was not slow to see the strong bond blossoming between Angela and Hannah and it both worried and infuriated him. Now, when he tried to do something to discredit Hannah or cause her to be an object of scorn, Angela would say that he was unkind and she didn't want to hear him say things like that.

God, when this holiday was over, he'd have something to say about the whole thing! He'd tell Hannah to back out of Angela's life. Angela left in a flurry of hugs for Hannah and genuine tears of regret about leaving her. Arthur tackled Hannah about stealing Angela's love that same evening when he returned home from delivering her to school.

'You can't steal a person's love, Arthur,' Hannah said unabashed. 'Angela is growing into a young woman. You could control the child, but it becomes harder as they grow and form their own opinions. It's natural too for a girl of Angela's age to be closer to her mother.'

But the link between them was fragile, both were feeling their way and for that reason, she didn't want to upset her before the confirmation. 'But she'll know. You'll be much larger by then,' Vic said when Hannah told him.

'If she notices it at all, she'll just think I've put weight on,' Hannah said.

'Look, Hannah, I'm tired of waiting,' Vic said. 'We'll tell Arthur together and soon. I want you to visit my parents next weekend.'

'All right,' Hannah said with a sigh. She knew Vic was right. It was becoming harder and harder for her to leave him too. She longed to be with him all the time. 'We'll see him Friday night.'

'Promise?'

'You sound like Angela,' Hannah said with a laugh. 'I promise.'

But Arthur knew two days before Friday. He'd received a letter he'd not mentioned to Hannah from a well-wisher who thought he ought to know about the number of times the doctor's car stood outside their house of an evening and the times Hannah left the house after he'd gone out, sometimes in the doctor's car and sometimes in a taxi. It even had gone on in the holidays when he'd taken the little lass away for a few days.

Did he care? Yes, he bloody well did. He cared about being made a laughing stock, so that even the neighbours knew and were probably sniggering behind their hands at him. Damn and blast her to Hell's flames! He knew he had to emerge from this whole thing whiter than the driven snow. But then reason took hold – her and the doctor. There was a law about a doctor and women patients, wasn't there? By God, he'd find out and if he was right, he held the trump card.

He was waiting for her Wednesday night. He had returned for the two previous nights and seen the doctor's car outside just as the anonymous letter writer had said, but he'd retreated those nights, not wishing to confront Vic until he'd spoken to Hannah on her own.

That night, though, the house was in darkness when he let himself in, having parked his car around the corner so that Hannah wouldn't know he was there.

She came in happy and warmed through by Vic's gentle lovemaking. She was smiling and humming a little tune to herself as she filled the kettle.

'Where have you been?'

The words, though quietly spoken, almost made Hannah drop the kettle as she faced Arthur, framed in the doorway.

She took her time answering, putting the kettle on the gas and lighting it before she spoke. Excuses flew into her head, but to use them was only putting off the inevitable and she felt Arthur deserved the truth, so replied, 'I've been with Vic, you know, the doctor, Vic Humphries.'

'Whore!'

Arthur took a step towards her and she retreated. 'No! No! It's not like that. We love each other, we're getting marr . . .'

She got no further, for the fist slammed into her face with such ferocity that she staggered. 'You filthy, dirty harlot! Laughing behind my back, you sodding whore!' Arthur almost screamed. 'Half the neighbourhood knows of your carry-on – you and the doctor shagging each other.'

Out of swollen and bleeding lips, Hannah pleaded, 'Let him come round – explain it. Arthur, believe me we had no intention for it to be this way.'

'Whatever you intended it is this way,' Arthur said. 'And he'll come around when I decide and by then he'll not be able to recognise you, because I'm going to beat you to a pulp.'

Hannah knew Arthur meant it for a demonic light shone in his eyes and there was froth on his lips – it was the angriest she'd ever seen him. She fought like a wildcat, but she was no match for Arthur and he at last beat her down so that she crouched to the ground and tried to protect her stomach as much as she could. He gave her a violent shove so that she overbalanced.

He was astride her in seconds and Hannah remembered with revulsion that violence had always aroused Arthur and she looked at him with eyes just mere slits and said, 'Please, Arthur, no – I'm pregnant.'

Pregnant! Pregnant with some other man's bastard and living in his house, cooking his meals, talking and laughing with his daughter, tainting her innocence!

'Pregnant, eh,' he said with relish. 'Well, I can do no harm then.'

'No, Arthur, please.'

'I'm your husband in case you've forgotten,' said Arthur, pulling up Hannah's skirt as he spoke. He yanked her knickers down and unzipped himself. Hannah couldn't believe it. He was going to rape her and she was helpless to stop him.

'Has he a bigger cock than me?' Arthur said, spittle from his slack lips spraying her. 'Is that it?'

She didn't answer, but let out a groan of pain as he entered her. 'Can he do this and this and this?' Arthur cried at every thrust, sending arrows of pain shooting through Hannah. And then he was unable to speak, taken up as he was by excitement, and his thrusting got wilder and faster.

Hannah lay passive and told herself eventually it would be over. She just had to lie and wait. It couldn't last forever and the pain would go. Everywhere ached and throbbed anyway, particularly her face. But what Arthur was doing was making her feel degraded and dirty.

Arthur gave a shout, a final thrust, and lay still for a moment, spent. Hannah wriggling beneath him roused him to get off her, zipping up his trousers. 'Get up.'

Hannah pulled up her knickers and stumbled painfully to her feet. 'Come into the breakfast room, I wish to speak to you.'

Hannah moved to obey him as if she was a robot and sat opposite him. She could only guess what she looked like, she felt like death and wished she could sink into a soft bed and sleep forever.

Arthur was talking to her. 'You can take all you can pack into one suitcase,' he said, 'and that is all. Once you leave, it will be as if you are dead. I don't want to hear or see you ever again and you will have no contact with Angela.'

'You can't do this,' Hannah cried. 'I'll go to court.'

'I don't think so, my dear.'

'Don't you "my dear" me, you vicious sadistic brute. I want Vic here. He'll sort you out.'

'Your Vic will do nothing,' Arthur said. 'That is if he wants to continue as a doctor.'

'What are you on about now?'

'I see he hasn't told you,' Arthur said. 'Well, let me put you in the picture. By starting a relationship with you, a patient of his, Vic has broken the law and it would be hard to deny any sexual relations took place when your belly is full.'

'You're lying. It's something you made up,' Hannah cried. But then she remembered the odd way Vic had reacted to the news that he was to be a father. He'd said he'd just been surprised by it all and she'd accepted it at the time.

'I assure you, I am not lying and I have made nothing up,' Arthur said. 'Vic will say the same – phone him.'

And Vic did say the same eventually. The frantic telephone call roused him from sleep and when he drowsily answered, 'Erdington 3501, Doctor Humphries speaking,' he couldn't at first understand the message mumbled through Hannah's swollen lips. 'Vic, it's Hannah. Arthur knows. It's bad. Please come.'

That she was crying registered with him. 'What is it? What is it? Oh, damn it! Hang on, Hannah, I'll be there in a jiffy.'

He was out of bed as she spoke, searching the floor for his clothes.

When Hannah opened the door to him and he saw her face, he was rendered speechless for a moment. Tears of relief ran down her face. 'Oh, Vic, Vic.'

'My darling.' Vic's arms were around her and despite the bruises all over Hannah, she leant against him seeking comfort.

Vic's shock at Hannah's condition was receding to be replaced by raging anger. 'Where is he?' he said.

'In the breakfast room,' Hannah said. 'But it's no good.'

'I'm sorry, Hannah, I can't let this go,' Vic said,

putting her gently from him. She tried to catch at his sleeve and when that didn't work she ran down the corridor after him and arrived at the door to see him holding Arthur against the wall with his powerful arms.

Arthur appeared completely unafraid. 'I should take your hands off me if I were you,' he said calmly. 'If you value your job, that is.'

Vic's hands sank to his side. The bugger knows I've broken the law by sleeping with Hannah, he thought, and as the supercilious smile slid across Arthur's face, he had the idea to send his teeth down his throat and hang the consequences.

And what then? Not only would he be out of a job, his parents disgraced and ashamed, but possibly behind bars. What Arthur had done to Hannah would be judged by some circles to be acceptable – a man deceived and now to have his wife admit to be carrying another man's child. Well, what was a man to do in the circumstances but give her a good hiding? And for the one who'd wronged him in the first place to then set about him. If Arthur was to take it to court, and he would, Vic knew, they would throw the book at him.

He couldn't do that, not to Hannah, nor his parents. 'I see you're sensible about all this,' Arthur said, as Vic relaxed his hands and Arthur stood straightening his tie and rearranging his jacket that Vic had rumpled.

'What about Hannah? What right have you to beat her?'

'The right of a husband,' Arthur said. 'She promised before God to love, honour and obey me in sickness and in health, till death do us part. Do you call what she did loving me, honouring me?'

'You have led her a life of hell.'

'In your opinion,' Arthur said. 'And of course you've helped her, by sleeping with her, making her pregnant.'

'Will you both stop talking as if I wasn't here,' Hannah said angrily. 'Look it's over; Arthur's had his revenge, I'm going to pack now ready to leave.'

'One suitcase remember,' Arthur said. 'You'll never get a penny piece from me and you'll not see or speak to Angela again. You're not to contact her by letter or phone, or send her birthday or Christmas cards or presents.'

Hannah gasped in shock and she looked at Arthur out of horrified eyes. 'I can't believe you can be this cruel,' she said, forcing the words through her swollen lips.

'Well, now you know,' Arthur said.

'Please, Arthur, for God's sake, don't do this,' Hannah pleaded. 'I promised Angela I'd go to her confirmation.'

Arthur shrugged. 'You'll break that promise and when she hears nothing from you, not even a card for her birthday, she'll know what sort of mother she has and I will tell her that her mother cares nothing for her.'

'Come now,' Vic said, catching sight of Hannah's anguished face. 'This is inhuman.'

'I don't care for your opinions,' said Arthur. 'Those are my conditions. Break them in any way and there will be a call made to the Medical Board.'

Hannah looked at Arthur and knew he meant every

word he said. She'd burnt her boats anyway. Her life now lay with Vic and from the moment she left, she'd cease to exist as far as Angela was concerned. Without another word, she stumbled from the room and went upstairs to pack her life up in one case.

Vic felt frustrated at his helplessness. Arthur should pay a price for the punishment he inflicted on Hannah and yet he could do nothing about it. Then, later that night as they lay together in Gloria's bed, Vic's arms encircling Hannah for comfort only, she told him of the rape and he felt rage pound through his body.

The man was vindictively, inhumanely cruel, he realised. Hannah's injuries would eventually heal, even the emotional trauma of the rape would fade, but he didn't know whether she'd ever get over the block he'd put on her seeing or contacting Angela. Knowing her history, Vic worried about her mental state over this loss, as it were, of a second child. For the first time, he looked forward with eagerness to the birth of their own child and hoped it would help to heal the hole that would be left in her life because access to Angela had been denied her.

Chapter Twenty-One

One glorious day in the middle of June 1959, Hannah opened the door to see the priest on the threshold. She wasn't surprised. She'd been expecting him to visit before this. She still went to Mass on Sunday, but to the earliest one held at seven o'clock and she always scurried away after it, giving Father Fitzgerald no opportunity to ask if he could have a wee word with her, which she knew he was dying to do. She was glad it was Father Fitzgerald who came to see her, because although she knew what he'd come for, she couldn't help but like him. She knew nothing of the conversation the priest had had with Arthur before they were married, but she always felt the priest took an interest in them all, especially in Josie, so she smiled as she said, 'Come in, Father. I'll take your coat and put the kettle on,' and ushered him into the room that had been Gloria's private sitting room that Hannah loved so much.

When she came back in with a tray of coffee and plate of biscuits, the priest was still standing in the middle of the room looking about him. It was a warm comfortable room, decorated in terracotta and cream.

Hannah had retained Gloria's terracotta-coloured sofa, with its array of bright cushions. There was no fire in the grate, for it was summer, but a beautifully decorated fire screen sat behind the gleaming brass fender. More brass decorated the mantel shelf either side of the carriage clock and a large gilt-edged mirror was above it all on the wall, while in the glass-fronted cupboards either side of the fireplace, Hannah had put her favourite ornaments.

Hannah set the tray down on one of the occasional tables and the priest sat down on the sofa beside it. 'You have it very nice, Hannah.'

'I can't claim much credit, Father,' Hannah told him. 'This is mainly Gloria's stuff. I always loved this room so I changed very little. Most of the other rooms have been cleared. It was a mammoth task. But this room was Gloria's favourite. Not everyone was invited in here, but the pair of us used to have some famous chats in here, so we did. I still miss her quite dreadfully at times.'

'You were good friends,' the priest said gently. 'Were you surprised to inherit the house, Hannah?'

'Totally,' Hannah said. 'She never gave me any indication that that was what she intended to do.'

'And yet,' the priest went on, slowly accepting the cup of tea Hannah handed him, 'maybe it wasn't such a good thing. After all, it enabled you to leave your husband.'

'Father, that was on the cards anyway.'

'But why, Hannah? Could you not have talked any problems through?'

'No, Father. It went deeper than that,' Hannah said.

'I never loved Arthur, so I suppose I did him a disservice marrying him, though I never lied and told him I did. He knew I didn't love him. But that wasn't it, Father, at least not the whole of it. If he'd been kind to me, I could have lived with him contentedly, I believe.'

'Unkind? Did he hit you? Beat you?'

'He hit me three times,' Hannah said, and a shudder passed through her as she remembered the last time when he'd also raped her. 'If you'd seen me a couple of weeks ago, his handiwork would have been evident,' she went on. 'But there's worse things than a slap or punch, Father. Arthur began being verbally abusive not long after we were married. He became spiteful and vindictive when we were alone. In company he was totally different. In the end, I could stand no more.'

'As I understand it, Hannah, in the end you negated your marriage vows.'

Hannah lowered her head. 'It wasn't like that, Father,' she said earnestly. 'I never went looking for another man. Anyway, now Arthur is divorcing me.'

But though she gave the priest this news without a tremor in her voice, she remembered how she thought she'd die of shame when she received the papers from the solicitor's office and realised she'd been named in them as an adulteress, this adultery leading to a breakdown in their marriage. Vic had been terrifically supportive then as he'd held her in his arms and soothed her. He told her not to worry. It was, he said, the last time Arthur would have the power to hurt her in any way.

'Divorcing you? You know there is no divorce in the Catholic Church.'

'There is in the civil court, Father. I'm being named as an adulteress, which I suppose is only fair. But as soon as it happens, Vic and I will be married in the registry office.'

'You'll not be married in the sight of God,' the priest said, appalled. 'You will be living in sin.'

'I know that, Father.'

'Does that not worry you, child?'

'A bit,' Hannah admitted. 'That's why I held off so long.'

'That isn't the way I heard it,' the priest said.

'Well, it wouldn't be, would it?' Hannah said bitterly. 'Look, Father,' she went on. 'I never went out looking for another husband. I took the job with Vic Humphries for two reasons. The first was boredom, for with Angela out all day at school and Pauline there to see to things anyway, there wasn't enough for me to do. The second reason was that I needed the money because Arthur gave me none. Vic and I became friends, as two people who work closely together often do, and that's all it was then, a deep friendship.'

'When did it change?' the priest asked.

'The day I found out Gloria was dying,' Hannah said. 'Vic found me crying and . . . and he comforted me.' She was silent then, but her face flamed crimson and the priest surmised a lot by that flush.

'But,' Hannah went on, 'things really came to a head at Christmas. Arthur took Angela away for four days. I felt so alone, so isolated and unloved. I couldn't bear it and I phoned Vic and asked him to come.'

'And did you spend the night together?'

'Yes, Father.'

'And is he living here with you now?'

'Yes, Father.'

'Child, your soul is in mortal danger,' the priest said, shaking his head sorrowfully. And then he looked at Hannah's swollen stomach and said, 'Are you expecting Doctor Humphries' baby?'

'Yes,' Hannah said and lifted her head defiantly. 'And I'm proud to be, Father. Vic is a good man.'

'You can't really expect me to agree with you on that,' Father Fitzgerald said sternly. 'A man who entices a woman to flee from her husband and child is not one I would term "good".'

'He did no enticing, Father.'

'Hannah, have you not thought of Angela's reaction to all this? She's at a very impressionable age.'

'I know that, Father.'

'Arthur tells me she is being confirmed next Sunday?'

Hannah knew that too. She'd circled the date on the calendar. Not that she'd needed to, it was etched in her memory. 'You'll be going to that I presume?'

'No, Father,' Hannah said. 'The only regret I have about this whole business is that I am not able to see or contact my daughter in any way.'

'And why is that?'

'Arthur forbids it.'

'No, Hannah,' Father Fitzgerald said. 'Arthur cannot forbid that.'

'Oh, but he can, Father,' said Hannah. 'Apparently, because Vic is my doctor, it was illegal for us to begin a relationship. Arthur threatened to report Vic if I tried to have any sort of contact with Angela.'

The priest could hardly credit it. He'd heard of such

a rule, but to separate a mother from her child was an inhuman thing to do. 'I'll speak to him,' he said.

'No, Father,' Hannah said. 'Arthur is a vindictive and spiteful man. I don't know how he'd react to the news that I'd even mentioned it to you. It might make things worse.'

'So you'll do nothing?'

'That's about the strength of it, Father,' Hannah said. 'I'll do nothing because there is nothing I can do.'

She held on to her tears until she'd shown the priest out and then she cried brokenheartedly. Other people, besides the priest, showed their feelings openly too. Hannah got a very distressing letter from Elizabeth Banks, who'd obviously got totally the wrong idea of the state of their marriage from Arthur. The letter reduced her to tears and she thought of replying to it and putting her side, but Vic said it would do no good. 'She will believe what Arthur has told her,' he said. 'Don't stoop to trying to justify your actions. Believe me, my darling, she won't be the last to castigate us and we must prepare ourselves for it.'

Many of Vic's patients disapproved of what he had done and voted with their feet, leaving the practice before he had time to sell it. Hannah had not returned to work since that dreadful night she left Arthur, not that she could have appeared anyway with her face as battered as it had been. And yet she knew if any had seen it, a fair few would have said it served her right.

Instead, she moved into Gloria's house in Grange Road and lived there alone, while Vic stayed above the surgery, which he was desperately trying to sell, so that he could establish himself in Grange Road in a new practice before the baby was born.

Once he was free of the practice, he moved into the room to the side of the house, which in Gloria's day was used as the breakfast room for the guests. It was perfect for though it had a door into the hall of the house, there was another that led outside so it could be totally private. Hannah engaged a carpenter to partition the large room so that part of it was reception and a waiting room and the other was for Vic's consulting room.

Vic worried at times that any one of his remaining patients, or those offended enough to transfer doctors knowing he was now living with Hannah, might do what Arthur threatened and tell the Medical Council of his association. If so, it would probably destroy him, but at least Arthur's power over them both and his ban on Hannah seeing Angela would be null and void.

But, none of his remaining patients or neighbours reported Vic. They either didn't know his relationship with Hannah was illegal or weren't that interested in reporting it. Nevertheless, he knew how they felt, for few patients followed him from his old practice in Wood End Lane. People, it seemed, were loath to consult a doctor who'd lured a woman from husband and child to live with him, especially as she was shamelessly carrying his baby.

It was soon made obvious that Vic's parents thought that way too. Hannah and Vic went to see them together as soon as Hannah's face was back to normal. Hannah was nervous of the meeting, aware that she wouldn't appear much of a 'catch' for their son.

And she wasn't and Vic's mother, Flo, who she was careful to address as Mrs Humphries, made it very apparent early on. It was obvious, too, in just a few seconds that his mother ruled not only the house, not only his father, Eric, but also his two colourless, browbeaten sisters, Betsy and Dorothy. They were both quite a few years older than Vic and already settled into spinsterhood.

Hannah felt sorry for them. She knew their lives would revolve around these four walls, bullied and dominated by their mother, with no possibility of escape.

She knew too she had to win Vic's mother over if she was to fit into the family. She naturally said nothing about the baby she'd had in 1944, but did tell her about Angela. She didn't discuss her marriage, other than to say that she and Arthur had decided to part and said her daughter had been left in the care of her husband, though she was away at boarding school most of the time. She didn't explain why and Vic felt he shouldn't interfere, though he saw his mother's eyes widen in shock and disbelief and severe disapproval and knew that Hannah had blown it.

The whole visit after that was stiff and formal and the meal they sat down to was conducted almost in silence. Hannah was never asked to go there again. Vic was asked alone and though Hannah wanted him to go, he said he wouldn't go anywhere she wasn't welcome and refused. It was yet another nail in Hannah's coffin, because Flo was convinced that Hannah was keeping her son away from her.

Hannah knew that Vic hated the separation from his

parents. He knew he owed them a huge debt for supporting him through his studies that he'd never be able to repay. Maybe it wouldn't have mattered quite so much if his waiting room was full of people daily and he was too busy to worry overmuch about his parents' reaction, but that wasn't happening either.

Vic didn't want to worry Hannah over these problems, but she was no fool and well aware of what Vic was going through in the practice. He'd engaged a part-time receptionist when Hannah'd left, but the girl was just that and Hannah still did the accounts and she knew how grim things were becoming.

'Don't worry,' Vic would say, 'we're not on our beam ends yet. Once you have the decree absolute, we will marry. The gossip will die down eventually. It will be a nine day wonder, you'll see.'

Hannah wasn't totally convinced. Her new neighbours ignored her and not long after Vic moved in, she'd come face to face with some of her old neighbours from Erdington Village, Mary's mother amongst them. They didn't speak to her, but about her as they began to talk in loud voices saying it wasn't right that decent people should have to mix with shameless hussies and harlots. Hannah turned away from her tormentors and one of them spat at her retreating back.

She never told Vic. He had worries of his own and anyway could do nothing about it, but ever after the incident she went into Birmingham city centre to do her shopping, which became very tiring as her pregnancy advanced. Meanwhile Vic, despite his reassuring words to Hannah, became increasingly concerned about their finances and took a part-time consulting job at Good Hope Hospital in nearby Sutton Coldfield.

Hannah was glad of Amy next door, who mainly kept her own counsel about Hannah's behaviour, but she often remembered the things Gloria had mentioned and the rare times she'd seen Hannah with her husband and told her not to worry so much about people's reactions. 'They shouldn't be so quick to judge,' she said once. 'Few know what goes on behind someone's front door. But don't fret, someone else will be doing something worse before long and a child is a great healer.'

In a boarding school in Leeds, a young girl cried herself to sleep one day in late June while Hannah was coping with hostility from all around her. It was her confirmation day, though she'd taken the beautiful white dress and lace veil off before she'd thrown herself face down on the bed and allowed the tears to fall. She was the only one in that school whose mother hadn't come to her confirmation and after her promising, too. There were spiteful girls amongst her friends who said they doubted she even had a mother and Angela thought it might be preferable not having a mother at all, to having one that couldn't be bothered with her.

She'd wondered for some time why she hadn't had the weekly letter from her mother that she always looked forward to. She assumed she'd been too busy and intended to say a few sharp words about it when she came up for her confirmation. If her father didn't go into a blue fizz any time her mother's name was mentioned, she could have discussed it with him, but that she knew was out of the question.

But when she didn't come on the day, Angela risked her father's wrath to tearfully ask him why. 'She's moved out of the house to live with that doctor chap she worked for,' he told her bluntly. 'And she's having his baby now. She won't be bothering with you or me again.'

Angela's mouth dropped open with shock. 'What do you mean? Of course she will.'

'Oh,' Arthur said, looking around in an exaggerated way. 'Is she here then after promising you she would be?'

'You know she isn't,' Angela said and tears ran down her face as she added plaintively, 'and she promised, promised faithfully.'

She needed to see her mother even more now after the dreadful things her father had said. Her Mommy couldn't have moved out! She lived with them. All mothers lived with their children and she couldn't be having another baby either. That would be . . . well, almost obscene, to think of her and the doctor . . . it was better not to think of it.

Arthur laughed humourlessly, breaking in on the thoughts jumbling about in Angela's head. 'Promises,' he barked. 'What does she care for promises? What about the promises she made me and in front of a priest, too? I tell you, she doesn't want anything to do with you anymore, she's made a new life for herself, and Josie doesn't either. Both of them have made it quite plain. So we'll just rub them out of our lives and never think of either of them again.'

But that wasn't an easy thing for Angela to do. She wasn't angry, just hurt, bitterly hurt and let down. She needed to know why her mother had done the things her daddy said she'd done. Surely she owed her some sort of explanation? She would write to her. She knew where she was, her father had told her she was living in Gloria's house now.

But the letter was never sent. The nuns, by blocking the letter, were carrying out Arthur's orders, which they fully agreed with. They could quite understand why he didn't want his daughter to associate with his wife who they'd seen just the once and had marked down already as an unfeeling mother to never once visit her child, especially with her husband coming every week.

But now she'd gone one step further. She'd actually left her husband for another man, and as she was expecting this man's child, she'd already committed adultery with him. Certainly, she was an immoral woman and not the example the father wanted for his daughter. But Arthur had warned them that her mother or her mother's niece might write to Angela, attempting to turn her mind to accept immorality to be all right and purity and innocence to be scorned.

Oh yes, the nuns agreed. It was a daily fight against such things. If any letters like that came they would be handed to Arthur. And similarly, he said if Angela should write, for after all, bad as she is, she is the child's mother. Oh, they assured him, such a letter written by Angela would not leave the convent.

The letter therefore that Angela wrote to Hannah was placed in her father's hand on his weekend visit and when he opened it later, he felt the hurt and disappointment leaping from the page. He knew he'd been right to distance her from her mother who might have easily turned the child's head. In time, she'd get over the pain.

But it took some time. Each day, when the letters were distributed, Angela expected a reply. Eventually, not understanding her mother's silence, she wrote another letter, but it went the same way as the first and gradually anger and bitterness took the place of the hurt. 'I hate her, hate her,' she confided to Hillary. 'If she was here now, I wouldn't speak to her. I might spit in her eyes, but I wouldn't speak to her.'

Hillary couldn't blame her. Mothers didn't just up and leave their families and live with other people. It didn't happen. She'd always known there was something odd with Angela's family.

Hannah still saw a lot of Josie, especially as Hannah's time grew near, and she was glad of her for she was nervous about giving birth again and how she would react after it. 'I haven't got a good track record in caring for babies,' she said to her once.

'Oh for pity's sake, Hannah.'

'It's all right for you,' Hannah retorted. 'What if it happens again?'

'If what happens again?' Josie asked, though she knew full well. Vic had told her that as the summer was coming to an end, the obsession Hannah had about getting depression again was affecting her sleep and she woke up crying and screaming in the bed quite often. 'I've tried to reassure her,' he said. 'But to no avail. You have a go.'

So when Hannah said, 'You know. What if I respond to this baby the way I did with Angela?'

'Why on earth should you?' Josie asked. 'Have you spoken to Vic about it?'

'Yes, he says that just because it happened once that's not to say it will happen again.'

'Well then?'

'I'm still scared,' Hannah said. 'I don't think I could go through that again.'

'Oh God, Hannah, you won't have to,' Josie said, putting an arm about her shoulders. 'That other business was Arthur's fault and the terrible time he gave you. If you hadn't got away from him when you did, I think that you would have had a complete nervous collapse and that would have helped no one.'

'I know I had to go,' Hannah said. 'Even if there hadn't been Vic, I don't think I could have stayed much longer. But, I never thought it would hurt so much not to be able to see Angela. I know she is away at boarding school and I see little of her anyway, but it's hard to think she's at home now, yards from me, and I cannot see her, talk to her, or contact her in any way.'

'It's the price you had to pay,' Josie told her. 'Vic had to give up things for you too. And don't worry, Arthur won't be able to hold on to Angela for ever,' she said. 'If he thinks he will, he's in for a shock.'

Hannah knew Josie was right. Angela or no Angela, she couldn't have stayed with Arthur and held on to her sanity. Arthur always made her feel worthless as a person and useless at everything she did. Vic had taught her to value and like herself. Tilly, too, had been a great comfort and Hannah's great confidante from the time she'd met her again in Leeds and she'd poured out her feelings in the letter she sent when she wrote and told her she'd left Arthur. Tilly's reply was swift:

> *Good for you and about bleeding time. Now stick to your guns and don't go back to that sadistic bugger, not for anyone.*

She couldn't go back, the gate was firmly shut against her. She wrote and told Pauline too, though she didn't go into details. Pauline had known how things had been between Arthur and Hannah for years and thought a split between them inevitable.

Martin and Siobhan were slightly shocked, though not terribly surprised, after talking to Arthur at the wedding. They'd known then that Hannah wasn't happy and yet a Catholic marriage was for life. Josie had told them, for since the wedding they'd corresponded regularly with their little sister and she was delighted about that. She laid it on the line just the sort of man Arthur was and pulled no punches as Hannah might have done and also said in her opinion she had been a saint to put up with it for so long. After Josie's letter, both Martin and Siobhan wrote Hannah letters of support and that meant a lot to her.

Vic had insisted that Hannah be booked into a small maternity hospital in Heathfield Road in Handsworth in plenty of time. The doctors checking her medical notes decided a Caesarean section was advisable. Vic agreed, but was more concerned that she didn't sink into depression as she'd done after Angela's birth. 'I must be there when she wakes,' he said. 'And I wish every assistance be given to her should she wish to breast-feed.'

It was amazing, he thought, how being in the medical profession himself gave him such authority and how the nurses deferred to him. He waited restlessly outside the theatre one day in mid-September until it was over and he could sit beside Hannah.

When Hannah opened her eyes, it was to see Vic by her side holding a blanket-wrapped bundle in his arms. Though still a little tired, she asked the question all mothers ask. 'What is it?'

'A boy.'

'A boy! I have a son,' and then catching sight of Vic's face amended it. 'I mean, we have a son. Is he all right? Can I see him?'

'He's perfect and you can do more than see him,' Vic told her, 'you can feed him. He's beginning to protest already.' The words were scarcely out of Vic's mouth before the baby began to flail in his arms and newborn wails filled the room.

'Vic, I can't feed him.'

'Of course you can, as long as we're careful about your stitches,' Vic said reassuringly. 'It wouldn't be sensible for you to sit up yet, but with the help of pillows, I'm sure we'll manage.'

And they did manage. Hannah looked down at her small son, his cries still, his eyes closed in contentment as he sucked, so that his auburn lashes lay in a crescent shape on his cheeks. His little snub nose was squashed up slightly and she lifted the tiny hands holding her breast with the even tinier nails, marvelling at him. Her son!

She felt the rush of love, as powerful as she'd felt for his half-brother Michael fifteen years before, for this child, that they'd decided to call Adam, amazingly was born on Michael's birthday. Hannah didn't know if she was pleased or not about that fact. She did know, however, that this child was worth everything that she and Vic had gone through. She looked across from the baby to Vic and saw his eyes were wet, glistening with unshed tears and full of love and concern for her, and she felt loved and cherished. 'Oh, Vic, isn't he just wonderful?'

'He's marvellous, darling, and so are you.'

'You don't regret anything?'

Vic kissed her nose. 'The very idea! The only regret I have is that we didn't come together earlier.'

'Oh, Vic.' He was essentially good this man of hers, Hannah decided, and she pulled his head down towards her and kissed him gently on his lips.

Hannah was to find Amy to be right about a child being a great healer. The people in Grange Road tended to keep themselves to themselves more than those in Harrison Road, but after Adam was born, even some of them had thawed enough to knock on the door to ask about the baby and offer a gift, or stop Hannah in the street to peep in the pram.

The consensus seemed to be firstly that it wasn't the child's fault and then that Hannah was pleasant enough and really you couldn't believe all you heard. Even knowing she'd left her child wasn't so bad when you realised the child was at boarding school and that was the father's choice they believed.

But even with the people in Grange Road, now smiling at her, or calling out the odd greeting, Hannah was still wary of braving Erdington High Street, but she couldn't go to town with a baby in tow. She'd found it a strain the last weeks of her pregnancy.

Still, she was full of trepidation when she made her first trip up there, but because she'd chosen her time well she met few old neighbours. But she did bump into some patients from the old practice. Some smiled and some ignored her, but there were no nasty comments and she told herself she could cope with that.

Vic knew, though, that Hannah had still not really settled into her new life, despite the fact that she was now at least on nodding terms with the neighbours, and he suggested having a christening-cum-housewarming party when Adam was a month old. 'We'll invite the neighbours,' he said. 'Then they'll see for themselves that we are a solid and rather boring family unit.'

Hannah agreed that it was a good idea in principle, though she didn't think even Father Fitzgerald would be interested in baptising a child he considered a bastard. But he had no problem with that for in his opinion none of it was the child's fault. 'What date had you in mind?' he asked them, consulting his diary.

'The second Sunday in October would be good,' Vic said. 'The shops might be selling fireworks by then and we may be able to get some for the party.'

Hannah went suddenly cold. Fireworks always made her think of Angela because November 6th was her birthday. Another child I can't send a birthday card to, Hannah thought, and she hugged Adam so tight, he struggled against her. But she said nothing to Vic. She didn't expect him to remember Angela's birthday, nor did she want him to think that Angela was on her mind so much. He might think then she was unhappy and it wasn't that at all.

She just wished she could see her, talk with her, watch her develop into the young woman she was now teetering on the edge of becoming, but Hannah didn't blame Vic for not being able to do these things; she knew who was to blame. Vic caught the look of sadness on Hannah's face, however, and knowing her well, did a quick calculation and cursed himself for being an insensitive fool. There would be no fireworks at this party, he decided. He would do nothing to add to Hannah's unhappiness about the situation with Angela.

Hannah refused to ask any people from Harrison Road to the party, so not even the Byrnes got an invitation. Amy and Tom came, of course, and some other new neighbours who'd been particularly friendly and Josie and Phil and baby Phillip in a carrycot, and Josie's friend Cynthia and her brother Peter. Vic invited two colleagues, one was married and brought his wife and another who was a bachelor by the name of Colin Ferguson. Hannah found him an interesting man and one who was passionate about the National Health Service and had deliberately chosen to take an inner ring practice in the poorest part of Edgbaston.

Though he had no wife to support, Vic had told her Colin had ailing parents and a young brother trying to establish himself as a barrister who he was giving financial help to, and as he had no private patients in his area to supplement his income, it was proving difficult. Hannah thought he sounded such a considerate and generous man that she went out of her way to talk to him and make him welcome.

He didn't advertise any of the altruistic things he did, but he did say that he'd had to give up his car the other day as his brother needed a large deposit to put down on a flat. 'Had to come over though, didn't I, with Vic asking me to be godfather and all.'

'But how will you manage without a car?' Hannah asked.

'I won't of course. At least not for any length of time. I'm looking at a cheaper model in the morning. Not that I use my car to do the bulk of my visiting, I usually walk. The streets are too narrow for one thing and the children are so unused to seeing cars there, they leap all over it. They've broken countless mirrors and scratched it all over more than once.'

'So how will you get home today, perhaps you'd like to stay the night?'

'That's kind of you,' Colin said. 'But I won't stay this time if you don't mind. I've got the car to see early, before surgery. I won't be able to stay on too late though, because I'm not sure of the time of the last bus.'

Josie, passing at the time, heard this and stopped. 'No need for that, Colin. We can give you a lift.'

'No, no, I can't put you out like that.'

'It's nothing,' Josie assured him. 'It'll take forever to get home this time of night when the buses are none too frequent and then once in town, you'll have to walk right across the city centre to get another. No, we'll take you.'

And so it was arranged and when they drove Colin home, it was the early hours of the morning. It was as they drove along Pershore Road that Josie spotted Arthur coming out down the steps of a house there. 'There's Arthur,' she said, turning around and pointing him out to Colin. 'Slow down, Phil, and let Colin have a deck at the creep.'

'Hannah's ex-husband, you mean?'

'Yes, I wonder what he was doing in there,' Josie mused. 'It doesn't look his type of place.'

And it didn't. Even in the light of the street lamp, they could see the steps were a dingy grey and pitted and broken and the paint on the door was peeling. The whole place looked shabby and seedy.

But then the whole neighbourhood was the same, a place where no one lingered and decent women seldom left the house once darkness had fallen. The streets of houses were shabby and run-down and peopled at night by prostitutes. The whole area reeked of poverty and pubs stood on every corner. Driving through it, you could see the scantily clad, often very young girls approaching the cars cruising slowly along the kerb. Then, with the price arranged between them, they would climb in and be spirited away God alone knew where. And lolling on street corners would be the pimps watching them with narrow, fox-like eyes.

This was the practice Colin Ferguson had chosen to work in and Josie thought the man deserved a medal and yet she still couldn't understand why Arthur Bradley, who'd always had ideas above his station, should be in such a place.

Colin had heard varied and fantastic rumours about

what went on behind some of those doors, but in the main he discounted rumour and in that part of the city it was wiser and healthier to do so. He'd had no occasion to visit the places, but now he suggested, 'Maybe he has another woman?'

Josie recalled the early days of Hannah's marriage and said, 'I don't think he's interested in that side of things very much.'

The man moved under the street lamp to light a cigarette and Colin had a good look at him. A docile, unpretentious kind of man, it was hard to credit him with some of the things Vic said he did. Not that Colin disbelieved Vic. He knew him to be honest and trustworthy, but he knew many who would choose to doubt Hannah's word if she began to explain what her life had been like with him, just because of his appearance and manner. His brown hair was very thin on top and the glasses fastened over ears that stuck out slightly were balanced on a thin straight nose. He took a drag of his cigarette through lips so thin they spoke of primness, pocketed the cigarettes and matches, turned up his coat collar, though the autumn night was warm, and sloped off.

And this man, who Colin could never remember seeing before, he saw regularly after that night, sometimes coming up or down the same steps, or sometimes in his car. He told Vic, but cautioned him not to say anything to Hannah in case the news should upset her. Besides, he didn't know what went on behind the shabby door and would probably never know, and feeding Hannah with rumour and speculation would do her no favours.

Josie and Phil never mentioned the sighting of Arthur to Hannah either, though Josie puzzled over it for weeks and if Phil had his own ideas, he kept them to himself. 'It couldn't be another woman, nothing like that,' Josie said a few weeks later. 'He doesn't . . . Well, you know? More can't really, I suppose.'

'It might be completely innocent,' Phil replied. 'Maybe Hannah knows all about it?'

'No, she doesn't,' Josie declared stoutly. 'That I do know. Sometimes he went out every night of the week and Hannah never knew where he went. She never asked him, but if she had, he'd probably not have answered her.'

'Well, I shouldn't think what he does now would interest her in the slightest,' Phil pointed out. 'All the same, I wouldn't say anything. It might bring it all flooding back again and start her fretting all over again about seeing Angela.'

'No, I shan't,' Josie said. 'Arthur can take a long jump off a short pier for my money. Hannah's far better off without him. She deserves some happiness in her life.'

'And so do I,' Phil said, but with a smile. 'I'm feeling neglected. If you're not worrying about Phillip, it's Hannah.'

'Okay,' Josie said and though she knew the answer she said, 'What's your problem?'

'Frustration. The need to make love to my wife.'

'Okay. I'm up to that as long as his lordship stays asleep,' Josie said and taking Phil's hand, she snapped off the light.

* * *

Angela kept a thread of hope alive until her birthday in November. Though she'd received no answer to her letters, she was sure her mother hadn't forgotten her totally. She wouldn't forget the day she'd been born, no mother ever did that. Maybe she'd even send her a present? She received cards from her father, Reg and Elizabeth Banks, and Pauline, but none from her mother or Josie and she couldn't believe it. It was just like her father said, she didn't exist for them anymore. Well, she thought, she wouldn't care about them either. She wouldn't. No, she bloody well wouldn't. Her father had written to tell her he would be along to see her at the weekend and bring all her presents with him. But a leaden weight of disappointment settled inside Angela and in time developed into a dense hatred.

Chapter Twenty-Two

Hannah didn't often analyse her life, it was too full to leave her much time to do this, but had she been asked, she'd have said she was happy, content and satisfied.

She'd married Vic in April 1960, just a week after her fortieth birthday. It had been a quiet ceremony and quite soulless, Hannah thought. None of Vic's family attended, neither the ceremony nor the reception. But Tilly, together with her husband and children, and Pauline came after Hannah had said they had plenty of room in the house to put them up for the weekend. Hannah was especially glad to see Pauline for the busyness of her life meant she'd rather lost touch with her. Amy and Tom and of course Josie and Phil and baby Phillip were invited too.

Vic had also asked some colleagues from the hospital and in the end the reception proved to be a lively gathering. Vic had eventually persuaded Hannah to go away for a long weekend, a short honeymoon to the Lake District. He said they both needed the break, but Hannah had been difficult to persuade, for though Josie had offered to look after Adam and she had absolute faith in her, she didn't like letting the child go out of her sight.

However, she loved Vic and realised they needed time alone together. Vic's job was stressful, she knew that better than most, and made worse, Vic said, by the fact that he'd not had a decent secretary since the day she'd had to leave. She still did his accounts, as this function seemed to be beyond the capabilities of any secretary Vic engaged.

She was due to take a more active role when Adam was a little older and so she was staggered when in the spring of 1961, she missed a period. Vic examined her and to his dismay found she was pregnant again.

Hannah was delighted and even more so when she found Josie was pregnant too, both children expected in October and within days of each other. Vic was not so delighted with Hannah's pregnancy. She would be forty-one years old before the child was born, and as a doctor he knew the risks. He told Hannah there could be no more children after this one.

Though Hannah had to have another Caesarean section, Frances Humphries, named after Hannah's sister, was born without any problems in the pearly dawn of a mid-October morning in the maternity unit of Good Hope Hospital. The baby, though smaller than her brother, was hale and hearty and Hannah felt wonderful. Again Vic was there when she awoke, holding the baby, and that meant a great deal to her. He'd told the staff his wife would probably want to breast-feed the baby. But he needn't have worried, breast-feeding was fashionable once more and the nurses applauded Hannah's decision to feed Frances and gave her all the help she needed.

The following day, Josie gave birth to a baby girl at home, as she'd had no problems with Phillip, and she called the baby Leonie.

She gave up work now that she had two children to care for and consequently saw more of Hannah. The two of them pooled clothes, toys and ideas and looked after one another's children. The birth of Frances also brought about a thaw between Hannah and Vic's family. Vic's two sisters were both still unmarried and Vic's mother saw the chance of either of them making her a grandmother was remote. She also missed her son, and after all, she decided, since the war, while divorce wasn't commonplace, it certainly wasn't a rarity anymore.

There was, of course, the problem of the Catholic Church, but even then Flo made it clear to her disapproving parish priest that her son's happiness came before any doctrine and Church rules. 'Surely it's not a good thing to be estranged from my son as I once was,' she said. 'And after all, what's done is done now. We have to accept it as you do.' Vic's father and sisters followed Flo's lead and Hannah was glad, not for herself – she'd never really taken to Vic's parents – but for Vic's sake.

His sisters, Betsy and Dorothy, were dowdy girls who'd had the life sucked out of them by their domineering mother, but all their lives they'd doted on Vic, their young and favoured brother, and accepted Hannah now they were able to do so and adored the children. They were grateful for the kind and sincere welcome Hannah gave them, not being brought up to expect kindness, and Hannah again felt sorry for them both.

They were only too willing to baby-sit so that Vic

and Hannah could go out now and again, and once Hannah got over the fear that something would happen to separate her from her children forever if she turned her back for a minute, she took full advantage of it.

It enabled her to accompany Vic both to medical functions and also to put time aside to go out together. Vic was fond of saying a relationship had to be worked at like anything else and they needed time alone. Vic loved Hannah even more than he had when he'd married her. Her hair was still as auburn as ever, without a hint of grey, her skin as flawless and her eyes as clear and shining.

In turn, Hannah found she loved Vic more and more with each passing week, month, year. He was a wonderful husband and lovely father and took pride both in his impetuous, boisterous son and his quieter, reflective daughter. But for Hannah's sake, he wanted her to risk no further pregnancies and after Frances's birth, he encouraged Hannah to take the new contraceptive pill, which had only gone on sale in the United Kingdom that year.

Hannah had been sceptical that taking a tiny pill could prevent pregnancy, but to please Vic she took it and as the months and years passed, she had to accept it worked.

It had been heralded as a breakthrough for women, though it was slammed by the Catholic Church who were against planning one's family. Vic was angry about that. 'They should see some of the sights I've seen,' he complained. 'Women old before their time, worn out by child-bearing year after year, bringing children into the world they can't afford to feed or clothe. This will be the making of people, you'll see.' Hannah thought of Miriam's lot and agreed with Vic.

It seemed Vic was right as family planning clinics began opening up and what had begun as a trickle had become a flood as women believed for the first time that they could choose how many children to have.

People generally were feeling more optimistic about the future. The austere post-war years were behind them and most people looked forward to the future

The emancipation of women was just one aspect of it all. Cosmetics, once frowned on by some as being 'fast', were worn by the majority of women, and there was more choice available. Now powder was dusted across faces moisturised with Pond's Cold Cream, rouge rubbed into cheeks, and lipstick, eyeshadow and mascara were used as a matter of course.

The world seemed to belong to the young and they spent their evenings jiving and rocking and rolling to Billy Fury, Neil Sedaka and a bit of a girl called Helen Shapiro. When the new dance 'The Twist' was launched by a man that went by the unlikely name of Chubby Checker, it caused a storm.

It was as different from the world in which Hannah grew up as it was possible to be. Even Josie had spent her teenage years in a world where rationing and shortages were a fact of life and where boys disappeared at eighteen for national service.

Now that national service had been abolished in 1960, the young had more freedom than ever before. Teddy boys were a thing of the past. Now at the dances some boys wore Oxford bags and two-tone shoes with pointed toes called winkle-pickers became the thing.

Many of the girls wore silky, brightly coloured skirts with layers of starched petticoats underneath them so that their dresses stuck way out. They were very popular amongst the boys as, when they were thrown about with vigour when jiving, there was often more than a glimpse of suspenders. These were called bouffant dresses to match the bouffant or beehive hairstyles the girls sported, achieved by vicious backcombing.

But, there were other types of teenagers. Whether boy or girl, these wore their hair long and like a throwback to the beatnik era, they wore 'bovver' boots, jeans and large baggy jumpers called sloppy joes.

Hannah seldom saw teenagers without wondering what Angela wore, what Angela liked doing, what music, films, books she enjoyed. The only time that Hannah was sad in her new and very happy life was when she thought of Angela.

In the summer of 1963, Hannah, desperate for news of her daughter, wrote to Pauline and asked if she'd had any contact with Arthur or Angela. Her daughter was now going on for sixteen and she longed to hear about her life. Many times over the years Hannah had thought of trying to find out what had happened to her daughter and had always been stopped by the threat of Arthur informing the Medical Council about her and Vic. She didn't know if it would matter as the years passed, but with Vic's livelihood at stake, she couldn't take the chance. Writing to Pauline was a long shot for she didn't know whether or not she'd kept in touch with Angela or Arthur but now, her daughter teetering on the verge of adulthood, she was desperate to know how she was. Hannah didn't know just how much of a long shot it was, for Pauline hadn't kept in contact with the family and had heard nothing of them until a fortnight previously when Arthur had written to her pleading for help.

He'd been asked to remove Angela from the convent school before she was expelled, he wrote. He was distraught. Angela had been accused of unacceptable behaviour, obscene language and a flagrant disregard of school rules. Pauline hadn't been surprised. She'd seen the way Angela was heading when she'd left the house, but took no pleasure in being able to say, 'I told you so.'

Arthur told her that in September he'd decided to send Angela to a boarding school in Hastings, famed for its academic achievements and discipline, but Angela was proving difficult and refusing to go. Pauline felt her heart plummet. Angela had been raised in a way where she had everything she wanted just by a click of her fingers. If she'd bucked against rules at the convent school, what would she do when she was sent to an even stricter place?

Arthur wanted to know if Pauline would come back for a while through the summer and talk to Angela. Maybe she could persuade her to go to the school to secure her future? He said he would make it worth Pauline's while.

But Pauline's sister had died the previous year and she was financially independent now, older and softer, and had little desire to try and talk sense into a resentful, truculent teenager, however much she'd loved her when she was younger, and she wrote a tactful refusal to Arthur's offer.

She thought long and hard when she received Hannah's request about whether she should tell her of the letter Arthur sent. She decided it wouldn't help Hannah to know her daughter was going off the rails. She'd had little to do with her daughter's upbringing and virtually no influence on her behaviour. Angela was the product of her father. She knew if she was to tell Hannah, though, she'd be racked with guilt that it was somehow all her fault. She remembered the radiant joy that had shone out of her on her wedding day. She deserved happiness and had found a fine and decent man who obviously loved her to bits. So why land this cloud on her horizon? No, she decided, she'd not tell Hannah anything about it. And she folded up the letter and put it away in a drawer.

Angela was desperately unhappy at her new school and she showed her unhappiness by cheeking and disobeying the teachers, being disruptive in lessons and using obscene language and gestures and being generally objectionable and aggressive. Each time she was punished her behaviour deteriorated.

But this school was of sterner stuff than the convent and didn't give in easily. On Angela's sixteenth birthday in November, they wouldn't allow her to leave the school with her father, as was usual, because her behaviour had been so bad. Arthur would not go against the school, for he hardly knew how to handle his unruly, angry daughter.

Angela took little interest in the gold watch and matching bracelet her father had given her for her birthday and her behaviour became worse than ever. While the rest of the country was reeling from the shock of President J.F. Kennedy being gunned down in Dallas, Texas on 22nd November 1963, Arthur was reading through another letter from the school, detailing Angela's latest misdemeanours.

He dreaded having her home for Christmas and was right to dread it. Not really understanding Angela's tastes now, he asked for Elizabeth Banks's help and she chose pretty underwear and perfume she was sure Angela would like, while her sons advised on the latest records. Arthur bought everything they suggested and hoped to appease Angela with them.

However, Angela liked nothing and the holiday was a disaster. They celebrated alone because Angela was so unpredictable that Arthur was too nervous to take up the Banks' offer to go there for Christmas, or even book into a hotel. He had a horror of being embarrassed in front of people whereas his daughter didn't seem to care. In fact, having her brooding, complaining presence in the house was like walking around an unexploded bomb that might erupt at any time and Arthur was totally exhausted.

He tried to hide his sigh of relief when the holiday was over and he could return his daughter to the school. But his relief was shortlived for in late January he received a telegram demanding that he come to the school and remove his daughter, for she had gone beyond the bounds of decency.

This time she had teamed up with another girl and the pair of them had actually left the school, sneaking away after lights out, using a convenient drainpipe as their means of escape, and gone into town and undoubtedly got up to all sorts of mischief, the headmistress was sure.

When she was missed at breakfast and the teachers then discovered that her bed had not been slept in, they were thinking of contacting the police, but then she and the other girl returned dishevelled, their clothes in disarray, and in an intoxicated state. They could not keep such girls in their school, they said. They were a bad example to the other girls and in moral danger themselves.

Arthur was now a worried man for he was at a loss to know how to deal with his daughter. If he'd had his way, he'd have locked her in her room, for much as he loved her, he thought she'd inherited bad blood from her mother. But he doubted Angela would stay in her room or obey any order she didn't agree with.

The housekeeper, Mrs Mackie, who had come to look after the house after Hannah left, took one look at Angela's petulant face and curling lip and said she'd been engaged to look after the house, not baby-sit teenagers who didn't know when they were well off.

'I didn't ask you to bloody well look after me, you stupid old cow,' Angela cried, turning on the woman she'd never really got on with. 'I don't need a bleeding nursemaid.'

'Angela, please!' Arthur said, shocked to the core at his daughter's angry outburst.

'That settles it,' Mrs Mackie said. 'I'm off. There's plenty of jobs where you don't have to stand the likes of language and behaviour like that.'

Angela laughed at the housekeeper's outraged face and with a baleful look at his daughter, Arthur rushed from the room to mollify Mrs Mackie who'd gone off to pack her case.

Mrs Mackie stayed, persuaded with a substantial pay rise, and Angela was left to her own devices while Arthur looked for some other place to send her. Not that he had much hope of another school keeping Angela, for she refused to conform. 'You send me to another bleeding prison and they'll just throw me out again and I'll make sure of it. I've had enough of sodding education!'

'Please Angela. At least modify your language.'

'Why? Shocks you, does it?' Angela said and added, 'You're easily bloody shocked though, aren't you? If you knew half of what I got up to your hair would turn white.'

Arthur didn't doubt it, but refrained from asking Angela to elaborate and didn't object when she suggested staying with her friend Hillary in Yorkshire for a while. In fact he was quite relieved: Hillary had been expelled from the school in Leeds along with Angela, but she wasn't sent anywhere else. Arthur had no idea of the laxity of the home Angela was going to. He had no idea that her mother, never one to bother with her daughter when she was younger, had even less to do with her as a teenager. Hillary's father, even when he was home, which wasn't often, didn't take much notice of her. On her removal from school he'd just remarked that Hillary had probably learnt enough to get by and hook a wealthy husband and that anyway most men didn't like brainy girls, so maybe it was all to the good her schooldays were over.

Hillary's brothers had finished with school too and

were now encouraged to sow their wild oats before settling down to further study at university or entering their father's firm. They attended many wild parties and were not that averse to their pretty sister accompanying them. Hillary's letters to Angela, while she was incarcerated on the south coast, told her of a life she could only dream of. Hillary's parents, like many more of her friends', were just the means of financing a life full of fun with no worries and no responsibility.

Hillary spoke of the lavish parties that went on all night and where the drink flowed constantly. She spoke of the little pills called 'purple hearts' that everyone took that made you feel wonderful and the other pill that she took each day now that she was sixteen, which meant that there was no possibility of pregnancy after her nights of steamy sex with all and sundry.

And this was the world Angela entered and threw herself into, though she was shocked at first by some of the things that went on. But she didn't want to appear square to her new friends.

'Are you sure those contraceptive pills work?' Angela asked Hillary not long after her arrival. She watched Hillary popping one into her mouth and couldn't believe such a tiny thing could stop pregnancy.

''Course I am.'

'How do they work then?'

'How the bloody hell should I know? They just do, that's all.'

'And the doctor gave them to you just like that?'

'Not the doctor,' Hillary said. 'I mean, they might, but we go to the family planning clinic. There's a Marie Stopes place in York. They don't ask many questions.'

'And they don't care that you're not married?'

'They don't know,' Hillary said. 'At least . . . Look, I've got my great gran's wedding ring, but lots of the girls just get a ring from Woolworth's for a tanner and call themselves Mrs Something. They know at the clinic, they must do, but they don't say anything.'

Angela found it was just as her friend said. Armed with a bogus wedding ring and fictitious husband, she came away from the clinic with three months' supply of pills for twelve and six.

'Now you can really let yourself go, girl,' Hillary said in delight.

'Not for the first month,' Angela said. 'She said to be careful.'

'Careful be damned!' Hillary declared. 'Plenty of time to be careful when you're old and past it.'

'Yeah,' Angela said. 'Yeah, you're right.'

'Anyway, there's a big party Saturday,' Hillary said, handing Angela a glass of cider. 'It's at Charlie's place and his folks are away for the week. God knows how long his party will go on. Certainly all night.'

'Won't your parents . . .?'

'I've told them to expect us when they see us.'

Never had Angela experienced the freedom Hillary enjoyed. Whether at school or home, her movements had always been carefully monitored. She couldn't believe that Hillary's parents were not the least bit interested in her movements, or those of her brothers. The cook complained she never knew how many to cook for, but her voice was the only one to raise any sort of complaint and one Hillary didn't care about anyway. Since Angela's arrival the week before she'd seen neither parent. There was always booze available and Angela, desperate for excitement, was ripe to try it all: cider, beer, wine, vodka, white rum, gin and brandy, or even the lethal cocktails Hillary's brothers made called punch. Angela would drink glasses of it and she liked the effect it had. It tasted sweet like fruit juice, but had a kick like a mule, laced as it was with anything to hand.

Angela was also smoking heavily, but so far she'd refused the purple hearts and the odd joints that had begun to appear among some of Hillary's friends which they passed around the group. 'Lighten up,' they encouraged her. 'Live a little.' Angela didn't know why she continued to shake her head, for she longed to experience all life had to offer, so she took her first joint at the party and mixed with alcohol, it had a dramatic effect.

On Saturday evening, Charlie's house was softly lit, there was a pungent smell of joss sticks smoking on the mantelpiece and 'She Loves You' by the Beatles was pulsating around the room. Angela had met many of Hillary's friends in the days when she'd stayed at her friend's house regularly and she was introduced to many others and had a glass thrust into her hand.

It was a good party and two hours into it, Angela had danced and drunk more than she'd ever done in her whole life. As the night went on, she noticed couples detach themselves from the group and drape themselves over sofas or armchairs, or cuddle up in corners of the room. She saw them strip off clothes and though she couldn't see much, she knew most of them would be naked or virtually naked and from the cries, moans and groans, it was blatantly obvious what they were about.

It didn't bother Angela, or any of the others. Her initial shock had disappeared at Hillary's, where her brothers would often come in with a girl they'd lead upstairs by the hand and even Hillary had told Angela to get lost a couple of times when she took a boy to her room. 'It's been the prerogative of a man for long enough,' she told Angela, who hadn't yet experienced sex. 'The pill has opened life up for girls too now. You don't know what you're missing.'

Angela thought she might be right, and no one seemed to worry about it and that night, anaesthetised further by alcohol, she began to giggle as a couple in the throes of intercourse rolled into her and almost knocked her over.

The boy beside her steadied her and she stopped and put a hand to her head. 'All right?' he asked.

'Yeah. A bit drunk, I think, my head's spinning.'

'Rubbish,' said the boy. 'You're just relaxed that's all. But I'll give you something that will relax you more,' and Angela saw a little pile of purple hearts in his hand.

Without thinking about it, Angela took two and washed them down with half a pint of cider. Almost immediately, she felt as if she was lifted up, hovering above the party, part of it and yet not. She felt marvellous, wonderful, and nothing seemed to matter, certainly not the boy who had wandered away from his previous partner and led her to a vacant sofa and began to kiss her and fondle her as he removed her clothes.

She didn't stop him, she helped him, and then pulled

his clothes off and gazed in awe, seeing a man, an aroused man, naked for the first time. When his arms came around her and his tongue teased her lips, she felt an explosion inside her.

They fell to the floor, but it hardly mattered, nothing mattered to Angela, but satisfying the throbbing ache inside her. She cried out just once and then was overtaken by waves and waves of exquisite joy and over and over she moaned in ecstasy.

She danced some more afterwards until another boy took her in his arms. She lost count of the times she sank willingly to the floor. She didn't feel tired, but alive, wonderfully alive.

Around dawn she found herself sitting on the floor beside Hillary. She was naked and had no idea where her clothes were and had wrapped a throw from the chair around herself. Hillary, semi-dressed, gave her a lopsided grin. 'You okay?' she said, her voice slurred.

'C . . . couldn't be better,' Angela said, taking a sip from the glass in her hand. She had no idea now what she was drinking and neither did she care.

'You're smashed,' Hillary said.

'So are you,' Angela retorted and both girls fell against each other giggling. 'Here,' Hillary said. 'Look what I've got,' and she produced a joint from her pocket. 'Want a smoke?' she asked. 'This will blow you away.'

Angela nodded and between them they finished the joint and their drinks and afterwards Angela could remember nothing until she woke up naked in bed beside a man late on Sunday night.

Afterwards back at her house, Hillary told her she'd shed the cover and danced naked around the room.

'You were wild,' she said. 'You even got up on the table once, but you nearly fell off.'

'Oh God, I'll never be able to look people in the face again,' Angela said, embarrassed. 'I've never behaved like that before.'

'Don't be bloody stupid. No one will care what you did. They were doing the same or worse. God, I'm just glad you decided to let yourself go a bit.'

'I know but . . .'

'But nothing,' Hillary said. 'We could be blown to bits any day. Look at the cockup our parents made of the last war and now they have the bomb no one's bloody safe. Even the President of the United States isn't safe these days.

'So the thing to do is eat, drink a lot, have great sex, enjoy yourself and don't feel guilty about it, right?' Hillary told Angela, handing her a glass of cider.

'Right,' Angela said. 'Bloody right!' and the two girls clinked glasses and giggled together.

Angela had been away three months, it was now mid-June and yet she showed no sign of coming back home. In Harrison Road, Erdington, Arthur worried about his daughter and what she was doing and he wondered where his little girl had gone, the child he'd wanted to raise in innocence and purity. He faced the fact that she was innocent and pure no longer. Any girl that sneaks out from a school in the dead of night and doesn't return till morning is up to no good.

No, it was definitely better to have her away from the house for a bit and though Hillary hadn't proved a good influence at school, now she was at home, he was sure her parents would see that she toed the line.

At least, he consoled himself, she wasn't mixing with the hooligan element, the mods and the rockers that had come to blows in Clacton, Margate and lots of other coastal resorts that spring. Nor had Angela asked for a scooter and a parka, favoured by the mods or, Heaven forbid, a motorbike and leather gear the rockers preferred. He couldn't have borne that she'd go out dressed in such a way, and he'd never have a moment's peace if she had one of those death trap machines.

Of course, he thought, it was all Hannah's fault the child was the way she was. Despite all he tried to do to prevent Angela being contaminated by Hannah, Angela had obviously inherited her bad blood. Thank God, he'd been able to forbid any contact between them. At least Angela didn't see her mother openly living with another man. True, he'd obtained a divorce, but he'd done it only to bring shame to her and also so that others, his work colleagues and in particular the Banks, would see him as the wronged party.

It had worked too, for although Elizabeth and Reg Banks had been shocked, or horrified would be more the word, their sympathies had been all for Arthur. 'I never thought, never for a minute, that Hannah would do such a thing,' Elizabeth had said, her face slightly pink with embarrassment at the news Arthur had brought. 'She said she was actually expecting the man's baby?' she asked incredulously.

'She did and she wasn't at all ashamed.'

'Poor Arthur. And you were always such a devoted husband to her.'

'Poor Arthur' shrugged and chose not to tell the

Banks about how he'd punched his young wife almost senseless and then raped her on the floor. 'That's life,' he said.

'Damned life that is,' Reg said. 'Good God man, you gave her everything, lovely home, even help in the house for years which was more than Elizabeth had in the early days. Didn't she even think of that lovely child of yours?'

'No,' Arthur said. 'To be truthful, Hannah's never been that keen on Angela. That's why I always did so much with the child. I mean, I never said anything, for that's just the way Hannah was, but she's quite willing to throw her aside now. Actually, she doesn't want anything to do with her anymore.'

'Never!' Elizabeth had never heard anything like it. To renege on her wedding vows and to leave Arthur was bad enough, but that did happen. Regrettably, that's how life was today, but to not just leave your child, but abandon her totally, was unheard of. It wasn't normal. And Elizabeth wouldn't be a bit surprised if Angela wasn't seriously disturbed in some way by it.

As the years passed and news of Angela's near expulsion from the school in Leeds filtered through to the Banks and later when they heard Arthur had been asked to remove Angela from the second school too, Elizabeth laid the blame for the girl's behaviour totally on her mother's head.

'It might have been worse if she'd stayed,' Reg said. 'Bad example and all that.'

'There is that,' Elizabeth agreed. 'Poor Arthur. But he had no option but to divorce her.'

But Arthur didn't agree with divorce really. He

followed the Church's ruling on that and considered himself still married to Hannah. He'd spoken to Father Fitzgerald about it.

He had made the Church's position clear. Hannah was living in sin, neither the divorce nor the civil marriage ceremony were recognised and therefore the baby she was expecting was illegitimate. Arthur felt justified in protecting Angela from such wickedness.

It was one day in late June when Vic came home from the hospital, where he'd been visiting a patient, with news for Hannah. He wasn't sure how she'd react to it, so he said nothing until the children were in bed.

Then, as she went to turn on the television for *Billy Cotton's Band Show*, he said, 'Could you leave that a minute, Hannah, I need to talk to you.'

This wasn't news for Hannah. She knew Vic had something on his mind and knew, too, he would tell her about it in his own time and she turned to him with a smile. 'Go on then.' And so he told her and he watched as her eyes widened in disbelief and her jaw dropped open.

She shook her head from side to side. 'I . . . I just can't believe it.'

'I assure you, Colin was quite adamant. He'd hardly lie about such a thing.'

'No,' Hannah said, for Colin Ferguson, who she'd not met until the night of the housewarming party, was now a fairly regular visitor. Hannah liked him very much and knew him to be trustworthy and yet she said, 'But he hardly knows Arthur. I mean, he doesn't really know what he looks like.'

'Yes, but he does,' Vic said earnestly. 'After the house-warming party, Phil and Josie drove him back home because he was without a car if you remember. They saw Arthur then, going down the steps of a house in Pershore Road – a shabby place by all accounts. Josie pointed him out to Colin and he took a good look then. That would have probably been that, except that he kept on seeing him after that, and always in the same place. He told me a little while ago, but never mentioned it to you and asked me not to in case you'd be upset. I said I didn't think you would, but there you are. Colin is quite an old-fashioned man in some ways. He must have been shaken by the last development.'

'You're telling me a man died of a heart attack lying naked and tied to a bed and Arthur was tied up in a similar way in another room?'

'That's what Colin found when he went there in response to a frantic and anonymous phone call. Even worse, the man that died was a Member of Parliament. The house had emptied, of course, and Colin untied Arthur without letting on that he knew him or anything and he disappeared before the police arrived. Arthur tried to give Colin money, but of course he didn't take it. He just told him to clear off and fast. The police told Colin they've had their eye on the house for some time.'

'Why are the police so interested?'

'Hannah, the things they get up to are against the law,' Vic said. 'It's for people with twisted minds who like being tied up, whipped and tortured and performing all manner of perverted and unnatural sexual acts. You remember how you said once that Arthur was aroused by violence?'

'Yes,' Hannah said, 'but that was him inflicting it on me, though I must admit, I never took a turn beating him up. Really, Vic this is making me feel sick. Arthur was, and probably still is, a prude. Look how he went on about my not being a virgin on marriage. God, how he has made me suffer for that one small slip, while he . . . No. Vic, he's a devout Catholic. Even when he was going to see Angela every weekend, he never missed Mass and always went to Communion, because Angela used to mention it in her letters home. He's fanatical about purity, about being chaste. It doesn't ring true.'

'Look, Hannah,' Vic said. 'You used the right word when you said Arthur was a fanatic. Maybe he has a split personality? Perhaps he goes on about purity to cover his tracks? I don't know, but what I do know is if Colin said he was there, then he was.'

Hannah knew that Vic was right. Arthur, the man spewing filth at her in the early days of the marriage, was the same one that charmed the neighbours and the staff at the hospital. The besotted father who gave in to his daughter's every whim was the same man who was so cruel to her and delighted in keeping her away from Angela and yet would live a lie in front of the Banks and pretend that they were a devoted couple.

It still sounded incredible though. It was like something you'd read in the more lurid Sunday papers. You would never imagine that you'd know someone who did this kind of thing. She thought she knew Arthur. God, she lived with him for years. She didn't like him much, but she thought she knew him. But he'd gone somewhere all those evenings when he'd left the house. She knew now where, all right. 'Where do they find places like this?' she asked Vic. 'I wouldn't know where to start.'

'There's adverts all over if you only know where to look,' Vic said. 'They even target certain people and approach them. Kids leaving local authority homes, often without a relative in the world to care what happens to them, or runaways who want to hide anyway. They befriend them and before they know where they are, they're sucked in. Colin has picked up quite a few casualties this way and some of them are so young. Now I'm not saying Arthur is into any of this, I'm just telling you what goes on and explaining why the police are so concerned.'

'I think it's appalling! Disgusting!'

'I agree and so do the police,' Vic said. 'But, Hannah, don't you see we've got him?'

'Got him?'

'Arthur. We can threaten to expose him if he continues to refuse to let you see or at least contact Angela.'

'And what do I do, Vic, vilify the father Angela loves, or perhaps go to the police and report what Colin told you?' Hannah cried. 'You know I can't do that. If Angela knew about this, it would destroy her. She's the one that matters here and the one that I will protect as far as possible.

'She knows nothing of her father's ban. Probably the Medical Council wouldn't be interested now, we're married and so on, but I wouldn't want to risk it. Arthur could make a good case against you, him being the aggrieved party and everything. Believe me, Vic, you don't know him like I do. He can be charming and very believable.

'Can you imagine what he'd do if I threw this at him? He'd use Angela in this, too. Remember, Vic, she's never had much time for me and probably by now thinks I'm the lowest of the low. Some day I might have the chance to put my side. But if we were to threaten Arthur, I dread to think what he'd say. He'd poison her mind right and proper.'

He covered her small hands with his own. 'We had no choice in what we did, darling,' he said gently.

Hannah pulled her hands away impatiently and rubbed the tears from her eyes. 'I know that, but this man is evil. And yet Angela believes every word he says, or at least she did when she was younger. What if he was to tell her I'd been carrying on for years, even before she was born?'

'She'd never believe that.'

'Why wouldn't she, Vic?' Hannah said. 'Why would she doubt anything her precious father tells her? I'm telling you, Arthur could convince her black was white if he'd set his mind to it.

'Then of course there's Colin's involvement in all this. There is only his word that he was there in the house that time and he couldn't say anything – not now. He'd be in trouble for perverting the course of justice.'

'So you'll do nothing to see more of your daughter?'

'Listen,' Hannah said. 'When Angela is eighteen, I'll make contact with her. She will be more able to decide then whether she wants a relationship with me or not.'

'What if Arthur still forbids her?'

Hannah smiled. 'He might try, but at eighteen, he'll have little, or no control over her, I'd imagine. And she'll be seventeen this November and it's not so long to wait.'

'So for now we say nothing?'

'That's about it,' Hannah said. 'But I'm glad I know. It's hard to think I shared the same house, the same bed for a few weeks with a creep like that,' and she gave a shudder of utter disgust and Vic, knowing that she was more upset than she was admitting to, drew her into his embrace and kissed her gently.

Chapter Twenty-Three

Angela was in love. She'd met Matthew Olaffson at one of many parties of the time and when she spotted him she just stood stock still and stared. He was, she decided, one of the most handsome men she'd ever seen. His hair was blond, worn in the Beatles style, his eyes brilliant blue and his smile as he caught sight of her across the room was the sort to die for. 'Who is he?' she hissed to Hillary beside her.

'A looker, isn't he?' Hillary replied. 'He's Ralph Olaffson's cousin. Staying with him, I believe.'

'Ralph Olaffson?' Angela knew Ralph all right. He was one of the set, but not one she was greatly enamoured with. He was always looking for bigger and better and hairier things to do to liven up his boring existence. A few months before, he'd tried to get Angela to take LSD, but she'd refused. He mocked and bullied the rest into taking it, but Angela stood firm. She didn't mind purple hearts, she'd even tried speed a couple of times and smoked a joint or two, but LSD she was wary of. She'd heard of people who'd leapt through windows thinking they could fly under its influence and others where it affected their mind ever after. Ralph treated her with scorn and called her a scaredy cat and she supposed she was but didn't care. 'There's no way I'm taking that muck,' she cried out at Ralph in exasperation.

'All right, keep your hair on,' Ralph said with a shrug. 'Your loss.'

Later, though, Angela knew she'd been right when she saw the effect it had on some of the people at the party, Hillary included. She'd begun screaming and then started sobbing hysterically and Angela sat with her for hours, holding her shivering frame. Ralph was the least concerned of anyone in the room and said it was, 'No sweat. She's just had a bad trip.'

She didn't want to get mixed up with anyone connected with Ralph and yet Matthew could hardly be responsible for his cousin and the man *was* gorgeous.

'He's coming over,' Hillary suddenly hissed and gave Angela a sharp jab in the ribs.

And then he was before the two girls, but it was obvious it was Angela he was interested in.

'Hallo.'

Angela just knew his voice would have a musical quality to it and she smiled back. 'Hallo.' They might have been the only people in the room, their eyes were locked together and Angela felt her heart hammering against her ribs.

Hillary walked away when she saw the way it was between them. She might as well have been invisible. The man had barely acknowledged her and had not spoken at all. But she was philosophical about it, plenty more fish in the sea. Matthew and Angela stood gazing at each other, while the noise went on around them and neither noticed it.

'Smoke?' Angela said, offering Matthew one from her Benson and Hedges packet.

'No. No, thank you. I don't.'

'You don't,' said Angela in surprise, lighting one for herself. 'You must be the only man I know who doesn't.'

Matthew didn't doubt it. He knew drugs were circulating too. It was totally alien to him. There had been opportunity to indulge at college, almost any drug could be obtained, but he'd never taken part.

'You're staying with Ralph, I believe?' Angela said, breaking in on his thoughts, and she took Matthew's hand and led him to a vacant sofa.

'Yes,' Matthew said. 'My mother insisted. I'm on vacation from university, you see.'

'Oh, clever clogs, eh?'

'No, not so clever,' Matthew said, though he knew he was very intelligent. 'Just lucky, I suppose. I just went to a good school, run by the Jesuit Fathers.'

'Oh Jesus, how ghastly!' Angela exclaimed. 'I've heard about them.'

Matthew smiled again and Angela's heart skipped another beat. 'Stay here, don't go away. I'll get us both a drink. You do drink, I suppose?'

'Yes, I drink,' Matthew said and might have added, 'But not in the copious amounts my cousin and his friends do.'

In fact, he'd been so shocked by many things his cousin said and later by what he saw. His cousin Ralph had scarcely believed him when he'd told him he'd never tried drugs. 'What you on about?' he said incredulously. 'All the students are at it.'

'Not this one,' Matthew said. 'None of my friends do either.'

'You don't know what you're missing then, that's all I can say.'

Matthew shrugged. He knew enough to know Ralph was into everything he could get his hands on. He was one of the worst of the set. It was incredible to believe his stern authoritarian father was the brother of Ralph's father, his Uncle Maurice.

They'd never got on. His mother invited them down to the house a few times when they first moved into the house in Sutton Coldfield, but it had never been a success. Ralph, three years older than Matthew, had bullied him mercilessly and his father and uncle had always ended up arguing. He knew his mother's hair would turn white if he was to do half the things Ralph did. In fact, if he was to tell her, she would certainly have recalled him to heel pretty quickly, but he was no sneak.

It was such an odd thing, he thought, for his mother to send him here in the first place when since his father's death two years before, she'd required his presence more rather than less. 'But won't you be lonely?' he'd asked.

'Of course not,' Marian Olaffson had said. 'I'm at the works all day.'

'Well, shouldn't I be coming now? Getting the hang of it?'

'Not, not yet a while,' Marian told her son. 'Have a holiday first. Enjoy yourself.'

'But why with Ralph? We've never got on.'

'Well, I know that, dear, but that was when you were

children. I do know he bullied you a little then. But you're both adults now and we've been sadly negligent at keeping in touch with our relatives.'

Matthew didn't say he had no desire to keep in touch with the boy he'd been frightened of in his childhood, because obedience had been banged into him since birth. He'd also been brought up to respect and defer to his mother and as she seemed so set on him making peace with their relatives, he left his Sutton Coldfield home and travelled to Leeds.

Marian waved him off at New Street Station with tears in her eyes. She was so sorry she had to send him away. He'd been the light of her life since the first time she held him in her arms. But she'd been brought up not to show emotion.

She often envied the nanny her husband Ernest had insisted they employ who could scoop her son up effortlessly and hug him, or play down on the floor with him for hours. She felt an actual pain on the nights she'd come into the nursery, often dressed up for some function, to see the nanny sitting snuggled with a drowsy Matthew on her knee, reading him a bedtime story.

He was always glad to see her. 'Oh, Mummy, you look beautiful,' he'd say and she never corrected him, though she knew Ernest said the child should say 'Mother'.

More than once, she was tempted to go down and tell Ernest to go alone, she was putting her own son to bed. But she never did. Ernest had a short fuse and a very nasty temper she was careful not to inflame.

So, she'd kiss the child lightly, careful not to pick him up and hug him, though she longed to, because he'd probably crush her clothes. She'd leave the room, dabbing at her eyes once she was outside the door with her hanky, lest Ernest see the tears and be vexed.

But at least she'd protect her son as long as she could from this secret she'd carried for months. 'I could offer you an operation,' the surgeon had said just a couple of weeks before Matthew came home for the summer. 'The tumour in your kidneys is too large and touching too many organs to remove, but an operation might shrink it, give you more time.'

'How much time?'

'Eighteen months, possibly two years. Certainly no longer.'

Marian thought only of her son, soon to be an orphan. The only relation left was Ernest's brother, Maurice, in Leeds. Ernest had always considered him feckless. 'Spoilt you see,' he'd said. 'Mother's pet. The child she never thought she'd have. While I was in the trenches in France, my baby brother was being petted and pampered in the nursery.'

But now, with Ernest dead and her soon to follow, Maurice, his wife, Phyllis, and son, Ralph, were all Matthew had in the way of family. When Marian knew she was dying, she wrote and begged her brother-in-law to look out for her son. She'd not seen him since Ernest's funeral and even then they'd only attended the service and returned the same day and there was no time to talk. Now though, she must ask for his help.

It came by return of post, a letter so warm and welcoming that she shed tears of relief and gratitude. Matthew must regard their home as his own, Maurice said, and there was another letter from Phyllis full of compassion and sympathy and Marian regretted the years she'd not tried harder to maintain a relationship with them.

But, she stressed, Matthew must not know, not yet. She would have had the operation to postpone her death a little longer and be home and recovered as far as she would ever recover before he came home again in the autumn to begin his second year at university.

Matthew knew none of this. He thought the request to come to the city he'd been born in, to an uncle and aunt he could scarcely remember and to a cousin he remembered too well and with dread, was a ridiculous one.

He needn't have worried about his cousin though. He had much more pleasant diversions to distract him than that of beating up a young boy and his aunt and uncle's welcome was sincere enough. He just wasn't used to such laxity, such a free and easy way of going about things.

Then he met Angela Bradley. Even her name, Angela, suited her, for that's what he thought of her as, an angel. And yet he doubted many angels had such vibrant beauty as she had and certainly not the gorgeous auburn hair that hung down her back in waves that were tinged with gold. Despite her excesses of the past weeks, Angela's skin was flawless and her eyes sparkled. She was perfect, absolutely perfect. They sat side by side, drinking wine and Angela smoking endless cigarettes, while they found out about one another.

'So you don't live here?' Angela asked and her heart soared when Matthew said, 'No, I live with my mother in a house in Somerville Road, Sutton Coldfield.'

'I live in Erdington,' Angela said, but she didn't mention the name of the road, suddenly embarrassed because the houses in Somerville Road were enormous. 'I bet you live in a mansion,' she said.

Matthew flushed uncomfortably. 'It is quite big,' he said, 'three storeys. There used to be an army of servants to look after a house like that, now there's just a daily and a cook. Oh, and a gardener because the garden is huge and goes down to the lake at the edge of Sutton Park.'

'Oh!' Angela said, for she knew all about Sutton Park because she had been there many times with her father. Roads ran through that massive green lung of the Royal Borough of Sutton Coldfield and it was threaded with streams that fed the five large lakes. 'To live so close to that must be marvellous,' Angela said.

'It is, I suppose,' Matthew said. 'We tend to take it all for granted. We've even got a landing stage for a yacht.'

'And have you a yacht?' Angela exclaimed in surprise.

'No, more's the pity,' Matthew said. 'I used to watch some Sunday afternoons and see the yachts bobbing about and the dads teaching their sons how to sail, or I'd see the fishermen on the other side. Lots of dads had their sons with them. I often wished it could be like that with mine.'

'And it wasn't?'

'No, it wasn't,' Matthew said rather wistfully. 'I always wanted to gain his approval. I mean, I know, or I supposed I knew, he loved me in his way, but he never said it or showed it much. He'd haul me over the coals quickly enough if I did anything bad, but he never said anything good.' He shrugged. 'Too late to ask him why he was the way he was now he's dead. What's your father like?'

'My father,' Angela said, 'would give me anything I desired. All my life he's been there. Lately,' she said almost guiltily, 'I've given him a tough time, but he's so possessive, he wants to own me. He doesn't realise I'm growing up. I had to get away, so I came to stay with Hillary. We were at school together.' Angela thought that this was not the time to tell Matthew she'd been virtually expelled. She had the feeling he wouldn't approve, and she was so attracted to the man, she wanted to look good in his eyes.

'I've read fathers are often like that with their daughters,' Matthew said. He could understand any father being besotted with the beautiful creature Angela, for he was fast becoming that way himself. He was glad, too, that Angela was here on a visit like himself. He guessed her father would be as shocked as his mother about the goings-on. He noticed that Angela never mentioned her mother. He assumed that she was dead and decided not to quiz Angela about it, in case it should upset her.

Matthew had the desire to take Angela away from all this. Away from this depravity and lax behaviour. She was very young, she couldn't be tainted by it yet. It was true she smoked, but then many girls did that. If he'd been asked, he would have said Angela had a pure, unsullied look about her, he wouldn't believe she'd drink excessively, would ever have taken drugs, or sleep around.

For Angela, it was the soberest party she'd gone to since she'd arrived. She drank only sparingly, refused the joint circulating and warned the others not to offer her any pills. Together with Matthew, she watched her friends getting spaced out or blind drunk. When they all began stripping off, Matthew pulled Angela to her feet. 'Let's get out of here.'

Angela giggled. He was treating her like a vestal virgin. Dear God, if only he knew. Normally, she'd have been joining in like all the rest, for she was finding sex very nice indeed and was equally as rampant as her friend, Hillary.

But Matthew must never know that. For there was just one man she wanted now. She fancied Matthew like mad and if he wanted to think she was as pure as the driven snow and sober as a judge, then that was the part she would act. It wouldn't be hard once they got back home. No one knew about her there. She decided to talk to him about going back to Birmingham. Surely he wasn't expected to stay away until September?

But for once, Arthur didn't want Angela home. God, he'd had a terrible fright that night in Pershore Road. Bloody good job that doctor untied him and he was able to get away. Fancy the old fellow kicking the bucket like that, right there. Still, he thought, I bet he died with a smile on his face.

They wouldn't have made such a stink of it, of course, if he hadn't been an MP. Splashed all over the *Evening Mail* it was. For days, weeks, he'd feared a knock on the door, policemen feeling his collar. 'Answer a few questions at the station, sir.' He'd barely slept, barely eaten, certain that the doctor would say something, that he'd been identified.

Not of course that he'd used his real name and address there. No one did. Mug's game that. But he'd been going for years, he was a regular. His car would have been spotted. If anyone had had the nous to take his number plate and given it to the police, he was done for.

He didn't want his daughter to come back to this just in case. He was a nervous wreck. He must write, put her off, but gently. Wouldn't do to arouse her suspicions.

'My father doesn't want me home just yet,' Angela said to Matthew. 'I can't understand it. I've been here months and every week he's written and said how much he misses me and for the last month, he's been asking when I'll be home and now . . .' She was confused. She thought her father would be pleased, delighted to have her back home. 'He said he's really busy at the moment,' she went on. 'Said to leave it a week or two. He could spend more time with me then.'

Well, she thought, she was damned if she would. By then, Matthew would have a good idea of the kind of girl she was and then the chance with him might be gone. Anyway, what right had he to say she couldn't come home? It was her home too. Well she'd go back, and damn him. What could he do? She didn't care if he worked twenty-four hours a day, she'd have Matthew at hand and that was how she wanted it. Matthew had also written to his mother saying despite the welcome from his aunt and uncle, their ways were strange to him and he and Ralph were poles apart. He said he thought he'd done enough bridge-building for now and wanted to come home.

Marian was out of hospital, the operation to hopefully prolong her life over, but she was far from well. She wrote to Maurice and in his reply, he said he was willing to keep the lad indefinitely, but he was restless, anxious to be home. And so resigned to it and longing anyway for the sight, sound and feel of her son, she said he could come back and welcome.

Angela and Matthew returned together and sat holding hands during the long journey, talking non-stop. Matthew was expected, but Angela wasn't and so, unsure of her father's reaction, she said, as the train pulled into New Street Station, 'We'd better separate and go to our homes by ourselves.'

Matthew agreed. Neither Angela nor Matthew had told their respective parents about each other, feeling that it would be better to tell them face to face.

And so, a little later, Arthur faced his daughter across the room, astounded that she'd gone against his advice. 'Aren't you pleased to see me, Daddy?' Angela asked. Till now she'd always been sure her father would be obviously delighted to see her. If it had not been convenient or not a good idea, he'd never let her feel it. She was the most important person in the world to him and she was well aware of it. But now, for the first time, she was unsure.

'Of course I'm pleased, my dear,' Arthur said. 'Delighted, in fact. It's just as I told you, I'm busy and . . .'

'Oh Daddy. I don't care about that,' Angela said. 'Don't think you have to entertain me. As a matter of fact I've met someone, someone special. He lives here, I mean in Birmingham, and he was visiting cousins in Leeds when I met him.'

'Oh,' Arthur said guardedly. Angela had never brought a boy home. In fact, she'd never brought anyone home. She had openly said she was ashamed of the place.

Thinking of her behaviour over the past months, he hadn't high hopes for the type of boy Angela would attract, yet he had to feign interest.

'His name is Matthew, Matthew Olaffson.'

'Foreign? Norwegian?' Arthur said, unaware that he'd lifted his nose in the air and given a slight disdainful sniff.

Angela, though, had noticed nothing amiss. 'His great-grandfather was,' she said. 'Or maybe the great one before that. They lived in Leeds originally and his grandfather owned an engineering works. After the war, Matthew's father came to Birmingham to open another factory.'

'You mean Matthew's grandfather owns an engineering works?'

'He did. He's dead and so is Matthew's father. His mother runs the Birmingham side, because Matthew is at Birmingham University, studying for an engineering degree.'

Now that, Arthur thought, was more like it. Not that he had a lot of time for students either, long-haired layabouts most of them. But at least the lad was studying and engineering what's more, not some airy fairy nonsense. And he seemed to have a ready-made factory to step into when he was qualified.

'The point is, Daddy, he wants to meet you,' Angela said. 'We've been going out for the few months I've been away.' This was a lie but she considered it a necessary one. She wanted her father to think she knew Matthew Olaffson inside out, for then she went on to say, 'We want to make it more permanent. We could get married next September when he's twenty-one. He gets his inheritance then, all the money his father left him.'

Matthew had never actually mentioned engagement or marriage, but that was a minor point as far as Angela was concerned. She usually had little trouble getting boys to do as she wanted. She would have said the same about her father too, but since she'd grown up and developed a life and ideas of her own, he'd got incredibly stuffy.

Arthur was dumbfounded. His little girl! His baby. But then he faced the realisation that she hadn't been his little girl for a few years now and the older Angela was difficult to even like at times, her defiance wearying and upsetting and her behaviour frankly disgusted him.

But he'd never visualised her with another man, not permanently, not to leave him, not for another man to be more important in her life than he was. And yet he'd sensed a difference in Angela since she'd returned, as if she'd taken a jump nearer maturity. She'd not sworn at him, or shouted at him since she'd entered the house, nor had she smoked a cigarette.

He wondered if it was the influence of the boy Angela mentioned or just a question of her growing up that had changed her. He didn't know, but it was such a relief to have her talking to him rather than snarling at him that he knew he had to be amenable and agree to see the boy. He'd even countenance engagement if she wanted it so badly, but marriage before she was eighteen, that he wouldn't agree to, but there was no need to tell her that yet.

He cleared his throat. 'Well, Angela,' he said. 'If the boy means so much to you, I'd better meet him, I suppose.'

'Oh Daddy,' Angela cried and with a smile of pure delight, she ran across the room to kiss Arthur on his cheek. Arthur held her close for the first time in months and hoped fervently for Angela's sake and his own that he liked this boy.

Matthew was at that moment saying to his mother, 'I think we should get the doctor to look at you.'

He'd been shocked by the sight of his mother who'd looked robust enough when he'd left home. Now, less than three weeks later, he noticed how thin she was. Not of course that she could lose so much weight in three weeks, but she'd not had that putty-coloured skin when he'd left and her eyes weren't sunken into her head like that. She was listless, had no energy.

'Don't fuss,' said Marian. 'I've had this summer 'flu. I said nothing because I didn't want to worry you. It does take it out of one, but I'll be better in no time, you'll see.'

Matthew still looked doubtful. 'You look awful, Mother, really. Let me ring the doctor.'

Marian laughed. It was an effort, but she did it. 'Matthew,' she said in mock severity. 'No woman likes being told she looks awful. As for the doctor, what can he do for 'flu, for goodness' sake? He'd just say to rest and have plenty of fluids and take aspirin for the temperature – that's all he can prescribe. Mrs Foley in the kitchen has made sure I've plenty of rest and the delicious food she's cooked has tempted my appetite, I'll tell you.'

'Well, it hasn't fattened you up any.'

'It's fashionable to be thin.'

'Well, that settles it,' Matthew said. 'You are doing too much at the works. You're to take a break now. Certainly while I'm here. I should be in every day learning the trade. "From the ground up", Father always said.'

'If that's what you wish,' Marian said. She was tired, deathly tired, and at any rate, she knew that soon Matthew would have to learn every aspect of the business. A degree was all very well; Ernest had insisted on a degree for his son and heir, but there was no substitute for actually working there day after day.

In an attempt to lighten the atmosphere and take Matthew's mind from how frail and ill she looked, she patted the bed and said, 'Come on, sit down and tell me all about your stay.'

Matthew sat obediently. He'd been worried to be met at the door by their cook, Mrs Foley, who told him his mother was in bed recovering from a dose of 'flu. Mrs Foley had been cook in the family for years since losing her husband to the selfsame thing that was now killing her mistress. She'd guessed there was something serious the matter with Marian before Marian'd been aware of it herself, but had said nothing.

Marian had told her in the end and also said Matthew wasn't to be told. Mrs Foley had not been too happy about that. After all, Matthew was no young lad any more and she thought Marian Olaffson could have done with her son's support. But she was adamant and so now with Matthew returned long before he was due, she had to go on with this façade and say the mistress had the 'flu. She could see Matthew wasn't taken in entirely and now he was up there talking to his mother. She'd taken a tray with sandwiches and some fancies and a pot of tea for the two of them. She knew that Marian might drink the tea, but she'd eat nothing and probably tell Matthew she'd eaten earlier.

Mrs Foley was right, that was exactly what Marian did say. She listened to her son telling her of Maurice and his wife and Ralph. Matthew wasn't one to tell tales and he didn't now and though he mentioned the parties he'd gone to, he didn't say what went on and he praised his uncle and aunt for their genuine welcome.

He was not aware how expressive his vivid blue eyes were and how well his mother knew him after nearly twenty years of rearing him. She knew much of the way it was from what her son didn't say and her heart sank, for she knew Matthew could never settle in the north with Maurice and Phyllis when it was all over. She hated the thought of leaving him all alone.

But then she heard a new note in his voice. He described his meeting with Angela and she saw the light dance in his eyes as he described her beauty and simplicity and Marian knew her son was smitten by this girl, this Angela Bradley, and a stab of jealousy pierced her. She crushed it down. What was the point of her being jealous of the girl her son had chosen? Maybe she would be the one who could help him afterwards. She'd have to see the girl, assess her. She reached for her son's hand and squeezed it. 'I'm happy for you,' she said. 'All your life all I've ever wanted is your happiness. This girl seems really important to you.'

'Oh she is, Mother,' Matthew replied eagerly, marvelling at how well his mother had taken the news, for he knew many mothers were jealous of their sons' girlfriends. He'd never had anyone serious before, but he'd heard the chaps at school talk about it and even those at uni.

'And now,' Marian said, 'I'd like to meet her.'

'Oh you will, Mother,' Matthew assured her. 'And I'm sure you'll love her like I do. She's speaking to her father tonight and she'll phone me when it's time for me to go round and see him.'

Marian watched her son leave the room shortly afterwards with a spring in his step. Oh, let her be the one, she prayed, I know he's young, they're both young, but time isn't something I have a lot of. If I could see him settled, I'd die with an easier mind.

Chapter Twenty-Four

Matthew had been very nervous meeting Arthur for the first time. Angela had explained about his possessiveness and he knew few fathers think any boy good enough for their daughter. He took care with his appearance that night. He wore a dark blue suit – not his usual style, but he thought the occasion warranted it – first impressions were everything.

Arthur was impressed. The boy, for that's all he was, wore the suit well and the pure white silk shirt beneath it. The striped blue tie matched the handkerchief in his pocket and if he was any judge, the cuff links and tie stud were solid gold and his black shoes shone so you could imagine you'd see your face in them.

This young man he knew was no riffraff and better than he could have hoped for Angela to hook. Not that she didn't have the looks, but looks weren't everything and he knew her behaviour hadn't been the best. Thank goodness that Hillary had come up tops in the end, he thought, and introduced Angela to the right kind of people. 'Smoke?' he asked Matthew, flicking his silver cigarette box open.

'No thanks,' Matthew said. 'I don't.'

'Nor me, Daddy,' Angela put in. 'Not any more anyway.'

'Oh,' Arthur's eyebrows arched in surprise. It was too soon to see if Angela had changed for good, for she'd been home less than twenty-four hours, but she'd not shouted and sworn at him once since she had returned and now she said she'd given up smoking. He smiled at her benignly. 'I'm delighted to hear that, my dear,' he said. 'Maybe we could have a coffee or perhaps, Matthew, you'd like something stronger?'

Matthew would have dearly liked a double brandy to stop his limbs shaking so much, but appearance was everything. 'No thank you, sir, a coffee would be fine.'

Angela took the cue and she flashed her smile across at her father, the one that ensured she always got her own way, and said as she got to her feet, 'Well, I'll not be long, I'm sure you have plenty to talk about.'

And Matthew talked. He told Arthur about his parents and how the premature demise of his father meant the burden of the factory had fallen on his mother, as it had been his father's dearest wish that he gain an engineering degree.

'How far through it are you?'

'I've finished my first year,' Matthew said. 'I'm nearly twenty, my birthday is in September.'

'And you like my daughter it seems?'

'I do, sir. Really who wouldn't like her?'

His answer pleased Arthur and he was laughing and chuckling as Angela entered the room, a tray of coffee in her hands. 'I see you two have hit it off,' she said happily. 'That's good. I told Daddy yesterday that I don't want to be married right off, that we'll have to wait until you have your inheritance next year, but I'd like to be engaged by my birthday in November.'

Matthew had been so surprised at her words, the coffee had slopped in his saucer, and he looked at her open-mouthed before adjusting his gaze to Arthur, certain he'd make some remark, some comment. But he saw Arthur gazing with rapt attention at his daughter, a smile playing around his lips.

Arthur *was* pleased, pleased that Angela, despite her dubious past behaviour, had found herself a decent boy at last. He faced the fact that his daughter was a sensual girl, bad blood inherited from her mother. It could be seen now even as they sat on the settee. She was snuggled against him, stroking his arm, clasping his hand with her own and almost devouring him with her eyes.

If she wasn't to bring disgrace upon the house, she needed to be respectably married and speedily. Who better than this young, intelligent, upright man, who would one day be wealthy? Added to that, they were more than fond of each other, anyone with half an eye could see that. Before he'd met and been impressed by Matthew, he'd thought to delay the marriage, but seeing them together he knew that would be a mistake. Matthew got a settlement on his twenty-first birthday next September and Angela would be eighteen the following November. They could have a winter wedding.

Matthew eventually found his voice. 'I . . . I'll still have almost a full year at university after my birthday.'

'That's no matter,' Arthur said dismissively. 'Being married shouldn't affect your studies.'

'I'd thought to graduate before I marry,' Matthew said. In fact, he'd had no thought of marrying anyone at all yet, but he felt he couldn't say this.

'Your inheritance is a sizeable one, I believe,' Arthur said. 'You'll not need to graduate and be earning good money before you can afford a wife.'

'You don't think us too young to settle down?'

'Not at all, you'll grow up together,' Arthur said. 'Not that I won't miss my minx of a daughter you know, but I'm afraid when my Angela decides on something, then she has to have it. She likes her own way.'

No way was he going to rock Angela's boat and turn her back into the raging virago she'd become when she came home from the school in Hastings. If she wanted marriage to this young man and she'd been so much better since she'd met him, then she would have marriage and really, Arthur reflected to himself, she could have done a lot worse.

Matthew said nothing more. He was confident that his mother would see it his way, that she would say that he was too young to settle down, that the whole thing was ridiculous. She'd make both of them see that.

But Marian didn't see it that way at all. She liked the lovely Angela – who was on her best behaviour every time they met. True, the girl was young and wouldn't have an idea how to run a house, but in their case that hardly mattered. When she was gone, this house, in fact everything would belong to Matthew and she was sure Mrs Foley would help Angela fit the role of lady of the house.

Far, far more important was that Angela so evidently loved her son and it relieved her mind that he would have that love to bolster him when her time was up. And a wedding just over a year away was splendid, time enough to organise the lavish occasion and she should still be well enough to attend.

Matthew couldn't understand his mother's attitude, nor Angela's. He'd thought to travel after his degree. He'd seen nothing of the world, because his father had disapproved of holidays. But with the money he would have, he wanted to buy a car and first travel around Britain and then try the continent. Then he wanted to go further afield; Canada, America, Mexico and the Caribbean.

Could he still do this with Angela in tow? He doubted it. He just knew Angela would expect plush hotels, her every whim attended to. But you didn't really see a country like that. He'd intended to rough it, to sleep in a small tent, to go off the beaten track for most tourists. For years, this dream had sustained him every autumn term at school when he'd listened to his friends as they recounted their adventures in the holidays they shared with their parents.

He saw the dream crumble. He saw the constraints of a home and maybe a family fall around his shoulders like a dead weight. He'd thought to have a few carefree bachelor years – possibly sharing a flat with some of the friends he'd made at uni. Girlfriends would figure of course and he did feel something special for Angela, but as yet the feelings were new, fragile, and he'd thought to take one day at a time as they got to know about each other, not make long-term plans on such a short acquaintance.

However, obedience had been demanded of Matthew

and from an early age he'd learnt the worst thing he could possibly do was to upset his mother. He could stand the odd beatings his father gave him, but to see his beautiful mother's eyes awash with tears, and hear the hurt and dismay in her voice at something he'd done, he'd always found hard to cope with.

And now, his mother appeared frailer than ever and he knew still spent much of the day in bed. How could he go against something she was so much in agreement with?

He couldn't. He might want to but he couldn't. He had to let them all arrange his life, his marriage to the lovely Angela Bradley and hope that they'd get along together. He gave a sigh, knowing this was the life he was committing himself to.

By the end of November, Angela sported a large diamond ring on her left hand. Matthew was back at university and that weekend they were out together looking for Christmas presents.

Angela had never shopped in Erdington Village since her mother's defection. She was terrified of meeting her. She didn't know how she'd react. But that day, the weather was cold and the skies heavy and leaden grey and Matthew, who wasn't keen on shopping at the best of times, had balked at the idea of going to town when they had an array of shops on their doorstep. 'It's madness, Angela,' he'd said. 'You can see that sky is going to empty itself any minute. Let's go and get the wretched shopping and be done with it.'

Hannah, too, was shopping. Normally, she'd leave the children behind with Vic, but he'd had a call-out that day, and so she pushed Frances in the pushchair and Adam danced by her side as they reached the High Street, making for Tesco's near Six Ways.

Angela and Matthew had been into Gardner's Milk Bar for a coffee and to get out of the horrible weather for a while. 'I told you we should have gone into Birmingham,' Angela complained. 'What can you get in this crummy town? I wanted a cashmere cardigan for Daddy and Rackham's is the only place.'

'We can go next weekend,' Matthew said. 'Might be better weather then.'

'Hardly likely.'

Matthew laughed. 'Come on, grumpy, I wanted a beautiful shawl for my mother too, but I'm not moaning.'

'Is your mother no better?'

'A little,' Matthew said. 'She was picking up a bit, but this cold weather doesn't help. That's why I wanted the shawl. Something pretty and soft. Angora wool, or something similar. I'll know the right thing when I see it.'

'Well, you won't see it here, will you? A wonderful collection of shawls Erdington has to offer.'

'Drink your coffee and stop harping on,' Matthew said, but good-humouredly. 'Today's the day for going back to your house and listening to records. Have you got the Beatles' latest?'

'"Hard Day's Night",' Angela said. 'Yes, I bought it yesterday. I'd like to see the film too when it comes to the Palace.'

'I think we can manage that,' Matthew said. 'And next Saturday, rain or shine, we'll go into town and buy the things we couldn't find here.'

They were laughing as they went out of the café, each thinking how nice it would be to cuddle up on the sofa and listen to the Beatles that both Matthew and Angela were mad about, while they explored each other's bodies. Angela, much more experienced than Matthew, tried to keep that fact secret, but it was hard. Matthew went very slowly, almost too slowly for Angela, and she often wanted to urge him to go further, but so far she'd restrained herself. She'd hate for Matthew to think her fast.

When they'd first had the house to themselves, she'd taken him to her bedroom. The first tentative kisses had grown more ardent and they'd fallen back on the bed together and Matthew, in a fever of excitement, had unbuttoned Angela's shirt and unhooked her brassiere so that her breasts lay exposed. Angela, aroused beyond measure, unbuttoned her jeans and began to wriggle out of them as she felt Matthew harden against her.

Suddenly, Matthew had stopped caressing Angela's breasts, swung his legs away from her and sat on the edge of the bed. 'What is it?' she cried, pulling her jeans up as she spoke and putting her arms around him, heedless of her semi-nakedness. 'Don't you want me?'

'Of course I want you,' Matthew said. 'That's why I couldn't lie there next to you a moment longer.'

'You could have me if you liked.'

'You wouldn't mind?'

'Not with you I wouldn't,' Angela said. 'After all, we're going to get married. It's different.'

'It's still wrong,' Matthew insisted. 'I'm sorry, I forgot

myself.' He looked at Angela's luscious breasts inches away from his face and he knew if he reached out and touched them as he wanted to, he would be lost. There would be no turning back this time. 'Please get dressed,' he said. 'We mustn't come up here again. It's too much of a temptation.'

And they never had and their lovemaking hadn't progressed much further than that, yet they often had the house completely to themselves. Mrs Mackie never worked weekends, for when Arthur had employed her, he was off to Leeds every weekend. She always left the makings of a meal, or during the winter, a pie or casserole to just put in the oven for Saturday and Arthur and Angela, if she was home, always had their Sunday lunch out.

Arthur was often needed at the office now on Saturday mornings and many afternoons he told Angela he was visiting his club. It was a different club to the one she would have envisaged though and its address wasn't Pershore Road any more, that had been too risky. He went instead to a similar place in Belgrave Road, where every sexual perversion could be bought, at a price.

But for Matthew and Angela, it meant a whole day of freedom and Angela couldn't know how hard it was for Matthew not to take their lovemaking further when he held her beautiful and pliant body next to his and his whole body was on fire for her. But each time Matthew wanted to go forward, he was haunted by the scenes at some of the parties he went to with Ralph. The blatant depravity engaged in by some of the couples in view of everyone else had sickened him and because of it, he curtailed his lovemaking with Angela. They had, he told himself, plenty of time and he had no wish to frighten Angela by behaving like an enraged, out of control beast.

Angela knew nothing of Matthew's thoughts and while their lovemaking never went far enough in her opinion, used as she was to regular sexual gratification, she began, as the weeks slipped by, to value Matthew for other qualities. He was innately kind and considerate and generous, for he'd been brought up to treat women well, and those were things Hillary's friends often didn't do.

He also had a good sense of humour and could always coax Angela from a mood. They mostly liked the same type of music, though Matthew liked the Rolling Stones, thinking they were almost as good as the Beatles, while Angela thought them awful – brash and common. Angela had also met some of Matthew's university friends and found most of them interesting and fun. Matthew didn't tell Angela of his friends' open-mouthed astonishment at the news of his engagement and impending marriage. 'God, man! What is it with you?' one asked. 'I mean, I know she's a cracker, but marriage? Jesus, man!'

While another said with a slight smirk, 'You don't have to marry them these days. You can love them and leave them. They have the pill today.'

Matthew knew that there was no way on God's earth that he could make his friends understand how he'd been coerced into marriage, when he could barely understand it himself, so he said nothing.

Instead, he and Angela entered a courtship. No wild

parties or heavy drinking bouts or drug-taking. Instead, they met groups of friends in coffee bars and pooled their money for the jukebox, or they went to the cinema, or out dancing and occasionally Matthew borrowed Marian's car and they went to the theatre or to dinner. Then of course there was the entertainment at the university; concerts, balls, dances, variety acts, live groups – they sampled them all and daily Angela realised Matthew was becoming more and more important to her.

That day they left the milk bar, arm in arm, snuggled together for warmth, laughing hilariously about something and so engrossed with each other that they failed to notice the woman turning the corner with the pushchair. 'Oh sorry,' Matthew said. 'Didn't see you there.'

Angela said nothing and neither did the woman. They both just stood and stared at one another and Matthew then stared too. The woman was the spitting image of his Angela, he thought, or maybe it was the other way round? But whatever way it was, they were like two peas in a pod. The woman was older, although her hair was still the same vivid auburn and the eyes sparkling green, the skin as clear, and even the nose and mouth the same shape. It was like looking at what Angela would be in twenty years' time.

Hannah looked at her daughter in shock, but it was nothing to the shock she got when she tore her eyes from her daughter and they slid across to Matthew. Then her eyes widened, while the blood drained from her face.

It was as if she'd slipped back to the war years and the man before her was her beloved Mike, her first love and the father of her son. Her son! Oh my God! She told herself not to be so silly. The boy had a resemblance to Mike, that was all. Didn't people say everyone had a double? That was all it was. There was no need to get into a state about it.

There was at any rate no time to give the matter more thought, for suddenly Angela, her flashing eyes furious and resentful, turned to her companion and almost spat out, 'Matthew, this is my mother!'

Matthew turned his gaze on the woman. The atmosphere between them was charged. He couldn't understand why she was looking at him with an almost frightened look. The child in the pushchair began to grizzle and the little boy, who'd heard what Angela had said, cried, 'She's not your mother.'

Hannah barely heard the children, though she automatically jiggled the pushchair, and in the silence Matthew burst out incredulously, 'Your mother? I thought your mother was . . .'

'Dead? She is,' Angela spat out. 'Or at least she might as well be.'

Matthew had been sure Angela had no mother. He'd discussed it with his own. 'But is she dead?' Marian had persisted.

'I suppose so. She never talks about her.'

'Well, it must be sorted out by the wedding,' Marian said. 'Ask her.'

But Matthew hadn't. He'd wanted to, but always his courage failed him. He had no desire to upset Angela. But this woman beside him now was no ghost, no figment of the imagination. Angela had a mother and one that looked just like her and it was more than obvious Angela had little time for her.

Hannah was trying to find a response to Angela – some way of reaching out to the child she'd left behind and knew she'd hurt badly, when Frances, cold and frightened by something she could barely understand, set up a wail. Adam, on the other hand, wasn't frightened, he was angry. He didn't see the resemblance between his mother and Angela, he only heard Angela's words. And he sprang forward. 'Don't you say that!' he yelled. 'She's not your mother, she's mine and Frances's.'

'Only for a while,' Angela told the confused little boy. 'Make the most of it, I should. One day she'll just take off.'

'No she won't,' Adam said and he aimed a kick at Angela's leg, but Hannah jerked him back before it connected. She saw Adam's face was crimson with bewilderment and temper and Frances was fretful and shivering, despite the blanket covering her, and she said, 'Angela, we need to talk.'

'There's years I've needed to talk to you. Where were you?'

'Please, not here. Let me try and explain at least?' Hannah pleaded.

'Huh. Explain? Explain why you just walked off?'

'It wasn't like that,' Hannah said. 'Please come home with me for a little while? It's too cold to stand here.'

Matthew watched the exchange between the young woman and the older one and saw the yearning in Hannah's eyes. Surely they could discuss whatever it was that had happened in the past? 'Angela,' he said. 'I think you should talk to your mother.'

'Why the hell should I?'

'Because you might regret it if you don't,' Matthew said, but gently because he could feel Angela's body trembling against his own and knew she was upset.

'I won't regret it,' Angela said defiantly. 'Why should I? What is she to me anyway? She's nothing.' She sprung forward away from the protection of Matthew's arms and, her face inches away from Hannah's, spat out, 'You hear that? You're nothing to me! Nothing!'

Hannah recoiled slightly, not at all sure Angela wasn't going to hit her. Not so her small son, who began pushing Angela away, and though tears rained down his face, he was shouting, 'You're horrible, horrible, stinking horrible,' and Frances began to scream.

They were attracting attention. Many people weary of shopping and worn down by the cold weather were happy to stop for a few minutes and watch the entertainment. Hannah and Matthew were only too aware of it and were embarrassed, while Angela couldn't seem to care less.

Matthew drew her away from Hannah, who held on to Adam, and said, 'You're upsetting the children and whatever happened between you is nothing to do with them. Why don't you go somewhere more private and talk it over?'

Angela turned to him. Her face flushed and she snapped, 'You know nothing about it.'

'No,' he agreed. 'I don't need to know perhaps, but you do.'

Angela dropped her gaze from Matthew and he asked Hannah, 'Where do you live?'

'Grange Road.'

'Well then, Angela, why don't you go home with

your mother and I'll see you later?'

'No,' Angela said to Matthew and then reluctantly continued, 'Okay, okay, I'll go if you think it's so important, but I'm not going on my own. You've got to come too.'

It was the last thing Matthew wanted to do, to go to some strange woman's house and listen to the pair of them re-hashing some old injustice, maybe getting angry, tearful even. But he knew this thing between them had to be faced. Angela's mother had walked out on her, that much he'd picked up, but she wanted to explain why and Angela had a right to know and she was afraid to face it alone. 'All right,' he said at last with a brief nod and without another word, Hannah turned the pushchair around.

The walk back was torturous and almost silent. Hannah, too busy formulating what she was to say to her estranged daughter to make conversation, and Angela too angry and resentful at being talked into going back with her. Matthew concentrated his efforts at breaking the pregnant and uneasy silence by trying to talk with the little boy. He walked obediently beside his mother, but his mouth was mutinous and he cast many a baleful look at Angela.

But he had nothing against Matthew and answered his questions about school and Christmas, not that far away, pleasantly enough. Hannah barely heard the two talking, for her mind was racing and she could have wept with relief when she saw Vic's car in the drive, for she didn't know how she'd explain everything to Angela, the way she needed to, with the children around.

* * *

'I don't know what the bloody hell I'm doing here,' Angela said, standing awkwardly in the middle of the sitting room Hannah had shown them into.

The use of the swear word in front of Matthew showed her level of distress, but he said nothing about that. Instead, he said, 'It's better this way. You were bound to meet one day, living as you do only a relatively short distance apart.'

'Daddy will go mad when he hears.'

'Why should he?'

'Oh Matthew, you don't know Daddy. I've never been allowed to even speak Mommy's name since the day she left.'

'A bit harsh that,' Matthew commented. 'So you were never able to ask questions about why she left?'

'No.'

'Did you want to?'

'What do you think?' Angela said. 'At the time, I was so upset, but he said that as far as I was concerned she was as dead as if she was laid in the cemetery and I was not to think of her again.'

The pain of that time showed clearly in Angela's eyes and Matthew felt so sorry for her that his arms encircled her and she buried her face in his coat.

And that's how Hannah found them when she came in with a tray of coffee and tea and biscuits. 'Take off your coats,' she said. 'You'll not feel the benefit when you go out. I'll poke up the fire. It will warm up in no time.'

Angela had drawn out of Matthew's embrace at her mother's entrance and she said, 'We won't bother, we're not staying long.'

But Matthew was already unfastening his coat and the look he cast in Angela's direction was so like Mike Murphy's that Hannah's heart skipped a beat. 'Come on, Angela,' he said. 'We might as well see this through now we're here.'

With a shrug, Angela unfastened her coat and Hannah took them both and laid them over a chair and Angela and Matthew sat side by side on the settee. It was as Hannah took Angela's coat that she noticed the beautiful engagement ring on her left hand. A large cluster of diamonds surrounding a red stone, and Hannah's heart fell for she knew the relationship was not a casual one, not if they were engaged.

She also knew the ring was an expensive one, like the clothes Matthew wore. Everything spoke of quality; his coat was pure wool and he wore an Aran sweater and blue trousers in the modern tight-bottomed style and soft leather boots.

'Would you like coffee or tea?' Hannah asked.

Matthew would have been glad of either for the day was raw but Angela snapped, 'Don't bother with either. We're not stopping. Say what you've got to say and then I can leave and get on with my life again.'

Hannah sighed. 'Angela . . .' she began, but Angela burst in again, 'I don't owe you anything. I hope you know that.'

'I know you owe me nothing, Angela, believe that, please,' Hannah said. 'Just give me one brief half an hour to explain what happened five years ago.' She knew she was on shaky ground, for if she was to tell the truth, and she had to do that, she would have to speak against Arthur.

She began gently. 'You know your father and I had not got on for years,' she said. 'You know we had separate rooms?'

'I hope you're not going to blame all this on Daddy?'

'No,' Hannah said. 'I'll take my share of the blame, but usually it is never just one person's fault. Will you hear me out?'

Angela would have made some rude retort if it hadn't been for Matthew's hand that had covered hers and Hannah swallowed a lump of nervousness in her throat and went on.

She went back to her pregnancy with Angela. 'That's when Arthur moved out of the bedroom,' she said. 'He . . . he was never interested in that side of marriage.'

Angela shifted uncomfortably in embarrassment, but Hannah plunged on. Angela learned of her mother's deep and long depression after her birth and of Pauline being engaged to look after her and the part that she and Arthur played in Angela's rearing. 'I was ill for so long and then when I was feeling better, you rejected me,' Hannah said. 'Before I got to know you properly, Arthur had got you into a school full-time and after a little while, there was little for me to do at home. Pauline ran the house and was there to see to you, that was until your father came home, because then you wanted no one else.

'I took the job at the doctor's to get me out of the house and to have money of my own because your father never gave me much. From the first I got on with Vic. We were friends – that's all. It developed from there. Your father was often cruel, not that he hit me regularly or anything, but he was cruel in what he said and did. Vic was always so kind, compassionate and gentle.

'I often felt a failure as a mother and your father helped my insecurities along. Vic and I knew we'd become attracted to each other, but I told Vic I was a wife and mother and however bad I was, I wouldn't make myself worse by beginning an affair.'

'Huh,' snorted Angela. But Matthew saw the unshed tears shining in Hannah's eyes and he squeezed Angela's hand to show his support and said gently, 'Let her finish, pet.'

Hannah smiled at him, but he saw her smile was watery as she went on. 'Believe me, Angela, I wanted no part in an affair, but the time your father took you away for Christmas – you remember that time?'

Angela nodded and Hannah continued, 'I was so lonely. Pauline had gone by then and Josie had her own plans and in the end . . . in the end, I phoned Vic and he came. That was the start of it. I loved Vic dearly, Angela, and I still do. I do want you to realise that. I wanted to be with him, live with him, marry him eventually. But I also loved you very, very much and Vic understood that. We'd worked it out. If I wasn't living with your father, he could not prevent me from going to the school to see you.

'I would have fought through the courts for access and then you could have possibly spent the holidays with us too, part of them at any rate. Vic was in total agreement with me on this. If you love someone, you want the best for them and he knew I could never just toss you aside. But in the end I could do none of the things I'd planned because I became pregnant with Vic's child and was forced to leave.'

Angela remembered the long lonely years without Hannah and said, 'You could have taken me when you went away, other mothers do.'

'And believe me, I wanted to,' Hannah said earnestly. 'Your father prevented me.'

'Oh yeah,' Angela said sarcastically. 'That's a good one. Blame Daddy, why don't you? How could he stop you?'

'Angela, he'd spent years trying to keep us apart, trying to drive a wedge between us. If you think back, you'll know I'm right.'

Angela did, and remembered various instances, not fully understood at the time, where her father had been undeniably cruel to her mother and she knew now her mother spoke the truth. 'But this time,' Hannah said, 'he had the law on his side. Vic was my doctor and as such not allowed to have any sort of sexual relationship with his female patients. Your father said I could leave any time I wished, but that if I tried to contact you in any way, any way at all, he would report Vic to the Medical Council. He would have been struck off.

'I couldn't put him through that. Being a doctor was all he ever wanted to do and he knew his parents couldn't stand the disgrace either. They were so proud of him and had made vast sacrifices to enable him to become a doctor in the first place. They are not wealthy people. Anyway, I had to leave. Your father told me I could take only what I could get into one suitcase and I left the same night.'

'You could have written at least. I wouldn't have said,' Angela said mulishly.

'The nuns would have,' Hannah said. 'I couldn't take the risk. Josie wasn't allowed to contact you either.'

'I wrote you letters at first.'

'I never got them. Your father would have dealt with that sort of thing.'

Angela nodded slowly. 'Yes,' she said. 'Yes, he probably did. What about now though? What if I were to tell him about this? Would it matter after all this time?'

'Probably not,' Hannah said. 'But even if it did, I couldn't pass up the chance of seeing you, talking to you, trying to explain. If . . . if you tell your father, I don't know what it will mean now. After all, your father divorced me and Vic and I married. I know in the Catholic Church our divorce and marriage are not recognised, but they are legal. Maybe as we are now a stable unit, Vic wouldn't lose his job, I really don't know.'

Angela was silent for a moment and then said, 'Maybe we should put it to the test?'

'Maybe we should,' said Hannah. 'But whatever happens, I certainly don't want to lose contact with you now.'

Angela didn't answer and Hannah let her ponder and turned to Matthew. 'Tell me about yourself,' she said. 'You must be some sort of superman to have talked Arthur into letting you and Angela become engaged?'

'How did you know?' Angela demanded.

'Angela, you are sporting the biggest diamond I've ever seen,' Hannah said with a smile.

'And I suppose you are going to disapprove?' Angela

snapped. 'Say we're too young. We don't know our own minds.'

'No,' Hannah said. 'I've lost the right years ago to disapprove of what you do. But I would like to know something about Matthew if he's going to join the family.'

She listened, her apprehension increasing as she heard of the family from Leeds where Matthew had lived for his early years before moving to Somerville Road in Sutton Coldfield. There was wealth in the family, but Hannah sensed a loneliness in the young man. Yes, he told her, he was an only child and as he spoke of his father she saw a child constantly trying to please an aloof parent, always falling short, and she saw also the deep devotion he had for his mother, who she heard was ill at the moment, and she saw too that Matthew was worried about it.

Her apprehension increased rather than diminished as he spoke. Not only by what he said, but by his gestures and the look in those large blue eyes that spoke again and again of Michael Murphy.

She told herself not to panic and jump to conclusions. Maybe it was just a dreadful coincidence. Sweet Jesus, she prayed silently, please let it be just that.

And then, Matthew pushed up the left sleeve of his jumper to check his watch and Hannah saw the mark on his arm and she felt a wave of fear envelop her as she asked, her voice sounding shaky, 'Your arm. Is it a burn?'

'No, a birthmark,' Matthew said, pushing up his sleeve to reveal the apple-shaped scar. 'I've always had it.' Hannah could have told him that. He had it when he was minutes old and when she'd held him in her arms for the one and only time. Every bit of him then was ingrained in her memory and she remembered leaning down and kissing that blemish that he displayed now for her.

After they'd gone, she sat for a long time in front of the fire thinking. He'd come from Leeds. His family were devout Catholics. He was an only child. It all fitted. He'd obviously never been told that he'd been adopted, but then that she knew was quite normal. Oh God, what should she do?

For a couple of days she did nothing, knowing that she was risking raising a hornet's nest, but also knowing she couldn't do nothing and let the two . . . God, it was against the law, against nature and against all decency. She had to find out.

She discussed it at length with Vic and Josie. 'I'm frightened, Josie,' she admitted. 'If I spoil this for Angela, she'll hate me for it.'

'That's a risk you have to take,' Josie said firmly. 'You can't let it go on, Hannah, you just can't. And it's best to do something quickly before they are in too deeply.'

Hannah knew Josie was right. But not wishing to rock the boat too much, too soon, she wrote to Tilly. She told her the whole story and asked if she could find out where her son had been taken and the name of the family.

Tilly tried. The nuns who were involved in the home in the first place had scattered and to find any of them was impossible. She did find Father Benedict, who Hannah had also told her about, who she said had helped her initially. He was an old man now and in a home for elderly and retired priests, and he took some time to recall Hannah. It had been years ago and she was just one of many, but when he heard of the urgency and reason for Tilly's enquiries he was upset he couldn't help her further.

When Tilly phoned and told her of her fruitless search, Hannah wasn't altogether surprised. She knew there was little likelihood of locating any of the nuns from the home. She remembered Gloria saying Sister Monica had gone to Ireland, but she'd never mentioned the name of the convent. But even if one of them had been found, could they help? They might want to, if they were aware of the consequences if they didn't, but would they remember? Would there be any form of records kept and would she be able to have access to them?

She doubted it, because Tilly, bless her, also tried social services and the local authorities and came up against a brick wall.

It was now mid-December and Hannah knew there was only one avenue open now and that was to go and see Matthew's mother and ask point blank if he was her adopted son. And she had to do it quickly. She didn't know the number of the house, but Angela had given her a description of where it was and told her it was called 'Stonehaven'. Hannah knew she had to go there and find out the truth. She was desperately worried about Angela's reaction should Matthew prove to be her son for since the first visit, Angela had been back only once and Hannah was sure that that had been at Matthew's instigation.

He was a good influence on her daughter, she thought, and a lovely, lovely boy and they were definitely very fond of each other. She wondered if she was about to blow their world apart.

Chapter Twenty-Five

Hannah got off the bus and looked about her, dreading what she must do. Icy relentless rain fell in sharp spears and the leaden grey sky did little to lighten her mood as she pulled her coat around herself a little more and shivered.

This was unfamiliar territory for her. She'd been into the centre of Sutton Coldfield a few times before for bits of shopping she couldn't get in the village, but this was a bus stop or so before the terminus. She'd asked the help of the bus conductor and he pointed out the way as she alighted by the small parade of shops.

As directed, she walked past the girls' grammar school and on up the hill, over the railway line and there, just as he said, was Somerville Road. The houses were expensive and the road select, which from Matthew's demeanour and speech Hannah would have expected. Wealthy people lived behind those walls and hedges. Had her son grown up in such surroundings? Well, she'd soon know.

Matthew had told her his house backed onto the lake in Sutton Park and Hannah had checked that on the *A-Z* and knew his house had to be past another road called Monmouth Drive. She strode out purposefully, wishing now she'd taken up Vic's offer to go with her to see Mrs Olaffson and drive her to the door. Somehow, though, she'd known she had to do this alone.

Hannah just had Angela's description of the house to go on yet she recognised it as soon as she came to it. As she'd said, the house was set behind tall, but well-kept hedges with a short fence before them that ended in a wrought-iron gate with the house name 'Stonehaven' on a brass plaque across it.

She opened the gate and looked at the sweep of gravel path that scrunched under her feet as she stepped forward, shutting the gate behind her. The house itself was magnificent, proud and majestic with three storeys and many windows and a host of chimneys on top of the red-tiled roof. The studded oaken door with gleaming brass letterbox was approached via three stone steps and Hannah would allow herself no hesitation as she stepped forward and pressed the bell and heard it resound in the house.

She'd taken care with her appearance that morning, knowing that it would give her more confidence. She'd chosen a dove grey woollen costume, worn with a gold-coloured blouse, and this was covered with a black fur-trimmed coat and matching hat while her gloves, handbag and shoes were steel grey.

This was the figure Mrs Foley saw as she opened the door. She knew at once the young woman before her was no down-and-out, nor anyone trying to sell her encyclopaedias or religion, and so she smiled and asked, 'Can I help you?'

Hannah didn't know if the person before her was

Mrs Olaffson or not, and so a little hesitantly she said, 'I need to see a Mrs Olaffson.'

It was the last thing Mrs Foley expected. In her lifetime of working for the Olaffsons, they'd had few visitors. Family in the early days, the brother of Mr Olaffson and his wife and son and occasional business associates, but no friends called. Not that this young woman looked to be a friend exactly. But no matter, Mrs Olaffson was not to be disturbed or upset in any way, so she said, 'I'm afraid Mrs Olaffson cannot see anyone this morning. She is indisposed.'

Hannah more or less expected that Mrs Olaffson would not welcome her with open arms. She'd discussed it over and over with Vic the night before and he'd agreed it really was the only thing to do. She could not allow herself to be put off. The happiness of Angela and Matthew was at stake, so she said firmly, 'I'm sorry, and I do not wish to disturb her, but I really must see her, it's of the utmost importance.'

Mrs Foley stared at her, the words, the tone, even the young woman's stance said that she'd stand no nonsense. But she said firmly, 'I'm sorry but Mrs Olaffson is ill.'

Matthew had said his mother was ill and she had no wish to worsen her condition, but if she did nothing the consequences didn't bear thinking about. It had taken great reserves of courage to come to the house that morning and she doubted she'd ever have the courage again. 'I'll keep her no more than a few minutes,' she said. 'Please. I'll try not to tire her.'

Something in the sincerity and earnestness in Hannah's voice caused Mrs Foley to relent and say,

'Wait here. I'll see if she's up to meeting you.'

When Marian first saw Hannah framed in the doorway, she reminded her of somebody, but she couldn't think who. She wondered what she wanted. Normally, Mrs Foley guarded her from others like a mother hen. But when she told her about the woman at the door and what she'd said, she'd been intrigued enough to agree to see her. She hoped that whatever she had to say would help keep her mind off the raging beast inside her tearing her innards apart. She had constant and extreme pain now which the doctor's tablets gave her little ease from.

She was still in bed. Sometimes she didn't rise until Matthew was due home when they ate together, or rather he ate and she pushed the food around her plate and hoped he wouldn't notice. Mrs Foley helped her sit up and while she went to usher Hannah upstairs, she put a silken bed jacket around her and combed her hair.

Hannah knew as soon as she saw Marian Olaffson that she was looking at a woman who was terminally ill. She was painfully thin. Hannah saw that by the wrists peeping beneath the bed jacket sleeves and by the gaunt look of her yellow tinged face. Her red-rimmed eyes were raised to Hannah in enquiry and she saw the pain reflected in them and her heart ached for what she had to ask this woman. She was positive, despite what she'd said to the woman who opened the door, that she was going to upset her.

She cleared her throat as she sat on the chair by the bed as Marian indicated and decided to go straight to the reason she was there. 'Thank you for seeing me,' she said. 'I'm sorry I've had to disturb you, but it's a matter of grave urgency.'

Marian's eyes were more puzzled than ever and Hannah went on, 'You don't know me, my name is Hannah Humphries and I'm married to a doctor in Erdington. I say this just to put your mind at rest that I am a respectable person, for I must ask you what you might consider a very impertinent question.'

'Yes?'

'You have a son, Matthew?'

'Yes,' Marian said, leaning forward slightly.

'Is he . . . Was he adopted as a baby?'

Whatever Marian had expected the woman to ask about her son, it wasn't this. She was angry. How dare a stranger that she'd agreed to see march into her bedroom and ask her things she'd rather not think about? Matthew had been but days old when he'd been placed into her arms that ached for a child and from the minute their eyes met, she'd pushed to the back of her mind the child's birth mother. She didn't exist. Matthew Olaffson was her son.

Hannah saw the blood drain from the woman's face, except for two angry spots of red on her cheeks, as she said haughtily, 'I really think that my personal affairs are none of your concern.'

Behind the clipped tone, Hannah heard the uncertainty and she said, 'I understand how you feel, believe me, and I wouldn't upset you unnecessarily. But, twenty years ago, in a home for unmarried mothers, I gave birth to a baby boy. I couldn't keep him and he was taken from me, hours after his birth, to be adopted. All the years since then, I've thought of him often and then a few days ago I met your son and he was the image of my fiancé Mike Murphy, the baby's father.'

'This is preposterous!' Marian said, frightened that this woman could claim her son after all these years. 'Even if Matthew does bear a resemblance to someone in your past, it doesn't signify anything. Anyway,' she went on, 'we came to Birmingham when Matthew was just a young boy. Before that I lived in Leeds.'

'Yes,' Hannah said quietly. 'So did I.' And then she continued, 'Don't worry, I know I relinquished all rights to Matthew years ago. I met him recently because he is engaged to my daughter, Angela Bradley, and I want to be certain there is no way that they are brother and sister before the relationship goes any further.'

'Oh God!' Marian clapped her hand to her mouth. 'Oh God!' She knew then that Hannah spoke the truth and she knew she was Angela's mother. That was who she'd reminded her of when she'd first come in.

Hannah felt so sorry for the woman's obvious distress that she'd inadvertently caused and without thinking, she grasped the hand plucking agitatedly at the eiderdown. She glanced around, certain the woman who'd opened the door to her would throw her out of it if she was to see the state her employer was in.

'Please,' Hannah begged. 'Please stay calm. I know the situation is abhorrent. It is to me as well, but it's not irretrievable.'

'You think not? They are promised in marriage.'

'Yes, I know, but it can't be allowed if I'm right,' Hannah said. 'That is why I had to know the truth.' She grasped Marian's hand tighter and looking deep into her eyes said, 'Your son, Matthew, he is adopted, isn't he?' Marian gave one brief nod and Hannah's head sank in her chest and her breath left her body in a huge sigh.

'What . . . what are we to do?' Marian asked plaintively.

'They must be told the truth. It is the only way.'

'Matthew doesn't know that he's adopted,' Marian said, and raising her eyes to Hannah went on, 'How am I to tell my child his real mother didn't want him and had given him away?'

'It wasn't like that,' Hannah said, stung to snap back in spite of her good intentions. 'My lover was killed. We'd planned to marry by special licence. He was due a forty-eight hour pass, but leave was cancelled. He was blown up on the beaches of Normandy on D-Day. I have no family to speak of, my mother died just after I was born, and I was brought up in a small Irish village by my sister. The shame of my arriving there pregnant with an illegitimate child would have been beyond bearing.'

'Hadn't you anyone else to turn to?' Marian asked. 'What of the young man? Had he no parents?'

'Oh yes, and they would probably have cared for me and loved Mike's son,' Hannah said, 'but Mike's father died of a heart attack the day they received the telegram telling them of Mike's death and his mother, severely traumatised, was taken away by her sister after the funeral and no one knew where.' She looked Marian straight in the face and said, 'I was destitute. If there had been any way on God's earth that I could have kept my son, I would have done. When they took him from me, they tore the heart out of me and that, Mrs Olaffson, is what you can tell my son.'

'I'm sorry,' mumbled Marian, moved in spite of herself by the sadness in Hannah's voice. 'But,' she continued in an effort to explain, 'I had years and years of trying for a child. No one understood the torment.' She sighed. 'That's all I wanted you see, a child. I'd known the Olaffson family fairly well, because we lived nearby, although our circumstances were hardly the same. My parents had also died and I was reared by a maiden aunt who had limited resources. I used to hang around outside if I heard Ernest was to come home on leave. He looked so handsome in his uniform. He was an officer, you see, and I was little more than a child.'

Hannah nodded, sensing Marian needed to tell her how it had been for her.

'In 1918, when the war ended, I was thirteen years old and I loved Ernest Olaffson with a young girl's passion. He was twenty-two and embittered by his experiences. I had little contact with young men, my aunt couldn't afford to take me to places where I might meet them, and of course there was no money to present me at court.

'So, when Ernest asked for my hand in 1926, it was like a dream come true for me. He was thirty then and I was twenty-one years old and I thought I was on the shelf. I knew nothing of lovemaking, but I endured it, welcomed it even, to have a child of my very own.'

Hannah knew that longing. 'And what happened?' she asked.

'Nothing!' Marian said bluntly. 'Year after year, I implored God, pleaded on my knees, said novenas, lit candles, had Masses said, made bargains, things I wouldn't do if God had just let me have a child. No one could understand and certainly not my aunt, who'd never even been married, who wouldn't even discuss the issue. Nor Ernest, not that he wouldn't have minded a son of his own of course, but if it wasn't to happen, he wouldn't be as devastated as I was.

'Then in the spring of 1939, Ernest's brother Maurice married a girl called Phyllis. He was fifteen years younger than Ernest and at twenty-eight knew when war come, as everyone knew it would, he would be called up. There were many such marriages at that time.'

Hannah nodded. She knew of plenty.

'I liked Phyllis,' Marian went on. 'We all lived together, you see, in the big house. I liked Maurice too, to tell you the truth. Ernest never had a good word for him, but I always liked him, because he had a wonderful sense of fun.

'When he was called up and Ernest was at the factory all day, Phyllis and I were company for one another, though she was just twenty-one and seemed a young girl to my thirty-four years.'

She stopped and seemed far away and Hannah said nothing. She just waited, sensing that Marian was coming to a particularly painful part of the story. Eventually she said in a voice just above a whisper, 'Maurice was one of the lucky ones rescued from the beaches of Dunkirk and he had a week's leave after it in June 1946. Phyllis was ecstatic to have him home and his parents held a party for him.

'When he returned to his unit, Phyllis was tearful and upset and I sympathised with her worry and concern, until I found out that in Maurice's scant week home, she'd become pregnant. And there was me, trying for years. It was like a mockery.

'When she gave birth to a baby born in the spring of 1941, I fell into such a deep depression that eventually I was admitted to hospital in the autumn of 1942. Ernest thought I was going mad.'

Hannah remembered her own depression after Angela's birth and Arthur's reaction to it and sympathised with Marian.

'I don't remember much about it,' Marian said, 'but I know I was there a long time, months and months. It was like a fog surrounding me. Phyllis came to visit, but I didn't know her, even Ernest came a time or two, I believe.

'I submitted to everything, all their pills and potions, sessions with a psychiatrist and even that dreaded painful electric shock treatment, but my mind was still unable to function. That was until the priest came to see me. A man I'd never seen before and he said, "What do you want, Mrs Olaffson? What is making you so unhappy?"

'No priest had ever listened to me before. They'd told me it was God's will that I was barren. This one though was different. "I want a child," I told him. "Just a child."

'"And you can't have one?" he asked.

'I shook my head and told him how many years I'd been trying. He really seemed to care and he held my hands while he prayed for me. I don't know if he spoke to Ernest and we never spoke about it afterwards, but Ernest came to take me home for the next weekend. I was so glad to leave the hospital, but I was far from well.

'That was the start of many weekends home and then in the autumn of 1944, the nuns came. They were carrying your son,' she said, glancing up. 'From the moment I held him close, I felt the swirling fog around me melt away and the shroud covering my mind and body slipping off. I was whole, complete. A woman with a child. Matthew was just four days old and I imagined he was totally mine, that I'd given birth to him.' She glanced up at Hannah and said, 'Never once did I give a thought to you.'

Tears were trickling down the cheeks of both women and it seemed the most natural thing in the world for Hannah to put her arms around this woman she felt so sorry for. They cried together, two women who'd been strangers just a short time before, but who were inexorably linked together.

Hannah pulled away first, dabbing at her eyes with a lace handkerchief. 'And your husband?' she asked huskily. 'Did he resent my son, or did he come to love him? Was he kind to him?'

'Kind?' Marian said. 'Ernest didn't understand kindness. No one had been kind to him his whole life. He hardly knew his parents, brought up by a nanny and off to school by the age of eight, but when Maurice was born, it was completely different. Ernest's strict, aloof parents were never away from the nursery then. According to Ernest, Maurice got his own way in everything and was bought anything he asked for. Ernest understandably resented the way he was being reared and equally resented the man he turned out to be and was terrified Matthew would go to the bad unless he was brought up strictly.'

'Was that because he didn't know where he came from? His parentage?' Hannah asked.

'Well yes,' Marian admitted. 'And yet it wasn't just that. Ernest was against extravagance in any shape or form. He disapproved of holidays, for example.'

She looked at Hannah steadily and said, 'Ernest loved your son as much as he was able to love anyone. Fortunately, Matthew was a compliant child – anxious to please. He loved and admired Ernest and was always trying to gain his approval.'

'Did he get it?'

'Not often if I'm honest,' Marian said. 'Approval was not something Ernest gave readily. But,' she added, 'I don't want you to feel sorry for your son, Hannah, for I loved him with all my heart and soul and he loved me I know.

'Soon when I'm gone he will be a rich man,' Marian said. 'It won't be long now and I know that hasn't come as a surprise to you. I saw the shock register on your face when you came in.

'Of course, Ernest never meant to die till he was a good age and he was affronted that he who'd controlled so much in his life had no power to defy the doctors and stop the Grim Reaper.' She sighed. 'And now it's my turn.' She turned to Hannah and said, 'Matthew doesn't know how ill I am.'

'Doesn't he see it?'

'I'm skilful with make-up,' Marian said. 'I've tried to shield him. Maybe I'm wrong. Ernest's brother said I was being silly about it and that Matthew is a boy no longer. But to me he will always be a boy.

'However, perhaps this is the right time to tell him

everything. I'd hoped to see him safely married before I had to break the news of my impending death to him, but now that cannot happen.'

'Do you think they will be terribly upset?' Hannah asked.

'Well,' Marian answered. 'They're fond of each other certainly, but they're young.'

'Ah, but passions are high when you are young,' Hannah said, remembering her own youth. 'It's the very devil that they had to meet at all. What made you come to Birmingham from Leeds?'

'Oh, that was because Ernest and Maurice couldn't agree. After Maurice was demobbed, it was dreadful. They were at each other's throats daily. If I'm honest, Ernest used to goad Maurice. In the end, he told his father either Maurice went or he did. Well, he didn't want that, but could see they'd never agree, and he'd made plenty of money during the war, so he asked Ernest to come and establish a new factory in Birmingham.

'Ernest was glad to go and by that time so was I. Matthew was little more than a baby and in one way I was glad to get away from the city of his birth. No one knew about him here. He was just our son. It was how I wanted it.'

'I do understand that,' Hannah said.

'Do you? I don't know that I'd be so understanding,' Marian said.

'But I do understand,' Hannah said. 'I'd probably have done the same. And were things easier between your husband and his brother once you moved?'

'No,' said Marian with a sigh. 'I tried at first; I used to invite them down for the weekend. It was always dreadful. Their parents had died within a week of one another not long after we came to live here, so there was just the two of them then. I'd have loved a brother or sister and I thought they should make some effort, if only for the sake of our sons.'

Hannah thought of the family of brothers and sisters she had who she never got even a scribe of a letter from. The only one who'd cared was Frances and she was no more. 'Sometimes siblings aren't so great,' she said. 'Different characters, different attitudes. They haven't got to get on.'

'Well, Ernest and Maurice didn't,' Marian said. 'Like chalk and cheese they were. But when I knew I was dying, I wrote to Maurice and Phyllis, told them how things were and asked them to look out for Matthew. They were lovely and they made my boy welcome while I went into hospital to have an operation to help me live a little longer. That's how he met your daughter.'

'I wondered about that,' Hannah said. 'Although there was a girl, Hillary, that she used to spend some of the holidays with.'

'Yes, Hillary, that was a name Matthew mentioned. And Angela did too.'

'I wish it hadn't happened.'

'So do I,' Marian said. 'But it has and we must face it.'

'I know.'

'Despite the awful news you brought, I'm glad I've met you,' Marian said quietly. 'I feel privileged.'

'And I you, Marian,' Hannah said and she bent and kissed Marian gently on her cheek. 'Thank you for rearing my son to be the fine, upstanding young man he is. I'm not surprised you are proud of him.'

'How do you think Angela will take the news?'

'Badly,' Hannah said. 'I've steeled myself to the thought that I'll lose her all over again, but we cannot let this go on.'

'No, no, indeed not,' Marian said.

For a while, both women were silent, each thinking their own private thoughts, and then Marian said, 'I think we should have tea together. Take off your coat and I'll ring for tea and I'll tell you about my son and your son, Matthew. I wanted marriage with Angela for I didn't want him alone when I'm gone, but now he'll have you. I thought I would resent you, feel jealous of you if ever I met you, but I don't.'

'You have no need to feel jealous of me,' Hannah said gently. 'You brought my son up. I just gave birth to him.'

'Thank you for giving him away,' Marian said. 'I know now the courage and heartache it took, but he made my life complete. Matthew means everything to me,' and she reached out to Hannah. 'Soon he will have only you.' It was too much; Hannah marvelling at Marian's courage, felt tears trickling from her eyes again and Marian gripped her arm tight. 'Don't cry, my dear. Please don't cry.'

Mrs Foley, summoned and asked to make tea, was surprised on taking it in to find both of them in tears and the bed littered with photographs of Matthew. She knew they had previously been kept in the albums that Mrs Olaffson took such pleasure in that were kept on a shelf above her dressing table.

What's more, despite the tears her employer was

shedding, she looked more alive than she'd seen her in ages. Somehow happier. And Marian was happier, happy and relieved to have met Hannah. She thought her a fine woman.

'Tell me honestly now,' she said. 'Do you think Matthew will hate me for not telling him sooner he was adopted?'

'No. No, of course not. He is, as you said, your child and he loves you dearly. That is very clear. That will never change for a person he hardly knows who just happened to give birth to him,' Hannah said, though it hurt her to say it. 'Take heart, Marian, Matthew is too generous and open-hearted a person to bear a grudge against you. I fear my daughter won't feel the same.'

'I don't understand, have never understood, why you left your daughter behind,' Marian said. 'Matthew told me you fell in love with another man, though he never mentioned names. He thought at first you were dead because Angela never spoke of you.'

Hannah began the story and told Marian of the frightened, ashamed and traumatised young woman who arrived at Gloria's door and the tea grew cold in the pot and the scones remained uneaten as Marian listened to Hannah's life unfold. She heard of the sham of a marriage she had had with Arthur Bradley and how Arthur had connived to gain full control over Angela, due to Hannah's affair with her doctor. 'He'll be outraged over this latest snippet of news,' Hannah said. 'As I explained, he knew I wasn't a virgin when I married him, but I told him nothing about a son. He has to know now, though, but I doubt he'd open the door to me.'

'Then who will tell him and Angela?'

'Vic suggested our parish priest, Father Fitzgerald. He does know the family and has always taken a keen interest in us. He doesn't know about my past of course, there has never been any reason for him to know until now. When I leave here, I'll go straight round and see him and tell him everything.'

'Will he be shocked?'

Hannah shrugged. 'Who knows? But shocked or not, he'll see he'll have to do something about it. I just hope he can break it to them as gently as he can.'

'I don't know that priests are very good at that sort of thing,' Marian said. 'To be honest, I had little time for them until that lovely priest came to see me in that hell hole I was in at that time. I'm sure he contacted the nuns and told them how desperate I was for a baby. No one else would bother. Ernest once admitted he agreed to have Matthew only to please me. Apparently, the doctor had told him I was close to going over the edge into madness. He threw that knowledge at me one day when he was annoyed at something Matthew had done. I had wondered at his change of heart, for I'd suggested adoption before and he'd dismissed it out of hand.'

'Father Fitzgerald is different,' Hannah said, 'although he doesn't approve of me for divorce is not recognised in the Church and the children are therefore illegitimate. But when there was a bit of trouble about getting the Abbey school to take Adam because of it, he stepped in. He's a good man and a kind one, but he has to follow the rules, yet even in his disapproval, he will help.'

'Wouldn't it be better for you to break it to Angela?' Marian asked tentatively.

'Maybe, but Arthur would never let me see her,' Hannah said. 'Besides, I'd be afraid. He's been violent towards me in the past.'

'Ah, then it's better to get someone else to convey the news,' Marian agreed.

'And thinking of that, I must be off,' Hannah said, getting to her feet. She'd seen tiredness etched on Marian's face and thought she'd stayed long enough and she bent and kissed her goodbye.

Marian watched the door close behind Hannah and lay back on the pillows with a sigh. She hadn't felt so exhausted in a long time, but despite the fatigue, she wouldn't have missed the encounter for all the tea in China.

Later, when Mrs Foley come in to clear away the tea things, she found Marian in a deep sleep, such as she'd not enjoyed for many weeks now. 'And without her pill too,' Mrs Foley remarked to herself as she carried the tea things from the room. 'So that young woman did some good after all. I did wonder when I saw the mistress in tears, but whatever she came for and whatever she said worked.'

Father Fitzgerald listened to Hannah's tale without any sign of shock, though he felt his insides tighten. Such a thing that happened to Hannah had happened to many in the turmoil of war. What a tragedy the man hadn't been able to marry her. And what a double tragedy that her daughter should meet her own half-brother and become engaged to him – of all the coincidences in the world!

However, he knew Arthur and the high moral stance

he put on everything, the standards he had that few others aspired to. The priest knew he had no patience with people not as morally stalwart as himself. Sometimes he'd become irritated with his lack of charity for the unfortunates in society.

He also found him hypocritical in divorcing Hannah and he'd spoken about it at the time. He had though felt sorry for the way the man had been left, and had popped round to see him on many occasions after Hannah's defection, so Arthur wasn't that surprised to see him at the door that evening. 'Hello, Father. Come along in.'

Father Fitzgerald stepped over the threshold with a heavy heart for he knew there was no way he could soften the blow for Arthur or Angela.

And he was right, Arthur was outraged, livid, and he ranted and raved. Angela shared her father's views and said she was disgusted, both by Hannah having a baby and then giving it away.

She had no knowledge of how hard life had been then and how easy it was to become pregnant without the pill that she and Hillary and many of their friends had used so successfully. But when the priest identified the child as the man she was promised to marry, she'd become hysterical.

The priest begged Angela to be calm with no effect and eventually Arthur slapped her face, shocking her into silence, and then he grabbed her arms tight and shook her. His face was puce and spittle formed on his lips as he spat out, 'You see what she is to you, your mother? A dirty filthy trollop, that's what. That's the woman you've been sneaking behind my back to see.

Some mother! She gave away her son and had no time for you either when you were born. Pauline brought you up. But now she's scuppered your wedding plans right enough,' he went on. 'You can hardly marry your own brother.'

Father Fitzgerald tried to free Arthur's grasp on Angela, because he was shaking her like a rag doll. 'Leave go, man! For God's sake, Arthur!' Arthur appeared not to hear the priest and Angela, in shock, was making no effort to protect herself. When Arthur flung her away from him as if in disgust, she sank to the floor in a dead faint and it was the priest who went to her aid.

Father Fitzgerald waited until the doctor had been summoned before he left the house and although he could feel sorry for all of them in this business, the one he felt for most was Hannah and he could imagine how she was suffering and his heart went out to her.

All evening, Hannah waited. She'd put the children to bed early and Vic, knowing she needed to be alone but not wishing to leave her altogether, stayed in the surgery, dealing with paperwork. She was grateful to him. He seemed to know instinctively what she needed. However, when the knock finally came to the door at about half-past nine, Hannah's legs turned to jelly when she tried to stand. It was Vic, hearing the bell ring the second time, who crossed the hall and opened the door to Matthew Olaffson.

The young man faced Hannah across the living room and asked bluntly, 'Is all of this true?'

She nodded. 'It's true and I'm sorry. I'm not sorry I'm your mother, but I'm sorry for Marian who adopted you and loves you as if she'd given birth to you and I'm sorry that you had to find out this way and I'm sorry for you and Angela.'

Matthew said nothing. He was thinking of the most devastating news he'd been given that day and that was that the only mother he had ever known had cancer and hadn't long to live.

He could barely take it in. They had talked and talked about it and both had cried and hugged each other. Matthew, at first, suggested getting a second opinion, private consultants, even trying for treatment abroad, until Marian convinced him all avenues had been tried, and the diagnosis was one and the same. 'That's why I pushed for the marriage with Angela,' she said. 'So that you wouldn't be alone. But now that can never be.'

'Why?' Even amidst his distress, Matthew was puzzled.

Marian didn't answer his question. Instead she said, 'There is someone else who has a claim on you now. Though not a claim as such, she's actually said she's relinquished any claim, but she cares about you. And that, Matthew, is Angela's mother, Hannah.'

'Angela's mother? What has she to do with all this? She has no claim on me.'

'Listen,' Marian said. 'What I am going to tell you is something I should have told you years ago.'

'What?'

'Matthew, I was many years waiting for a child,' Marian said. 'I've told you this often and told you that's why you were precious to me. And all that is true, Matthew, but the point is I never gave birth to you,

Hannah is your birth mother. She was without support in the world and had to give you up for adoption.'

'Hannah is my birth mother?' Matthew repeated and Marian just nodded and then slowly Matthew said, 'Then Angela is . . .'

'Your half-sister,' Marian said. 'That is why you cannot marry her,' and then Marian grasped one of her son's hands and looking into his face said, 'Say you don't hate me for deceiving you?'

'How could I hate you?' Matthew asked, squeezing Marian's hand. 'You're still my mother, the only one I know and the only one I love, the one I will always love.'

But Marian knew the news had shaken Matthew, she'd seen it in his eyes and when later he said, 'I must go round to Angela's mother, talk to her,' Marian wasn't surprised. It was what she had expected he'd do. 'I think you're right,' she said.

He'd whipped himself into a state by the time he arrived at Grange Road. Shock had taken hold and he shook all over as he stood on the doorstep. Funny that he'd never doubted a word his mother had said. How could Hannah be so convinced he was her son? He thought once you gave a child up for adoption that was it, you never were able to know what happened to them. Well, he'd find out.

And he did. 'How are you so sure I am your son?' he asked as he sat on the settee she'd indicated and accepted a glass of whisky and was glad of it for waves of emotion still ran through him.

'Because you are the image of your father,' Hannah said. And then, because she'd been expecting Matthew, she showed him the few precious photographs of Mike that she had.

For Matthew, it was like looking at a picture of himself, he was so like the dashing young soldier, his cap set jauntily on his fair hair. There were some of him taken with Hannah, his arms possessively around her, and Matthew thought with a start that they could be pictures of himself and Angela.

But then he told himself stranger incidences had happened before surely. 'You can't be absolutely certain,' he said.

'You have the same birthday and you were born in Leeds where I was at the time in a home for unmarried mothers run by nuns,' Hannah said. 'That alone would almost prove the point, but the real proof was the birthmark.'

Immediately, Matthew clapped his right hand over his left arm and Hannah had the desire to take his hand away and trace the mark with her fingers. But she couldn't do that. Instead she said softly and sadly, 'I held you after your birth, just once, and because I knew I'd never be able to do it again, I examined every bit of you so that the picture would stay with me. You had the birthmark then.' Then more softly, she asked, 'Did you love Angela so very much?'

Matthew realised that with all he'd been told and had to cope with, what it meant to him and Angela mattered very, very little. In fact, if he was honest, he felt relief. He'd felt he was being hustled into something he wasn't ready for. 'No,' he found himself saying. 'No, it isn't that. It's just I need to be sure.'

'I'm sure, Matthew,' Hannah said.

'Can you . . . would you mind telling me about my father?' Matthew said. 'I never really measured up for my adoptive father. I think I understand a little more now why he was the way he was.'

Hannah remembered Marian's words earlier that day and her heart ached for her son and she said, 'Your father would have loved you, Matthew. He was a fine man and you can be proud that you are his son and I'll tell you all you want to know.'

And so she did. Now and again, she would get up to shake more coal on to the fire and once Vic brought in a tray of coffee and biscuits and Matthew was encouraged to help himself from the whisky decanter and still Hannah talked, answering any questions Matthew asked her as well as she could.

Matthew realised when he eventually took his leave that his birth mother was a wonderful woman too. She had not been loose-living or fast and had his father survived the war, he would have grown up with them as his parents. But then he wouldn't have known Marian Olaffson and although she hadn't given birth to him, he knew she loved him as much as if she had.

How tangled his emotions were! He felt as if he'd been put through the mangle. And he knew he had yet to see Angela and as soon as possible. He couldn't just avoid her forever. That was the coward's way out and now he knew he was Mike Murphy's son, he couldn't ever allow himself to stand accused of cowardice.

Angela didn't come to see her mother but the following morning, fully recovered from her faint, she phoned, spewing out her vitriolic rage and disgust at the mother she claimed had ruined her life. Hannah was shaken by the venom in Angela's voice and shocked by the language she used. She could not reason with her, although she tried. Angela was only interested in having her say and when she shouted at her mother that she never in all her life wanted to see her again, she eventually reduced Hannah to tears.

She was glad Matthew was mature enough to hold no one responsible and considerate enough to see that other people's lives were affected and not just his. He came to see Hannah again and invited the family to Christmas dinner at their house. Marian insisted, he said, and Mrs Foley would be in her element cooking for a large number and especially having children in the house on Christmas Day. So Vic and Hannah did as Marian wished and Hannah watched Marian move everything around her plate and the pain-filled, laboured way she moved and felt great sympathy.

She also couldn't help but be impressed by the brave way Marian faced her imminent death. From the beginning, she'd never felt sorry for herself, only anxiety for Matthew, and she knew she was a truly selfless woman.

She was glad that if her son had to be reared anywhere away from her, it was Marian who had a hand in his rearing. Her attitude contrasted sharply with Vic's parents who visited them on Boxing Day. She'd discussed the issue with Vic and they decided they had to be told about the existence of Matthew now, before they heard it from someone else.

There might have been an element of sympathy in Vic's sisters but it was quickly crushed by Flo Humphries, who behaved as if Hannah had done the whole thing on purpose in order to disgrace them. The very thought of it, she said, sickened her. In fact, it was making her feel quite ill and she was sure it would bring on one of her headaches. Hannah felt the woman was milking the situation for all it was worth and was surprised she hadn't sent one of her daughters running for the smelling salts to prevent an attack of the vapours.

She was glad when the day was over and as she snuggled up to Vic that night she said, 'Your parents think you had a bad deal with me. Unmarried mother, who also abandons her second child, to hook the affluent doctor, who risks ruining his career for her sake.'

'Oh God, Hannah, it was hardly like that. Anyway, I wasn't so affluent.'

'Yes, but you might have been if you hadn't married me.'

'Hannah, will you stop thinking every damned thing that happens is your fault? Who cares what my parents think anyway? They're only in this century by accident.'

Hannah knew though that what Vic's mother thought would be echoed by many more when Matthew Olaffson's relationship with her became common knowledge. But no way would she deny him, not again. In fact she'd be proud to claim him as her son and all those who didn't like it could go to Hell.

Chapter Twenty-Six

Angela felt that life really wasn't worth living. Brought up as a pampered, indulged girl, she was ill-equipped to deal with disappointment and disillusionment. She couldn't remember a time before when she'd desired something and it had been denied her. But she was denied Matthew all right and it was all her mother's fault. Matthew had come around and talked with her and even Angela had to admit he'd been nice about it. Maybe, he'd said, in time they could be friends, particularly as they were half-brother and -sister.

The point was, Angela wasn't used to looking at Matthew in a sisterly way, but she thanked God now that they hadn't become lovers. Dear God, the thought of that made her feel sick.

But with Matthew gone from her life, she was completely friendless. She had no desire to go back to Hillary's set and have them all sniggering at her for falling for her big brother and she knew they'd all know, because Ralph would tell them.

Even if she'd wanted to go, though, she doubted her dad would allow it. Since the outburst in front of the priest, he'd been different with her. He always wanted to know where she was going and who with and would give her a time to be in. She never went far and never anywhere very exciting, just hanging around the shops, or going to the cinema.

She was so achingly lonely that one Saturday morning in February, she made her way to Josie's flat. She wouldn't lower herself to visit her mother anymore, and anyway, from what she'd understood from Matthew, he was a fairly regular visitor there. So, even though she considered Josie almost as guilty as her mother for she could bet she knew all about Hannah having a baby before she was married who turned out to be Matthew Olaffson, she couldn't stand her own company a minute longer.

Josie did know of course and said so. 'So why didn't you tell me?' Angela demanded.

'Well, first of all, it wasn't my tale to tell, was it?' Josie said, calm in the face of Angela's evident anger and hurt. 'And secondly, I think Hannah hoped you'd never have to know.'

'Yeah, well that went a bit wrong, don't you think?'

'Okay. But you got to admit it was one massive coincidence to meet Matthew Olaffson like that.'

'And if I hadn't, I'd never have known?'

'Maybe not. It hasn't made your life any better now, has it? And in your hands the knowledge would only have been one more stick to beat Hannah with.'

'What do you mean?'

'Come on, Angela, you're not daft. Hannah's been pushed out of your life from the day you were born . . .'

'Daddy said she didn't want me.'

'Then your Dad is a big fat liar,' Josie said hotly.

'Right, young lady, you want to know the truth about how it was for Hannah, I'll tell you. For a start your hallowed father is not too hot in the sexual department and I know you're no innocent, so you'll know what I'm talking about. He has to get violent before he can do anything and from the day you were conceived, when he discovered Hannah wasn't a virgin, he never slept with her again. He used to call her a whore and a harlot and far, far worse. I used to hear him and he said she would have nothing to do with his child, he wouldn't allow her to be near you to taint your life. He meant it, but Hannah couldn't really believe anyone could be vindictive enough to try and separate a mother and her child.

'Hannah had to give her first child away, so she longed for your birth. But she had a bad time and had to have an operation when you were born, so she couldn't see you for a while and when she could . . . There's an illness, a depression some women have after they give birth. The know more about it now, but seventeen years ago they didn't.'

'I know,' Angela said sullenly. 'She told me.'

'Yes well, that's what happened,' Josie said. 'And did she tell you your father kept telling her what a useless mother she was and that she believed him because she couldn't care for you, or feel anything for you? He engaged Pauline Lawson, not to help Hannah, though she needed help at that time, but to stop Hannah having much influence over you. That's the reason you went to nursery school so young and away to board when you were just seven.'

'Why did she let him do it?' Angela said. 'I wouldn't

have. Some girls at school didn't think I had a mother.'

'It's not as easy as that,' Josie said. 'If someone tells you you're useless and a bad mother, a bad woman, often enough you believe it, especially if no one is able to tell you different. You were brought up as a spoiled brat and even as a child you'd take the pattern from your father to goad and hurt Hannah. It was only when Hannah met Vic that she gained a few grains of self-respect.'

'Yeah? Well she didn't have to go and marry him and leave me behind.'

'She had to leave, because she couldn't stand life with your father any longer.'

'But what about me?' Angela cried. 'She promised to come to my confirmation, promised faithfully. She never even sent me birthday cards. It was as if I didn't exist any more, like Daddy said. I wrote her letters and she never even replied. She said she never got them.' Angela shrugged. 'I don't know whether she was lying or not.'

'She didn't get any letters from you,' Josie said. 'I know that for a fact. I'm guessing here, but I bet the nuns had orders from your father. The same orders that said neither Hannah nor I were allowed to contact you in any way.'

'She told me about that too,' Angela said. 'About Daddy reporting Vic or something. Is that true?'

'I'm afraid it is,' Josie said. 'Your father loved you. If he ever loved anyone in the world it was you. He was, if we're absolutely truthful, fanatical about you, and he was becoming jealous of the way you were beginning to turn to your mother. It wasn't how he'd planned things. He wanted you all to himself. In a way, Hannah played right into his hands.'

'Yeah, well he's worse now,' Angela said. 'He doesn't know what to do with me, see, and he definitely thinks I've inherited my mother's bad blood.'

'There was no bad blood in Hannah,' Josie said. 'She never behaved as you did for a start.'

'How do you know what I did?'

'I know enough,' Josie said. 'You almost boasted to Hannah that you were virtually expelled from two schools. You wouldn't say why, but I bet it wasn't for nothing.'

'Yeah, well it was Daddy's fault,' Angela said petulantly. 'The convent was bad enough, but that place in Hastings was just like a bleeding prison. Do this! Do that! All the sodding day long.'

'Really! How awful!' Josie said sarcastically. 'I bet they liked your choice of language too. Remember, you wouldn't have been sent there if you'd behaved yourself at the convent and if you don't mend your ways, you'll end up in a heap of trouble and it will be no one's fault but your own.'

'You don't understand,' Angela cried. 'No one does. Daddy sent me to a really posh school and nearly everyone there lived in mansions. They were wealthy, had servants, swimming pools and ponies of their own. How could I be friends with them and invite them home to my poxy house in a poxy street? Even before Mom left it was impossible. And she was an embarrassment too, working in the doctor's surgery. I mean as if she needed the money.'

'She did, you bloody little fool,' Josie cried angrily.

'She was never given any money unless it was at your father's discretion, because they were invited somewhere special, like the Banks' for dinner. Even then, every receipt had to be scrutinised by him and any change returned. That was Hannah's life, Angela. You had whatever you desired with a click of your elegant little fingers.'

'That wasn't my fault.'

'No, of course it wasn't,' Josie said scornfully. 'None of it was your fault. It was Hannah's, your friends at school's, the house you lived in. Grow up, Angela, for God's sake! If you couldn't bring yourself to tell your friends at school where and how you lived then I'm sorry for you. True friends wouldn't care. But there's no reason on God's earth why you didn't take advantage of the first-rate education the school provided. Many girls would have given their eyeteeth for your advantages and you threw it all away.'

'I was upset after Mom left. You don't know how much I missed her.'

'I'll grant you that you might have been upset,' Josie said. 'And it was cruel of Arthur to forbid contact. But, for all that, you never bothered with Hannah much before. Your father always came first with you. Sometimes you scarcely had a kind word to say to her.'

'Well, I did miss her,' Angela shouted at Josie. 'You can think what you like, but I did. And then Daddy came up at weekends and every week, he'd go on about Mommy's bad blood and how he hoped I hadn't inherited it. It made me want to show him so I played up all the time. I was pissed off by the whole place by then anyway and so was Hillary. I was bloody glad they told Daddy to come and get me before they threw me out. He came up all apologetic and thought I should be hanging my head in shame or something, but me and Hillary just thought it was one big laugh.

'I couldn't believe it when Daddy sent me somewhere else. And it was bloody well worse than the sodding convent. I wanted to get myself expelled and I misbehaved even more. They kept writing to Daddy, but never talked of getting rid of me. Instead, I got all my privileges stopped and I was kept in isolation for a bit and in detention loads of times. I also had lines at least twice a week and even had my pocket money confiscated more than once. I'd palled up with this girl who was as pissed off as me and one night, she suggested creeping out after lights out and going into town for a bit of fun. I thought, "Why not?" Not much fun to be had in that dump, I can tell you.

'It was great too, till we got back to school and had a reception committee waiting for us. Normally, I suppose I would have been a bit scared and nervous, but that night, we'd met some fellows in a pub. They took us into this club and bought us anything we wanted to drink. They wanted something else too, but we weren't daft. We climbed out of the window of the ladies' while they were buying the last round before the place shut and hightailed it back to school. But by then, of course, it was light. We must have been in the club hours.

'We were still pretty squiffy and when the teachers started on us, we really laid into them. I'd already been in big trouble for constantly breaking every rule in the book and that was the last straw.'

'Well,' Josie said. 'I imagine your father imagines his predictions have come true. That should be gratifying for him.'

'What do you know about anything anyway?' Angela snapped mutinously. 'Don't be so bloody sneering.'

'Well, don't be such an idiot yourself,' Josie snapped. 'And what d'you intend to do with yourself now?'

'In what way?'

'In the way of a job, Angela,' Josie said. 'You know, the things that most ordinary mortals have to do to keep from starving while they keep a roof over their heads?'

'Why are you so nasty to me?'

'Because you're still a spoiled brat,' Josie said. 'If you'd used just half the brain you were born with, you'd have seen that if you wanted to be really free of your father, you should have worked for qualifications to get you to university – a place very few ordinary kids can afford to go to – as I know. We have a fair few of them here who just come for a good feed and a bit of warmth. But you could have gone easily and comfortably and at the end of it all, you'd have a degree and the chance of a good job, with a decent salary. You would be totally independent.

'That would have shown your father that he'd brought up an industrious and intelligent child, who was also blessed with a measure of commonsense, and you'd have gained respect for yourself. I suppose,' she added, 'you do intend working for a living? You're not surely intending to live off Arthur until you ride off into the sunset with your knight in shining armour?'

'Of course I'll get a job,' Angela said. 'Stop being so bloody patronising all the time.'

But in reality, Angela had not thought about a job until Josie had spoken. None of Hillary's set seemed to have a job and none seemed to worry about it. Now, though, a job seemed a far pleasanter prospect than hanging around the house day after day, but she hadn't a clue where to start. She'd managed to get herself expelled without taking her O levels. Not that she imagined for a minute she would have passed them; she'd done little work, either in the class, or out of it. Now here she was, seventeen and without a qualification to her name, despite the years of private education under her belt. Probably, she thought, not even Woolworth's would employ me.

'Come on,' Josie broke in briskly. 'Stop feeling sorry for yourself. Spare a thought for Hannah who has seemed to wait all her life for a kind word from you.'

'You can't expect me to forgive her for this?' Angela said incredulously.

'Why not? It was hardly her fault that you and Matthew were to meet. That was never her intention.'

'She was unmarried and had a baby.'

'So what? She was just one of many. She was unlucky that was all,' Josie said. 'You weren't here during the war and neither was I, but I've heard people talking about it. It was a different sort of life, lived as if any minute might be your last, as indeed it might have been. Don't you see then that every hour was precious to you? Can't you see that in that sort of atmosphere, when two people in love have only twenty-four or forty-eight hours together in God alone knows how many months – years – their feelings might get the better of them?'

Oh yes, Angela could. She wasn't going to say so

though and so she tried another tack. 'She still abandoned her baby and then years later left my father and me behind. Excuse that if you can.'

Josie looked at her cousin and couldn't believe what she'd heard her say. She'd said nothing about Hannah's plight, had no vestige of understanding. With her, it was self, self, self. Still, she thought, not to be wondered at after the upbringing she has had.

'Okay,' Josie said with a resigned sigh. 'Lecture over. If you cannot feel in your heart to see any of this from Hannah's point of view, I feel sorry for you, but I can do little about it.'

Funnily enough, Josie's words made Angela feel a real heel – a novel experience for her and one she was certainly not going to admit to. No one had ever spoken to her as Josie had, or made her feel she was responsible for her own actions. But she didn't resent Josie going for her because, Angela thought, it showed at least that she cared about her and she wasn't sure any more if anyone else did.

Once, she would have said her father would love her and care for her till Hell froze over and no matter how she behaved. But since she'd made contact with her mother his attitude to her had changed.

He'd gone mad when he found out she'd visited her mother after the priest's visit. When she'd recovered from her faint, he had gone on and on about it, accusing her of going looking for her mother and seeming not to hear when she said they'd met her while shopping. They'd gone home with her and to Arthur that was unforgivable. She couldn't begin to reason with him these days.

'Would you like to stay to tea?' Josie asked and Angela wanted to very much. She certainly didn't want to go back home to her father's stiff disapproval and his list of endless questions or the silent treatment he'd indulged in lately, but it wouldn't do to be too enthusiastic. She shrugged. 'If you like,' she said nonchalantly. 'I'll have to phone Daddy first.'

But the phone rang unanswered. 'Must have gone out,' Angela said. 'He was pottering about in the garden when I slipped out earlier.'

'So he doesn't know you're here?'

'No, I tell you, he's changed,' Angela said. 'Sometimes I think he's going off his rocker. Hearing all this about Mommy seems to have sent him over the edge. He might have even physically stopped me from coming to see you, and at the very least, I would have been treated to one of his famous lectures that linger on for days.'

'So are you stopping for tea or not?'

'Might as well,' Angela said ungraciously. 'Nothing much to go home for.'

The following night, just as Hannah was thinking of making a last drink for her and Vic before bed, the phone rang. Vic had been out on house calls the last two nights and he groaned. 'My idea of paradise is a week of undisturbed sleep,' he said, as he made his way to the phone. 'Don't you think that's a sad fantasy to have?'

But, this time, it wasn't one of Vic's patients, but a concerned Josie on the other end of the line. She told Vic about Angela's visit the previous day and briefly what had transpired between them. 'Phil ran her home later in the evening,' she said. 'The house was in darkness. Angela said not to worry, that her father was often in late. The point is though, he didn't come home, not all night, nor today either.'

'Has there been no phone call, no explanation?'

'No.'

'That's funny. He'd know Angela would be worried.'

Hannah had moved across to Vic when she heard Vic mention Josie's name and he handed the receiver to her. 'It's Josie,' he said. 'Arthur's not been home last night, nor all day today with no word.'

'Where are you now, Josie?' Hannah asked.

'With Angela. I could hardly leave her rattling around in an empty house by herself,' Josie said. 'I've told her, I can stay the night with her if she wants me to, but I'll have to go early in the morning before Phil leaves for work. Hannah, can you come?'

'She hardly wants me,' Hannah said. 'I bet she's not asked for me?'

'No,' Josie admitted. 'She wouldn't, would she? But she's just seventeen and she's frightened and worried and doesn't know how much she needs you.'

'What if Arthur comes back and finds me there?'

'What if he did? What could he do to you now?'

Hannah, who knew just what Arthur was capable of, said nothing further. She knew she had to go to her daughter, regardless of this risk to herself and of her daughter's reaction when she saw her. 'I'll be there as soon as possible.'

By the time Hannah returned from next door with a sleepy Amy in her wake to listen out for the children, Vic had been busy. He'd made a list of all the hospitals in the area and was working his way through them. 'You don't think he's had an accident?' Hannah asked fearfully.

'No, I don't,' Vic said firmly. 'I just feel that it's as well to make sure.'

But no, Arthur Bradley wasn't in any of the hospitals and Hannah didn't know whether that was a good thing or a bad one.

'Maybe,' said Hannah, 'the Banks might know something.'

'Is it likely?'

'Well, as he disappeared on a Saturday night, it could be that the company had a function somewhere.'

'Wouldn't he have told Angela?'

'According to Josie, Angela didn't tell him she was going out. Maybe he intended to tell her.'

But Elizabeth Banks knew nothing. She was cool with Hannah, until she told her the reason for the call and then she was as concerned as Hannah was fast becoming. No, there was no function. They hadn't seen Arthur socially for some weeks now.

'Has he a special colleague, a friend he goes out with?' Hannah asked.

'No, no one really,' Elizabeth said. 'Not in the company certainly. He is quite a loner, Arthur.'

Hannah knew that quite well, but it was worth a shot in the dark. 'Well, thank you anyway, Elizabeth.'

'There's one other place I haven't tried,' Vic said as they set off in the car. 'And that's the police station.'

'Would they tell you if he was in there?'

'I don't know,' Vic said. 'But we can try.'

Steelhouse Lane Police Station was a squat, grey,

grim-looking building and Hannah shivered as she walked up the steps. I'd hate to be incarcerated in one of these cells, she thought. But then, to be locked up anywhere would be desperate. I'd go daft, I would, and in a way she hoped Arthur wasn't there either.

But he was. Nobody wanted to tell them, until Hannah pleaded with them. 'I'm his ex-wife,' she said. 'And between us we have a daughter of seventeen who lives with her father and she is frantic as she's had no news of him.'

'He had the opportunity to tell her,' the policeman said. 'Every prisoner has that right.'

'Then he is here?'

'Yes, he's here. We asked if there was anyone he wanted to phone, or if there was no phone, we'd have called around, but he said nothing. Wouldn't answer any questions or anything. Then tonight he said he wanted to see his solicitor. He's on his way now.'

'Can I ask what he's been charged with?'

'You can ask,' the policeman said. 'But I'm not at liberty to say. You can see the prisoner if you wish and he may tell you.'

'I don't think either of us would be welcome,' Hannah said. 'What happens now?'

'He'll be in court in the morning,' the policeman said. 'Because of the nature of the crimes he is accused of, he will probably stay in custody until the trial.'

Hannah's head was reeling, but the one she was sorry for was her daughter. 'How can I tell her this, Vic?' she said as they drove towards Erdington. 'Do you think this is connected to the previous business, you know, from last summer?'

'I don't know, pet,' Vic said, though privately he thought it could be little else. 'But surely it's better she hears it from you than read about it in the paper?'

'Surely to God the papers won't be interested?' Hannah cried and then with her head in her hands she gave a mournful moan, 'Oh Vic, Angela will hate me afresh for this.'

'Darling, maybe this will build bridges between you.'

'And maybe pigs can fly.'

'Would you like me to tell her?' Vic asked.

'Oh Vic, would you?'

'I'll try if you want me to.'

Hannah was glad Vic had offered to speak to Angela because she was apprehensive of even meeting her daughter. The last communication had been the abusive telephone call she'd had. Since then, there had been silence but Hannah had no reason to think Angela felt one jot better about her than when she screamed down the phone that she'd ruined her whole life.

Josie opened the door to them, much to Hannah's relief, and she said quietly, 'I've told her you were coming over. She was a bit upset, but she's all right.'

'Not for long she won't be,' Hannah said, 'not when she hears our news,' and then seeing Josie's surprised expression, she explained, 'We know where Arthur is.'

'Where?'

'Prison,' Hannah said briefly and went on to tell Josie as much as she'd been told.

'Oh God!' Josie said. 'On what charge?'

'They wouldn't say, but I think we can make a good guess.'

'Poor, poor Angela,' Josie said and she led the way

down the passage to the breakfast room.

A white-faced Angela sat before the fire hugging her hands between her knees. She looked a picture of misery and when she lifted up her beautiful green eyes, shadowed as they were by worry, Hannah was smote with pity for her.

Angela saw the look, and though she didn't fully understand it, she burst out, 'I don't know why you've come. Pretending to care all of a sudden.'

'I do care about you, Angela. I always have and I can see how worried you are.'

Angela's resistance crumbled before her mother's obvious concern and she suddenly felt very young, too young to deal with her father's disappearance by herself. 'He's never done this before when I've been home,' she said uncertainly. 'I keep waiting for the phone to ring, or to hear his key in the door. I mean, what if he's had an accident?'

'He hasn't, Angela,' Vic said. 'We checked the hospitals before we left.' He glanced at Hannah, waiting for the signal to go on, and she gave a nod. There was no way she could shield her daughter from this and maybe it would be easier for Angela if Vic told her. 'We know where your father is,' he said. 'He's in Steelhouse Lane Police Station.'

'The police station? Why?' Angela demanded. 'Has there been an accident?'

'No, Angela. Your father has been arrested.'

'Arrested!' Angela cried, leaping to her feet. 'What are you talking about?'

'We know little about it,' Vic said truthfully. 'He goes before the court tomorrow.'

'And then he'll come home, right?' Angela said. 'I mean, it's got to be some silly mistake.'

Vic knew he couldn't let Angela harbour the idea that this was some minor motoring offence, such as being given a ticket for speeding. 'No, Angela,' he said. 'It's not a mistake and it's highly unlikely that your father will be home tomorrow. The policeman we spoke to said they'd probably keep him in jail until the trial.'

'Trial? What is this? Daddy's never done any harm!'

'We won't know what he's done till tomorrow,' Vic said. 'We honestly don't know any more than we're telling you.'

Angela glanced over at Hannah and she could tell by the flush staining her cheeks and the way she was biting on her bottom lip in agitation that she was uncomfortable. She wondered if it were anything to do with what Josie had told her the previous day and even her mother had hinted at about her father not liking sex. But surely no one could arrest you for that. 'Is this anything to do with sex?' she said, turning to her mother.

Hannah swallowed deeply. God, this was awful. She was about to inflict terrific pain on the daughter she loved. 'He . . . your father didn't like normal sex,' she said.

'And could that be something to do with why he was arrested?

'Angela, we don't know.'

'But could it?'

Hannah glanced at Vic and his eyes met hers, full of sympathy. Perhaps, she thought, it might be better to prepare Angela for the revelations that would come out in the morning. She was certain that finding some form of outlet for his perverted sexual appetite was the reason he was behind bars. She gave a sigh and said, 'Yes, Angela, it could, but let's just wait and see.'

But Angela remembered the kinky sex some of Hillary's set had engaged in that even in the throes of drink and drugs, she'd refused to indulge in and even hearing about what they did had made her feel sick. To think her father took part in things like that – it was disgusting. To think of a parent having any sort of a sex life was embarrassment enough, but this . . . She felt nausea rise in her throat and she fled for the bathroom.

Hannah followed her and held her hair back as she vomited into the lavatory bowl and later wiped her face as she sat recovering on the toilet seat. 'You're enjoying this?' she accused.

'I assure you I'm not.'

The tears began then. 'Why is he like this, Mommy? Why?'

Hannah sighed. 'We'll probably never know,' she said.

'I'm so lonely,' Angela said plaintively. 'I have no one now.'

'You have me.'

'You don't want me. You never have.'

'That's not true. It's another lie your father has fed you.'

'Does Matthew still come to see you?'

'Yes, he does,' Hannah said. 'He's my son and you're my daughter just as much as little Frances and Adam are. Matthew will also soon be alone in the world. His mother is dying. She has only months to live.'

That was a shock to Angela, for though she'd known Matthew's mother was ill, she hadn't known it was so serious. Suddenly, though, she envied her, because she felt she couldn't stand the shame and humiliation which would be heaped on her head because of her father. She just couldn't bear it! She couldn't!

'Oh, Mommy,' she cried, using the term she hadn't used for years. 'Oh Mommy, I wish I was dead.'

Hannah cradled her weeping daughter and tried not to be glad at the circumstance that had caused her daughter to turn to her. She crooned to her, rocking her as she hadn't done since she'd been a little child and then not often. She told Angela she had much to live for, her life was before her and many people loved her. Listening to her, Angela realised how she'd missed her mother over the years. 'Can you stay tonight?' she asked.

'Darling, I can't,' Hannah said. 'If Vic should be called out, there is no one to see to the children. Amy is listening out now, but we can't expect her to do it all night. We said we wouldn't be long.'

'Then . . . then can I come home with you?' Angela said. 'I don't want to be alone tonight.'

It was what Hannah had hoped for and thought would never happen. 'Of course you can, darling,' she said. 'Let's go and put a few things in a suitcase,' and as she followed her daughter out of the bathroom, her heart soared in joy.

Chapter Twenty-Seven

Angela, with red-rimmed, black-smudged eyes standing out in her head, thought she'd die with shame as she listened to what her father was accused of. Horrible bestial activities, they said, he was engaged in, things that defied normal comprehension and other crimes that involved children.

That was the worst of all and she'd wanted the floor to open up and swallow her. She felt the bile rise in her throat and swayed on her feet and was glad of Hannah one side of her and Josie the other, for without them she was sure she would have fallen.

Her father wasn't the only one in the dock, but he was the only one she saw, except that she barely recognised the grey-faced, stooped man who seemed to have aged twenty years. But she felt no pity for him, only revulsion, and she wondered if he knew she was there listening to the dreadful things they said he did, or if he'd given her any sort of thought at all.

Hannah hadn't wanted Angela to come to court that morning, but Vic said she had a right to be there if she wanted to go. 'You can't protect her from this,' Vic had said. 'Even if she'd listen to you, which I doubt. Just be there by her side supporting her.'

And how glad Hannah was when the list of crimes was read out. Never in her wildest dreams had she believed people did such things and certainly not people she knew. She wondered how Angela was bearing it at all. She wished she could put her arms around her, but she was afraid. She knew that although Angela had cried in her arms the night before, that had been in the nature of a drowning man clinging to a raft, not a true indication of her feelings.

Hannah felt she had thrown away the right to be a mother to Angela, to give her advice and certainly the right to give her a hug and tell her things would be all right. That would be a lie anyway, for would it ever be all right again? But then she saw Angela suddenly sway on her feet and risking rejection, Hannah grasped one of Angela's hands tight and though Angela made no sign, she was glad of the small measure of comfort it gave her.

Arthur's case was adjourned for medical and psychiatric reports and his solicitor, Mr Morriatty, was glad, for he was very worried about Arthur's mental state. Arthur had told him that when he'd been arrested on Saturday evening, he'd been in a state of shock, a state that rendered him almost incapable of speech and certainly of coherent thought and that was why he hadn't asked the police to ring him. It had been when the cell door slammed shut that he thought he'd go mad. But he'd resisted the desire he had to beat on it and scream and cry and beg to be let out. Instead, he'd lain down on the bed and let a numbness – the aftermath of shock – steal all over him. It lasted all of

Sunday. He spoke when he was spoken to, ate what he was given, but nothing touched him. He seemed outside of this current situation as if it was happening to someone else.

By eleven o'clock on Sunday, he knew it wasn't and he hammered on the door. This was ignored for some time, except by fellow prisoners, some of whom hammered with him, while others protested at the noise.

Eventually, a policeman came to see the cause of the disturbance. 'I want to see my solicitor,' Arthur demanded.

'Are you bloody crazy, man? It's the middle of the night.'

'I have a right.'

'So does he, I should think. A right to a decent night's sleep.'

'I insist you phone him.'

'You ain't in a position to insist on much, mate,' the copper said. But he knew he'd have to phone. The man would be up before the magistrate in the morning and if he said he'd been refused legal advice, then the policeman knew he'd be in big trouble. The others arrested with him had all had their solicitors brought in straight away, but this one hadn't spoken. They'd brought in a police solicitor, but the prisoner hadn't looked at him, let alone spoken. The entire time the solicitor was there, Arthur had lay and stared at the ceiling.

Now it appeared the man had his own solicitor all the time. 'All right,' the policeman snapped. 'Give me his name and number and I'll ring him. But if he won't come, he won't come and I can't make him. D'you understand?'

But Mr Morriatty had come. He hadn't been pleased because he'd been about to go to bed. But it wouldn't be the first time he'd been summoned this way, though he'd never thought such a call would come from Arthur Bradley. He'd worked for the man for years, usually for his business interests and certainly not for anything of this nature.

However, solicitors are trained to hide their feelings of shock and even revulsion that they might feel in a client's dealings, and Mr Morriatty was no exception. He'd known over the years he'd dealt with Arthur's affairs about his feelings for his daughter – in fact, he often thought you'd have to be deaf, dumb and blind not to realise how Arthur doted on the child. He'd been staggered then to find that Arthur had chosen not to inform Angela of his whereabouts. 'I told you I wasn't thinking straight,' Arthur snapped angrily. 'Anyway, how could I tell her about all this?'

Mr Morriatty was incensed on the girl's behalf, incensed enough to let his veneer drop slightly. 'Good God, man, you don't have to give it to her chapter and verse. Couldn't you just say the police had asked you to come in for questioning? You can't just say nothing at all. The girl must be worried sick.'

Arthur couldn't begin to explain why he didn't want to talk to Angela. He didn't want her involved at all for, despite her behaviour over the past months, he cherished the idea in his head that she was his one triumph. She was no longer as pure and innocent as he'd have liked, but still he'd have never wanted her to know of this side of his life.

But the solicitor was right. She had to be told, but

he didn't want to see her or speak to her, he couldn't cope with seeing her scorn, her disgust. 'You tell her,' he told the solicitor. 'But not by phone. Go up to the house.'

'It's the early hours of the morning.'

'Well, if she's as worried as you say she is, she'll hardly be deep in sleep, will she?'

Mr Morriatty dreaded the visit, dreaded what he had to tell Angela and he was both relieved and worried when no one answered the door. The house was shut up and in darkness and it stayed that way, but as he turned away, he couldn't help wondering where the girl had spent the night.

Next morning, he only had a few minutes with Arthur before the hearing, but he did tell him that Angela hadn't been at the house. He'd seen a tic begin to beat at the side of Arthur's head and his hands curl into fists and uncurl again. 'Calm yourself, Mr Bradley.'

'Calm myself! Calm myself, you say!' Arthur snarled. 'So where has the little trollop been? Tell me that if you like.'

'Mr Bradley, I hardly think . . . Has the girl any friends or family?'

'None,' Arthur snapped. 'She has no one.'

Mr Morriatty knew of course of the mother who had abandoned her daughter, but maybe in the circumstances of her father's disappearance – well, blood was thicker than water, people said.

But there was no point discussing this with Arthur, and anyway there were things they had to go over and they had little enough time before the case was to be called. But the worry about the whereabouts of Arthur's daughter remained in the solicitor's mind.

When he went into court therefore, he was relieved to see that Angela Bradley was not only alive and well, but had someone with her to support her. And although he'd never met Hannah, he could make a calculated guess that one of the women with Angela was her long-lost mother, for she was too like her to be anyone else. He saw the malevolent look Arthur cast their way and thought that he'd never understand the man.

In fact when he saw him after the adjournment, Arthur seemed more concerned about Hannah getting her claws into Angela after all he'd done to prevent it than he was about what would happen to him now. He seemed not to be aware of the severity of the charges levelled against him, nor come to terms with the fact that even with all the skill and efforts of Mr Morriatty and a clever barrister, he was still facing a hefty prison sentence. Surely it was better that the girl had someone to turn to?

Apparently not in Arthur's mind. Mr Morriatty was very glad that Arthur's trial had been adjourned for psychiatric reports for in his opinion his reactions were anything but normal!

As the three women emerged on the court steps, they were joined by Vic who'd come after morning surgery.

All were in a state of shock. It was hard to see someone you know up in the dock and particularly for such unspeakable crimes. Previously, all three women had only seen inside a courtroom on the television and the experience had unnerved them all. Angela wasn't really functioning properly, for her mind was going over the list of crimes read out. She held on to her tears with difficulty, for she had the feeling if she began to cry she'd never stop. But Hannah was amazed and had great respect for her daughter's self-control, for she knew the whole experience must have hit her like a hammer blow.

Angela forced her mind back to her present predicament. She had to decide what she must do now. Where was she to stay? She must at least collect some clothes, she'd brought little with her the previous night. But when she asked Vic if they could stop at the house, he shook his head. 'I wouldn't, Angela,' he said. 'I drove down your road on the way here and the press are already converging on the house.'

Angela was shaken. She'd not realised they'd be newsworthy – or at least not so quickly.

'Oh. Aren't they horrid?'

'They're out to sell papers, that's all,' Vic said. 'They don't care who gets hurt in the process.'

'Thank God, she's well out of it with us then,' Hannah said.

'They'll soon find out where she is,' Vic warned. 'The neighbours will talk and they'll know where she'll make for.'

'Maybe I'd be harder to trace,' Josie put in. 'Angela could stay with us for a while if she wants to. I know Phil won't mind in the least. How do you feel about it, Angela?'

'After this morning, I don't feel anything about anything,' Angela said forlornly. 'I'm sort of numb inside.'

Hannah longed to hold tight to her child who was

hurting so very much. She also wanted her under her own roof where she could look after her, but she knew Josie's suggestion was a sensible one. 'What about my things?' Angela said as they drove towards Moseley. 'I've left nearly everything I own behind.'

'Well, we can manage clothes for a few days,' Josie said. 'You can borrow some of mine.'

'How long d'you think I'll have to hide out like this?'

'Oh, not so long, I shouldn't think,' Vic said confidently. 'Something else will happen before too long and this will all be old news.'

'But until then I'm like a prisoner,' Angela thought and then another thought overtook her. She had very little money. She tended to spend her monthly allowance as soon as she got it, knowing she could always tap her father for more, but now . . . Well, that part of her life was all over. Josie was right, she thought, as Vic drew up outside Josie's little house. If I'd tried harder at school, I could be working now. Who would employ a seventeen-year-old no hoper?

Hannah had only been in a few minutes when there was a knock on the door. Mindful of Vic's warnings about the press, Hannah opened it cautiously to find Elizabeth Banks on the doorstep. 'Oh Hannah, my dear, I'm sorry to trouble you, but have you had word from Arthur? He hasn't turned in for work this morning and in view of your phone call yesterday, we were rather concerned.'

There was little point in not telling her. So far, she'd told only Amy and Tom, but now the press had wind of it, the whole can of worms would be open to the world soon enough. 'Come in, Elizabeth,' she said. 'I'll make us coffee, although for what I am about to tell you, something stronger might be in order.'

To say Elizabeth was shocked at Hannah's news was putting it mildly. 'I can't believe it, I just can't believe it,' she said and then she leaned across the table and patted Hannah's hand. 'I can quite see, my dear, why you felt driven to leave him.'

'I didn't leave him for this,' Hannah said. 'I didn't know. He used to go out many evenings in the week, but I didn't know where. I didn't much care either, I was happier when he was out of the way. No, Elizabeth, I left Arthur because of cruelty. Not physical cruelty, though he has used his fists on me occasionally, but he put me through mental agonies. He went to extreme lengths to separate me from Angela. That was the hardest thing to bear.'

'Dear, dear,' Elizabeth said. 'Arthur told us you never bothered with the child.'

'I was never allowed to bother,' Hannah said bitterly and went on to explain why Angela had been sent away to school and how she was never allowed to go with Arthur when he went to see her at weekends and about the Christmas when Arthur took Angela away and she began the affair with Vic Humphries.

'I took the job with Vic, not just because I wasn't needed at home with Angela being at school all day and Pauline still in the house, but also because I was short of money,' Hannah told Elizabeth. 'Arthur never gave me any unless we were coming to see you. I had to be decently dressed then and he would play the part of the devoted husband and that's all it was – an act.'

'Vic and I had fought the attraction we had begun to feel between us initially, but that Christmas Day, I was just so incredibly lonely. Of course, the inevitable happened. I became pregnant and Arthur threatened to report Vic to the Medical Council if I had any contact at all with Angela. The ban extended to Josie as well.'

'That isn't how I heard it.'

'I bet,' Hannah said bitterly. 'And now Elizabeth, you may as well hear it all,' and she went on to tell her about Mike Murphy and the son she had who was now called Matthew Olaffson.

'By pure chance, the family who adopted my son moved here from Leeds as I did and Angela and he met – neither of them knowing of the association between them. They were engaged to marry before I met Matthew, again by chance in Erdington, and I guessed straight away that he was my son. I checked of course, I didn't go on likeness alone.'

'Does Arthur know?'

'He does now,' Hannah said. 'He had to know, because the association between Angela and Matthew could not be allowed to continue.'

'Never have I felt so stupid,' Elizabeth said. 'Reg and I thought you such a lovely couple.'

'It was the image Arthur wanted to promote,' Hannah said. 'He said if I told the truth and he was to lose face, I'd never see Angela again.'

'Surely he couldn't . . .'

'Oh, he could,' Hannah said. 'Angela wasn't too keen on me when she was younger anyway – helped along by Daddy, of course. Then there was the lucrative job Arthur had, enabling Angela to go to private school, and the house that was his alone. I would have nothing to offer, besides which, he threatened to bring it up about my mental history, you know, the depression I had after Angela's birth, making it difficult for me to even have contact with her. After losing my first child, I couldn't have borne it.'

'I really don't know what to say,' Elizabeth said. 'I feel I've been really stupid. Reg will feel that too. We have both been taken in quite dreadfully.'

'Don't feel too bad about it,' Hannah said. 'Arthur could be charming when he wanted to be. To tell you the truth, the one I am most worried about in all this is Angela.'

'She's never staying in the house by herself?'

'No. She'd never get in the place,' Hannah said. 'It's besieged by the press. Angela's hiding out in Moseley with Josie. Vic says they'll come here. Some of the neighbours are bound to say where I am.'

And they obviously did. The day hadn't finished before Hannah was contacted. The phone calls were bad enough, but worse were those belonging to the knot of press hanging about the gate who actually knocked on the door.

'I have a life to live,' Hannah complained. 'I have to get Adam to and from school and Frances to her playgroup. I also have to go shopping and every time I leave the house, they're hustling around me, firing questions, shouting after me.'

'It will calm down eventually,' Vic said. 'You'll see. It will be a nine day wonder.'

'Well, if this keeps up, they will be the longest nine days of my life,' Hannah said, and so it proved and she was grateful for the letters of support she got from Tilly and Pauline when she wrote and told them both of the latest developments.

If you want me to come down for the trial, Hannah, you've only got to say the word,

Tilly wrote and Pauline also offered to come down for a few days if it would help.

If things had been right between Angela and her, Hannah would have been happy to have seen both women and knew she would feel more able to cope with a couple of good friends at her back. But for now, her energies had to be directed towards Angela and building the relationship with her. She couldn't allow anything to come before that.

Marian understood how she felt and Hannah valued her friendship. She knew when Marian died Matthew wouldn't be the only one devastated, for she'd miss her greatly.

The papers were very concerned with the lurid details of the arrests and crimes the people were accused of and not just names, but photographs too, were in some of the Sunday papers, much to Angela's dismay. But eventually the interest in the cases died down as something more sensationalist came into their line of vision.

One Sunday afternoon, two weeks after the whole nightmare had begun, there was a knock at Hannah's door and she opened it to Father Fitzgerald. 'My dear Mrs Humphries, Hannah, I've come to see how you are coping.'

'With the latest outrage you mean, Father?' Hannah

asked. 'Come through to the kitchen and I'll make us a drink.'

Father Fitzgerald had come to see Hannah because he felt he must, for he'd been shocked to the core, but he was as embarrassed as hell to be there. He'd wondered before he came how much Hannah had been aware of, but when she told him about it as he drank the tea she made him and nibbled the proffered biscuits, he realised she'd known very little. 'It's Angela I feel sorry for really,' Hannah said at the end of her tale.

'Ah, yes,' the priest said. 'Is she here?'

'No,' Hannah said. 'Because of the media interest, you know. We thought it would be better if she stayed with Josie.'

Father Fitzgerald had always had a soft spot for Josie and had popped in to see her quite a few times in the house since she'd married. 'I'm sure both Josie and Angela would love to see you,' Hannah said.

'Yes, indeed I'll go, the first chance I get,' Father Fitzgerald said, draining his cup and getting to his feet. 'I do understand more now, Hannah, why you felt you could no longer live with Arthur. It is regrettable. Maybe in cases like this, there could be special dispensation . . .'

'No, Father. Leave it as it is,' Hannah said. 'I'm divorced now and married to Vic and happy with it.'

'But . . .'

'I know what you're going to say, Father, but don't. I know the Church's views on divorce, but it isn't mine or Vic's. Please leave us to sort our lives out and deal with Angela.'

'If that's how you really feel?'

'It is, Father.'

'Well, then, we'll leave it so, Hannah,' the priest said and he took hold of Hannah's hand at the door and shook it as he said, 'I'll pray for all of you.'

Hannah watched the priest walk down the path and thought that a few prayers for them wouldn't go amiss at the present time.

'The waiting is the worst part,' Angela said to Josie about a month later. 'I feel as if I can't get on with anything until it's settled.'

Josie understood, but she said, 'Angela, whatever happens, you have a life to live.'

'I know that,' Angela said with a sigh. 'But for a long time Daddy was the centre of my world. It was like looking at a stranger, hearing things about a stranger – it was weird. I feel as if I'm cast adrift. As if my father is dead. And for ages I thought I'd never be able to raise my head again, I felt so ashamed. I still do at times, but it's slowly getting better.'

'But you have no reason to be ashamed, surely you know that?' Josie said. 'You're not responsible for your father. And now that the press has lost interest, you could go and live with Hannah if you want. I know she'd like it.'

'I'd prefer not to, unless you want rid of me,' Angela said.

'No, not particularly,' Josie answered. 'It's quite nice having you, really. You're another pair of hands, but I think Hannah feels it.'

'I see her every week.'

'I think she wants more than that.'

'Yeah, well . . .'

'What is it, Angela?'

'She's always going on about Matthew. Have you noticed how much she mentions him?'

'You can't be jealous of Matthew?'

'Well, I can and Adam and Frances, too,' Angela replied. And she was, insanely jealous. She'd never really learnt to share. She'd never had much practice at it and at home amongst her family, she'd been used to taking centre stage. It had changed when Hannah had left, but she'd still come first with her father. 'My mother doesn't need me,' she said.

'She does, Angela,' Josie insisted. 'Love isn't something you just get so much of and if you love one person, it has to be taken off another. If I had another child now, I wouldn't love my two any less.'

'That's different.'

'It's no different,' Josie said firmly. 'This isn't because you still hold a candle for Matthew, is it?'

'No!' Angela said, but was honest enough to admit, 'I did in the beginning. When I found out about him being my brother. I thought he was the love of my life, but I know now how silly I was then.'

Josie hid a smile, for Angela was talking about just months before, but even she had to admit this last business had matured Angela overnight. She had the feeling she was marking time as they all were. She was glad she got on so well with the students who called and seemed to like nothing better than sitting with them drinking coffee and discussing the world situation.

Vietnam was on everyone's lips then and Angela couldn't see what good America's involvement would be.

Surely it would escalate the problem and make it worse? And she was more than keen to join the march organised for April that year to demonstrate against US policy.

She kept her eyes and mind focused on the march, because it helped keep thoughts of her father at bay. Mr Morriatty had been to see her, to explain procedure. He was concerned too about the house being left empty for so long – not that he wanted Angela to live there, a young girl alone, especially as the housekeeper had left in high dudgeon, as soon as she'd found out what had happened. She swept out, saying she'd always been a respectable woman and had always worked for respectable people and she wouldn't have put her foot over the threshold if she'd had the least idea of what Arthur was into.

So Angela couldn't stay there, it would never do, but neither was it good to leave a house vacant for any length of time. Arthur must make a decision to either let the property or put it on the market. But then, Mr Morriatty, worried about Angela's welfare, was trying to get Arthur to make some provision for her, but the man seemed to have almost forgotten the girl.

In fact, if it hadn't been for the priest, Father Fitzgerald, who Arthur seemed to have a measure of respect for, and who'd talked to him after the solicitor had had a word, he doubted he would have got him to agree to anything. But the priest seemed a genuine kind of chap and a friend of the whole family. He'd known Angela since she was born, so he was obviously going to be concerned for her and apparently he'd been to see her quite a few times.

He really was relieved that Angela had such support,

for he doubted at the end of all this if her father would be any good to her. He wouldn't agree to see her – not that Angela showed much desire to visit him and you could hardly blame her, but he wouldn't agree to write or phone either. And there were times when Arthur was barely lucid, raving about his wife much of the time.

He knew the psychiatrists were worried. Arthur wasn't reacting terribly well to the tests they were giving him and they were as concerned as he was.

This he kept from Angela as much as possible, feeling she had enough to cope with. He thought it a good thing her family had stepped in, whatever had gone before, because if it had been left to her father, she could have gone to the devil.

Hannah was surprised that Angela was taking such an interest in world affairs and presumed it was the influence of Josie. To an extent it was; Angela apparently had a high regard for Josie and Phil, and also for the students they hung around with. Few of them knew why Angela was there, being more interested in world affairs than scandal, and even fewer cared, and Angela was grateful for their acceptance of her and gradually her self-esteem began seeping back.

Because of them she had a glimpse of what life could have been like for her, if she'd worked, if she'd taken her O levels and her A levels and gained a place at university. Instead of the indulged and vacuous life she had led that had given her so little satisfaction, she could have worked for a degree. But perhaps all wasn't lost and she could still do that. Maybe she could talk it through with Josie and her mother after the trial.

And then suddenly, there was to be no trial. Mr Morriatty explained to Angela that Arthur had suffered a complete physical and mental collapse. His mind had finally snapped under the strain.

'What does it mean?' Hannah asked when Angela came with Josie to give her the news.

'The medical people think he's unfit for the rigours of a trial,' Josie explained. 'He's been sent to Broadmoor, a place for the criminally insane.'

Hannah gave a shudder for it sounded so horrific, but it was really only what he deserved.

'And what about you?'

'Mr Morriatty is applying to set up some allowance for me from Daddy's funds,' Angela said. 'He will be in charge of it until I am twenty-five. He doesn't think Daddy will ever be well enough to leave the hospital, but you can never be sure. I can't sell the house, for example, or strip his bank account, but the house could be let out and I've told Mr Morriatty to push ahead with it.'

'What will you do with the money?' Hannah asked.

'Well, I've been toying with the idea of going back to college to take O levels,' Angela said. 'The allowance would come in very handy.'

Hannah was pleased that Angela seemed to have a goal to aim for, but knew better than to go overboard about it. That would be the surest way for her to back off.

She talked it over with Vic that night. 'If she was to

take the courses at Sutton College and agree to live here, I'd be perfectly happy,' Hannah said.

'I thought you wanted her and Matthew to get on,' Vic reminded her.

'I did,' Hannah said with a sigh, 'but with the relationship they had, maybe that's rather a tall order. The age of miracles is probably past.'

They amassed in various parks all over the city with their banners and their slogans, chanting and singing songs. 'It's very well organised,' Josie said. 'Groups are all meeting up at scheduled points so that everyone can converge on the city centre, finishing up in Chamberlain Square.'

Angela was amazed by the people. It wasn't just students, but many, judging by their clothes, from all walks of life and though the police were out in force, they didn't appear threatening.

It was as they were getting ready to move off that Angela spotted Matthew in a crowd with Birmingham University scarves around their necks. Angela saw with fury that there were nudges towards her and sniggers from some of Matthew's friends. They'd known Angela to be Matthew's girlfriend, even fiancée, and had to be told the story that they were related and couldn't marry.

Angela stamped over to them in anger. 'What are you doing here?' she demanded of Matthew.

'Same as you, I expect.'

'Don't give me that. You're not bothered about things like this.'

'How do you know what I'm interested in?'

'I knew you quite well at one time.'

'Not deeply,' Matthew said. 'We were only scratching the surface. I happen to believe that the Vietnam War, which we are staring in the face now, will be long and bloody. I think it will kill many people and will solve nothing in the end and I think the US should keep out of it. They won't, but at least we should register our disapproval.'

'Is that really what you think?'

'Yes. I wouldn't be here if I didn't. Why?'

'It's just so exactly what I think.'

'Well, there you are then. We're on the same side for a change, so you can stop attacking me. How about it?'

Matthew was looking at Angela with the half-smile on his face that used to make her heart turn somersaults yet she now felt nothing. Matthew was as good-looking as ever, but the chemistry between them was gone and she found herself smiling back.

'Shall we be friends then?' Matthew asked and Angela shrugged. 'If you like.'

Matthew linked his arm through Angela's and she waited for the icy thrill to run through her body, but it never came. 'Your friends have gone on,' she said.

'I'll catch up with them again,' Matthew said carelessly. 'Come on, they're almost ready to move off.'

Josie saw the confrontation between Angela and Matthew and would have joined them, but Phil held her back. 'Let them be. They'll sort it out better on their own,' he said. 'You know, I feel more sorry for Angela than Matthew. He at least had the love of a mother till he was almost grown and now that his mother is on the way out, he finds his birth mother.

Few are as lucky. Angela's life has been really screwed up these last years. She's still fighting the demons inside her.'

'Well, she's winning,' Josie said. 'One of those demons is her mother and Angela told me earlier she's prepared to live back at Hannah's for a while and see how it goes. Hannah will be beside herself. She's meeting us in town with all the children and Angela is telling her then.'

And Hannah saw them, her son and her daughter, together as she never thought to see them, as they turned down towards Chamberlain Square where she and Vic with Josie's children and their own waited to greet them.

Hannah suddenly felt as if her life was very blessed and she silently thanked God for the good things in her life. In her mind's eye, Hannah could see the future rolling in front of her as she thought it would never be. She saw *all* her family sitting down to a meal for the first time, being together for Christmas, maybe even having a family holiday.

The one depressing thing in her life, and Matthew's of course, was Marian's imminent death and Hannah hoped when it happened she would be of some help to the son she was becoming so very fond of. She knew she'd gained his respect and could only hope it would blossom into love. But if it didn't, she was grateful for what she had now, for it was far more than she'd ever dared hope for.

Angela, too, now spoke to her as if she was a human being and not like a slug that had crawled from under a stone, or some object of hatred. She hoped in time she might have a proper relationship with her daughter too. She loved her so very much and prayed that eventually she'd come to believe it.

But above it all was the all-abiding and consuming love she and Vic had for one another. Hannah knew some people would never experience what she had and she considered it worth all she had gone through. Vic was such a lovely, special person, always there when she needed him and generous-hearted to a fault. She hugged him close to her and he smiled down at her, the smile that still had the power to turn her legs to jelly. He too had seen Angela and Matthew arm in arm and he knew how it would affect Hannah and bending towards her, he said, 'Have I told you today that I love you, Mrs Humphries?' and at the small shake of her head, he kissed her gently on the lips.

The rally was over, the people were dispersing. Matthew still had hold of Angela's hand and he was pulling her through the milling crowd. Angela was laughing, her eyes shining and then she caught sight of Hannah and raised her free hand in a wave. 'Mum!' she shouted.

It was too much for Hannah to see her daughter and son, so happy and easy together, and then for her daughter to wave and address her like any other daughter might have done and tears trickled down her cheeks. This hadn't gone unnoticed by Adam. 'Dad,' he cried. 'Our Mom's crying. What you crying for, Mom?'

Hannah tried to take a grip on herself. 'Because I'm so happy,' she said at last. Adam had never heard of anyone crying because they were happy before and he looked uncomprehendingly at his mother and saw then that apart from the tears, she didn't look sad at all and he couldn't understand it. 'That's plain daft,' he decided in the end.

But Hannah barely heard him, for Matthew and Angela had reached her and both had put their arms around her in a hug as if it was the most natural thing in the world. Hannah held them tight and thought she would burst with happiness and then her eyes met Vic's and she saw the shine of tears there too.

Suddenly Josie and Phil were beside them to reclaim their children and Hannah looked at her whole family surrounding her and thought she must be one of the happiest and luckiest women in the world. And she knew she had been wrong; the age of miracles was alive and well.